DEVIL'S INTERVAL

To Diann and Wilton
who found two keys to life—
each other.

Nelson

DEVIL'S INTERVAL

A Novel

Nelson Canton

iUniverse, Inc.
New York Bloomington

Devil's Interval

iUniverse books may be ordered through booksellers or by contacting:

iUniverse
1663 Liberty Drive
Bloomington, IN 47403
www.iuniverse.com
1-800-Authors (1-800-288-4677)

Because of the dynamic nature of the Internet, any Web addresses
or links contained in this book may have changed
since publication and may no longer be valid.

This is a work of fiction. All of the characters, names, incidents,
organizations, and dialogue in this novel are either the products
of the author's imagination or are used fictitiously.

Cover design by Tom Gladden Graphics

ISBN: 978-0-595-46395-4 (pbk)
ISBN: 978-0-595-70201-5 (cloth)
ISBN: 978-0-595-90687-1 (ebk)

Printed in the United States of America

To my grandmother, Neoline Foey James, and my mother, Jacqueline Olivia Canton, to whom I owe everything

Sincere thanks go to Earl "Bud" Rovit for years of readings, responses, and encouragement, and to Mary Faber for her much valued proofreading of an earlier manuscript of the novel.

"You taught me language; and my profit on't
Is, I know how to curse: the red plague rid you,
For learning me your language."
William Shakespeare, *The Tempest*

"I want you to overcome 'em with yeses,
undermine 'em with grins, agree 'em to death and destruction."
Ralph Ellison, *Invisible Man*

CHAPTER 1

▼

The competing calls of millionaires awoke Watt as he dozed. "He's eating himself again!" cried Stetson

"Where's my slap!" bellowed Willard Camalian.

"I want service!" yelled Lena Messa.

As Watt jumped up, Stetson cried, "Hurry! Before he bites a sinew!" prompting Watt to race down the stairs of Dr. Otto Von Geber's New York City townhouse on Sutton Place to do his job.

"I'm calling you!" cried Stetson. "You should be here!"

As Watt passed Lena Messa's room, she opened the door and cooed, "I *expect* service, too."

"The thumb might be done!" cried Stetson as Watt ran down another flight of stairs, thinking, *I ought to let him eat himself until nothing's left but his teeth and backside.*

Reaching Sir Ainsley Bridges' room, he cracked the door. Through a red light, he saw Bridges and his crew: Stetson, his loyal manservant, and Pearl Fryman, his concubine. Scratching his head, Stetson pleaded with Bridges who stood atop the bed, "Sir Ainsley, think of the corporations that depend on you." And Pearl Fryman, in a sexy negligee, asked, "Who'll teach your grandchildren about *power,* if not you?"

"Let them learn for themselves!" screamed Ainsley Bridges. Standing atop the bed, he had a sheet wrapped around him, like a toga. A black bowler hat sat on his head. With his mouth wide open, he was about to bite into a loaf of pumpernickel bread with mustard oozing out of the sides, containing for meat his own natural hand.

"Please let the hand go, sir," implored Stetson.

"Do it for me," urged Pearl Fryman. But Bridges simply glared at them both. Then he asked, "Do you know the price people pay to work for me?"

"No, Mr. Bridges."

"Well, each of you has paid it a *thousand* times," he laughed, and Pearl and Stetson began laughing, too. Keeping their eyes peeled on Bridges, they awaited their cue when to stop.

"Let's begin with religion," said Bridges, "because *I* think it's important. Before I give a Christian a job, he has to shit on the Ten Commandments; Muslims must eat pigs' feet; Buddhists must replace meditation with video games; Hindus must eat mounds of beef, and Jews must throw darts at the Star of David.

"People must give up *all* beliefs to work for me. They must pay the price for not learning what I did at an early age. Do you want to know what that is?"

"Yes, Mr. Bridges," they said in perfect unison. And without warning, Ainsley Bridges burst out with, "ONE and ONE makes TWO dollars! And *KILL! KILL! KILL!*" Screaming, he raised his hand sandwich and brought it down as if wielding a dagger.

Watt had to stop him before it was too late. That was his job. An out-of-control millionaire is dangerous. *Didn't I handle two of them last month*, he told himself. As the clock in the den hissed and the parrot cried "Ordnung!" he pushed open the door and stood there like a gunfighter. All heads turned. Raising his hand sandwich, Bridges cried, "We're terrible animals! We've put other animals into TV dinners!" As Bridges laughed, Watt moved into the center of the room, saying, "What's going on? Go back to bed!" Grabbing Bridges by the toga, he yanked him from the bed. Unfastening the tape, he threw down the bread. Snarling, Bridges cried, "You've ruined a dramatic moment in my life, Watt. And *you* will pay!"

"Not in *this* lifetime," said Watt as Bridges grinned, saying: "I don't need bread to eat an arm or mustard to season it. All I need are teeth." He did a jig with a clumsy final step, saying, "Isn't this how your people do it, Watt? You do know Sambos can never be Rambos."

Taking a deep breath, Watt reared back and slapped Bridges, sending him reeling across the bed. As Pearl gulped and Stetson covered his eyes, Ainsley Bridges lay there making baby sounds. *This ought to keep him quiet*, thought Watt, shaking a silver tin over him. Gently tossing, Ainsley Bridges fell asleep in a shower of baby powder. He was snoring as Watt and Stetson tiptoed from the room.

While Stetson carried the broken bread downstairs, Watt went upstairs, thinking, *these crazy millionaires, why do I have to straighten them out? What gives them the right?* Then, one word leapt through his lips: "MONEY."

What is money anyway? It's power. It's everything. It's the sixth sense without which the other five can't live, as Dr. Von Geber often said. It's nice to be philosophic and believe in the *mind* and *love.* Without money, they're just illusions in a world of pain. When love wanes, people automatically fight over money because it can buy anything—even *more* love, or a woman like Pearl Fryman, whom *PEEPHOLE Magazine* described as "the best (you know what) with money that money can buy."

The article said a lot of other things about Pearl, but it left out the most important item: She'll do anything for money. She dreams of money every night. Her mind swirls to an orgasmic height, and then trickles down in a shower of money. The way a plant bends toward light, she bends toward money.

Yes, Watt has seen her and others like her, too, sitting in discriminating country clubs, laughing at people who work, tossing illusions into the air like banana peels, without any concern for whom they hurt. And yes, sometimes they slip on their own banana peels, landing on their asses with a thump. But someone always helps them up. Do they do it for friendship, love, or their extraordinary minds? No. They do it for the *money*—to be close to it and figure out a way to get some.

Perhaps the best-kept secret going today is the mental disease called Chronic Millionaire Burnout, or CMB. The fact that wealth and power are difficult burdens to bear isn't something the media want the average citizen to hear. Such knowledge could undermine the global economy. Besides, who would believe that a millionaire could have problems?

But imagine: people always watching you, reporters everywhere. No one really cares about you. Slicksters hide investments in your tax shelter or piggyback through computers on your accounts. You search in vain for a purpose, some uninherited fruit from your own brain. Then one day you find one, but the guy with whom you found it turns out to be in the Mafia. To your chagrin, you learn you're in the Mafia, too. You receive mail addressed to the Godfather. The word *Don* becomes a prefix to your name. Everybody kisses your hand, but you can't trust a soul—not your lawyers, not your accountants, not your wives, and especially not your money-sucking kids. Life is meaningless, but you don't have the guts to end it. Then, suddenly, it's there before you like an iceberg drifting in fog. You knew it was coming but had miscalculated when. It's too late now. It's got you. Burnout!

It can happen that easily. But before the average millionaire does something crazy, he usually seeks the help of Dr. Otto Von Geber, the greatest mind to leave Germany at the conclusion of the Second World War. Having written about everything, he began treating CMB after meeting a Texas oil millionaire suffering from the disease. Dr. Von Geber cured Tex and documented his case history in a book titled: *In the Coffin with Caesar,* which also tells the story of CMB.

According to Dr. Von Geber, Rameses, the Egyptian Pharaoh, may have been an early CMB victim and the ravages of the disease probably affected his dealings with Moses. Unlike the holocaust survivor, the CMB victim is anguished, not by why he has survived, but by why he has so much wealth. It's a peculiar form of guilt whose symptoms in their mildest form reveal themselves as an unbridled desire to give cheese to the poor or take a bath with rats. (One millionaire, suffering from the disease, cut off his hands to lose weight.) But at its more severe stages, the disease can drive a millionaire to leaping from the Golden Gate Bridge in a Superman costume or traipsing through Morningside Park in search of love.

And CMB has powers that are even more far-reaching. It can affect church policy or church investments. It can sway Congress or any parliament. It can even change the mood of *the people,* or a trend in the fashion industry. Following World War II, the Civil Rights Movement accelerated at a time when a large number of millionaires were suffering from the disease. Some, consuming inconspicuously during the 1960s, began dressing like the poor: in jeans and rags. They were wolves in cheap clothing. And what happened? Did the poor benefit? No. By the Seventies, the price of jeans went through the roof. Rags became so expensive the poor couldn't afford them any more and were compelled to buy less expensive, dressier clothing. But those are the breaks.

Perhaps the economy is the next patient Dr. Von Geber will treat—after he stamps out CMB. But why should he stamp it out when he charges five million dollars per millionaire for the cure? That's cheap when you consider the stakes.

While millionaires are receiving the cure at Dr. Von Geber's Sutton Place townhouse (AKA The Treatment Center), Watt's job is to prevent them from hurting themselves. They may hurt other people. That's not his concern. He wears a long white coat similar to Dr. Von Geber's with *Watt* written over the pocket. He's a professional even though he dropped out of high school. His gimmick: He has developed a special technique for restraining millionaires—he slaps them. Technically calibrated, therapeutically administered slaps put food on his table. Energy that could have been wasted on Harlem streets—or prison—he channels into slapping millionaires, and he loves it, looks forward to it, although he's sometimes awakened in the middle of the night. The power! *the power!*—and a good job, too, not like beating patients in a mental institution for the poor, but as Dana, the street poet, put it in a poem titled, "The Art of Smacking a Millionaire," so much more.

> *There's an art to smacking a Millionaire,*
> *Hit him too hard or too soft and you're in trouble,*
> *Step back and time your blow just right*
> *So that he reels and staggers and feels contrite*

It's nice to have a job that you like. Although Watt did not know all the steps in the cure, most of them consisted of Dr. Von Geber telling millionaires not to worry about the poor. It also included Born Again Fantasy Sessions in which nude millionaires swam through a plastic orifice in the basement pool and emerged from the water to receive Watt's blessing: damp cigarette ashes scraped across their faces. Just thinking about them made Watt laugh. Of all the comic creatures on God's Earth, there's nothing funnier than a Born Again Millionaire. Even dry-cleaned, their self-righteousness stinks!

Looking back, Watt remembered some of the early millionaires he knew. Like their ancestors of the Twenties, they came to Harlem seeking a noble savage—someone with whom they could climb into garbage cans and get funky-low. In truth, they came to find their ids, which no one had taken but they had misplaced. Every Wednesday night they came during those incendiary summers, rolling up to Morningside Park in chauffeured limousines. They got out of their luxury cars to talk with some of Harlem's toughest kids. Conversing first on the edge of the park, they later entered the id oasis and found some spot in the dark where the kids could tell their stories while the millionaires patiently listened.

Had the Pollution Plane, which nightly fills Harlem's air with strange gas, flown overhead and the pilot spied the scene, he would have seen the glitter—a necklace of limousines around the park.

The misery of children ignited the burned-out millionaires. Stories that began *my father's a dopefiend* or *my mother's a whore* seemed to turn the millionaires on, making their manicured hands move in commiseration. Only once was there a problem. Some kid told his story, and then started yelling, "Because of *you!*" But the police, usually harder to find than employment, quickly appeared and took him away.

After that incident, everything got worse. Misery, misery, all became misery—on television, in the movies, and on the streets. The cons increased exponentially while the suckers decreased geometrically. Bleeding hearts and creaming genitals dried up. Proud men started to beg. But nowhere was the pain greater than inside Morningside Park.

Eventually, the kids tried to mug the burned-out millionaires. Revolution! Revolution! Revolution! Watt remembered how shocked some of the kids were to learn that millionaires never carry money. They are their *own* currency and can charge anything with just their names or faces.

Meanwhile, the kids continued to tell their sad stories to the millionaires, who gave them a little money—"just enough for the cit-tay." Then the kids and millionaires started playing fantasy games. The Pollution Plane probably saw it—all those millionaires being slapped and enjoying the pain.

But everything must change. In time, the kids' lives grew so horrific they couldn't talk about them anymore, and the millionaires got tired of getting slapped. Compassion withered. Then it finally happened. The kids became burned-out victims of racism, sociology, fallacious reasoning, and their own uncultivated corruption. Finally, they couldn't make it in Harlem anymore.

Number-runners (mathematical geniuses!), who could load their brains with hundreds of books of numbers, suddenly lost track of their numbers and control of their numerate brains. Shrewd hustlers, who could always turn a dollar for profit, couldn't even turn around. Then, some of the younger kids developed trouble with reading; a few appeared to be lame. Was it the shock of integration? Maybe. But telling their stories to the sick millionaires was the beginning. The kids saw their lives in a new vein. Heroin, alcohol, crack, cocaine. angel dust, you name it, filled the void of their days with pain. Spikes, pipes, and fools rushed in where wise men feared to tread.

Although the police stood by in broadest daylight while drugs were being sold, no one blamed them. And even though the trucks that delivered the dope were driven by the same men who chauffeured the millionaires at night, no one blamed them either. An amorphous nonentity called *Society* was blamed. As for the millionaires, they stopped coming to Harlem. Bored by the stories or the lack thereof, they returned to their yachts and villas off the coast of Spain. They forgot about the kids who barely remember anything.

But who needs to bitch about the past? Those are the breaks. You have to accept them, like a truck of shiny clichés. You're the sum total of whatever you have left, whether you can take it to the bank or not. You have to use what you have, no matter what the color or dimensions, to change a negative into a positive and survive. That's the way you win while you lose—because you will lose. You're going to die.

Watt learned how to win while he lost. Like other Harlem kids, he staked out a millionaire, visited his home and told sad stories to his family over dinner. Upon request, he made love to the millionaire's wife (while the great man of wealth watched). That millionaire led him to his present job as psychological surrogate to the world famous Dr. Otto Von Geber and his first encounter with a high-powered German mind. The discipline! The control! The Horror!

Perhaps the best symbols of it are Dr. Von Geber's cuckoo clock and bird. The German cuckoo clock hangs in the den over Dr. Von Geber's desk. Many years ago, one of his patients snatched out the cuckoo in a fit of rage. But the wooden stick upon which the painted bird once perched continued to shoot out and hiss, like a drunk snoring. Rather than remove the broken clock from the wall, Dr. Von Geber bought a parrot and taught it one word and when to say it: "Ordnung!" (*order* in *German*). Every hour on the hour the exhausted bird cries "Ordnung!" then goes back to sleep.

Like the parrot, Watt had a job to do, too. When he applied for it, Dr. Von Geber told him he would hire him if he answered one question correctly. "Tell me, Watt," asked Dr. Von Geber, "Do you believe in the American Dream?"

Perhaps it was the question coming when Watt least expected it, or maybe it was the fact that he had seen the American dream upside-down all his life. Whatever it was, Watt burst out laughing. When Erika Von Geber opened the den door carrying a refreshment tray, she saw the young man from Harlem and the Wittenberg professor slapping each other on the thigh and laughing while the cuckoo clock hissed and the parrot cried "Ordnung!"

As Watt's employer, Dr. Von Geber was always testing him, saying things like: "Did you know, Watt, Blacks account for 60-percent of the disorganized crime in our society?" Then he might hand Watt a computer printout containing figures that proved the point. Snatching it, Watt would yell, "Bullshit!" and tear it up as Dr. Von Geber laughed. "You are right not to trust figures, Watt," said Dr. Von Geber. "They can be made to do anything, even shake your hand. Besides, Watt, organized crime creates disorganized crime, not the other way around."

Perhaps once in a century Nature endows a human being with the ability to know everything, but seldom does it give that person the ruthlessness to do anything. Such a person is Dr. Otto Von Geber, whose power is so formidable that presidents and dictators the world over seek his counsel and advice. He understands all the nuances and limits of power and enjoys explaining them to Watt. "Like a car," he once told Watt, "History is driven. Fear and anxiety burn in the gas tank. Religions console the passengers, but do little to prevent the car from toppling over the brink. All religion, Watt, is the product of anxiety and inaccurate reporting. Not *one* would exist if there had been a cheap little camera around to record the miracles—or if the right people had been given a little money at the right time."

Dr. Von Geber didn't stop there. He constantly detonated things in Watt's mind and made him realize that the way he perceived the world was not the only way. And Dr. Von Geber made him read. (Watt probably had the equivalent of two PhDs.) Dr. Von Geber had that effect on everyone. Whether leading a millionaire through his brownstone or walking a carefully measured step behind a president, he always had an explanation ready—con and genius honed to perfection.

One day, Watt decided to test Dr. Von Geber's genius and asked, "Tell me, Doc, who's Bugs Bunny?" Slowly, Dr. Otto Von Geber's hand moved to his chin. He tugged his Freudian chin whiskers with a smile, countering," Don't *you* know?"

"If I knew, I wouldn't ask," said Watt.

"Bugs Bunny," announced Dr. Von Geber, "is a direct descendant of Brer Rabbit, the ultimate fugitive slave going back to Aesop. *You*, Watt, are Brer Rabbit," he said, pointing his finger. "But in the minds of most whites you are also King Kong. So be careful. *What's up, Doc* has a different meaning when you're talking about B.F. Skinner." Saying that, he advised Watt to reread Shakespeare and Machiavelli and learn how wars in Europe sometimes began. Who would have thought that a king could say he wanted to screw another king's queen and not expect it to reach the second king's ear. Gossip dominated events even back then. That's no different from the kind of stuff that happens in Harlem. But instead of one person getting pissed off, the offended king declared WAR and thousands died, and for what, territorial violations? No, for the best (you know what) with money that money could buy in those days. Of course, History was dry cleaned. It's always dry cleaned so future generations don't discover how much their ancestors screwed around.

But times have changed, or have they? One thing remains the same. Morningside Park still isn't safe. Creatures and characters from around the globe forage through it at night, conducting unspeakable rites. The most dangerous is an Indian named Laughing Gravy. A descendant of the great Apache chief Geronimo, he swore vengeance on the white man five years ago and single-handedly wiped out a nest of freaky millionaires. Cutting their throats and taking their scalps, he made Morningside Park look like a Little Bighorn.

In an effort to capture him, New York's Mayor Modal Glow sent the New York Calvary into the park. What was the use? Daniel Boone teamed with Davy Crockett couldn't find Laughing Gravy in that park even in broad daylight, let alone in the dark.

Perhaps Sir Ainsley Bridges will catch him. When he's not trying to eat himself, he's seething with anger and dreaming of settling a score. One night while he was roaming through Morningside Park, Laughing Gravy scalped him without slitting his throat, an Apache insult. Sir Ainsley Bridges was not worth killing, Laughing Gravy said.

Aside from Sir Ainsley Bridges, the multinational head, the current crop of millionaires receiving treatment from Dr. Von Geber also included Lena Messa, the founder of the Messa Speed Reading Schools, where people learn to read by focusing on subjects and verbs only. The problem is they speak and write that way eventually and make Tarzan-talk, which Lena spews in bed. Current patients also include Willard Camalian, a lowlife filmmaker whose latest work is a full-length feature film animating the works of Picasso in a brutal plot that opens with the exploded horse from Guernica galloping through the blue period while a cubist man slaps a cubist woman on her snout. Dr. Von Geber's family is also in the house: his wife, Erika, and son, Fritz.

As Watt reached the top of the stairs, he thought, *had I been born a few years earlier, I might have been an analyst.* He would have liked to espouse a few psychological theories in barbershops, the academies of the ghetto. He even had a theory he could hustle if only he had the right credentials. (Credentials: You're not supposed to think without them.) His theory: *Every black man really has three black men locked within him: a black man watching, a Negro disapproving, and a nigger having fun.*

The nigger having fun is always the hard part. Neither the black man nor the Negro can live with him. The real problem is still integration, how to let all three out at once without somebody getting killed. Liberation, that's the goal of analysis, but in truth it often cripples. Enough thinking—he was so tired he couldn't pay attention to his own thoughts.

Passing Willard Camalian's door, he heard him mumble: "There's nothing left. Hermaphrodites, fuck yourselves." Then, in a voice charged with exultation and power, he cried, "I am a bowelful man. I am one of the most bowelful men in the world!" Opening the door, Watt found Willard Camalian kneeling at the foot of his bed, wearing a priest's collar. "So you finally got around to me, Blackie," he turned and said. Before he could say another word, Watt slapped him. Sighing in ecstasy, Camalian fell back and began twitching. He twitched himself to sleep as Watt opened the door and left.

A few minutes later, Watt climbed into bed with Lena for her therapy, thinking, *a bowelful man? Yes, he's full of shit.*

CHAPTER 2

▼

Watt awoke exhausted, hearing Lena sing some old, worn out song, "Please stay. Don't go" as he climbed out of bed saying, "I've got better things to do than listen to Tarzan-Talk from a millionaire."

"In Harlem!" she exclaimed. "I go, too!"

"No you won't! I'll be damned if I'd walk around Harlem with *you*," he said. "What would the *sisters* say?" Immediately Lena got depressed. She removed a packet of Alka Selzer from the night table and popped one into her mouth. Alka Seltzer was her remedy for everything. She chewed it as a candy. She drank it as a soft drink. She bathed with it for soap. As the Alka Seltzer fizzed and formed a froth that dripped from her lips, Watt said: "Don't get depressed. You've got money. There's a lot for *you* to do in New York."

Climbing from bed, Lena asked, "What do you have against millionaires?"

"Nothing," snapped Watt, "nothing for you and nothing against you."

"Then stay with me," she begged as Watt shook his head.

Passing Willard Camalian's door, he heard him mumble, "Rome sends flowers." And from the top of the stairs he saw Stetson gingerly knocking on Ainsley Bridges' door. "There's a call from your solicitor, Sir Ainsley, Mr. Chubby Hands." On the floor below, he saw an Arab sheik and a Chinese businessman hastily writing checks and handing them to Erika Von Geber. As Watt went out the rear door, he heard a racket from little Fritz's computer game, which had replaced the Saturday morning cartoons and maybe even little Fritz's brain.

Walking through Sutton Place, where millionaires fester like disease, Watt heard a voice scream, "NOTHING CAME OUT!" And looking up, he saw a white man in a Superman costume dive from a luxury penthouse apartment and splatter on the ground in front of a Rolls Royce. A minute later, a beautiful blonde came running out of the building. Looking down at the splattered corpse, she cried, "Why didn't you call Dr. Otto Von Geber? You knew you had CMB!"

Reaching Second Avenue, Watt caught a bus down to 42nd Street and walked over to Times Square, the anus of the Apple. Hands diced in doorways waving hot goods. Silhouettes of copulating couples gyrated on theater marquees. Pimps, muggers, and drug dealers searched for prey. And at the end of the block, horse trailers and lamb trucks delivered animals for the bizarre sex acts. At the center of this hellish sanctum, a church choir sang,

Just a closer walk with Thee
Grant it, Jesus, if you please
Daily walking close to Thee
Let it be, Dear Lord, let it be

But while they sang, pickpockets plied their trade.

Listening to the choir, Watt thought, *Music can be faith. At an ice-skating rink, it keeps people apart; for nervous lovers, it opens the heart; in the street, it can serve as a force-field; in a troubled home, it can even be a shield. Everyone hears his own music and struggles to charm his own savage beast.*

Watt had his faith, too—not in music, but in his ability to survive. He would survive in this world of doom-drops, where every man ate the man above him and shat it out on the man below, where every day he saw headless bodies stooped, smoking from the implosion of corporate rites. Shit was good in New York's palate, "Today New York, tomorrow the world," as some cocksucker said.

As he turned onto Eighth Avenue, he heard sirens. A phalanx of motorcycles spearheaded the path of New York's Mayor, Modal Glow. The procession screeched to a halt in front of Rusty's Peep Show Joint. A mayoral assistant opened the car door, and a trembling Mayor Glow hurried into Rusty's Peep-show Joint as reporters snapped his picture.

Ten minutes later he came out after his private session looking refreshed and relieved. His political facade reinforced, he calmly ordered the sirens turned off. Then he met the press. With Jehoover, his top police captain standing by, he talked of how the city was winning its war against crime. As reporters snickered, he got back into the car and drove off.

"Thank God we've got the Black Hole!" cried a woman, and the crowd cheered.

"Yeah, if we didn't have her," said a man, "one of our leaders might get uptight and do something stupid—like bomb New Jersey."

"Maybe the president should use the Black Hole for a summit."

"Where does the Black Hole come from?" someone asked, and Watt remembered a story he had heard. The Black Hole was born to parents of an unknown racial stock somewhere in upstate New York. She came into the world without any sense of taste, touch, sight, smell, or hearing. A vegetable with an oversized digestive tract, consuming any substance near her mouth, she ate with a rapacity seldom seen in zoos.

Suffering from the beginning, her parents called her their curse for transgressing nature and having their first baby so late. Ashamed, they never gave her a name or food. Hoping she would die, both went to work and came home each night only to find her alive. Having devoured her crib and whatever food they left on the floor, her mouth was always wide open for more. And the cost of feeding her became outrageous, taking the larger portion of both their incomes. So they began giving her cat food and dog food and bird seed for snacks. But even that became expensive.

And they were tired. Cleaning behind her was wearing them out. For as fast as she ate one thing she shat another out—on the floor, of course, in the room in which she had sat since the day they brought her home from the hospital in a bag, the only room she had ever known, where the heaps of food were placed and where her father, with his nostrils closed, shoveled her waste into a plastic bag each night and hosed the room out with water on weekends after moving her into a corner against the wall.

Unbearable, she drove her parents to drink. Desperate, they thought a circus might take her and wrote letters to every big tent circus and county carnival for which they could find a listing, now referring to their child as the human piranha.

Dear Sir:

Would you be interested in our daughter? With teeth sharper than razors and glands that produce saliva by the bucket, she can tear cheap meat to pieces and suck a circus lollipop thinner than a dime. She even chews the stick.

Unfortunately, sir, none of her senses work. But we'd be happy to ship her to you, all expenses paid, if you'll just give us your shipping address. Please let us know as soon as possible, for we think our daughter would be a great addition to your show.

Sincerely,
Osgood P. Conklin

Alas, they didn't receive one bite and came to accept their lot. Ceasing to call it their curse, they made the best of a bad situation that didn't get worse, cutting cord on her teeth when no scissors was handy and sharpening pencils in her mouth. And because her father lost his sense of smell, cleaning her room was no longer a problem, and they became closer, having one lost sense in common.

But one day her father died, and her mother cried, "Don't leave me with the human piranha!" Then she died, too, leaving the little girl with no one to care for her. She was sent to a state home where the superintendent put her to use as a garbage disposal. Recognizing a vegetable-of-a-gold mine when he saw one, Chump, an attendant at the home, kidnapped her on her eighteenth birthday and took her to New York's 42nd Street where she produced money like a mint and received the appellation of the Black Hole, working in the back of Rusty's Peep Show Joint off Times Square.

A human vacuole into which men, not a little perverse, thrust themselves, she became famous for giving the best head in the nation, eventually the world. Arab emirs and Singapore businessmen sang her praises. Old men near death crawled into her darkness for that final shot of life. Scientists, assuming that which exists on Earth exists in Space, re-postulated scientific theories. For better or worse, the Black Hole had left her mark on the Earth.

When the mayor's procession disappeared, old Rusty, crumpled money in hand, stumbled out and posted a sign:

NEW BLACK HOLE HOURS FOR THE PUBLIC:
5:30 P.M.–7:30 P.M.
BY APPOINTMENT ONLY

Approaching Rusty, Watt asked, "Seen Perry"

"I ain't seen him," said Rusty, rolling his eyes from Watt's head to his toes. "But if you see him, tell him I want my money. And if he doesn't pay me, I'll call Joe Vine."

Mean Joe Vine was a leg breaker with a downtown office decorated with human anatomical charts. His customers studied the charts, and then pointed to the parts they wanted broken on someone else. Joe would break a leg for $200.00; two for $350.00. At $100, a broken nose was a bargain. But if Joe missed the nose and hit the mouth you had to pay extra for the teeth.

"Now don't forget to tell Perry what I told you," said Rusty.

"Fuck you!" snapped Watt, and Rusty hustled back inside. "If you mess with Perry, you mess with me!"

Watt walked to the subway and caught the "A" Train uptown. (Yes, the "A" Train—hurry, hurry, hurry.) But the screeching rail car that crawled into 42nd Street wasn't worthy of Billy Strayhorn's great song. And if the Duke were alive—you can bet he wouldn't have got on board.

The doors opened. Passengers gasped for air and stumbled out. Other passengers entered and waited for the doors to close. A man, racing down the stairs, cried, "Holder the doors!" Peering from the train, the conductor grinned sadistically. Then, as the running man leaped to enter the train, the conductor closed the doors, catching the passenger in mid-flight. Half of him was inside the subway car; the other half was out.

"Releaser me! Releaser me!" he cried as the train sped through darkness.

CHAPTER 3

▼

Watt got off the train in Harlem. As he climbed the subway stairs to exit, shot gun blasts exploded in the air. Dopefiends scrambled in all directions. As the last dopefiend turned the corner, Watt saw Captain Jehoover and Towntamer, his black lieutenant. Reloading their weapons in a cloud of smoke, they pursued fleeing dopefiends around the corner.

Moments later, the street returned to normal. The sun peered out from behind a barricade of clouds. A kid, dribbling a basketball, ran desperately toward the park. Hardworking people returned from laundry or supermarket chores, and life seemed normal for awhile. Then the Pollution Plane flew overhead and people started coughing.

Watt was looking for Perry, but first he had to meet Sylvia. As he crossed the street, a sanitation department truck rounded the corner, cutting its sweepers into the guts of the curb. When the truck passed, he saw her standing in front of the pharmacy. And in that instant, he saw what had attracted him. Her smooth, ebony-colored skin, her keen features and light brown eyes, her well-proportioned body neither skinny nor fat made her look like a Madonna and gave credence to those stories about Jesus being black.

Before he could say a word, she asked, "Do you want me to have your baby or not?" And the question struck him like a bullet to the head. He said nothing, but in his mind he heard a circus ring master bark, *Ladies and gentlemen and children of all ages.*

"What do you want?" asked Sylvia.

"I don't know what I want," he said. "I know I'm not ready. I haven't made myself yet."

"You may never *make* yourself," she said. "You don't have to be rich for me. I want you the way you are."

Why? he thought, imagining himself rushing to get somewhere, pulling an old suit from the closet with mothballs falling off. Placing his hand into the dark trouser pocket, he found a mothball in it. Playfully, he stuffed it up his nose and couldn't get it out. The smell of camphor raced through his brain suffocating him. It was 1984. Something was supposed to happen this year. He didn't remember what it was. But he knew it wasn't for Sylvia to have his baby. "I'm hungry," she said. "Let's go to Dreamland."

As they walked toward Seventh Avenue, the sun made its retreat and the wind sucked drapes from windows and made them wave like tongues at the litter below. Sylvia grabbed his hand and made his insides jump. He cringed and wanted to run but kept walking with her.

"What's wrong?" asked Sylvia.

"Nothing," he said.

Rounding the corner of 116th Street and Seventh Avenue, they passed the Optimo Candy Store. An old man lay dying on the concrete while some children played around him, placing empty soda cans and candy wrappers by his head. A speaker propped against a record store thumped a beat: "Before you die," the voice screeched, "sat-tis-fyyyy yourself! just sat-tis-fy yourself!"

As they neared Central Park, a ragtime line of old politicians leapt into Watt's mind. Cakewalking in Vaudevillian time, a fat one said, *Ladies and gentlemen, today is a proud day for the Harlem community. East, going downtown, they have their Fifth Avenue; west, coming uptown, they have their Central Park West; and south, parallel to this very spot on which I'm standing, they have their Central Park South. Now, good people, we are honored and honor all of those who fought with us these many years for this—our Central Park North."* And his arm swept wide in a gesture toward the part of the park where people get mugged most.

Reaching Dreamland, they went in and took a table.

"Do you know how many men want me," said Sylvia, "offer me cars and houses—anything I want—if I'll just marry them. And I turn them down, and for what? For *you*."

What am I doing here? thought Watt as a diminutive waitress with dyed red hair came over.

"A coke and a cheeseburger, please," said Sylvia.

"I'll have the same," said Watt. As the waitress walked away, he said, "Maybe you should hook up with some of those dudes. I can't give you anything but...."

His voice trailed off into silence.

"But what?" she asked.

"Nothing," he said.

"I want *you*," she said. "It's *your* baby I'm carrying."

He started to say "So what!" but bit into his lower lip to keep quiet.

"What do you want?" she asked.

"Why don't you have an abortion," he said.

"Have an abortion!" she cried, as heads turned. "That's all you can say? Have an abortion! What do you think I am? I'm a woman, Watt! I've already had one abortion because of a man like you! I won't have another!"

"Then have the baby."

"You mean, have the baby, without *you*."

Casually, the waitress brought over their drinks with an expression of *Hmmmmmmmmmmmmmm ... poe thang* on her face, then sauntered to another table.

"If that's what you want," said Watt, "go for it."

"Bastard!" cried Sylvia. "You can't love anyone, can you?!" Suddenly, layers of scab exploded in Watt's brain. "Why? Because I don't love *you*!" he yelled.

"You finally said it!"

"And I'd say a lot more, too! But I'm leaving." He stood up and she grabbed him. As if by reflex, he slapped her and she fell backwards, the sodas toppling in her lap.

"No-good cocksucker!" screamed the waitress, running over, and he slapped her, too, yelling, "Mind your business, bitch!" As he went out the door, the waitress ran to the kitchen.

If he had turned, he would have seen the waitress, running after him with a butcher knife in her hand. But he wasn't thinking about her. He was thinking about the child—his child, Sylvia's child. He descended subway stairs, put a token in the turnstile, and boarded a train that seemed to be waiting for him. Looking back, he saw the waitress, face contorted, climb over the turnstile pursuing him, yelling, "Nigger, I'm gonna getcha! So help me I'm gonna cutcha!" The doors closed, and she banged on them cursing and screaming, waving the butcher knife in the air. Two transit policemen grabbed her from the rear. One wrenched the knife from her hand while the other raised a pair of handcuffs in the air. Then the train began moving.

As Watt got off the train at 125th Street, a man sang

I need love so bad
I'm willin' to give some.
Are you willin' to share?

No, thought Watt, *Hell no!* Exiting the platform, he walked over to Seventh Avenue, thinking about the child—his child, Sylvia's child. When he reached Seventh Avenue, he saw a crowd assembled, listening to Brother Kahlil.

"Brothers and sisters!" cried Kahlil, "The white man's time has come! He's being pushed out of Asia, out of Africa, down deep into the troubled recesses of his own sick mind.

"He's a desperate beast, my people, a wounded beast, who for centuries didn't have the decency to eat the *whole* man.

"Many of our brothers have been seduced by the beast's foul daughters. To those who have, I say, take your Hodgkin's disease, take your cancer, and leave Harlem! And if any of you try to return to our beautiful, black sisters after cooking in the sheets with the beast—you sisters, cut it off! Cut it off and let him know that you don't want him after he fucks the White Devil!"

A roar went up. The words "White Devil!" swung across Seventh Avenue, like meat and blood delivered separately on a trapeze, and stopped in the mouth of an old shoeshine man: "White Devil!"

People in the crowd raised clenched fists and slapped fives while policemen—black and white—smiled, as if they knew a secret. In the back of the crowd, old West Indians gathered. "Yahse, dee brawther cun talk," one said, "but not like Garvey or Malcolm."

"Where does Kahlil get his money?" another asked.

Shaking hands, Kahlil got into a black Mercedes Benz and drove off.

The sun going down dispersed the crowd, casting bloodstained rays into boot-black slopes. Walking across 125th Street, Watt passed the spot where A.J. Lester's Clothing Store used to be.

Ain't dat some stuff, ain't dat some shit! Look at them shirts! Look at them suits! I'd be cleaner than the board o'health if I could afford em. But tell me somethin'—as fly as his clothes are, as hip as his shit is—how's he gonna have a name like Abraham Jesus Lester? Dat don't sound right. Don't sound right. Do it, Bro?

Gay tones, light and airy, floated from the Club Baby Grande as young men in tight pants switched across the street. "If he likes me, he'll pay for my shots. That's all there is to it."

"All—I'm ever given' out—is ass! And I don't do no rim jobs on Sunday. If he wants his ass sucked Sunday, he'll have to see *another* lady!"

Watt walked down Manhattan Avenue. As the street lights came on, an old man preached from atop a stoop: "I tell you when New York was a city of darkness and you couldn't see a white fist wavin' in your black face, there was no crime. *LIGHT BRINGS CRIME.*"

Going into his building, he heard little Cecil call, but ignored him. Climbing dark and urine-splattered stairs, he heard feet shuffling, breath trickling, and people moaning. A sound, like a miniature jackhammer, thumped repeatedly. As he took out his knife, a flashlight shone in his eyes. Then the flashlight rotated up to a face.

"Perry?" said Watt.

"Still a king!" cried Perry.

"What's going on?" asked Watt.

"Come up and see," said Perry.

Climbing higher, Watt saw Rosaline lying on the stairs with her legs in the air. A copy of the *New York Times* was under her ass, and nine men stood in a line listening to her peeling moans.

Condom-clad, one man finished and rose while another fell between her legs. His back snapped into place and began jacking as rusty giggles blew through loins of pipe behind.

After several minutes, one of the men said: "C'mon, Gene, Don't wear it out. Save some for us. You been on it ten minutes. That's long enough."

"Shut up, mafuck, fore I kill ya!" groaned Gene. "I'm almost there!" Then BADNIGGER stepped to the front of the line and slapped Gene on his ass with a blow that sounded like a whip lash. "Kill me, faggot!" he said and dragged Gene off as he was coming. Another back plopped into place and began jacking. Some plaster fell from the ceiling and slid between his thighs, making him yell "Woh!" and move further into Rosaline double-clutched below. As BADNIGGER threw Gene down the stairs, the men on line smacked their lips, and Rosaline growled, "More plaster, goddammit!" as BADNIGGER got back on line.

"You fuck her?" asked Watt.

"I got mine first in the basement," said Perry.

"Then how did she get up here?" asked Watt.

"These dudes fucked her up the stairs and rode her across the landing," said Perry.

"How much you chargin'?"

"Even with inflation," said Perry, "a little night train has got to be worth ten dollars. Want any?"

"I wouldn't fuck her with *your* dick," said Watt. "Besides, BADNIGGER's gonna stretch the pussy for miles."

"Then forget about the pussy," said Perry. "She's got a hot tub in her mouth. Be cool and let me see if I can get her to give you a little head for nothin'."

Tossing a man off, Rosaline extended her legs to haul down a middle class looking man in a dark, business suit. Holding an attaché case, he stared at Rosaline, lustfully smacking his lips.

"It's that bourgeois motherfucker from Washington again," said Perry. "Either get down or get out! Don't hold up the line."

As BADNIGGER stepped forward, the middle-class man ran down the stairs. "Don't come back either!" roared Perry as the downstairs door opened and shut. "That's what's wrong with those middle-class niggers," said Perry. "They just wanna watch."

Six grunts later and BADNIGGER, it was over. The *Times* and Rosaline's ass were in shreds. "Rosaline," whispered Perry as BADNIGGER zipped up his pants. "Ros-a-line," he repeated as BADNIGGER went down the stairs. "Rosaline," he said, as the downstairs door shut and BADNIGGER went into the night. "I know you're kinda wasted, baby. But how's about givin' my man, Watt, the ten-minute head?" Sitting up dazed, Rosaline said: "If I do, Skip's a faggot." Bitch-slapping her once, Perry said, "Skip's a faggot!" and Rosaline's mouth sprang open.

Watt unzipped his pants and climbed three steps above her.

Arise, you more than dead! This is the music of ten-minute head. The sea of faith is rising, beating its way. Take my nerves and pluck them. Who knows what you'll find. But what you find, you keep. Swallow the way a bird swallows. And after you swallow, listen to the music of cells cease—the release, the release. And you can get it. You can get it if you stand still. Yes, still. For a tide comes through the tunnel with wind and beaten flesh. A tide comes pounding, bursting through despair. Yes, it's coming! It's coming! It's flying through the air.

"Yeah!" screamed Watt as Rosaline milked him. Then she rolled her head back and swished his semen around in her mouth before spitting it out between the railing spokes on the stairs. And as she spat, Watt heard old public school dozens echo through his ears:

Your mama's a one-titty bandit!
Your mama smells like a herd of wild sneakers!
Your mama is so bowlegged I can look up her legs and see her heart beat!

Holding the banister, Watt zipped up his pants as Rosaline wiped her mouth and threw the tissue down, saying, "Ain't one of you could take me by yourself, except BADNIGGER. That's why I gave him his ten dollars back. He ain't never got to pay me as long as I got pussy and he's got the biggest dick in the world."

"Shut up, bitch!" snapped Perry, as Watt laughed. "How's that lovely lady of yours?" asked Perry.

"Pregnant," said Watt.

"Well at least you know you ain't shootin' blanks."

"Ouch!" cried Rosaline as a splinter stuck her.

"Shut up!" snapped Perry.

"I saw Rusty coming uptown," said Watt. "He's threatening to put Mean Joe Vine on you if you don't pay him some money he says you owe."

"Fuck that Barnum & Bailey side-show freak motherfucker! I ain't payin' him shit! Who does he think he is—*Lipsky?*!"

"Nobody's Lipsky," said Watt, "*but* Lipsky."

"I wanna go!" said Rosaline.

"It just so happens that it's time to go," snapped Perry. "So get your ass off those fuckin' stairs."

"Where're you going?" asked Watt.

"Home," said Perry, "to get clean as a mosquito's peter."

"A skeeter ain't got no peter," interrupted Rosaline.

"Shut up, bitch!" snapped Perry. "Then I'm gonna take her around to the Outhide to see how much more I can make." He pulled out a fat wad of tens with one hand and slapped Watt's palm with the other. "I sure hope BADNIGGER didn't stretch the pussy too bad," he said going down the stairs.

"Later," said Watt. The downstairs door closed behind them and they moved into darkness, disappearing in a spot.

CHAPTER 4

▼

Perry was Watt's best friend. They had gone through elementary and high school together, suffering, triumphing and, ultimately, losing together.

"Miss Hastings."

"Yes, Mr. Kleindeck?"

"Send Watt and Perry Lamprey to my office immediately."

"Yes, Mr. Kleindeck."

The two boys entered, knowing why their high school principal had sent for them.

"Men," said Mr. Kleindeck, "as president and vice president of the student government, you have a responsibility to maintain. Up to now, you've done a good job. But yesterday you invited a man who advocates the violent overthrow of the United States government to speak at our commencement exercises next month. I—we—can't allow that. We have a...."

Watt didn't hear him. Loud sounds from the previous night clanged in his mind. A smithy's anvil opened, and bloated limbs and pus shot like geysers into the air. Dopefiends marched. And it was there in Kleindeck's office that he heard the wild music for the first time and wanted to run.

"So you see this Brother Kahlil is simply not the kind of speaker we want at our commencement exercises. I think it will look better if *you* withdraw his name and substitute State Senator Brown's. He's available. We've talked."

"But why can't Brother Kahlil speak?" asked Watt.

"I think I've explained," said Kleindeck. "He's a revolutionary, and he can't come to Nixon High."

"All he advocates is improvement," said Watt.

"Well, we don't need his kind of improvement at Nixon High," said Klein-deck. "This discussion is over. You two may go back to—"

"What do we need at Nixon High?" interrupted Watt. "We've already got a big drug problem."

"Hold on," said Kleindeck. "Our drug problem is not that serious. We have a few addicts...."

"A few addicts!" cried Watt.

"Hold on," said Kleindeck. "I support Civil Rights."

"I wasn't talking about Civil Rights," said Watt.

"I'm the principal here, not you! And I've had enough of these new policies for handling nig—"

"Say it!" cried Perry. "You've had enough of these new policies for handling niggers!"

Red-faced, Kleindeck jumped up and hopped to the door. Cracking it, he peered out. Then breathing a sigh of relief, he carefully shut the door and moved back behind his desk. "I never said that," he murmured softly, "and you can't prove I did." Watt and Perry looked at each other, and then turned their heads back to Kleindeck. "Let me explain something," he said. "When I was growing up, if a Negro didn't do what he was told, he was carted off to jail or lynched. Nobody *who mattered* cared if he was right or wrong. Nobody stood up for him. The only thing that counted was that a Negro had forgotten his place, and he had to pay for it.

"Now you two have full scholarships to two of the best universities in the country. You can get an excellent education, make a lot of money after gradua-tion, and enjoy all the benefits of the system. But if you don't forget about this Brother Kahlil and keep your mouths shut, you won't go anywhere. I'll see to that. Do you understand?"

"What do we have to do?" asked Watt.

"As you're told," said Kleindeck. "Just remember "everything passes—love, marriage, even the Civil Rights movement. They're just intervals in life—breaks in time between the way things are and the way they're *supposed* to be. And when those intervals pass, the only thing you have is the money in your pocket. You two can make it. Black kids with half your intelligence have gone to the top. They did what they were told and learned how to play the game."

Pausing, Kleindeck looked intently at the two boys. Then, lowering his voice, he said, "It just so happens that I've been asked to be on the lookout for bright black boys who might want to go places and serve their nation, too. The govern-ment needs people to help keep an eye on things."

"What do we have to do?" asked Watt.

"Watch your community, Harlem. Keep an eye out and give periodic reports. A lot goes on up there that we don't know about."

"How do we get started?" asked Watt.

"Be patient," said Kleindeck. "I'll make the arrangements."

"Can we work for the FBI?" asked Perry.

"You can work for *anybody,*" said Kleindeck, "and get *anything.* It can be arranged."

"What do you mean by *anything?*" asked Watt.

"The American Dream," said Kleindeck, smiling.

"You mean a house in Queens around black people who run from other black people?!" yelled Watt.

"Or a fucked up job doing meaningless work!" snapped Perry."

"With people passing each other all day, saying *Hello* each time they pass?!" jumped Watt.

"We ain't Uncle Toms," said Perry.

"And we don't eat cheese!" snapped Watt. If you want some rats, go down to the basement and catch some."

"No thank you, *Mr. Kleindeck!*" said Perry. "You can kiss our black asses!"

"Get out of my office!" yelled Kleindeck. "Get the hell out of here, you bastards!"

"We're going," said Watt.

"But before we do, Mister Kleindeck," said Perry, "I just want to remind you of one thing—you ain't white. You're Jewish. And *your* people have been fucked over just like ours."

An explosion went off in Kleindeck's head. "Get out of here, you dirty niggers!" he cried. "The only thing you understand is a whip and a chain! That's all you'll ever understand. You'll never be free because you're stupid!"

"Fuck you!" screamed Perry. Leaping onto Kleindeck's desk, he started kicking papers in all directions, and Kleindeck hollered, "I'll kill you, black bastard!" He reached into a golf bag by the window and pulled out a club. Watt grabbed Perry and pulled him off the desk as the swoosh of the putter grazed his head. Kleindeck fell over, then jumped up, and raised the golf club again, assuming a batter's position with his mouth wide open. Crying, Perry struggled to go to him, but Watt held him tightly, pulling him toward the door. As they left the office, Watt looked back and saw Kleindeck crouched in a corner with that look of *never again* in his eyes and the golf club raised above his head. "You two are through in this school!" he cried, "through in life! You're not going anywhere! Do you hear?! You might as well quit!"

They were kicked out of school the same day. But they kept coming to class until a judge ordered them to stay away. But the week before graduation they were outside Nixon High.

As their classmates filed out, they saw Watt and Perry in blue-jeans and berets standing like bookends on either side of Brother Kahlil who, raising both arms, beckoned to the students.

Standing atop a milk crate, Kahlil raised his bullhorn and cried, "They wouldn't let me speak to you in that school. So I've come to speak to you in the street. I've come to speak to you about three things: truth, knowledge, and wisdom—the truth of Nat Turner, the knowledge of Denmark Vesey, and the wisdom—the very potent wisdom—of Malcolm X.

"Those black men fought the white man until the day they died. They didn't have PhD's. All they had was a truth, knowledge, and a wisdom that could be summed up in six words, my brothers and sisters: *The white man is a devil!*"

As some students cheered and others drew back, Watt saw Kleindeck come out of the school's side doors flanked by two gym teachers and a school guard. He stared intensely at Watt and Perry, then looked at his watch and smiled.

"Only a devil!" cried Kahlil, "could cause the death of one-hundred million of our ancestors! Only a devil could enslave us for nearly 250 years, and lynch us, bomb us, mutilate us, and humiliate us for another 100 years. Only a devil could make us hate *ourselves* for the evil *he* did and continues to do to *us*.

"When has this devil ever acknowledged his sins? When has he even said, *I'm sorry for what I did to you?* Oh he'll go around the world to free *other* people. But he won't acknowledge the wrong he's done at home. He'll never admit that he did the same thing to black, red, and yellow people in America that Hitler did to Jews in *Germany!* Genocide!"

While a few students cheered, clapping their hands and nodding their heads the way they did in church, others, who never had a political thought in their lives, talked about revenge. But a few students, shaking their heads in disapproval, slowly walked away.

"But the devil never apologizes! Despite the hopes and dreams of Uncle Toms and the prayers of Aunt Jemimahs, the devil never apologizes! He thinks he's right—no matter what *you* say or history reveals.

"Well I'm not waiting for the devil to apologize. I'm not waiting for him to admit his sins. I'm not waiting for him to forgive *me* for what *he's* done to me. I'm gonna make him face me man-to-man. I'm gonna show him the price of—"

"Harvey Mason, you stop that talk this minute!" cried a voice from the crowd. It was Miss Winter, the oldest teacher in the school. Parting the crowd of students with wrinkled hands, she moved toward Kahlil, repeating: "You stop that talk right now!"

As her straight white hair blew in the June breeze, she stood before Kahlil defiantly, saying, "You can call yourself Brother Kahlil, instead of Harvey Mason. You can talk about pitchforks and call white people devils. But I won't allow you to ruin the lives of these children and poison them with *your* hate!"

"This woman is an Uncle Tom!" cried Kahlil, pointing at her. "I knew her years ago when I was a student in that school. And it's no wonder that she talks the way she does. Look at her light skin and straight hair. She's the product of rape and race mixing."

"You can talk about my hair and skin, Harvey Mason, and you can call me an Uncle Tom and a product of rape. But these children know that I love them. That's why I won't let you destroy them with your hate. You've already ruined the lives of two of our best students … now you're back to claim the rest. You're the devil, Harvey Mason!"

A student applauded, and then quickly stopped. "Yes, black people are oppressed—by white people *and* by each other. And racism, as always, is on the rise. But calling white people devils won't do a thing except foster more fear and confusion. And our children are frightened and confused enough already. We need to give them courage, not hate, Harvey Mason. We need to give them clarity, not confusion. So stop it! Leave these children alone! And don't corrupt them with *your* hate."

"This woman is a tom!" cried Kahlil. "She's got one foot in the grave. But with her last ounce of strength, she's still defending the white man."

"No, Harvey," said Miss Winter. "I'm not a tom. And the only proof I offer is that a teacher can fail. I failed *you*. We all failed you. We didn't save you when there was time. We didn't stop your family from destroying you. And you were hurt. You've spent your whole life trying to cover up that hurt, and now you want others to share your pain."

Leaning over, Kahlil whispered to Watt, "Shut that old bitch up!"

"How?" asked Watt.

"Punch her in the face!—I don't care how! That's an order!" Breaking his bookend stand, Watt looked at Kahlil as if he were crazy.

"Yes, I remember how your family abused you," continued Miss Winter. "I remember how they hurt you. But don't take it out on *these* kids. They deserve a chance to face the world without *your* hate and *your* pain. Let them find out what life has to offer them—not what it failed to give *you*. But it's not too late, Harvey. I'll help you."

"Somebody, shut her up!" cried Kahlil, placing his hands over his ears. "Shut her up!"

"You can *still* learn to read," said Miss Winter."

A hush fell over the crowd broken only by a giggle. Miss Winter stood there, seemingly unaware of the gravity of her words. Then more of the students began to giggle until their giggles blossomed into full-blown laughs.

"He can't read!" cried Miguel Vasquetelles. And the words "can't read" swung through the air, stopping Kahlil's throat. His revolutionary façade dropped as everyone—teachers and students alike—began to laugh and point at him. Watt saw Kleindeck and the gym teachers holding their sides, and slapping each other on the back. And he saw shame in Kahlil's eyes. His crime was trying to cover up his illiteracy, and his punishment was public humiliation. In the midst of the ribaldry, Watt and Perry took off their berets and started laughing, too. But their laughter was mixed with tears and pain that would haunt them the rest of their lives.

Moments later, everyone was still laughing when the first prowl car, siren blaring, entered the block. "Cops!" cried Miguel.

"Don't run!" called Miss Winter. "Leave the area quietly. You're not breaking any law."

But when a prowl car screeched to a halt in front of some students and a policeman leaped from it dressed in full riot gear, everyone started running. Chaos was in the air. Watt saw Brother Kahlil spin around as if riding a skate board and glide into an unlocked apartment building and lock the door behind him. Then buses, carrying what seemed like dozens of policemen, screeched to a halt in front of the school. Cops jumped out and formed a wedge, sealing off the street at both ends. Frightened students banged desperately on the school's locked doors while others tried to flee into any unlocked apartment building. Miss Winter tried to calm students and police, saying, "No Violence! No Violence!"

But it was useless. Watt saw a policeman's nightstick go up and come down on the head of Norman Reed who hit the pavement faster than a bag of dropped groceries. Then badge-less policemen appeared and started beating students up and down the street.

Watt saw old Miss Winter, her wrinkled hands outstretched, pleading with a policeman not to beat Michael Anglin anymore. And looking toward the school, he saw Kleindeck smiling and shaking hands with a police sergeant who seemed to say, "We've got everything under control." Then he saw Kleindeck's eyes searching for Perry and him. His arm shot out when he spotted Watt, and that same police sergeant, with four other cops, came running toward Watt who dodged a few of their tackles before being dragged down. They beat Watt with their nightsticks as he screamed. On the ground, nearly unconscious, he heard a cop yell, as if reminding him, "You're a nigger!"

And Watt saw Perry on the ground being beaten too. A cop kicked his head as if practicing football field goals while another beat the soles of his feet. In the midst of the ass whipping, Watt saw his revolutionary beret fly by and imagined Kahlil saying, "See, devil! See devil kick! See devil kick your ass!" Then sirens blared, sirens that, in the bitter-sweet years that lay ahead, the two boys would call "Our Song."

An ambulance carried them to a hospital. A paddy wagon took them to jail. Grandma bailed them out before their manhood could be taken. They went on trial the week they should have graduated. At the trial, no one mentioned Kahlil. A judge put them on probation.

Now they had to play the game that most black boys have to play: catch-up. Without any support system, they had to get their lives together and try to make sense of what had happened to them. They had to get a job or find a hustle to make money. They weren't going to college; they had to educate themselves. Books were the answer, and they went to bookstores all over town, buying books, reading them, and discussing them.

They were leaving a bookstore on Broadway, near Columbia University one day, when they saw a black man come out of the West End Bar & Grill with his arm throttled around a white woman's neck. Ebony and ivory, the couple moved in sync, kissing each other passionately as if on their way to a hotel. As the couple hopped into a car and the engine was turned on, the man's name exploded from the two boys' lips. "Kahlil, you dirty motherfucker!" they yelled, running after the car as it pulled away from the curb. With the driver looking back and the woman looking forward, the two boys cursed Kahlil who from that day on they regarded as the Devil or one of his chief disciples.

Walking back to Harlem, they were still cursing when they saw Dana, the street poet, Harlem's greatest word-wailer. Seeing the confusion in the two boys' faces, Dana stopped to give them a poem:

> *Brothers and sisters in social hell,*
> *private as well,*
> *fragmented notions of revolution,*

> *blocking the flow with circumlocution,*
> *penalous words, and idle devotions*
> *that fly with the birds*
> *These are the rocks that hurt since '54,*
> *The ironies in stone.*

Then the street poet was gone. He turned the corner, leaving an echo from his song, "the ironies in stone."

CHAPTER 5

▼

Bullshit. All bullshit, thought Watt, ascending the dark stairs. From the landing above, he heard bottle tops rolling in different directions. The smell of cooked heroin swept through the air, and he took out his knife again but put it away when he saw Blip stretched out on the stairs.

Blip was the resident dopefiend. He'd sit on the subway stairs during rush hour, with his hand extended like a cup, and beg anybody for money. "I'm a vet! Please, mistuh! Anything, lady! Thanks, kid."

As Watt stepped over him, Blip reached up and grabbed his pants leg, crying, "I gave my *veins* for my nation!" Watt grabbed the banister, saying, "Fuck is the matter with you, Blip? You can get killed doing shit like that!"

Blip laughed and choked at the same time, saying, "You never—cough, choke, haha—'ave much to say to me. You pass me by like you never s'pect me to talk. You not like Ralph's boy. Don't shock easy. You're just a mean city nigger, Watt."

Watt remembered what Grandma had said about Blip: *Blip's been on the dope since the day they dug up the bone.*

"I jest wanted to shock ya a little," said Blip, "jest wanted to touch ya."

He's taken his dope all over the world with him, said Grandma.

"See, Watt, I used ta play an instament. Nights round Minton's Playhouse, I used ta burn the gotdamn house down wit' my sassophone."

Until Charlie Parker walked in, said Grandma.

Niggers would hear me, Watt. Meeeee an' scream: Git the fire engines! Git the fire engines! This nigger's on fire!" said Blip.

Then he sort of got low and snaked out the kitchen door, said Grandma.

"And when I heard dat," said Blip, "I'd really pour it on! Teddy Hill use ta have ta open tha back door ta let some o' the steam out. I was a bad mafucker!"

Musically, son—and excuse your grandmother—He wasn't shit!

"I was a baad mafucker!" hollered Blip, craning his neck and rolling his eyes as if he could hear her. Then his head slowly drooped and he slouched on the stairs.

If only he had had the courage to stick with it, son, said Grandma. *He might have made something of himself.*

As Blip's head bobbed and bottle tops fell from his hand, Watt started to climb the final flight of stairs when Blip jumped up, yelling: "Wade a minute! Wade a minute! You think I'ma talk with *you*, risk talkin' with *you* and let you walk away so easy. I can only hang once and your grandma may drop some heavy shit on me for botherin' you. You do know about your grandma's shit, don'tcha?"

Watt didn't answer.

"Awright, awright, you don't wanna say nuthin'. I can dig it. Shhhhhhh. Play it cool. Right, my man? You don't think it's no accident that dopefiends have been kickin' down doors and swingin' in apartments for years and ain't nobody *evah* scratched your grandma's door.

"I r'member your grandma's husband. She ain't keep him long, haha. And once when she put 'im on the street for not actin' right, she tole him he better give her so much of so much money a week or it would be his ASS.

"Well, one day he took dat money and bought some tail from one o' those girls that only takes one leg out the pants ta fuck ya. Then the fool had the nerve to come around here ta see your ma. She wuz jest a few years younger than me."

Watt's left foot slipped off a step followed by his right. He clutched the sticky banister as Blip continued.

"I r'member your grandma comin' ta the top o' the stairs all in black, sayin', *Nigger, where is that money?* And when your grandfather he don't answer her, she says a bunch of fast words and ends it with *PROBATUM EST!* and walks away.

"Your grandpa's shakin' like he got palsy and my mother tells me ta git away from tha door and let him have what's comin' ta him. So I leaves and don't see him for a long time.

"But one day he's on the stoop cryin' and my ma goes over ta him and asks, *Do you need help? Can I call someone for you?* And he opens up his mouth ta cry and all that bridge work's crossed. So ma decides to take me upstairs and, as we're about ta enter tha building, we see your grandma comin' down the stairs in a long, black gown—tha kind they wear in movies. Her hair was gray—you know, boy, I swear I don't remember when your grandma's hair wasn't gray—and she's got this beautiful smile on her face, like your grandpa's the fattest vein in the world and she's gonna jab a needle in his arm no matter *what*.

"So he begins ta holler from tha bottom o' the stoop, and your grandma's smile turns up some more and she says, *Do you have what you owe me now, William?* And he's cryin' like he don't hear her, and he's about ta walk away holding his ankles when all of a sudden me and ma notice and we see that on his other side, the left one, he don't have no arm! So we back up closer. We were walkin' away and got closer! Das when we saw it! He had a *hand* wavin' outta his shoulder, a hand wit' no arm, like his body sucked it up ta tha wrist.

"Your grandma was still glowin' and took some more steps forward, sayin', *Do you have it now, William?* And your grandpa takes out a whole roll o' money and plops it in her hand. He gives it to her and jumps back screamin', *Zeporah, Zeporah! What about my arm?! What about my arm?!* And your grandma she looks down on him and waves him off. She goes back upstairs with that smile on her face and tha *money*. A few weeks later your grandpa he comes back and his left arm is long as usual and he's prompt and courteous and he never buys no pussy from those women who only takes one leg out tha pants ta fuck ya again!"

Blip's head drooped forward and remained suspended. As he returned to the land of nod, bottle tops fell from his hand. Watt climbed the final flight of stairs.

When he opened the door, he could feel the magnetism. Currents of energy swirled through the apartment. All the lights were out except in the living room where he could see the candles flicker as shadows rocked before burning wax and serpents of incense wiggled through the air.

He heard his grandmother's voice call, "Seruph," and a chorus of old women call, "Give us the fire." He heard his grandmother say, "You must obtain the ear of a black cat and boil it in the milk of a black cow, then make a thumb cover of it. Wear it and no one will be able to see you."

A young woman's voice asked Grandma something about her husband, saying he was unfaithful and sleeping with every woman on the block. "When he does it again," said Grandma, "wait until the first day of your menstruation cycle and take a large cauldron and fill it with boiling water. Remove the cauldron from the fire and squat over it for half an hour, allowing your menstrual juices to flow into the pot. Burn special incense, which I will give you, and then add fresh vegetables, saying the magic words, "Men and serpents, their sight, fools trapped between darkness and light—stars, foxes, hearts cut out, devices to put their feelings to rout." And behind her the old women chanted:

Jupiter, King Solomon, Felicity, Love Charm
Chapel Bouquet, Concentration, Rosemary, High John

"Rust from a dopefiend's spike, drop of infected blood, spoke from a child's old bike, bone from the back of a stud, wine from a life that's sad, woven into a charm to cure the lust of a no good lad."

Jupiter, King Solomon, Felicity, Love Charm
Chapel Bouquet, Concentration, Rosemary, High John

"Then add this," said Grandma. The plastic on the couch squeaked against the twang of the spring in the chair across from it as the woman took a parcel from Grandma.

The old monthly soup recipe, thought Watt. *After eating a few spoons, a man threw up every time his dick got hard for a woman other than his wife. If he didn't do another thing in life, he would be faithful to his wife.* Thinking about all those Harlem husbands who had eaten monthly soup and didn't know it, Watt began to laugh. The old ladies must have heard him because the living room door shut.

Now the voices were in whispers dusting the air. His grandmother chanted and the other ladies chanted in response. Their voices reached a crescendo and split open like eggs, releasing old moan yodels and eerie hums with a few of the old ladies even speaking in tongues.

The meeting ended. The lights came on, and the candles were snuffed. The living room door opened. Watt heard the old ladies coming down the hall. "He might have been impotent," said Mrs. Saunders, "but Dawson's husband had a good pension. He was a Pullman Porter."

"I heard Jenny Greene's husband died," said Mrs. Higgins.

"I went to the funeral," said Mrs. Vincent.

"How'd he look?" asked Mrs. Saunders.

"Natural," said Mrs. Vincent. "Like he was alive."

"He was a nice man," said Mrs. Higgins.

"Who did the work?" asked Mrs. Saunders, "Needby or Best Rest?"

"Needby," said Mrs. Vincent.

"They do fine work," said Mrs. Higgins.

"Jenny's livin' high on the insurance money," said Mrs. Saunders. "She doesn't come to our meetings anymore."

"Her sons are livin' high, too," said Mrs. Vincent. "Every one of them is a dopefiend."

"Jenny Greene's sons are crazy," said Mrs. Higgins. "They always were crazy."

"It just goes to show you," said Mrs. Vincent. "Sometimes a good family doesn't matter."

"What did Greene die of anyway?" asked Mrs. Saunders. The old ladies formed a circle, cocking their ears. The word "cancer" leaped out and deepened their fears, and they hurried out the door.

"Goodnight, ladies," called Watt. "And watch out for Blip below."

Grandma came out with fat Mrs. Dawson a little later. Fifty-five, she looked seventy-five and weighed three-hundred pounds at five-foot, two inches. Seeing Watt, she became excited: "My, how the years do go. I remember when he was just a baby. Look at him now! He looks just like his mother. Every time I see him, I swear ..."

As she talked, Watt felt like a rat in a Skinner Box. Screams were exploding in his soul. *Everyone takes you for a trip*, he thought. *Everyone wants you to eat their shit. That's what power is: the ability to make someone eat shit.* Then he thought of Billie Holiday, the patron saint and mother of dopefiends. She had the power to turn shit into sugar. He remembered the first time he heard one of her recordings, *Lady in Satin*. It sounded as if someone had put a gut up to a microphone and commanded it to sing.

Mrs. Dawson stopped recklessly eyeballing Watt and said good-night. Smiling, Watt and Grandma said good-night, too. Mrs. Dawson went down one flight and let out a shriek as Blip said, "I gave my veins for my nation!"

"I don't care if you are an ex-vet!" yelled Mrs. Dawson. "Get away from me with those nasty bottle tops!" And she hopped down the stairs from landing to landing.

Laughing, Watt and Grandma said good-night. The old lady slouched to her room for rest. Watt went to bed hearing Coltrane's music, his prayer as he descended into sleep. In his sleep, he imagined himself running—where, he did not know.

Neighbors in adjacent apartments made last minute threats, growling across the yard with their stereo sets. Then, dovetailing each other, they gradually lowered their volumes of madness until each warned the other with silence. As Watt tucked his head under a pillow, he heard, "O Harold! O Harold!" echo through the back yard. "More! O Harold! More!"

Then a head poked out a window and a voice cried, "Stop fuckin'! Stop fuckin'! Stop fuckin' over my head! You two pumpin' so hard up there ... might come through the ceiling!" The head reeled in, and the window shut.

CHAPTER 6

▼

"Ordnung!" cried Dr. Von Geber's parrot from the recesses of Watt's mind. "Ordnung!" the bird repeated as the telephone rang and Watt scrambled awake. He picked up the phone, growling, "Yeah," with mucus in his throat.

"This is Dr. Von Geber, Watt. I'm sorry to bother you at 3:00 a.m. on your day off. But Ainsley Bridges slipped out, saying he was going to Morningside Park to wait for you. I know you are not scheduled to resume work until Monday, but do you think you could meet him and give me a report? It's important for his therapy."

"Sure," said Watt, as Dr. Von Geber hung up.

Watt dressed quickly and went down the stairs, heading for the park. Few places scared him like Morningside Park. It was dark. It was beautiful, and it was dangerous.

"It wasn't always that way, son," Grandma once said. "There were summer days when the good people of Harlem picnicked in Morningside Park. Families used to come to the park and have all the fun you could imagine. Children used to run around while fathers played softball and mothers exchanged recipes. And there wasn't much crime.

"But somethin' happened after the war, son. The vets came home, and Morningside Park turned into Hell. Have you ever seen Hell marchin'? Well I have.

"Good people still went there. But at 6:00 p.m. they dropped whatever they were doin' and ran like wolfman was comin'. And if you looked down the street you'd see 'em comin', dopefiends with chains, razors, and switchblades so thick they sounded like wood snappin' when they opened. And the park became *worse* than Hell. But remember, son, good people always live in Hell until they decide to change it."

Morningside Park was where Watt had first met Ainsley Bridges for his CMB treatments. In those days, Bridges would come up to Harlem, flanked by twenty bodyguards, and wait for Watt in the park. Each outdoor therapy session used to begin with Bridges saying, "I head a multinational corporation. If my disposition is off a fraction, the price of oil could skyrocket and the world economy could crash. Nations would go bankrupt, and people around the globe would starve. So you see it's very important that I maintain a sense of balance.

"Nothing centers me more than being slapped. Slaps remind me that the world is a jungle, and you have to eat or be eaten to survive. So by all means, slap me, Watt. Slap me and save the world. And don't hold back your slaps— Remember I'm paying for them!" And Watt would slap his ass until he got tired, or Bridges, gasping, said, "Stop!."

'That crazy millionaire,' thought Watt, passing a sign that read:

YOU ARE NOW ENTERING
MORNINGSIDE PARK—
I DARE YOU!

"O father, if I sink into the center of the Earth, are you with me?" a voice prayed as Watt climbed the first flight of stairs, hearing an axe chopping at a tree as a poet sang:

> George Washington, the sound of your axe
> Still echoes in that tree
> A recording, George, technology
> After you take off your make-up
> And spit out your false teeth
> Your looted gums are empty
> Your limbs, bloated beef
> Rust hangs under your rouge
> You squeak whenever you move
> Nuts fall from your back
> not knowing what they lack
> These are your children, George
> Look at them!

As Watt went up the next flight of stairs, he heard the sound of metal clang and someone scream, "Help me!" Leaving the stairs, Watt jogged along a winding path and stopped. From the outskirts of a clearing, he saw a white man under the glare of a battered park lamp squirming on the ground. "Help me!" he cried, holding his leg, which was caught in an animal trap.

As he continued screaming and squirming, two husky white men in black tuxedos came out of the bushes. "It's not *him*," said one.

"We'll get him eventually," said the other. "This guy is just collateral damage."

"Do you think he's a millionaire?"

"Naw, he's looks like the broke-professor type—probably from that school up there."

Meanwhile, the man howling in the trap raised his arm and pointed at the two, crying, "It was *you!* And all the time we thought it was *them!*" A Tuxedo Mugger walked over to him and kicked him in the head. As he fell back unconscious, the Tuxedo Muggers pried open the trap's jaws and freed his leg.

Returning to the stairs, Watt thought: *Tuxedo Muggers, trickle down crime. They do the crime, and we do the time.*

Anxiety made him have to pee, so he stopped on the stairs, took out his dick, and sent a stream into the bushes. A voice in the foliage cried, "Goddamn you mothafucka you!" as Watt jumped back and raised his knife, then continued up the stairs.

Near the top of the park he saw two figures waiting. One wore a bowler hat and black wool cape coat that blew in the wind. The other wore an unlined, white raincoat in which he shivered.

"Once again, you are late," intoned Ainsley Bridges. "I shouldn't have to wait when I'm paying. However, before you waste any more of my time, let's get started."

"Where's my bowler hat?" asked Watt.

"You don't have a bowler hat," snapped Bridges.

"Why not?" asked Watt.

"It's not part of your culture," said Bridges.

"I don't give a fuck," snapped Watt. "I want a bowler hat."

"All right," said Bridges. "Stetson, have two-thousand bowler hats delivered to Watt."

"Yes, Sir Ainsley."

"Now can we get on with it?"

"Let's do it," said Watt.

"Do you remember your lines?" asked Bridges.

"I remember," said Watt.

"Remember, timing is everything," said Bridges."

"Step back, Stetson, and let him work."

"Yes, Mr. Bridges."

As Stetson moved to the side of the stairs, Bridges slouched down and assumed a victim's posture, cowering on the stairs with his hands above his head. Standing over him, Watt bitch-slapped him a few times. As Bridges moaned, Watt put a knee in his chest, saying, "Hurry up, it's time."

"Time for what?" asked Bridges.

"Time for you to wait in the shadows I've waited in for two thousand years."

"No!" cried Bridges.

"Time for you to experience the ignominy and powerlessness that I've known," said Watt.

"NO!" cried Bridges.

"Time for Western Civilization to go to the end of the line and wait its turn again," said Watt.

"I can't," whimpered Bridges.

"Time for you to give up your POWER," said Watt.

"When would I don the mantle of power again?" asked Bridges.

"In four thousand years if we survive," said Watt.

"Well I won't do it!" cried Ainsley Bridges, pushing Watt's knee from his chest and nearly toppling him. "I'll lie. I'll cheat. I'll change history, destroy art, and kill anyone before I give up my power!"

At that moment, Stetson came forward with a copy of Leonardo Da Vinci's *Mona Lisa*. "Fuck her!" said Bridges, tearing it to shreds. "Beauty is no longer truth." Then Stetson took out another print, one of a fat middle-aged couple slouched on a sofa, looking at television, flanked by two colossal cans of beer.

"Now *this* is Art," said Bridges. "Tell our PR department to see to it that *everyone* believes it ... and send the artist a check."

"Yes, Sir Ainsley," said Stetson.

"I feel better now," said Bridges sighing. "I remember why I do what I do. If *I* didn't screw them, they would screw me. We can go now, Stetson."

"Yes, Sir Ainsley."

Once again, the metal trap clanged in darkness, and a voice let out a cry, but this time it sounded as if it had come from the throat of an entire Indian nation.

"Could it be?" said Ainsley Bridges, smiling as Stetson ran down the stairs and came back up a few seconds later to announce, "They have him, Sir Ainsley! They have him!"

Ainsley Bridges clapped his hands and did a jig as the Tuxedo Muggers dragged Chief Laughing Gravy up the stairs, bound. Stopping a few steps below Bridges, they threw Laughing Gravy down. Bridges turned beet-red with excitement and asked, "Do you remember me? You scalped me—right here in this park." Bridges removed his bowler hat and bowed to reveal his chopped pate.

"Fuck you, white man!" snapped Laughing Gravy. "You scalped us first." Then Bridges pranced down a couple of stairs to slap him, but Laughing Gravy ducked and Bridges nearly fell. But Stetson pushed him back up and fell in his stead. As Stetson screamed, rolling down the stairs, one of the Tuxedo Muggers said, "We told you we'd get him."

"Yes, and you've done a splendid job," said Ainsley Bridges, "for which you will be paid."

Watt thought of trying to free Laughing Gravy for a moment. Some connection, perhaps in history, between black men and Indians beckoned him. But even if he could overpower the Tuxedo Muggers, Laughing Gravy was in no shape to run. As he tried to break away, a pipe attached to a cord around his neck fell to the ground. "Hold on," said Watt, picking up the pipe and reattaching it around his neck. "Thank you," said Laughing Gravy.

"You won't need that where you're going," said Bridges.

"Kill me now, white man!" said Laughing Gravy. "This is a good day to die."

"Nooooo. We're not going to do that yet," said Bridges. "First we're going to have some fun." At that moment, Stetson limped back up the stairs carrying a bag of herbs and seasonings. At a nod from Bridges, he started tossing some on Laughing Gravy

"Watt, your services are no longer needed this morning," said Ainsley Bridges, turning. "I'll put in a good word on your behalf with Dr. Von Geber. Make a note of it, Stetson."

"Yes, Sir Ainsley."

As Bridges and his entourage went up to Morningside Heights, Watt descended the stairs, hearing someone cry like a newspaper boy, "Violence! Get your violence!" At the bottom of the stairs, Watt saw bodies lying about like litter. A tree burned brightly, and a mad man, spewing epithets, swung a razor at the moon. Then sirens blared, and fire engines screeched to a halt at the park's entrance. But instead of entering the park to extinguish a blaze, firemen shot water cannons at the burning tree as voices in bushes near the flames cried out, "Goddamn you mothafuckas, you!"

The sun rose cautiously as Watt passed Grandma's building and headed for Sylvia's. Using a key, he entered her building and took the elevator up. His hands shook as he put another key into her door. Going into her apartment, he took off his clothes in the living room and groped in darkness to her bedroom His body needed release. In the darkness, her scent, radiating from the bed, hit him. He followed it to her body, which was nude and warm.

"Why didn't you tell me you were coming?" she asked, waking up.

"I didn't know," he said.

"After what you *said* and *did* to me this afternoon, you have the nerve to climb into my bed."

"I need you," he said.

"Why?" she asked.

"Because … because there's nobody else," he said.

"O Watt!" she cried, wrapping her legs and arms around him.

The smell of coffee woke him a few hours later. Sylvia entered the bedroom wearing nothing but an apron and carrying a tray, which she gently placed in his lap.

"Did you mean what you said—about there being nobody else?"

"Sure, I meant it," said Watt, with a smirk that placed him miles away from his words. Sylvia's took a deep breath, saying, "You son of a bitch!"

"I've got to go," he said, putting down the fork and removing the tray from his lap.

"Before you *go*," snapped Sylvia, "I want to ask you something. When was the last time you saw Perry?"

"Last night," said Watt. "Why?"

"I saw him with some dopefiends the other day."

"That doesn't mean anything," said Watt. "A lot of the guys we grew up with *are* dopefiends. He probably stopped to talk with them."

"No," said Sylvia. "He wasn't talking with them. He was *with* them. And when he saw me he tried to hide."

"You're wrong," said Watt. "Perry wouldn't shoot dope."

"I'm just telling you what I saw," said Sylvia.

"Okay," said Watt. "I've got to go."

"I had hoped we could do something together today," said Sylvia, "a movie, a museum, or just a walk."

"I can't," said Watt.

"What about tonight?" she asked.

"I'll call you and let you know later," he said.

"Why do I put up with this shit?" said Sylvia. "You don't love me."

"I've got to go now," said Watt, easing toward the door. He leaned over to kiss her, but she turned her head away, saying, "Just go." She closed the door behind him. As he waited for the elevator, he heard the tray of food crash against the door. He went home and back to bed.

CHAPTER 7

▼

The afternoon sun shone through a crack in the shade, drawing a sharp, white scar across the bridge of Watt's brown nose as he awoke. Cars growled, bottles broke, and garbage can tops clanged—the tumult of an angry day cresting upward to release its rage.

Watt heard a dog's leash jingle and the soft sashay of old legs swaying up the hall. His grandmother was returning with Happy, her blonde cocker spaniel dog. Walking past his room, she unleashed the dog and went into the kitchen.

Getting out of bed, Watt went into the kitchen, too. Grandma was sitting in a chair by the oven, heating a frying pan. Happy lay across the doorway on his back.

"Move, Happy, or I'll break your ass," said Watt.

"Don't hit my dog," said Grandma. "You just woke up and you're ready to kick ass."

The dog moved as Watt smiled, saying: "Good morning, Grandma."

"It's afternoon, son."

"The old ladies sure were howling last night. How much did we take in?"

"Never mind how much *we* took in," said Grandma. "That's what's wrong with your generation. Everything is money, money, money. Frankly, if I had my way I'd...."

"Yeah, I know," interrupted Watt. "You'd flush the whole damn generation down the toilet."

"I'd expect that from you," said Grandma, "a boy who ...

"Whose mother was a dopefiend," interrupted Watt, "and who was born a dopefiend, too."

"I'd never say that about *you*, son," said Grandma. "I'd never say that," she repeated, reaching out and turning off the flame. "I was thinking about your mother the other day. She'd be so proud of you."

Proud of wha?' thought Watt as his teeth ate the inside of his mouth. "I'm sorry, Grandma," he said.

"That's all right, son," said Grandma. "I know you didn't mean it. You got a brain, son, a good brain, and some day you'll show 'em all. More importantly, some day you'll know why I'm so proud of you."

Suddenly, a window broke across the street. Someone screamed, "PO-LEEEEECE!" singing the two syllables in raised fourths, the Devil's interval.

"If only your mother hadn't married that no-good father of yours. I told her he was a dog. But she wouldn't listen. She told me she loved him. Come Hell or high water, she loved that trash too big for an asshole."

Across the street, someone screamed, "I didn't mean to call PO-LEEEEECE! Please! Not my face!"

"The only time your father made sense" said Grandma, "was when he was listening to Jazz. He'd put on Charlie Parker's *Embraceable You* and walk around like he was playing a saxophone and, you know somethin', he'd seem human for awhile."

Watt became distracted. The wild music blared, and a vision of horror shot through his mind—pus-filled hands and limbs exploding in the air. "Watt," called Grandma. "Don't Mitty on me!"

"Mitty" was Grandma's word for daydreaming. She got it from an old movie called *The Secret Life of Walter Mitty*, which starred Danny Kaye, and she swung Watt's father by "Mitty" night and day. "Tell me, son," she said, with a mischievous grin. "If you were the loan shark and somebody refused to pay you, what would you do?"

From the time he was little, Grandma was always quizzing him. Smiling, Watt rubbed his chin in a manner similar to Dr. Von Geber. "I'd break his legs with a tire iron."

"Wrong!" jumped Grandma. "If you do that, he might come back and get you. What you do, son, is ease up behind him, when he doesn't expect it, and pipe him in the head. Remember, son, don't be fair with cheats."

"I hear you Grandma Bogart," laughed Watt.

"You got a heart, son. But you can't have a heart in this world. If you do, they'll cut it out and sell it. Remember, a man that cheats you has got to have cheated other folks, too. So don't hesitate. Pipe him. And if you pipe him right, he'll pay everyone off."

Still laughing, Watt said, "It's a good thing you're not a man, Grandma. You'd be out there opening people with can openers."

"I'm still here," said Grandma. "That's the proof. And I've done more than most men. Like this mornin'. I was out walkin' Happy by Morningside Park when I saw this doper flappin' his arms as if he was trying to fly. It was so funny, son, I had to laugh. I couldn't help it. Well, the doper saw me and yelled, *Old Bitch!* Then he took out a razor with nine diseases on it and started walking toward me. So I backed up and pulled my knife—the one I treat with garlic and onions so if I cut him he'll never heal. And son, I got to admit—I wanted a gun to blow his dopefiend ass out the park."

"Why didn't you put the roots on him?" asked Watt, "and wash him up for good?"

"That's what you don't understand, son. The roots are for long-term business. A dopefiend with a nasty razor is short-term. You've got to blow him away *there*.

"So I backed up some more, son, and Happy got ready to leap for his balls, and the doper started mutterin', *Mama! Mama!* with a crazy glow in his eyes, and I yelled, *I'm not your mama, bastard! You son of a watermelon seed! Come on! I'll carve you a new asshole!* Then, son ...*"

In the alley, a woman's voice cried, "Bastard!" A rope snapped and a voice screamed, "AHHHHHHHHHHHHHHHHHHHH!" and hit the bottom with a thud. Grandma hurried to the backyard window and ripped it open, hollering, "Are you all right, Mrs. Saunders?"

"Yes, I'm fine, Madame Zeporah. One of those dopers tried to climb down a rope and swing in my apartment, but I had the pot of lye on the stove like you told me."

"Lye is good for the heroin addicts," said Grandma, "but not the cocaine addicts. You've got to use something different on them." As the two old ladies talked about dopefiends as if they were insects, Watt thought of his baby, Sylvia's baby, their baby. "I'll see you later," said Grandma, shutting the window.

"It kind of reminds me of the time down at 72nd Street," said Grandma, "when this cracker wouldn't let me walk through the front door. Smart white people called on me in those days to take care of their long term business. Some of them are millionaires today."

Down in the yard, a voice growled: "Reggie! Wha hoppened to your face?"

"I swear, son," said Grandma, "sometimes I think dopefiends are an indestructible race. As if heroin weren't bad enough, now we have crack and angel dust, and dopefiends so high they think they can fly. But they're our children. My God, what will become of us?

"Anyway, son, this cracker wouldn't let me come through the front door and raised his hand to slap me. So I backed up some more, like a matador waitin' on a bull. When he charged me, I put my knife in him and turned it. I even stamped my foot for extra turns. Guts swirled, the cracker fell over, and I went home."

Maybe it was old age or the fact that so much had happened to her. But sometimes Grandma's mind wandered. Time ran together, and she didn't remember what she had done where. The man who got fresh with her when she was twenty might get confused with the man she pushed on the tracks at thirty-two. Whenever that happened, Watt had to remind her. "What happened in the park, Grandma?"

"Well, son, I was just about to put the knife in him and let Happy rip his balls when a friend of Blip's came tearin' down the street, screamin' at the doper. You know if he was a friend of Blip's he was a doper, too. I guess he remembered the time I put a spell on the neighborhood and nobody could get any dope the whole summer.

"Well, son, Blip's friend whispered something in the doper's ear and his eyebrows flew up so high they nearly came off the tracks. The doper started runnin' and flappin' his arms. He leaped over a six-foot fence and kept runnin'. I was so mad, son. *Come back, you son of a watermelon seed,* I yelled, *Cause I still ain't your mama!* Then I saw Blip's friend tryin' to sneak away. *Why didn't you mind your own business! I ought to cut you!* And son, he started runnin' and I thought I could get one slice before he got away, and Happy tugged to get him, and I accidentally cut *myself.*" She opened her hand and Watt saw the gash. "Don't worry, son, I've got some stuff to make it heal."

Down in the alley, angry voices roared, "C'mon, Reggie, shew us da window!" Raising a broken limb, Reggie pointed up to Mrs. Saunders' window, saying, "There!" as sunlight struck his lye-eaten face.

Tossing a pound of fat into a hot frying pan, Grandma went to the window with the fat sizzling. "You dopers get the hell out of that yard—now!" she yelled, and a couple of dopefiends recognized her and took off. A few looked up defiantly. The last thing they saw was the haze before the grease struck. Howling like animals, they pounded their scalded dopefiend hands and faces against the brick building. Then they began running—out of the alley, around the corner and back into their deserted tenement caskets. Watt went to the window and saw a final dopefiend heel kick behind a building.

Trembling, Grandma closed the window and groped her way to a chair. She opened her mouth to talk, but no words came out. She let out a moan, then snatched out her false teeth and threw them into a glass of fresh water. Food and grit rose in a cloud from the teeth and settled at the top of the glass. "Dope-fiends!" she shrieked.

At that moment the telephone rang, and Watt went to pick it up. "Yeah!" he said.

"Watt, why do we have to fight?" asked Sylvia. "I love you. I don't want to hurt you. I know what you've been through. I just want to be a part of your life—part of your dream."

"You might end up being part of my nightmare," said Watt.

"What nightmare?"

"Never mind."

"Whatever it is, I'm with you, Watt. I'm yours."

"I've got to go now."

"I'll call you later," she said.

"Yeah," he said. Putting down the phone, he thought, *Fuck Love!* as a moth-ball that had been lodged behind his eye decomposed and ran with mucus from his nose. He wiped it with a tissue and went back to his room.

Grandma was moaning in the chair as he went out of the door. Happy, on his back, had his paws in the air. Going down the stairs, Watt leapt over Blip on the landing, kicking a portion of yesterday's *New York Times*. He imagined he saw pieces of Rosaline's ass in the shredded *Times*.

Stopping at his mailbox, he removed a letter from Dr. Von Geber. It contained a fat check for his last two weeks of work. Putting the check into his pocket, he hit the streets, hearing little Cecil call, "Hey, Watt!" Ignoring him, he turned the corner and went to a bank to deposit the check.

Walking down Lenox Avenue, he saw a man in a three-piece suit running towards him, carrying an attaché case extended like a lance. It was the middle class man from Washington who was with Rosaline on the stairs. "What do you want?" asked Watt.

"Just take it—quickly! Before *he* comes," he said, extending the attaché case.

"Who?" asked Watt.

"The man I'm ashamed of. He's coming! He'll embarrass me! Take it before it's too late!" He offered Watt his attaché case. But Watt pushed it away, saying, "I can't stand you phony black bourgeoisie motherfuckers." Making an about-face and shouting, "No!" the middle-class man started running recklessly again with his attaché case extended, like a lance. Stumbling, he knocked over an old woman carrying shopping bags, and without apologizing, he jumped up and continued running.

"Bastard!" she cried.

"S. Burrows, come back!" called a man in rags. Earthy and earth-worn, he was in his forties and resembled Burrows. But in both movement and demeanor, he looked like someone who had just come out of a cotton field.

Shaking his head, Watt continued walking down Lenox Avenue. Passing 116th Street, he saw Dana, the street poet, reciting his latest composition.

> *Ain't no lightnin'*
> *When a word dies*
> *Comets beep:*
> *"Ain't hip!"*
> *'Leven thirty talks*
> *'Bout twelve like a dog*
> *You can't even pat yo foot.*

Watt didn't know why he even bothered to make poetry. No one listened anymore. They all took it for granted—like the smack of hands or the pat of feet. They could never conceive of a world without rhythm, even though, even now, one was being prepared at the backs of their minds where they could neither see nor hear.

As the street poet turned the corner reciting another composition, boogalooing with the language in quarter rhyme, Watt thought,

> *If there's a nation,*
> *it must be in our ears.*
> *It must be in those black sounds.*

"Hey boy!" called an old man, staggering out of a hallway. Wiping his mouth with one hand and waving a wine bottle with the other, he said, "You wanna know the trouble with black folks, son? The trouble with black folks is they *never* know what they got till white folks tell them they got it. And then it's *too* late. Lemme tell you some more. White folks spent more than three-hundred years starvin' black folks an' thirteen years feedin' them faster than they could eat. Them thirteen years was the Civil Rights Movement. Boy, come on over here and lemme tell you some more."

Smiling at the old man, Watt imagined the white minstrels who cakewalked behind the slaves who cakewalked behind the plantation owners who patterned their lives after the novels of Sir Walter Scott. Torn between myth and blood song, the old South rose and fell one vainglorious morn.

"I'm in a hurry. I don't have time, old fella."

"Who you callin' *old fella*?" barked the wino. He carefully put down his bottle, and then stood up straight to fight, staggering and throwing punches at the air. As Watt continued walking, he called, "Yeah, you better keep walkin', boy, cause I'll knock your block off! Cause thass what you younguns need—a good whippin'—a HARLEMASSWHIPPIN'—*cause you don't listen!*"

CHAPTER 8

▼

As Watt neared the House of Styles Barbershop and Beauty Salon, he saw Loray, the best beautician and most notorious faggot to bubble sperm in Harlem, standing in the doorway. Like a sentry, he wanted to be the first to know who was coming so he could run back inside and tell everyone else. A midnight rider of questionable equestrian skills, Loray loved to gallop into darkness between silk sheets while another man banged him in the rear.

Spotting Watt, he ran inside, then came out, standing in front of the striped barber's pole with his foot pointed. "My, oh my," he said, "the devil has a way of keeping in style." Then focusing his eyes between Watt's neck and knees, he licked out his tongue with a "slurp" sound, saying, "It's cold out here, Dreamweaver. How'd you like some hot breath on those chilly loins?"

"Go on with that shit," said Watt, walking by him. "I've told you since we were kids. I'm *not interested.*"

"Well a girl can keep trying, can't she? People do change, don't they? And I always wait." Then craning his neck and switching his thighs, he followed Watt into the barbershop with one arm dangling in the air.

"What's happening," said Watt, greeting Yank and Wilson, the barbers, Faye, the manicurist, a couple of customers: West Indian Claxton, Chump, and a few of the regulars.

"Yo, Bro, what's goin' on?" said Yank.

"I ain't s-s-s-s-seen you in a l-l-l-l-long time," stuttered Chump. "Where you been?"

"Around," said Watt, taking a seat as someone turned on the television news. Rattling off a grocery list of atrocities, the newscaster reported: *Last night in New*

York there were 200 stabbings, 300 shootings, 700 muggings, 69 rapes, 13 suicides, and two fatal automobile accidents. In Sports....

"A lot of people got f-f-f-f-fucked up last night," stuttered Chump.

"A lot of people get fucked up *every* night," said Yank as Loray ran into the beauty parlor section to check on a head he'd left frying.

"Yeah, but I'm still wondering," said old Wilson carefully snipping hair.

"Wondering what?" asked Yank.

"Will we ever hate whitey as much as we hate ourselves?"

"Who k-k-k-k-knows," stuttered Chump.

"I doubt it," said Faye, as the newscaster concluded with a light touch:

"What do OPEC, a camel, and a fifty-foot cake have in common?" asked a preppy-looking reporter, responding: "a billionaire. Last night, billionaire-playboy Wally Raunch celebrated his fiftieth birthday with a party at Madison Square Garden. You might say it was a big affair. Three-thousand millionaires from all over the world attended, feasting on cuisine that included food from seventy of the world's best restaurants.

"The highlight of the evening came when the birthday cake was brought out. Lit by thirty-thousand candles and four feet high, it covered an area half the size of a basketball court.

"But before the cake was cut, the guest of honor was given a unique present—a solid gold sewing needle from the Organization of Petroleum Exporting Countries (OPEC). I don't think he'll do much sewing with it though. For this gold needle stands fifteen feet high and its eye has a diameter of five feet.

"Before the festivities ended, a camel was brought out and led repeatedly through the needle's eye while millionaires applauded. The moral of this story: If a camel can get through the eye of a needle, even a solid gold one, then a rich man has a good chance of getting into Heaven. Bill Tetley reporting."

"Talk about waste," said Wilson.

"Some people make you sick," said West Indian Claxton. Babies dyin' with disease and neglect, and them squanderin' money that could save their lives. Don't get me wrong, mon. I ain't got nuttin' against millionaires, especially if they earned it. But shit, mon, how many of them do that? Most never work a day in their lives. They inherit money and talk shit about workin'. Meanwhile poor mon killin' each other, don't have nothin' and scared."

"Yeah," said Yank, "we oughta have a law that says a millionaire can only leave so much to his family. Throw the rest in a pit so we can fight for it—winner-take-all!"

"Whatever law you pass," said Wilson, "you've still got to work hard."

As heads nodded, a student walked into the shop loaded with books. "What are you, a human library?" asked Yank. But when Loray saw him, he lit up and licked out his tongue, saying, "Baby, if I sold my soul to the Devil in my sleep last night, I'm not responsible. I didn't know *you* were comin' tonight." But the student ignored him. Taking a seat, he opened a book, and started reading. "Well, there's nothin' as uppity as a book-carrying nigger," said Loray, and everyone laughed.

"U-U-U-U-Ugly women make g-g-g-g-good luv," stuttered Chump.

"Ugly men make good luv too," said Faye, as Chump dropped his head, and everyone laughed, save Loray who moved his hips to music only he heard. Walking to the glass door, he broke into song.

I know, yes I know
only God can make love
in slow motion
and draw each nerve
Out in fiddle whispers.
But I can relax you, Baby.
Pleeease give me a chance.
It's money in the back.

But the student ignored him, and Loray started to sob. Then Claxton stood up breathing dragon fire. "What 'ave we been fightin' for? Mon, tell me. Somebody tell me. All those black souls that die so that he can pack his ass unnaturally. Malcolm, King, DuBois, Garvey, Washington—ALL GONE!—and him showin' asshole for their pains. Shit, mon! It don't make sense! What have we been fightin' for?"

Ceasing to sob, Loray smiled. He forgot about the student and walked to the mirror and fixed his mascara. Then he turned to Claxton and said, "Maybe you been fightin' for me."

"I tell every woman I luv her in b-b-b-b-bed," stuttered Chump. "It makes them f-f-f-f-fuck harder." Then he told a story about his experiences in an up-state institution. "It was on f-f-f-f-fire. I had to h-h-h-h-hit her to g-g-g-g-get out!"

Finishing a manicure, Faye looked up, saying, "Stop lyin', you ain't stood on all three since you were two. And *I* know."

"F-f-f-f-fuck you, skinny b-b-b-b-bitch!" stuttered Chump. Getting low, he started whispering. His voice exploded from the circle of men. "That's r-r-r-r-right! I f-f-f-f-fucked her!"

"No, Chump!" snapped Faye. "I fucked *you*!—midget dick!—and it was very disappointing. You need to take that shit back to elementary school." As the barbershop became hysterical with laughter, Chump grabbed his coat and headed for the door.

"Just remember," said Faye, "some women ain't afraid to put it *all* on the line and can look up longer than you can look down."

As Chump left, he passed an old woman in front of the barbershop, trying to pick up a young G.I. "Ah, a young fryer's almost ready for the grease," laughed Yank. Loray quickly moved to the door, saying, "If he's ready for his mother, he's ready for *me*."

As if hypnotized, the G.I. turned to Loray. He ignored the old woman, who limped away, and focused his eyes on Loray who pressed his lips against the glass door, singing, *All of me, why not take all of me,* moving his hips and making sudden dips that aroused the G.I. even more. Then he signaled a kid who ran errands in the shop to bring his coat. The kid draped the leopard skin coat over Loray's shoulders and jumped back. When the G.I. nodded, Loray slipped through the door like an African princess or a trans-sexed version of a Mae West bloom.

They met by the winding-stripe barber's pole, embracing and kissing. "Dreamweaver," called Loray. "Where you been all my life?—cuttin' and killin' all over the world with me waitin' here for you. Say somethin', Dreamweaver, say somethin'! Oh, you make me feel like a natural woman!"

Then Loray, ass-throbbing, hips-shaking, and tongue-flashing, poked his head through the door, saying, "Tell my customers I'll be back in an hour." The G.I. touched his shoulder from behind, and Loray said, "Tell my customers I'll be back in an hour and one-half." As the G.I. touched him again, Loray turned and said, "Well I do have to come back sometime. I can't spend my *whole* day with you." Then turning, they went into the hotel next door.

"Now that's what I call godly intervention," said Faye, as everyone laughed.

Sucking his teeth, West Indian Claxton cried, "What are you laughing at? Thot is our strength go-wing down dee drain. The white mon has done a good job on us."

"We're not doing such a bad job on ourselves," said the student, raising his head from two books. Rearing up, Claxton scoffed, "You part of what I'm talkin' 'bout, too. Maybe you don't fuck G.I.'s, but you fuck those books—*white books*!—and the first thing you do when the white man slap a degree on your ass is leave Harlem and forget about your people."

"I'm black, and *anything* I do is black," said the student. "Anything I *read* becomes black because I translate the color. And I'm always thinking about helping my people and wondering how we got so fucked up. And I'm not going to let some handkerchief head West Indian tell me what blackness is or how I'm supposed to think, act, or live. Fuck you! I'm free!"

"Wait a minute," said Faye. "You ain't free. You're alone."

"No, I'm free *and* alone. I'm free from your lies *and* the white man's lies. I'm free from all the bullshit the two of you create. So don't tell me shit! Tell the fools taking drugs not to do it. Tell the kids killing each other not to do it. But leave me the fuck alone so I can do something positive.

"Well who's stopping you?" jumped Yank.

"All of you," said the student. "Black folks are so afraid they want to kill anybody who has courage. The only reason you fuck with me is because I carry books and not a gun, and you assume I won't shoot you. Well don't assume too much. I'll kill *anybody* for my freedom—even you."

"Who want *your* freedom, mon? It's the freedom of a paranoid," said Claxton.

"Maybe I'm paranoid," said the student. "But I'll tell you something most of you won't admit—*We're never going to be free.*"

A sudden hush fell over the barbershop. "What did he say?" asked Faye. "What did he say about the freedom of *my* people?"

"I said we're never going to be free," repeated the student, "until we stop disrespecting and hurting each other and start working together. It's that simple."

"Well I can't argue with that," said Faye.

"All of our problems," said the student, "stem from bad personal relationships. If personal relationships are bad, everything is bad—family, business, and community."

"You say t'ings we know already, mon. You talk this ivy tower bullshit, but you forget about the brothers who never have a chance, who born in shit and get locked in hell. They all innocent and 'ave no chance from the time they pop womb and yell. What you say to them, mon? What you say to the babies who innocent today but kill you tomorrow? What you *do* for them, mon?"

"We've got to stop being afraid of them so we can fight *for* them," said the student. "We've got to put ourselves on the line and fight for them from the moment they're born. But if they grow up and want to commit crime or hurt people, I say lock them up until they change. We can't help them until they're ready to help themselves.

"In the meantime, we've got to get ourselves together. We've got to improve ourselves and work to improve our people. Forget about being poor or middle class. Forget about how one brother talks properly while another speaks with a drawl. Forget about what people claim is in their hearts. Let's judge each other by what we do and stop being so fucking afraid. Let's work and improve ourselves. And let's do it, as Malcolm said, *by any means necessary.*"

"Now you talkin'," said Claxton, leaning back. "Garvey and Malcolm say those things, but a lot of people didn't listen. And those who did listen, like my great-grandfather who worked with Garvey, are long dead."

Suddenly, a little man in a peacoat stuck his head through the door and asked, "Brownie there?"

"Brownie's dead," said Wilson.

"Did he leave my money?"

"Naw," said Wilson, as the man sucked his teeth and slammed the door.

The student continued talking, but aside from Claxton, no one listened. But Watt heard him and remembered what Grandma had told him about Garvey, A. Phillip Randolph, and Malcolm X—and what he had read. And he remembered what she said when he asked her, "How much time do I have out here, Grandma?"

Smiling, she said, "You have as long as it takes whitey to get rid of his guilt and become his old self again. You see, son, in each generation, the white man allows a grace period and lets the coloreds get off their stuff for awhile, until he's certain that we'd do to him what he's done to us, but we can't do it. Then he returns to the business of his soul—*power!*

"But it's durin' this time, son, between his lettin' go and takin' hold again that you've got a chance to do somethin' with your life. It's during the Devil's Interval that you can break free while he's restin' and catchin' his breath. That's when you can run through the gates and find your dream. During the Devil's Interval is when you can turn your dream into reality.

"But watch out, son. He's meaner, crazier, more conservative, less compassionate, and more determined than ever before to keep those gates closed. He's mad like a bee whose honey's been stolen because so many black men and white women have got together."

White women, thought Watt, imagining the first enslaved African on American soil who, terrified at his plight, let out a field shout to relieve himself and looked up to see a white woman running excitedly toward his scream. In the prison of racism, the white woman dances before the bars.

But also in that prison, talented black people wait their turn, wait for the Devil's Interval to begin while below the ground that supports them the lash can be heard:

WOP! "I'm sorry, boss!"

WANG! "I'll tell you what they plannin'!"

WOFF! "No, Marsa, NO!"
WHIT!"And God said...."
WICK!" The white man skinned him wit' a knife!"

Then he heard a crueler, less obvious, strategy for maintaining control: *When the Blacks say they want freedom, give it to them. Overwhelm them with opportunities; undermine them with dependencies. Give them freedom until they bust wide open.*

"And a junkie shall lead them!" someone cried as applause swelled.

"Amen!"

Yes, Amen. Amen for the black flesh ripped like paper. Amen for smashed history and lost names. Amen for the oceans of booze and dope. And Amen for the Christ figure struggling to break free. All power to the Devil, who sometimes masquerades as God.

Watt imagined the Devil. He had always seen him as omnipotent. But now he realized that even the Devil was vulnerable and needed rest. Sometimes, exhausted, he slouches up from Hell, drops his pitch fork, and collapses under a tree to sleep.

The moment he closes his eyes, the grace period begins. The gates of Hell spring open and a few fortunate black people fly out. Laughing and tripping over their egos, they run towards the metropolis of the thought in pursuit of their dreams.

But eventually, the Devil wakes up. He spreads his cleft foot and yawns, rising, and then he tromps back down to Hell, slamming the gates behind him. Many years will pass before those gates open again.

Watt saw himself standing before those gates, trying to steal a glimpse of Hell. But neither sound nor image emitted. *Hell must exist*, thought Watt, *or what's a brain for?*

Frustrated, he started to weep when suddenly he heard thunder, black thunder, and staring up he saw thousands of black children who had found a new way out. Up from the earth, running across the fields, they looked like sweat pumping out craters of volcanic skin. So a part of the earth they seemed, so uniform their ebony rhythm.

The sun shone bright, striking their naked bodies. Each muscle glistened and allowed the sun to see itself. Naked and free, one ran ahead. It was Loray, Loray as he had never seen himself, uncocked and running like a Bison.

Then the darkness fell. A wooly wad of hair hit the floor, and Watt's mind turned as barbershop words splashed in, "Yeah, it's that wide, spread-eagle kind that sucks you in and takes off all your clothes."

"You mean like wide-wale pussy?"

"No, like WHALE pussy."

Swaggering back into the shop, Loray smelled as if he'd fallen into the Hudson River. He put down his purse and combed his hair, saying, "I told him to drive some runs for the tribe, and he took me serious. Some people think I'm Yankee Stadium. Some people think they can go on hittin' forever. Some people will fuck you till you die—if you let 'em. I give *good* fantasy. You know what I mean, baby. Black dreams began with Buddy Bolden, but black fantasies began with Little Richard, who is really BIG Richard if you know what I mean."

Everyone laughed except Claxton and the student. "Mon," said Claxton, "I 'ope you fall into your own asshole and drown one day!"

Spinning around, Loray jumped, "Thass alright, thass alright. Maybe *you* can't deal with it. But a lot of people can. Cause part of bein' free is bein' *all the things you are!*" He spread his arms as if concluding a song and the barbershop exploded with laughter. Claxton and the student hurdled the gyrating bodies as they went out the door. Loray, shifting his weight from thigh to thigh, teased them and waved goodbye, singing,

> *Do what you got to do.*
> *Go where you got to go.*

Watt put on his coat to leave and walked by Loray. "Well Mr. Hard-To-Get, but I bet soft-to-keep," said Loray, "have you finally realized that two holes are better than three if it's dipped in me cause I know how to use 'em!" Then his tongue flashed out and he touched Watt's crotch.

Grabbing Loray by the collar, Watt bitch-slapped him against the mirror. Throwing a heap of *motherfuckers!* on Loray, he grabbed a straight razor and pressed the blade against Loray's throat, saying, "Be funny now, *faggot!*"

The television was off. Everyone stood frozen as if posing for still shots as Loray, squirming on the glass, begged, "Please, Watt, not my face! Don't cut me! I was only kiddin'. Remember! We were kids together! I loved you *then* and I love you *now*. So don't KILL ME!"

"I told you I didn't go that way when we were kids," said Watt. "And I told you what I'd do to you if you ever played your faggot games with me. Now I'm gonna show you!"

"No, Watt, NO!" cried Loray. "I don't want to die for your fantasy! I don't want to die for your fantasy! You think you're killin' something else by killin' me! But you're not! And you can't kill it! No! It'll go on no matter what *you* do! It's sweeping the world. It may have *you* eventually!—God bless Oscar Wilde!" Then he made a strange sign with his free hand and tugged at a gold chain around his neck. From out of his shirt came a gold medallion, featuring a bull's head with a snake wrapped around the eyes.

Then Watt looked around the shop and imagined what each person would say if he killed Loray. "Gaiety is gone without Loray," Faye would say.

"The Club Baby Grande and Andre's will never be the same," Wilson would probably say.

"It's gonna be hard to get used to not seein' Loray crotch watchin' all day," Yank would volunteer.

Bullshit! thought Watt, releasing Loray and dropping the razor. As he headed for the door, a customer said, "shit!" with disappointment while another turned the television back on.

Why don't you listen? You never listen! said some TV character on a show.

"How can I listen," said Loray sobbing, "when one man wants to burn me and another wants to smoke my ashes?" Everyone laughed as Watt walked out the door.

From the street, Watt saw the G.I. return. Loray must have told him, "Where were you when I needed you? You're supposed to be my man! He was about to carve my ass like butter!" because the G.I. burst from the shop and ran right by Watt. Stopping at the corner, he looked up and down the street. Then he returned to the shop where Loray rewound some laughter in his belly and sprinkled new words on the G.I.'s shadow in the door as everyone laughed.

As Watt walked towards Central Park North, that Harlem politician crept into his mind, "So now, good people, we are honored and honor all of those who fought with us these many years for this...."

For what? asked Watt as the wild music blared and his legs started running.

CHAPTER 9

▼

He was still running along the park side when he heard the screams. It was Ralph, mad Ralph who, like an Arthurian knight, beat the heads of cars with old broomsticks, cursing as he hacked the lights and stomped the emblems. All cars were his enemy, and late at night while everyone slept padded behind three locks, Ralph waged war on Harlem streets and slew their cars like dragons.

Supported by the community garage owners because he generated business, Ralph could appear on any street at any hour to call a car to combat. Tooting his mouth like a trumpet, with a broomstick tucked under his arm, he fought with an unbridled passion and beat cars into metal bones. From Chryslers, Chevrolets, Fords—a Mercedes if he found one—to Hondas, Toyotas, or Volkswagens, the wages for being parked on a street where Ralph declared war was demolition.

Laughing, Watt stopped to watch Ralph challenge a Ford. With a fresh broomstick, he leaped on the car's hood and stomped it until it sprang open. Then he hacked the engine and tore out the fuel injectors. Fluids gushed as he dived under the hood and ripped out the car battery, which he tossed away. To cheers and laughter from people on the block, he raised his broomstick triumphantly, and then staggered to a nearby doorway.

Watt was laughing so hard he barely noticed someone behind him. His hand reached into his pocket for his knife as a voice gently said, "My name is Marv Goosebite, and I'm the new pastor at the Church of the Warm Savior. Can you tell me where it is, buddy?" A white man in a white raincoat stood before him. He looked like a human sacrifice.

"I don't know," said Watt. "But ask that brother over there leaning against the building. He knows the neighborhood better than I do."

"Thanks buddy," said Goosebite who got about four feet from Ralph when he saw the mad glow in his eyes. Shrieking, he made a beeline for the curb. But Ralph caught him. Reeling him in by his white raincoat, he asked, "Which car company do you work for?"

"Help!" cried Goosebite, his rubber heels skidding like tires. Goosebite was trembling, trembling so hard Watt could hear the coins in his pocket jingling. Ralph pinned him against a tree near a Mercury Cougar, asking, "Do you want to know what *REALLY* happened?"

Nodding feverishly, Goosebite screamed, "YES!"

"It was the morning my electric shaver leapt from my hand, drove for my throat, and purred for my life. I went to work *unshaved.*"

Suddenly, a motorcycle roared by with a white couple riding it. As Ralph tracked the bike like radar, Goosebite tried to make another break, but Ralph caught him and threw him back on the tree.

"Yes, unshaved! But crossing Fifth Avenue, in *your* neighborhood, the light was green, and all of the people who go to work to earn enough to go back started crossing when suddenly they heard a Moog synthesizer. Cars stopped. The god of metal smacked his lips, then gave the signal, and the slaughter began.

"Cadillacs raped our women, Volkswagens gobbled up children, and Chryslers ate men. I turned. I ran. I deserted them. I crouched in a doorway with my head in my arms. I'll never forget it. Never! From that moment I knew. *The automobile is the devil.*"

Letting out a shriek, Goosebite made another break, but Ralph caught him by his raincoat and dragged him back to the tree. "I was terror-stricken," said Ralph as Goosebite let out another shriek. "Yes, I used to sound like that!—How did you know?—and when I lifted my head, I saw the Yellow Cab patrols cruising around, picking up evidence. From that day I swore, like the Lone Ranger, to fight the beast *and injustice* wherever I found them and in the American way. But there's a problem. I have no Tonto. Have you ever fought the beast?"

"Many times!" cried Goosebite,

"Good!" said Ralph."There's an International Harvester truck parked at 111th Street. I'm always afraid to tackle trucks by myself, but with the two of us—you chopping at the rear while I hack at the front—we will prevail!"

"But I have to get to the Church of the Warm Savior," pleaded Goosebite.

"That can wait!" snapped Ralph, closing one eye and squinting out of the other. "What rank did you attain while fighting the beast?"

"General!" cried Goosebite, letting out another shriek.

"Which level of general generalship?"

"Major general!" screamed Goosebite.

"Then I'm your subordinate!" shouted Ralph, clicking his heels and saluting. "What are my orders, sir?" he asked, as another motorcycle sped by.

"It's an INVASION! Sir, for your safety, please get into that car." The rubber soles on Goosebite's shoes skidded as Ralph dragged him to a car, saying, "I've never heard of a red Pontiac bothering anyone." He smashed in the windshield and unlocked the doors as alarms went off. Then he threw Goosebite into the car, saying, "Lock the doors, sir."

As the alarm blared, and windows on the block opened in blinks, Ralph ran to a garbage heap and grabbed a fresh broomstick, screaming at the Pontiac, "You're just like your brothers!" Then he backed-up twenty paces, with the broomstick under his arm, and charged the car, head-on.

He took off a mirror on the first pass; the left tail light went on the second. On the third pass he hit the hood dead center and it flew open, making another alarm go off.

"You Devil!" cried Ralph. "You've ruined society by speeding things up!" And jumping into the hood, he drove his broomstick into the engine, tearing out caps, belts, and hoses as fluids gushed in the air.

From the inside of the car, Marv Goosebite screamed again, "I'll save you, sir!" responded Ralph. Leaping from the hood onto the convertible top, he drove his broomstick through the cloth roof as Goosebite dodged its jabs.

The block was hysterical with laughter, even the people whose cars were destroyed. "He's in the back, now the front. Swing the stick left!" they directed as Goosebite leapt around in the car.

Then a metal carpet-sweeper stick flew from a window and clanged on the pavement. Leaping from the car, Ralph picked it up. When he did, Marv Goosebite climbed through the convertible top, darted across the street, and ran into Central Park, screaming.

"Follow him!" shouted the crowd. "Follow the scream!" But Ralph's mind was on the metal carpet-sweeper stick. Finally, someone had given him what he always wanted—his own Excalibur broomstick. Taking out a knife, Ralph tried to plug it into the stick's hole, but it didn't fit. Then he turned to the Pontiac again. Leaping into the air, he descended into its womb, wielding the metal stick. When Ralph finished with the Pontiac, it was almost flat. To cheers and applause, he staggered away holding its battery and a fistful of wires. But suddenly, the roar of a motorcycle was heard again, and Ralph 's head turned with the sound. When the bike stopped at a light, Ralph ran toward it, yelling, "*Hiyoh sancho!*" swinging Excalibur in the air.

Five minutes later, everyone was still belly-laughing. Watt laughed so hard his sides felt as if someone had worked him over. Staggering to the Pontiac's remains, he picked up its license plate and laughed, "Who *owned* a red Pontiac with a license plate that says BJ9?" Laughing, he hurled the license plate back into the car's wreckage.

"Hey, boy!" yelled an old man in a window above him. "You better get the *hell* out of there and not ask twice!"

"What do you know about getting anywhere, old man," laughed Watt. "You're late for Death."

"See, boy, I tried to save your ass. But you *didn't listen!*"

"Save your own ass!" quipped Watt, giving the old man the finger.

Watt was still laughing when a man and woman came out of the Cambridge Hotel a couple of minutes later. The man, in a black, wide-brim hat, saw Watt and the wrecked car in a single frame and let out a "SHIIIIIT!" that sounded like an amplified roar. A hush fell over the neighborhood as he ran towards Watt, big hands extended.

That must be BJ9, thought Watt. Deciding not to run, he placed his hand on his knife. But as the man jogged toward him, with his woman hop scotching behind, they got bigger, and a tremor of fear struck Watt. *They're giants!* he thought, now ready to run. But it was too late. The man was on him, and shoulder to shoulder, he was twice Watt's size.

Looking up at him, Watt said, "Wait a minute, brother. I didn't do it. A crazy motherfucker named Ralph fucked up your car and ran into the park. If you don't believe me, ask anybody." As BJ9 studied the wreck, Watt looked up and yelled, "Somebody, tell him! Tell him who fucked up his car!"

"I don't know shit," somebody said. "My name's Bennit and I ain't in it."

"All I know," said an old man laughing, "is *I'm* supposed to be *late* for Death. I guess you're gonna be early, young mothafucker!"

"Listen, man," said Watt, backing up. "You do better to run through Hell in gasoline drawers than fuck with me! Yeah, motherfucker! You do better to run through the jungle in a pork chop suit than mess with me!" Backing up, Watt took two steps in prelude to a sprint. But BJ9's big hand grabbed him on the step and reeled him in. Reaching into his pocket, Watt popped his knife open. But BJ9 caught the hand and took the knife from him, breaking it in half. "Don't do it!" pleaded his woman. But BJ9 ignored her. Holding Watt with one hand and touching his wide-brimmed black hat with the other, he said, "This asshole's gonna pay!"

Planting his feet on the ground, Watt threw a hard right to BJ9's head. Snorting his nostrils, BJ9 sucked in some air with the blow as if contemplating its flavor. He smiled sadistically, revealing two gold teeth in the center of his head. Then he gave Watt a blow that cracked through his spine and traveled to his toes before doubling back to his brain with additional pain.

"It's a HARLEMASSWHIPPIN'!" screamed someone as Watt collapsed to the pavement. "I been waitin' for this since I come to New York. Martha, make some popcorn!"

Then BJ9 picked him up straight over his head and threw him about ten feet into an iron gate where he lay groaning as BJ9 pounced on him with finance company terror in each eye.

"No, BJ9!" cried his woman as a short, powerful blow knocked Watt unconscious.

Watt saw himself explaining life to Sylvia, *"There's no such thing as love. I work with Dr. Otto Von Geber, the baddest motherfucker on Earth, and do you know what he calls love? A dependency relationship."*

"But Watt, we don't have to accept anybody's definition but our own. All we have to do is believe and not be afraid to love."

"You're asking a hell of a lot," said Watt.

"You're afraid," said Sylvia.

"No, I'm not," said Watt.

"Most black men are afraid to love. It's in our history. Slavery's done this to us. But we can move on and go beyond that pain."

"I can see there's no use talking to you," said Watt.

"Someday, when you're old, maybe you'll learn that the only worthwhile thing a human being can do is love and be loved by someone in return. All the millionaires you work with can't change that."

As Watt contemplated her words, he felt cold concrete behind his neck. Sylvia's image poured like syrup from his eyes. He saw those two gold teeth as BJ9 bitch-slapped him with the back and front of his hand, making Watt's head snap to and fro while his body convulsed and he groaned in agony. BJ9 stood up and kicked him, and his woman cried, "Don't do it!" But BJ9 kicked him again. Watt spat some blood and a tooth into BJ9's face. Snarling, BJ9 reared back and hit Watt again. Then he stood up and walked around him, like a doctor about to perform a delicate operation.

"Let him go!" pleaded the residents. "We've seen enough!"

"You've been kickin' his ass for three hours already!"

"You've gone beyond a HARLEMASSWHIPPIN'!"

"To tell you the truth, Sonny," said an old man's voice, "*he* didn't do it."

Hawking and spitting, BJ9 stood up, his clothes drenched in Watt's blood. "If any of you want me to stop," he yelled, "come down here and take his place!" Then he knocked Watt unconscious again.

The door to another memory opened, and Watt thought about Ullysa, the girl he once loved.

"You can't blame white people for everything," she said, "because as long as we do, we can't take responsibility for ourselves or make them stop whatever they're doing to us."

Watt had invited Ullysa home to meet Grandma. Like him, she was a senior at Nixon High School. But unlike him, she was from a middle class family and lived on Harlem's Sugar Hill.

As they climbed the stairs, they saw Blip on the landing, nodding with a needle in his arm.

"Do something!" gasped Ullysa.

"Relax," said Watt. "That's normal for him."

As they entered the apartment, Happy greeted them at the door. Wagging his tail, he leapt all over Ullysa with excitement. "Get down, Happy! Down!" yelled Watt.

"Where's your grandmother?" asked Ullysa.

"She had to go out to take care of some long-term business," said Watt. "She'll be back soon."

Leading Ullysa to the living room, he put on a Marvin Gaye record, then left the room. While Ullysa listened to the music, he took off his clothes and put on a robe. Then he got the note that Pete the pimp had given him. After combing his hair and sucking on a Lifesaver, he walked into the living room with his dick standing up.

"What do you think you're doing?" asked Ullysa.

"Guess," said Watt as Happy let out a whine and collapsed on his side. Raising his back leg, he showed his dog erection.

"I can't believe this," said Ullysa, "I'm getting out of here."

"Before you go, read this," said Watt adopting a cool, suave demeanor. Cautiously, Ullysa took the paper and read.

Listen, baby, instead of me trying to hustle you, why don't we relax, listen to some nice music, and talk of developing a mutually beneficial relationship. I'm tired of playing these games. And you must be, too. I just want to hold you.

I know it sounds mechanical, but it's honest and true. You feel about me the way I feel about you. Let's stop all the pretenses. We don't need the fences. I wanna hold you.

You don't have to take off your clothes. But it's better if you do. We can pretend we're children playing at the zoo. I can grab you. You can grab me too. I want to develop a mutually beneficial relationship with you. But most of all, I wanna hold you—and get to know you.

Laughing, Ullysa put down the note, saying, "You're mad, Watt, but I may try you when I'm ready."

"What's wrong with right now?" asked Watt, tugging at his streamer and removing his robe

"It's not crooked," said Ullysa. Grabbing it, she jerked it hard a couple of times. The pain made the blood-fattening tide recede.

"Wow!" cried Ullysa. "Does it go up as fast as it goes down?"

"If you kiss it," groaned Watt.

"Not today," said Ullysa, releasing him. As she prepared to leave, Pete's words haunted Watt. "Young brother, let me tell you something. If the Beast had had this note, he could have stayed a beast and still got Beauty."

"Don't go," said Watt, grabbing her and feeling the hairs of her wool coat spike into his pores.

"So you'd take it?!" she said, looking into his eyes.

"I've been waiting a long time," he said. As he tried to kiss her, she reached down and grabbed his nuts, saying, "And you'll wait a little longer."

"Just go!" he cried as she released him and strolled to the door. Looking back, she smiled, stuck out her tongue, and said, "Let's go out next weekend." As she went down the stairs, Watt shook his head.

A new crowd had assembled to watch his HARLEMASSWHIPPIN'. Through bloody eyes, Watt saw a white policeman twirling his stick while some customers from the House of Styles Barbershop placed bets. The waitress from Dreamland stroked her hair, which was blonde now. Watt also saw Mean Joe Vine. Wearing a pimp-brown hat with a gold hatband, Joe squatted five feet from Watt's head, checking out BJ9's technique.

"Kill that no good cocksucker!" cried the waitress.

"Suck his blood out!" yelled Loray. "It's good for the Devil!" As BJ9 gave Watt another flurry of kicks, Loray sang, "I've got to go. I wish I could stay. But I've got to go. I've got an appointment. Maybe I can come back later. Keep it going for me, baby."

Then BJ9 held five fingers up to Watt's face. Five more car payments remained for the beast that Ralph had disemboweled. Breathing deeply, BJ9 rose and held up his hand for the crowd to see.

"Alright, baby, I'll stay if you make it quick!" cried Loray as BJ9 removed his black hat and his woman took it from him, saying, "Whatever happens, I still love you."

Leaning over Watt for the last time, BJ9 said, "Up to now, I've gone easy on you. But now I'm gonna give you all five fingers at once—right up your ass! And then we'll be even—my car for your ass!" Watt saw the two gold teeth come together and disappear behind a set of fat lips. Then the gold teeth appeared again, glowing with BJ9's eyes in the darkness.

"Somebody, stop him," moaned Watt, as Mean Joe Vine frowned, shook his head, and got up to leave, saying, "This is too much violence for me."

This is it. thought Watt, *my obituary in the Amsterdam News: Man Killed on Central Park North. Or maybe not even that.*

Looking into BJ9's face, he saw the gold teeth clap and the muscle-bound hair in BJ9's nose flex as he snorted. *My life is over*, thought Watt. Suddenly a bottle broke over BJ9's head, followed by another and another. Then a broomstick cracked over his arm.

It's Ralph! thought Watt, passing out. *Bless him. Bless mad Ralph.* When he awoke he saw BJ9 on one knee. Bottles continued to scrape across his face. Bricks bounced off his chest, and sticks cracked him in the head. Watt heard his woman say, "I only go with him. I don't fight for him."

Now BJ9 was on both knees, a colossus about to topple. A basketball ricocheted off his head, followed by a brick, and another basketball. He passed out next to Watt who managed to crane his neck and spit some blood on him.

"Hey, man," said a voice. "It's me. Just relax. The ambulance is coming. It'll be here in a minute." Through blood clogged eyes, Watt saw the liquid shadows of Perry, Sylvia, and his grandmother standing above him. Together they had beaten BJ9 to the ground. As a siren came closer, Watt raised his head, saying, "Perry, Perry! They're playing our song!" Then he passed out.

CHAPTER 10

▼

Watt awoke in the emergency room of Medical Center Presbyterian Hospital. He was born there in the same decade freedom riders boarded buses for the South and technology made television available for poor folks—two events that affected him greatly. One expanded the panorama of his reveries; the other extended the vagaries of his dreams.

His dream as a child was to be a cowboy. That was ridiculous then. The Black Rodeo didn't exist yet, and no black cowboy had a TV series. But Grandma got up early one Saturday morning and went up to the Schomburg Library. "My grandson wants to be a cowboy," she told the librarian. "Can you help me?" Later that afternoon, she came home with conclusive proof that many of America's greatest cowboys were black. And Watt turned up his imagination and saw tumbleweed roll across the floor in hunks of dirt, killed roaches for rattlesnakes, and dreamed of that great day when he'd ride a bucking bronco rat. But now he lay in the hospital where his life had begun.

An old man lay on a stretcher next to his. "That was some beatin' you took," he said. "What are you, a sparrin' partner? He sure musta paid you a lot to take that beatin'. What was his name? EK5? FU7? Oh yeah! It was BJ9." At the mention of the two letters and number, a tremor of fear ran up Watt's spine. He imagined those two gold teeth grinding him up.

"He sure musta paid you a lot," said the old man. "I ain't seen one like that since 1947, the time old BJ8, the ex-champ caught his ex-manager comin' out the hotel with his ex-wife and figured out who made all the ex'es.

Now that was the Original HARLEMASSWHIPPIN'. It went on for days. What'd you do to BJ9 anyway? Sleep with his wife? She musta been *somethin'* cause you didn't even put up your hands to make it look good. Now I'm from Georgia, and I ain't been one to bite my tongue since I stepped off the bus from Tennessee. If I'd seen ya on the street, I wouldn't take you for a man who'd lie down and fight a Go-rilla. But ya can't tell. People like weird things these days. You like people to beatcha, don'tcha? I bet you're one of those fellas with the keys. Well pull your stretcher closer and *I'll* beatcha! Just don't let me beat no bones."

Trying to tune out the old man, Watt thought about Sylvia, but her image curdled in the old man's words: "It's your fault I'm here! After I saw the first handful of your asswhippin', I went home and couldn't sleep. So I decided to buy some pussy and was on my way to the Honey Hole, walkin' along Central Park North, when this motorcycle come tearin' out the park with a white boy drivin' it, a white girl on his ass, and a mad Negro ridin' hers and wavin' a broomstick like Attilla, the hungry. 'Here come humanity!' I thought, tryin' to get out their ways. 'If only I had a hogmaw, I could stop 'em in their tracks.' But they got me … knocked me in the air. The last thing I remember was sleepin' upside down and thinkin' life was over. Now I wake up and all I see is you. And you ain't dead. Or are you? Is we *both* dead?"

Fortunately, an orderly took the old man away. Watt heard the bastard cry, "But I'm an accident victim!"

"No, it says here that you're to be operated on for spinal cancer." He wheeled the old man through a pair of doors that swung rapidly back and forth, then not at all.

A little later Watt felt a needle in his arm and he thought about his mother. He imagined her thousand needles jabbing in his soul, the rip from her womb, and the doctors giving him fresh blood because he was a junkie, too. He imagined his infant spasms and quaking, the withdrawal pangs, and the imageless hallucinations and wordless cries that preceded meaning. And he even imagined his mother, flat veined and reeling in her punched hide, moving through the tenements, carrying him like some chicken-in-the-basket: his mother—the daughter of another mother too strong, who threw her father into a Harlem street on Christmas day because he had been unemployed for three weeks and had come home with the smell of prostitutes all over him, and because he was a leech, as the mother said later, raising the little girl alone, giving her everything mechanical and due while choking her father in weekend spells for his general shiftlessness and general degeneracy, not knowing she was making her daughter susceptible to men even more shiftless and more degenerate.

Light pounded against closed eyelids. Darkness swirled with redness as a sponge swabbed his body. Then a man's voice said: "Alright, let's get him upstairs."

When his mother tried to sell him for a nickel bag of dope, his grandmother took him away, saying: "I'm not going to let you see this baby until you take care of *your* problem."

"My problem, Mama!" the daughter cried repeatedly until the mother slapped her.

"All right, *our* problem," said the mother. "And we'll solve it together ... or you'll die."

A few weeks later they found the daughter dead of a heroin overdose in the alley behind the RKO movie theater at 116th Street.

"My baby!" cried his grandmother. After the funeral, she dried her tears and continued to raise Watt—the blood from her blood that was dead yet still alive. She taught him how to scribble his first letters, count pennies up to 1,000, and to be a man before he was ten, all the while nurturing his imagination and listening to reports of what that imagination perceived.

> *History is on parade in the clouds,*
> *Africans and Indians*
> *Egyptians and Greeks,*
> *Norsemen and Asians*
> *They're all dancing In the clouds.*

He was drawing a cloud in school one day when he stepped into an argument between two boys. The bigger of the two boys pushed him, and he pushed him back. They agreed to do what boys in higher grades did: meet after school. They faced each other at 3:00 p.m. Each looked into the other's eyes wanting to forget and go home. But a circle of older children formed around them, and they had to fight. "Go on! You two ain't brothers! Fight!" demanded the higher graders.

Adults appeared, too: winos rising from stupors to watch any combustion. "Fight!" shouted one of them, raising a bottle to his head. Then the infamous hand in the crowd shoved Watt into the other boy who, bobbing and weaving like a midget Sugar Ray Robinson, caught Watt with some sharp jabs and hooks.

"Thass a bad mothafucka!" shouted one of the winos, as the boy changed styles, dancing backwards. "Woh! Thass a BADNIGGER!" the wino repeated, and "BADNIGGER, BADNIGGER," echoed through the crowd.

Then Miss Sommers, one of the few black teachers in the school, came out and stopped the fight. "You ought to be ashamed of yourselves!" she yelled, "especially you big kids!"

As the winos crept away, one said: "I useta go to school with that bitch, right there in P.S. 10. C'mon."

"Fighting like animals—You ought to be ashamed!"

Then, dragging BADNIGGER by the arms, she went into the school. "I'll see you tomorrow!" yelled BADNIGGER.

"I'll be waiting!" yelled Watt.

"Waiting for what?!" asked a voice, and Watt turned and saw a boy who looked as if he was in the fifth grade. "What's your name?" asked the boy.

"My name is Watt."

"My name is Spud," said the boy smiling and extending his hand. "You didn't have to be out here gettin' your ass kicked. I would've taken care of everything— Who's that?" The boy who had originally got into the fight with BADNIGGER approached. "What's your name?" asked Spud.

"Perry," the boy responded, and Spud extended his hand again, saying: "This may interest you, too, Perry. I'm willin' to protect you, look out for the *both* of you, for a quarter a week."

"No," said Watt.

"Whatchoo mean NO!" yelled Spud, punching Watt in the chest. The blow made Watt gasp for air. But he said "NO" again, inviting two punches.

"I'll cave in your chest!" yelled Spud as Perry tried to ease away.

"Don't run! You ain't goin' nowhere!" yelled Spud. "You'll be in school tomorrow, and it'll be worse if I have to chase you today."

As Perry walked back, Spud grabbed him "Lemme see what's in your pocket," he said, ripping one open. "Now take off your shoes." When Perry took them off, Spud found a dime and a nickel and punched him, saying, "I thought you said you didn't have any money! There's a tax for lyin'. Now you owe me twenty-five cents. Next time I'll check your socks! How much *you* got, sucker?" he said, turning to Watt. "Take off your shoes!" As Watt took them off, Spud rifled through his pockets, saying, "Nothing! You better have something for me tomorrow! And you better have my twenty-five cents! I don't like people that don't pay me my money!"

Turning in a dramatic sweep, Spud started down the street, bobbing up and down as if riding a camel. He got about twenty feet, then turned and bopped back. "So you won't forget," he said, punching both boys in the chest. Then he bopped around the corner.

Watt and Perry were in pain. But what hurt most was that no one cared. No one tried to stop it because in different ways it happened to everyone.

Then a bell rang, and the children dispersed with higher graders chasing each other for loot from the lower graders whom they had robbed, and Dewey Square, emptied of its contents, turned its face toward the Dewey Square Hotel for excitement. A trumpet hit a triple high C.

The two boys walked down 117th Street, trembling like rabbits. Near Eighth Avenue, they encountered a street gang dressed in red and white, the Sportsmen colors, poised before a great battle jingling bebop death. The leader of the gang, Teenangel, holding a chain in one hand and a stick in the other, cried, "Stomp the Baldies! Stomp the Fordham Baldies!" And an army of teenagers let out a cheer as Watt and Perry hurried back around to Dewey Square.

They went home the long way: past the Western Union Office on 116th, past the U.S. Post Office and Jagerman's Supermarket; past Dr. Irwin Benjamin's Optometrist Shop, and past J. Horn's Furniture Store.

The specter of Morningside Park loomed before them as they crossed Eighth Avenue. And Watt remembered Grandma telling him about a boy who watched Superman on television and crept out early one morning while his parents slept and went to Morningside Park. In pajamas and a robe tied like a cape, he tried to fly. Climbing the highest rock, he leapt to his death.

"Goddamn that Superman! Goddamn that bastard!" cried Grandma. "He's done it again!"

"Then who can fly?" asked Watt.

"Not a soul, not a goddamn soul!—And don't let me catch you playin' Superman!"

Splitting up on Manhattan Avenue, Watt went two blocks up and Perry two blocks down. Entering his building, Watt stopped and wet two fingers with saliva to wipe some dry blood from his nose. He expected Grandma to notice anyway and say, "I can't stop you from fighting, but I can tell you fighting never solved a thing. Like those World Wars I was tellin' you about, it puts a little Band-Aid on a big problem. Now if I go to school with you tomorrow, the other boys will call you sissy, maybe even gang up on you. And if I give you a nickel for each of them every day, I'll be workin' for an elementary school Mafia. So, you'll have to settle it yourself."

Going up the stairs, Watt saw a shadow bobbing between landings. A young man repeated to himself, "I'm Blip." as his mother stood in a doorway, tossing his clothes into the hall. "Don't come near me again!" she cried. "You're not my son! You're a dopefiend!" Then she slammed the door, leaving Blip mumbling in tears.

Passing him, Watt went up the stairs. He tapped on a door and Grandma opened it. "How's my little boy today?" she said hugging him. "Did you have a good day at school? Go wash up. Food is ready."

He went to the bathroom and peed, running water in the sink to make Grandma think he had washed his hands.

"Be sure to *really* wash your hands," she called, and he really washed them.

Grandma was at the stove with her back to him when he came into the kitchen and sat down. As she turned holding a plate of food, he playfully said, "I'm Blip," and bobbed his head up and down.

"Goddammit!" screamed Grandma, dropping the plate of food in his lap and slapping him. "You better not be *Blip* in my house! I won't have it! You better know who you are *all* the time! I'll put the wail on you if you forget! Your name is WATT."

Later that evening, he went into the living room and found Grandma watching television in the dark. The TV's rays shone on her bare feet, on the corns and calluses and bunions that had accumulated from footed demands that she had to meet. "How's my little boy?" she asked, giving him a hug. "Grandma didn't mean to hurt you."

The next day Watt and BADNIGGER pugged after school in Dewey Square; they made friends the following day, and two days later Perry poked his head out of the side door at P.S. 10. "See him?" asked Watt.

"No," said Perry. As they stepped outside, Spud yelled, "Punkfaggots!" and ran toward them. "Little motherfuckers, give it up!" he snarled. Collaring Perry, he growled, "Take off your shoes *and* socks!"

"Leave him alone!" yelled Watt.

"Whatchoo say?!" snapped Spud.

"Leave him alone!" repeated Watt, and Spud looked at him in disbelief.

"I'ma bust your ass!" he yelled as Watt started running with Spud trailing behind. He ran across 117th Street, past Mr. Sam's Candy Store and Harold's Barbershop, over to Morningside Park. To neutralize Spud's speed, Watt ran around parked cars repeatedly, taunting Spud with chants of "Your mama!"

"I'ma fuck you up!" yelled Spud who countered Watt's strategy by ducking below the windshield and out of sight so he could sneak up on Watt behind the car. But Watt thwarted that device by circling around another car.

Spud was still chasing him when two little boys crept up behind him carrying baseball bats. "You punks ain't gonna do *shit* with them bats!" snarled Spud. As

Perry gave one to Watt, BADNIGGER struck the first blow. Spud went down crying and holding his knee.

"How do you like it?" asked Perry, cracking him on his arm. Spud screamed for help, but no one heard him. Then he started running with the three smaller boys pursuing him and beating him with their bats. Eventually, they stopped beating him and left him lying in a pile of dog shit.

"Mess with one of us and we'll *all* get you!" BADNIGGER said as Watt awoke.

He was still lying on a stretcher in the hospital, hearing groans. In his mind, he saw the chain of life extending to the sky. A roach was at the bottom with a rat on its back. Man, naked and free, stood atop the chain, searching for meaning. Then the earth shook and the chain was altered. Sir Ainsley Bridges was on top, wearing a business suit and a smile. As he raised his arms triumphantly, the chain shook again. Now Loray was at the top, waving to an invisible audience and saying, *Thank you very much, ladies and gentlemen. And in conclusion, I'd just like to say one thing: Laissez Fairy! Laissez Fairy!*

Slowly, Watt's eyes opened. The light above him shone over an operating table. The groans he had heard belonged to three old men, a black, a white, and an Asian—who lay on stretchers around him with three signs that read: HEART. GUTS, KIDNEYS.

The operating room door swung open. Several doctors wearing masks entered. One carried a jar with fluid in it. "For his black brain," he said. And the eyes of the old black man shot open as his stretcher vibrated with fear. "No, no, not you," said a doctor consoling him. "You're different. You're a millionaire."

Then another doctor noticed Watt was conscious. "I told you he'd wake up, Selby. That beating wasn't as severe as you thought."

"But we've got to go through with it. We may never have another chance. We owe it to Science."

"Fuck *Science!*" said the old white man on a stretcher. "You owe it to *me*! I'm paying you!" As he waved his hand giving the command to proceed, Watt noticed a ring he was wearing. It had a diamond the size of a golf ball.

Briefly, the doctors conferred. Then Dr. Selby said, "We're agreed. We'll take it alive!"

'Take what?' wondered Watt as the old men groaned, "you, you, you." Maybe they intended to give Watt some parts from these old guys. *They can't use them much longer*, he thought,

One of the doctors gave Watt a needle, and he began falling, thinking, *It's me*, as a scalpel cut into his chest and moved in a circle around his heart.

Cleaning me like a chicken, he thought. As a pair of hands clutched his heart and began tugging at it, he heard Grandma cry, "That's my grandson's heart you're taking, BASTARDS! That's my grandson's heart!" Grandma stood in the doorway of the operating room with a white man who asked: "What's going on here, Dr. Selby?"

"We're attempting the first single-donor-multiple-transplant operation," said Dr. Selby.

"But like *this*, under *these* conditions, and with a *LIVE* patient?"

Sucking his teeth, one of the doctors ripped off his mask and threw it to the floor. A hush fell over the operating room. Then the three old men began groaning louder: "Who am I if I ain't better than a nigger?"

"If his heart ain't mine, then whose is?"

"Light, light becomes darkness."

"You pieces of shit!" yelled Grandma. "I'll show you who you are!" She pulled a purple vial from her pocketbook and ran towards the old men with her arm cocked. "Here's some Sybil juice for your assholes!"

Trying to restrain her, one of the doctors grabbed her from behind, causing some Sybil Juice to leap from the vial and splash on his arm. He screamed as his arm shriveled up and retracted into his shoulder, leaving only his hand waving.

"Bastards!" screamed Grandma, splashing the Sybil Juice in all directions. As the vial slipped from her hand and did a jig across the floor, the three old men groaned:

"Turn out the light!"

"Don't leave the water running!"

"And four squares of toilet tissue!"

CHAPTER 11

▼

"Where was Moses when the lights went out?" cried Loray as doctors pressed Watt's heart back into his chest.

"Where was Moses when the lights went out?" repeated Loray.

"Now I *know* you're crazy," said Yank. "They're on."

"I don't care," said Loray. "We're supposed to ask for MORE LIGHT, no matter what."

"But it's bright enough already. We've got double exposures. We need darkness so we don't blow ourselves up."

"Enjoy *your* ignorance," said Loray. "But give me *my* light. I can't sing in the dark."

"But you been singin' in the dark all your life."

"Not when *I* wanted to."

Then a curtain dropped, the lights went out, and Watt, plunged into darkness, heard Grandma cry, *"You bastards! You KILLED him!"*

"No, we were just starting."

"You opened up his heart!"

"That can be repaired. Trust me."

"He better live! My grandson better live or I'll...."

"No, Madame Zeporah! Don't throw any sibyl juice on me!"

As more light flashed through Watt's brain, Loray sang:

> *Where was Moses*
> *When the lights*
> *Came on-on?*

to the tune of "Dixie" while Yank, who wasn't worth a candle in the electric world, said, "You ain't shit."

"Whatchoo meeeeeean *I* ain't shit?" jumped Loray.

"You said LIGHTS before."

"So what?" said Loray.

"You *lie* faster than the speed of light—*that's so what!*"

"Sweetheart," said Loray, sliding on a liver and tripping on a bone, then laughing, "Weeeeeeeeeeee! With all them years, you'd think they'd make these bodies neater."

"But you still *ain't shit!*"

"Sweetheart," said Loray.

"Don't talk no stuff to me!" snapped Yank. "I said it and I'll say it again. You lie faster than the speed of light, and you *ain't shit!*"

"Sweetheart," said Loray, "what's all this talk about the speed of light? *What about the speed of darkness?*" Singing, "..things you are," Loray clapped his hands as Yank broke into a fit of epileptic laughter.

"Whatchoo laughin' at, sucker?"

"YOU," laughed Yank. "All these years I didn't know...."

"Didn't know *what*, SUCKER?"

"You can't SING!"

"Well that ain't all you don't know, *FAGGOT!*"

Watt saw them scuffling, the light beams clashing, and Yank howling as Loray got behind him and turned him over. "No, Ray!" cried Yank. But it was too late. Loray cold-cocked him. An x-rayed dick descended into an illuminated asshole as Yank screamed. Then a plug was pulled and the darkness returned.

"We've blown a fuse!"

"Call the technicians!"

"Get it right, you bastards!" cried Grandma as the darkness disappeared and the light returned—so bright it blinded Watt. Although blind, he could hear. But what he heard made him sick—a gravelly voice laughing over a car engine's roar.

"T.S., You motherfucker!" cried Watt. I'm glad you're dead!" As the voice continued laughing, Watt wanted to shake the thought from his head, but it would never leave. It would always be there, accompanied by the wild music and perpetual irresolution beyond his control.

He had first heard of T.S. in neighborhood whispers, then in curses and lamentations uttered by his grandmother for his dead mother. But he did not know who T.S. was or what he did until he was eight years old and roller-skating along the curb.

A huge white Cadillac Coupe Deville sailed to a stop in front of him. The Cadillac's window rolled down, and a brown-faced man in a wide-brimmed hat pointed at him, saying, "He's one of mine." His voice reminded Watt of the gravelly sound coal makes when it's poured down a chute.

"How do you know he's yours?" asked a young woman seated beside him.

"Look at his face," laughed T.S. as the Cadillac sped away. Nine years, ten Cadillacs, and countless young women would come and go before Watt sought out that man with the big hat and gravelly voice who was *supposed* to be his father.

He was seventeen and about to graduate from Nixon High. An honor student, he had received a full scholarship to college. But then it hit him—that cat-killing curiosity. He wanted to know about his father, not knowing how knowing would affect him. "I made it without you," he said, addressing his father in a mirror. "And I'm going to college." Perhaps it was the need to have the opportunity to utter those words, whether he said them or not, that drove him to seek out T.S. late one spring night.

He knew about his haunts. He passed them each day or heard about them in whispers from gossiping neighbors: the Outhide Bar & Grill, a Harlem "bucket o' blood" so dangerous that it offered five drinks for the price of one to entice customers, and Mel's Plaza off Seventh Avenue, the hotel where T.S. seduced young women with booze and dope.

Walking down Eighth Avenue past midnight in the fog, he saw a pawn shop's broken balls with rubble from a riot strewn beside it. A Great Dane tied to a gate barked incessantly as dopefiends moved in shadows, huddled in doorways, or lounged along the curb, hawking electrical appliances with plaster attached to the plugs.

Ahead of him, neon lights throbbed through the darkness. He reached the Outhide and entered a crowded, smoke-filled bar where a saxophone player had just finished a solo and a faggot, like Loray, howled for more. Two women sat like bookends at each end of the bar, their heads weighed down with booze for ballast. Between the two women, a pimp in a red suit held court. "Black women wanna go in the house. White women wanna go in the field. Shit! All I do is run a house-field exchange program."

Men holding cigarettes and sucking deeply on them as if they were reefers formed a smoky curtain around a table in the rear. One man sat dead-center at the table with his back to the wall. Observing everything under his wide-brimmed hat, he directed the others who did his bidding with an alacrity seldom enjoyed by kings.

As Watt stared at him, T.S. moved his head in fractions. Then one of his men signaled Watt to come over. Approaching, Watt coughed repeatedly as he penetrated the smoky curtain to see his father studying him with a look of contempt on his face, which was dominated by two stony jowls.

"Fuck you want?" he asked.

"To talk," said Watt.

"Talk!" said T.S. "Do I look like a bitch?" As the curtain of men laughed, the Bookend Sisters raised their heads and crashed them down on the bar again.

"No, sir," said Watt.

"Ain't he polite," said T.S., scowling and laughing simultaneously. "What's your name, kid?"

"I'm Watt."

"Fellas, this is one of my boys," said T.S. "Watt, these are my three main associates—Mr. Leopard, Mr. Lion, and Mr. Wolff." The three men closest to T.S. carefully looked at Watt and forced smiles onto faces that harbored secret passions.

"So what the fuck do you want?" repeated T.S.

"I just wanted you to know I made it," said Watt.

"Made *what*, motherfucker?" snapped T.S., looking around. "I don't see no car, no money, no jewelry, not even a fine bitch. So what the fuck do you have?"

"I'm going to college in September," said Watt.

"Goody-goody for you!" snapped T.S. "Who gives a fuck."

"I thought you...."

"You thought *wrong!*" interrupted T.S. "You thought you could come in here and tell me some bullshit about *how you made it,* and I'd give you some cash upfront. Well I'm not givin' you shit! You have my deepest sympathy. Now get the fuck away from me and let that man behind you step up."

As Watt stepped back with no sense of his feet ever moving, a dopefiend slithered forward. At first Watt saw only his hand, which held a twenty-dollar bill and shook as T.S.'s hand, swooped down, like a hawk, and took it from him. Then Wolff gave the junkie a bag of dope, saying, "Best heroin in town."

Feeling as if he could puke, Watt turned to escape and staggered back, mouth agape. Then he looked at the junkie. In his face he saw another version of his own. Then a voice within him yelled, "Run! Run! And don't stop running!"

As he ran from the bar, Leopard, Lion, and Wolff laughed. Someone boomed, "The Devil's on the moon!" And someone else asked the faggot if he was a Rough Rider. "A Rough Rider?—Shit! I've run up more hills than Teddy Roosevelt!"

Then Watt was outside, gasping for fresh air and running—past the dope-fiends hawking goods, past the pawn shop's broken balls, past the Great Dane barking relentlessly into oblivion.

CHAPTER 12

▼

"Where was Moses when the lights went out?" cried Loray from darkness risible.

"In the nut house," answered Yank, "where *you* belong."

Thass okay," said Loray. "Cause whatever *I* am, *you* are, too. And whither *you* go, *I* goeth too—or at least a part of me. We're married now, baby. So be faithful—Cause I can tell who you been with by the way you move."

Then Watt heard Sylvia ask, "Have either of you seen Watt?"

"How long you been standin' there?" asked Loray.

"Long enough," said Sylvia.

"See any trade secrets?"

"Is Watt there?" asked Sylvia.

"Honey, if Watt was here, would *I* be on top?"

"Were *you* on top? Then who was on the bottom?"

"Christ! Look what he's done to me!" groaned Yank.

"That's what you get for hanging out with a faggot," said Sylvia.

"Who you callin' a *faggot?!*" jumped Loray.

"*You!*" snapped Yank.

"Rub your ass when you say that, partner."

"Have either of you seen Watt?" asked Sylvia.

"I ain't seen him," said Yank.

"I've got to find his heart," cried Sylvia, "and I want you to help me."

"He ain't got no heart," laughed Loray.

"But he's got guts!" snapped Yank.

"Well I'm with ya, honey," said Loray. "After all, you showed me the way outta that darkness and into this light. But couldn't you have found some light with air-conditionin'? It's hotter than *Atomic Asshole* here."

"Christ! Look what he's done to me!" groaned Yank.

Then they went off with Yank rubbing his backside, Loray licking out his tongue, and Sylvia searching for some sign of Watt.

When they had gone, Watt tried to crawl away, but was too weak. He felt pain so acute that he wanted to give up. But then memory rescued him.

> Memory that sorts pain and spaces it out,
> Memory with recollections false and true
> The "I" that's different, yet the same,
> The "I" floating above
> In that Good-yarn Blimp.
> Speak, memory.

The next day he went to school, but his mind wasn't in class. It kept drifting back to the Outhide. The only time he stopped thinking about it was when he saw Ullysa. His girlfriend and lover now, she helped him to forget the pain of being born a dopefiend and approaching manhood without a mother or father. At concerts off Central Park's lake, in movie theaters holding hands, or playing Garden of Eden when her parents were out, she made him feel that he had a purpose and the right to dream. He dreamed of the day they would graduate from college and marry.

They were leaving 125th Street one afternoon when a white Cadillac Coupe Deville sailed by. When they reached 124th Street, both Cadillac and driver were waiting for them. "Son!" said T.S., struggling to smile. "I couldn't be soft in front of my boys. I couldn't last five minutes in Harlem if they thought I was soft. I had to be hard on you. Let's talk. I want to find out what you've been doing. Get in." Cautiously, Watt got into the Coupe Deville with Ullysa, and they sailed off.

Now everything was in order. The dream was almost complete. The dream of going to college had coupled with the dream of reconnecting with his father, and he had fallen even deeper into love with Ullysa who filled him with hope. Of course, Grandma did not know of his relationship with T.S. Nor could Watt tell her because of her hatred for his father.

Watt was feeling particularly good one June evening. He was on his way to Perry's house to get a book when he spotted his father's car sailing down the street. A young woman was with him. At first, Watt didn't believe his eyes. But as the car turned a corner, he saw it was true and cried out, "Ullysa!" With his heart pounding, he threw down his books and ran after the Coupe Deville.

The car sped ahead a block, then two blocks, but Watt kept it in sight, running under streetlamp after streetlamp and turning several corners. Then the car disappeared from his sight. He didn't know whether it had turned left or right. But he guessed where T.S. was taking her, and he ran as fast as he could to Mel's Plaza, a hotel off 117th Street and Seventh Avenue where his father was reputed to take young women and seduce them with booze and dope.

Reaching the hotel, he saw his father's car parked in front. Ullysa's books were on the back seat. Tearing up the stairs, Watt bumped into a man and woman exiting the hotel. "I'll kick your fucking ass!" the man threatened.

"Calm down, baby," said the woman. "He's just a kid."

"I'm sorry," said Watt. "Did you see a man with a young girl, about seventeen, come in here?"

"We didn't see anything, kid."

Then Watt ran to the hotel desk, breathing deeply and asking, "Which room is T.S. in?"

"I don't know any *T.S.*, young man," said the little clerk, a proper-talking faggot in his forties with a lisp. "Which room is T.S. in?!" shouted Watt.

"I said I don't know any T.S. Now get out of here—*this minute!*"

And Watt took off again. This time he ran up the stairs, screaming "Ullysa! Ullysa!" with the little clerk running behind, grabbing and punching him with blows he didn't feel. Dragging the clerk along, Watt knocked on almost every door of the four-story hotel, screaming, "Ullysa! Ullysa!"

Finally, a door opened. Watt entered and quickly flicked on the light. A fat man and a woman with her legs over her head were making love. When the light came on, the woman shrieked, and the man cried, "Don't shoot, William! It's the first time!"

"I *tried* to stop him." pleaded the clerk standing behind Watt. As the fat man got out of bed and grabbed a bottle, Watt hustled out of the room. He was half way down the stairs when he heard the bottle smash against the clerk's head. Then he was outside again, screaming to the windows above, "Ullysa!"

"Shut the fuck up!" yelled people from buildings nearby. Watt saw the clerk stagger back behind the counter with a towel wrapped around his head.

Hours passed. He saw the fat man cautiously leave the hotel by himself, followed by his woman five minutes later. And he saw couple after couple stop at the front desk to ask the clerk about the commotion. And he heard their curses as they descended the stairs.

It was past midnight when the door to Mel's Plaza swung open and T.S. appeared with a dazed Ullysa who could barely stand. The clerk stood behind them smiling, still holding the towel around his head. As they came down the stairs, T.S. tucked his hand under Ullysa's arm to support her. "You, mother-fucker!" cried Watt, running up the stairs. "Let her go! She's coming with me!"

"She's my woman now!" said T.S., his jowls protruding, and Watt balled his fist to hit him, but before he could land a blow, T.S. pulled a pistol from his pocket and struck Watt over the head. As Watt started to fall down the stairs, T.S. hit him again, and he started rolling down the stairs. Stopping at the bottom of the stairs, he lay there semi-conscious, hearing footsteps—a man walking and a woman being dragged. And he heard the car engine's roar, felt the heat from its exhaust, and saw a vision of the white car taking off. His mind told his body to get up. But his legs seemed miles away. Then he heard the clerk's shrill laughter, and he saw the towel dangling above him and felt little feet kicking him repeat-edly in the side. "Alright, alright," muttered Watt as the kicks stopped and little feet scampered up the stairs and through the door. Watt lay there a little longer, and then he pulled himself up and began staggering to the Outhide.

CHAPTER 13

▼

Blocks through which Watt had run hours earlier seemed miles in length. Putting one foot in front of the other and resting periodically on lampposts, Watt slouched toward the Outhide. And every few steps a voice within him angrily cried *how could that bitch have done this to me?!*

Staggering across 116th Street, he saw Spud, the bully of his boyhood, crossing toward him, wearing a faded denim suit from the boys department of some clothing store. Afflicted by the curse of the bully—no physical growth—Spud was under five-feet tall. He was practically the same height he was the day he robbed Watt and Perry in Dewey Square. But now his life and all that it contained—property, services, and income—were mortgaged to whoever was kicking his ass as repayment for what he had taken from them as children.

"Spud, help me," called Watt.

"I'll pay you next week!" shouted Spud, darting away.

Watt turned left at Eighth Avenue and continued walking. The pawnshop's broken balls were still on the pavement with the rubble from a riot. Watt pulled a bottle from the rubble and broke it against the curb. The brown glass glistened in the moonlight.

As he continued walking and his head became clearer, he noticed not one dopefiend was on the street. No shadows bobbed in doorways. No addicts hawked goods along the curb. In fact the streets around the Outhide were completely empty. But in the midst of wondering where the dopefiends had gone, Watt cried out, "How could that bitch have done this to me?!"

The fuse was lit; he was the bomb ready to explode. As he approached the Outhide, he saw the white Cadillac parked outside and thought, *He's in there, and maybe his whore is with him.* But before he could enter, the doors to the bar burst open and all the hustlers, pimps, and number-runners ran out. Hopping into luxury cars, they revved their engines and took off as if the street was a runway.

Others hit the pavement with shoe leather, kicking their legs. Watt saw Leopard, Lion, and Wolff race out, get into a gypsy cab and drive off. Even the Bookend Sisters were moving, feebly jogging and falling down the street.

The police must be coming, thought Watt. *But they don't run from the police. They own the police.*

A moment later, he heard the clamor and saw the mob. An army of dopefiends was marching on the Outhide, carrying knives, guns, chains, and bats. And they didn't look like normal addicts, but an army of grotesques. Each had a limb or some other part of his body inflated. Some had hands bigger than their chests. Others had heads that had doubled in size while still others moved on legs the width of fireplugs. A few even had faces that seemed to wrap around their necks. From all of the races, they looked like the mean side of the United Nations—or some of God's Silly Putty creations. *He sold them bad dope,* thought Watt, stepping into a doorway to watch.

The dopefiends stopped in front of the Outhide. "He's inside," said one. His hands were three times the size of normal hands.

"Let's get him," said another, with a head that was deformed..

But before they could do anything, T.S. appeared in the doorway holding an Assault rifle, yelling, "I don't run from dopefiends!"

"Kill that motherfucker!" cried a white dopefiend, coasting on feet the length of skis, and the dopefiend mob moved forward, chanting, "YEAH!"

Then Watt saw the young man he believed to be his half-brother step to the front. His right hand was inflated to half the size of his body and he moved it along the ground by creeping fingers on the pavement. "Look what you did to me!" he cried, running toward T.S.

"Stay away!" warned T.S. "Stay away or I'll kill you!"

But his half-brother didn't listen. As he raised his huge hand in judgment, T.S. fired the Assault rifle once. The shot hit his brother in the heart and he fell over, but not before his hand struck T.S. in the face and exploded, drenching the Harlem hipster with pus. Then shots were fired from both sides. T.S. crouched and unleashed the automatic fury of his Assault rifle, which cut some dopefiends in half or made others seem to explode.

T.S. went through three clips before they got him. When his rifle was empty, he swung the gun like a club until they took it. They lifted T.S. into the air as he screamed. Giant hands smashed against his head. He screamed even louder as a powerful dopefiend tore his jacket sleeve and arm from his shoulder simultaneously and tossed them away. Another dopefiend immediately began jumping up and down on the arm. T.S. was still screaming as several dopefiends with bloated feet stomped him. They continued stomping him until they knew he was dead.

Finally, dopefiends appeared carrying the broken pawnshop balls. They hoisted them above their heads and slammed them down on T.S.'s remains. Then they went after the Cadillac, turning the luxury vehicle into a tin can.

How long Watt stood on that corner, he didn't know. All he remembered was walking away but feeling he was still there and would remain there for the rest of his life. When the last dopefiend departed and the Pollution Plane flew overhead, he went home. Late that night, he awoke to find laughter pumping up from his stomach as tears streamed down his face. He was laughing and crying simultaneously, like the weather when it rains with the sun shining bright. He remembered wondering, *how could the sun be shining bright when it's raining?* And he recalled Grandma saying, "The Devil's beating his wife."

CHAPTER 14

▼

'The Devil probably beats his mother, too,' thought Watt, as the previous night's violence replayed itself through his mind: dopefiends marching and T.S. evil and blind—gone to his grave now, following a barely attended funeral courtesy of one of his *young* girls, presided over by a minister who sat down as soon as he stood up and said, "Thank God! It's over!"

But it wasn't over for Watt.

He went to school the next day, thinking, *I don't believe in shit!* And to make matters worse, Ullysa sent him a note, which he tore up thinking, *Bitches! I'll never trust one of you again!*

That was the mood he was in when he made a decision that forever changed his life. "Are you sure you can make it, Brother Kahlil?"

"Yes, my brother, I will be there. I will be honored to be the commencement speaker at Nixon High."

"Thank you, Right, Honorable Brother Kahlil."

"Thank *you,* my brother."

And after that decision, what forgiveness?—only Kleindeck holding a golf club, Kahlil's lying and hypocritical words, and the street poet's chanting,

> *These are the rocks*
> *that hurt since '54*
> *the ironies in stone*

Fuck it all! thought Watt, rolling in mind's darkness. Lost in his soul, he did not know where he was. He heard a lip-smacking, crunching sound—like someone eating cereal in a microphone. Then he heard a moan followed by the yell of a man having orgasm.

"Black Hole!" he cried. "Is that you, all senseless? Is that you? Did you come from a black hole, too?"

But there was no reply, and he continued crawling and wondering if he would ever find mercy in the darkness of his soul.

As he crawled into a tunnel, the cereal-chewing sound got louder and again he cried, "Black Hole, Black Hole, is that you, all senseless? *Did you come from a Black Hole, too?*" But there was no answer, and he crawled on.

Pulling himself out of the tunnel, he felt a hand grab him and heard Loray yell, "Gotcha, Dreamweaver!"

"Finally," sighed Sylvia.

"It's about time," said Yank.

"Let me go!" snapped Watt.

"We're here to help you," said Sylvia.

"Why?" asked Watt.

"Because I love you," said Sylvia.

"Then let me go," said Watt. "Leave me alone."

"That's not you talking," said Sylvia. "You're being goggled in the back of someone else's throat."

"Dreamweaver," jumped Loray, "whose throat you in, baby? Wanna try mine?"

"There you go again!" cried Yank.

"I can't help it," said Loray. "I been in love with him since the fourth grade."

"Shut up!" snapped Watt.

"You shut up!" jumped Loray. "I guess you forgot what happened the *last* time you *messed* with *me!*"

And out of the darkness BJ9 called, "Is Watt there?"

"Yeah," said Loray, "Like KILROY."

"We've got business to finish," said BJ9. "You know what you did to my car." BJ9 was about to pounce on Watt when BADNIGGER's voice boomed, "Leave him alone!"

And "WOH!" went up through the darkness, followed by shouts of "FIGHT! YOU TWO AIN'T BROTHERS!" As a bell clanged repeatedly, people from all over the world streamed into a dark arena. Some didn't speak English, but the spectacle spoke for itself. Watt heard the voices of Dr. Otto Von Geber and the CMB millionaires with whom he worked.

"What are you rich crackers doing in a black neighborhood?" asked Yank.

"This is not a black neighborhood," said Dr. Von Geber. "It's a BLACK BRAIN. And its owner plays an integral role in my CMB therapy."

Strangers came, too. "Ego sum lux mundi."

"Listen, honey," said Loray, "you gotto speak English."

"Aw, leave the chump alone," said Yank.

"Who you t-t-t-t-tellin' to leave me alone," stuttered Chump.

"I was talkin' to the chump in the robe," said Yank.

Instantly, Loray became the announcer, calling, "Ladies and gentlemen, and children of all ages, we got a *goody* tonight. Weighin' 249 pounds, fresh from inflictin' the first HARLEMASSWHIPPIN' in thirty years, with shoulders to match his height and gold teeth that glitter in the night—B … J … 9!"

As a bell clanged and the crowd cheered, Loray continued, "His opponent, weighin' 249 1/2 pounds, meaner than the day he was born and slapped the doctor, capable of inflictin' two HARLEMASSWHIPPINS at once, the pride of Harlem, the terror of wherever he's been—BAAAADNIGGER!"

As the bell clanged, and the crowd cheered, Loray, now serving as the referee, brought the two fighters together in darkness for their instructions. "We gotto have rules," said Loray. "We gotto have rules even when we're talkin' about eatin' a motherfucker. We gotto have rules so nobody don't eat no shit. So listen closely. We got two fighters and one pork chop, and one of you fighters ain't gonna get no pork chop—KILL EACH OTHER!" The bell rang again, and the two men went toe-to-toe, throwing haymakers and headhunting in the dark.

While they were fighting, Watt decided to escape. But he was so weak he could barely crawl. After crawling several minutes, he couldn't go on and had to rest. He curled up in a fetal position and fell into a deep sleep. The footsteps of departing fight fans awoke him. He heard Ainsley Bridges' voice say, "It was a good fight, but nobody died. I thought black people *always* killed each other when they fought."

"I could have died," said Yank, "when Loray struck a match and they were *both* knocked out."

"Too bad nobody knows who went down first," said Loray.

"What did BJ9 mumble?" asked Yank.

"We who are about to die," said a bearded man in a gown.

"Want some money," added Loray. "And honey, didn't I tell you to speak English before. Well I'm tellin' you again. I ain't from no island."

"Aw, he's just another chump." said Yank.

"No, he ain't!" said Loray. "Look at his robe. IT'S EXPENSIVE!"

"Well he ain't raisin' no hell," said Yank.

"Whatchoo talkin' about, baby," said Loray. "HELL HAS BEEN RAISED!"

"Well I ain't seen it" said Yank.

"You never *see* anything," said Loray. "You hardly *feel* anything any more. I guess that's what happens when you're married a long time."

"Don't mess with me!" jumped Yank.

"I'll MESS with you whenever I feel like it!" snapped Loray.

"Ego sum lux mundi," said the robed figure departing.

"Yeah, later to you, too," said Yank.

"Don't forget what I told you. Next time, speak English," said Loray. "Maybe I can help you get a Green card."

"He sure was strange," said Yank.

"You meet all kinds at a fight," said Loray. "But now I'm tired. My feet feel like they been walkin' with a flock of Jehovah Witnesses."

"Do you wanna pray?" asked Yank.

"I ain't lyin' down in nobody's green pastures," said Loray. "But if you wanna give me some head."

"All I wanna do is go home," said Yank.

"But we can't go home," said Sylvia. "What about Watt?"

"Ain't you heard, baby?" said Loray. "Watt's dead."

At first, Watt wondered what Loray meant. But then he realized both the darkness and the light were disappearing. Yes, he *was* dying.

The voice of a doctor started counting above him: "*One ... Two ... Three*" followed by an electric current that shot through his body, making him do a jig with the juice.

"Man, look at you down there," said Faye, "*stinkin' and stagnatin'* like the day you were born. You're alive. But what purpose do you serve?"

"I don't know," said Watt. "And I don't care. It's my life to waste."

He heard the count again: "One ... Two ... Three," as another surge of electricity coursed through his body, and Loray said, "So Dreamweaver, you're admittin' that you wasted your life?"

"But it's not over yet!" said Watt. "I might surprise you. After all, could a dead man dream up you motherfuckers and then sit back and watch you come to life?" asked Watt.

"Only God can make a tree, but even he can't make a man these days," said Loray.

"Well, could a dead man say, *Fuck you all!?*" asked Watt.

"Ain't no dead man ever said that," snapped Loray.

"Well I'm saying it," said Watt. "And because I can say it, I'm alive. Fuck you all!"

"I'm offended!" gasped Faye.

"W-w-w-w-why you gotto offend the l-l-l-l-lady?" stuttered Chump.

"Because that's what I do," said Watt. "I offend people by telling the truth about you, assassins."

"Who d-d-d-d-did we kill?" stuttered Chump.

"The individual," said Watt, "wherever you find him."

"Somebody shut him up," said Ainsley Bridges. "He's gone far beyond his station. He never did know his place."

"I'll d-d-d-d-do it," stuttered Chump.

"You're all afraid," said Watt. "But, beyond your bellies and your wallets, most of you don't even know what real fear is."

"Fear," said Dr. Otto Von Geber, "is the admission price to consciousness."

"Don't you talk about fear," said Sylvia. "I'm carrying your baby. And you won't even come close to me. You're afraid of your own heart."

"Truly a dramatic moment!" said Ainsley Bridges. "Somebody say something profound before we kill Watt."

"F-f-f-f-fuck him!" stuttered Chump.

"That will do," said Ainsley Bridges. "Now let's finish him."

But as they advanced to kill Watt, there was an explosion that curdled darkness and light. "They've dropped the bomb!" cried Loray. "I knew those crackers would do it!"

"But we *have not* dropped the bomb," said Dr. Otto Von Geber. "I spoke with the president this morning. He would have told me if he was going to launch a preemptive attack."

"Maybe another president struck first," said Yank.

"I spoke with *all* the presidents and the key terrorists, too," asserted Dr. Otto Von Geber.

"The world's a stage," said Loray. "They're not supposed to blow it up. They're just supposed to pump more electricity into it."

Again, Watt heard a doctor counting: "One ... Two ... Three," and again, he felt an electric shock. But this time it seemed to jettison him up. He opened his eyes and saw the light above an operating table. He saw Grandma standing behind three doctors masked in green.

"*Please step back, Madame Zeporah,*" said one of the doctors while another leaned over Watt and whispered, "*Wake up, nigger. Maybe your black eyes can find something.*"

Delirious, Watt wondered why he would say something like that. But then he imagined other doctors from every nation in the world filing by his operating table and saying the same thing in different languages.

"Vous vous levez, nigger!"

"Hey sun, nigger!"

"Despertarse, nigger!"

Although he wanted to kick their asses for calling him a nigger, he also wanted to know why he should wake up and do anything for them. He was tired. He had enough of the bullshit, enough of the struggle, and enough of life. He closed his eyes to die. But then he heard Grandma say, "Get up, son. We've been through a lot worse than this. You can't give up now."

"But they're not *worth* it," said Watt.

"I know," said Grandma. "But *you* are."

Then she called him the way she used to at dinner time when he was a boy. "Watt, come upstairs, son. There's something for you. It's a culture on a sineww-wwww."

"Is it wet?"

"Gettin' juicier by the moment, son."

"Is it hot?"

"Just the way you like it, son."

"Do I have to wash my hands?"

"You know you do."

"Alright, I'm coming up."

He awoke in the operating room to bouncing blips and doctors congratulating each other. "We did it!"

"He's alive!"

"It's bigger than the transplants!"

"I didn't think we could strip a human being down, take most of his key organs, and then give them back as if it they were never taken!"

"You can't," said Grandma. "He'll never be the same."

"But we did it! We saved him!"

"You sons of bitches killed him, too," said Grandma.

"Quick!" said Dr. Selby. "Let's get him to the Recovery Room."

As they wheeled Watt away, he heard Grandma say, "Son, I lied to you. This culture is cold."

CHAPTER 15

▼

"Oh baby, it's cold outside," he heard Ray Charles and Betty Carter sing as he lay in his hospital room attached to machines while blips danced across dark screens, and a clock, unlike the one at Von Geber's house, simply kept time. Outside of his door he heard a commotion.

"Reporters!" yelled Grandma. "You're animals!"

Opening his room door and shutting it behind her, Grandma slowly moved to Watt's bedside, saying, "Hello, son."

"They tried to strip me, like a car," said Watt.

"They sure did, son," said Grandma. "When I walked into the operating room, your chest looked like an open sewing basket, and one of the doctors was holding your heart. Another was measuring your private part, and when Herbert, the hospital director, asked what they were doing, that lowlife Selby threw your heart on the floor.

"They said it was broken, and they had to give you an artificial one. But I said, *No! Give him back his own heart—broken or not! And give him back the rest of his body parts while you're at it!* They spent thirty-four hours putting it back. The media got wind of it. That's why those reporters are outside the door. You're a celebrity, son. They've heard about you all over the world."

Then she took out a copy of *The Barely News,* and Watt saw his picture on the front page with a caption that read, *The Greatest Victim or the Smartest Survivor?*

"But why me?" groaned Watt.

"They came after you because you're black, son," said Grandma, "and because you looked helpless, lyin' in the Emergency Room half dead and alone. They figured nobody would care if anything *else* happened to you. See, son, that's why you always need people to look out for you."

"What about the ones who don't have anybody?" asked Watt.

"Dead meat," said Grandma, shaking her head. "You can't do nothin' for them, son. All you can do is be strong for yourself and those close to you."

"It's Hell," groaned Watt.

"It's always been Hell," said Grandma. "And you know the irony, son. Things are better today and *worse*. I remember when the stock market crashed and the little tramp went broke. Nobody had any money. But everybody worked together and shared. If a family didn't have any food, neighbors took turns feeding them—sometimes for weeks—until they could feed themselves. All that changed with integration. You help somebody today, and the first thing they do when they get back on their feet is give you a kick in the ass. People are mean and jealous today. Everybody's walkin' around actin' self-righteous. It's like Walter Mitty said: *The only exercise they get is jumping to conclusions.* There's no gratitude or appreciation and so little respect. Thank God I won't be here much longer."

"Grandma, I want revenge," said Watt.

"And I want you to have it," said Grandma. "It's like Giuseppe, the Italian butcher, used to say, *Revenge is a dish that's delicious even when served cold.*"

As Watt dreamed of revenge, Grandma said, "Don't mitty on me, son."

"You and Mitty," said Watt, smiling.

"Don't forget Bogie, son. Bogie won't let me take no shit off nobody, and Mitty won't let me take Bogie too seriously. A drop of Mitty and a pinch of Bogie, and you can rule the world."

As Watt's smile widened, Grandma said, "You're looking better, son. When you get out of here, we'll sue these bastards. "She looked away for a moment, then turned back saying, "And that BJ9, *he'll* pay. You get some rest now and don't worry." She leaned over and kissed him on the cheek. "Good-bye, son," she said, opening the door. "Get back, you animals!" she yelled at the reporters, opening and closing the door behind her.

Watt was half-asleep in his hospital bed a few nights later when the door to his room opened and two shadows tipped in. As Watt lay there helplessly, one of the shadows said, "My name is Digby Rugg, and this is Ty, my photographer. We're from *Chronos Magazine,* and we want to do a story on you. Tell us what really happened to you."

"Get out!" yelled Watt as the photographer, snapped his picture.

"How does it feel to be gutted? Do you think racism played a role in what happened to you?"

"Nurse!" yelled Watt.

"Listen," said Rugg. "This isn't just about *you!* Black kids are suffering in ghettos all over America today. What happened to you could happen to them. So talk to me so we can save those kids."

"Nurse!" yelled Watt again. The door finally opened, and two large nurses rushed in. Big-boned and wide-shouldered, they looked like football players. One picked up the photographer as if he were a toy and carried him out while the other clamped Rugg in a headlock. Burying his face in her pillow-size breasts, she walked him out the door.

After that incident, the nurses took special care of Watt in the months he remained in the hospital. For some, he became their baby brother; for others he became a recovering lover. As lovers, the nurses were hot. But few knew anything about giving good head. Watt had to take them from the top and teach them the ancient secrets.

> A woman must create an ocean in her mouth,
> Licking a man as if he's the shore,
> The cares of the world,
> The boats out at sea,
> And then the explosion of yesterday's debris

In thousands of man-butchering years, a woman's lips have remained juicyinspace. Man speeds down roads driven by those lips, crashes cars and planes driven by those lips, recovers or dies in hospitals driven by those lips, and O-O-O that Cleopatra lane.

The night before he was to go home, one of the nurses on the midnight shift came to his room with some wine. She poured a glass and he downed it, saying, "Pluck."

"What's pluck?"

"Cheap wine," he said.

"But this isn't *cheap* wine," she protested.

"Then let me pluck *you*," he said.

The next morning he was dressing to leave the hospital when one of the hospital workers brought him a copy of the *Barely News*. The headline leapt out at him:

BJ9 Found Slain

BJ9, former defensive tackle for the Chicago Body Snatchers and son of BJ8, the world class athlete, was found shot to death in the plush surroundings of his Central Park North apartment last night. Police ruled out robbery as a possible motive when they discovered nine-hundred dollars in a dresser drawer. Police speculate that Mr. Nine knew his assailant because there was no sign of struggle or forced entry. Neighbors said they didn't hear any unusual sounds. Mr. Nine, whose body was discovered by a neighbor, leaves no survivors. Police have no suspects and are engaged in questioning some of Mr. Nine's associates. Anyone wishing to give information on Mr. Nine's slaying, please contact the Harlem Murder Division at Collar-Green 6-8941. All information will be confidential.

Grandma did it, thought Watt. *But why didn't she use Sybil Juice or Circe Dust on him? But what does it matter. She made the hit for me.*

Before Watt checked out, he was asked to attend a press conference. The doctors who had tried to strip him were there, acting like celebrities. It was scripted, like the news. The reporters asked a few questions and the doctors, having received them in advance, answered with confidence and assurance. But no one asked Watt how he felt or what he thought.

Finally, Digby Rugg stood up and shot a question at Watt. "From your limited perspective, can you describe your gratitude to the doctors assembled in this room?"

"I'm not grateful to any of these ..."

"That concludes this press conference," interrupted Dr. Herbert.

Grandma wasn't feeling well that day and couldn't make it to the hospital. She asked Watt to take a taxi home. "No problem," he told her. To avoid another encounter with the press, he caught a private elevator that took him down to the street level and an exit at the hospital's rear.

Outside, he sucked in the end-of-winter cold air and contemplated his walk to the subway. As he stood there, happy to be alive, the elevator went up and came down again.

A white man, maybe in his seventies, stepped out. His face well-tanned, his hair perfectly coiffed, he wore the plushest white cashmere coat Watt had ever seen and looked as if he had fallen from a major fashion magazine. He was clearly a millionaire, but he moved with a swagger more befitting a young black man in the ghetto. And as he passed Watt, he said, "Catch you later, Home," in the style of a pimp.

A huge Rolls Royce pulled up to meet him, and a tall young foxy blonde in a big fur coat stepped out to greet him, saying, "Papa, you look great!"

"I feeeeeeel good!" sang the old man. Doing a spin and leaping into the air, he landed flush and kissed the blonde on the lips, saying, "I got energy to burn and tricks to turn. Let's go home and do some *serious* fucking, baby!"

"Hiram, is that *you?*" asked the blonde.

"Yeah, baby, it's me."

After they climbed into the limousine, with the chauffeur standing erect, the old man ordered a particular radio station to be put on. A rap tune's rhythms blared through the Rolls, and the old man started boogieing in the car. As the vehicle slowly moved away, the old millionaire, with a shock of white hair cascading down his forehead, lowered a car window and called to Watt, saying, "If not *you*, then *who?*" Watt wondered what he was talking about, but before he could ask him what he meant, the old man quipped, "somebody else. *That's who.* Thank you and no thank you, motherfucker." Raising his hand, he blew Watt a kiss. A diamond ring, the size of a golf ball, was on his hand, the same diamond ring Watt had seen in the operating room.

"You motherfucker!" cried Watt, running after the limousine. As the car sped away with the old man bobbing his head to rap music, Watt thought, *that old motherfucker just got away with some brother's heart.*

CHAPTER 16

▼

Looking back, he saw the slew of reporters roll out of the hospital in a dust bowl and scatter in the air. Jumping into cabs lining the hospital driveway, they raced off to new assignments and prey.

Digby Rugg and Ty, his photographer, came hustling out last. Seeing no cabs, they glanced at the subway and shook their heads. Then they spotted a cab pulling into the driveway, carrying an old blind man and a cripple. The moment the cab stopped, they opened the rear doors from both sides. Grabbing the disabled men, they threw them to the ground. Yelling "Press!" they climbed into the cab and began slapping the back of the driver's seat, signaling him to go.

"Are you crazy?!" exploded the cab driver. But Rugg stopped his anger with a crisp twenty dollar bill. "Where ya goin', Mac?" asked the cabbie.

"Downtown in ten minutes," said Rugg," and don't stop if you hit somebody." As the cab jetted from the driveway, two crutches and a pair of sunglasses flew out the windows.

Watt walked to the subway and caught the "A" Train to 125th Street.

Although you couldn't tell
from looking in his eyes,
old Duke was a hound dog
in disguise

Then he caught the "AA" Local to 116th Street. As he came out the subway, he heard, "Watt, O Watt." He turned and saw Mrs. Dawson. "I'm so glad to see you," she said. "The Lord's works are wondrous. I've been prayin' and askin' the Almighty to give you strength, and He answered my prayers. You look as healthy as ever. But button up your collar. You might catch cold. And stay off the streets, particularly Central Park North."

"How you doin', Mrs. Dawson?" asked Watt.

"Afraid," she answered. "We're all afraid. But why do we have to be afraid of *so much*? But faith in the Almighty keeps me goin'. I don't know what people do who don't have God. I'm startin' to sound like Rev. Puryear. But you listened. You always listened. That's your redeeming trait. Well, I've got to go. I'm on my way to church. Tell your grandma the stuff she gave me worked fine. The Lord willin', I'll see her next week at the meeting or in the Great Divine."

"Good-bye, Mrs. Dawson," said Watt as she hopped across the street. Stumbling, she almost fell. But she caught her balance.

Neither rain, nor sleet, nor snow
could cause her to stump her toe

Reaching his building, Watt saw little Cecil playing outside, batting pennies and calling, "Home run! Double! Extra bases!" When he saw Watt, a smile came across his face. "Watt!" he yelled, excitedly.

"Hey, punk," said Watt, coolly. "What are you doing batting money away?"

"They're just pennies."

"A lot of people would like to have those pennies. One-hundred makes a dollar, you know,"

"What's a dollar today?" asked Cecil.

"It's something that blinds you from seeing tomorrow, Punk," said Watt.

"I won't let you make a punk out of me *all* my life," said Cecil. "Some day I'm gonna have it big!"

"You were smarter when you were six," said Watt. "I work with people who have it *big,* and they're all fucked up. But if any of them saw a penny in the street, they'd pick it up. That's the difference between poor folks and rich folks. While our kids are learning one and one makes two, their kids are learning one and one makes *two dollars*. They're light years ahead of you because of the breaks they've had. But you can catch up if you stop bullshitting and work hard."

"I told you I'm gonna have it *big* some day," said Cecil.

"How?" asked Watt, "by selling dope and ruining lives?"

"People have to look out for *themselves*," said Cecil.

"That's why I call you punk," said Watt. "You don't know shit, and all you're going to do is fuck up your life. Just stay in school and get a good education, and don't mess up the way I did."

"How?" asked Cecil.

"By being stupid, like you," said Watt.

"Watt, what's happened to you?" asked Cecil. "You don't sound the same."

"I'm getting old," said Watt. "And I don't have much of a future."

He ascended the stairs, thinking, *why should I care about kids? I don't have any.* Then he thought about Sylvia, pregnant with his child.

"Here come the celebrity," said Blip, as Watt approached his landing. "Whas happenin', my man."

"I ain't your man," said Watt.

"Shit, you've known me since you wuz born," laughed Blip. "Maybe I'm your father!"

"Don't joke with me, old man," said Watt.

"You know, I'm old enough to be your father," said Blip. "I've told you a lot of shit, but you don't want ta gibb me my propers. You don't wanna tell me shit. You always 'spect me ta talk while you listen. Lucky for you, I'ma talkin' fool.

"You took a lickin', butchoo ain't stopped tickin'. Now you gonna be rich if you sue. You gonna hav' all tha shit money can buy—cars, houses, bitches—an' you gonna git it the legal way, not the way ya old man did."

"Shut up, dopefiend," snapped Watt.

"Yeah, I'ma dopefiend. An' I'm proud to be a dopefiend," said Blip. "Dope is the best thing that ever happened ta me. Dope is good. Dope *preserves* me. It's what I do. I don't kill nobody. I don't rob nobody. I just beg for money ta buy dope. I ask all those hard workin', lyin', cheatin', lowlife mothafuckas for some change, an' then I goes and buys my dope.

"Sumtimes it takes all day ta git tha money, sumtimes it takes all night. But no matter *how* long it takes, I always gets my dope. An' now you gonna get some money an' gibb old Blip a taste ta buy sum dope.

"Cause you ain't cheap like your pa. Boy, that mafucker would't gibb a cripple crab a crutch … if he *owned* a lumber yard. I remember how your pa first got his money."

Watt wanted to walk away, but once again, the word emanating from Blip's drooling orifice sucked him in. "We useta hab an elevator in this buildin' ober dere," said Blip, pointing. "Well, one night, your pa wuz about to take the elevator up to see your ma when he sensed somethin'. Tha elevator wuz dark, an' tha Take-off man wuz waitin' inside wit' a bat raised ober his head to coldcock a mothafucka dead an' rob 'im, an' he didn't care who.

"See, tha Take-off man had unscrewed all the bulbs so nobody could see. All you could smell in the dark was pee. But your pa—bein' tha kinda mafucker he wuz—carryin' a knife *an'* a black jack—got real low, lower than even tha Take-off man could go.

"Then your pa, he opened tha elevator door, an' tha Take-off man shuffled his feet, an' your pa, he jabbed the switchblade in his toe. When tha Take-off man howled an' dropped tha bat, your pa started beatin' his head wit' tha blackjack.

"Somebody punched a button, an' tha elevator started movin'. It went to every floor wit' tha Take-off man howlin', hittin' musical notes tha fat lady couldn't make. But your pa wuz beatin' him slow, cause he had his music, too.

Yes, tha bones keepa talkin'
but they can't starta walkin'
till I'm through

"Me an' ma heard tha Take-off man howlin' an' peeped out da door wit' a flashlight. Tha elevator stopped on our floor, an' we saw your pa standin' ober tha Take-off man. Tha blackjack looked like a big red pencil. Your pa, he landed a final blow and turned tha Take-off ovah. Then he slit his pockets to tha thigh.

Hold the light steady. he said like in a canyon, takin' out money an' countin' out loud. *Three hundred dollars, not bad*, he say.

How mutch ya say ya got, mon? axed tha West Indian down tha hall.

Never you mind, cocksucker, say your pa, draggin' tha Take-off man ta tha stairs an' kickin' 'im down. *Whatever's left is yours!* he say. But dere ain't nothing left— not a goddamn thing—but a head whupped worse than a guffball, a basket o' broken bones, an tha West Indian comin' ta get whas left.

"Then your pa, he come ovah to me an' Ma an' give us thirty bucks fa holdin' tha light an' actin' right, an' tha neck week your pa had the best dope in New York.

"An' thass how he got it. Thass how he got it! I *knows*. An' you jus like him, 'xcept you ain't cheap. You gonna look out for old Blip cause he looked out fa you. I didn't kick your ass when you were a kid. I gabe you r'spect. And now you gonna gibb me some money so I can buy some dope."

"I wouldn't give you *shit*, dopefiend!" said Watt.

"I thought we wuz tight," said Blip.

"You thought wrong, *dopefiend!*" said Watt, going up the stairs.

Blip broke out into some kind of dopefiend hysteria. He stood up, crying and flailing his needle-punctured arms. "You can't do dat to me! I won't hab it!" He tried to climb the stairs after Watt but slipped and slid back down to his landing, groaning.

"You're just a dopefiend," said Watt, "a blip on *nobody's* screen."

"As Watt turned and opened the door to Grandma's apartment, Blip curled into a fetal position and whispered, "You jest like your pa.""

CHAPTER 17

▼

Watt expected Happy to greet him as he went into the apartment. Instead, he heard the dog break into a fit of barks as Grandma yelled, *"Dopefiends!"* and a man shrieked, falling through the yard. Running to the kitchen, Watt found Grandma at the backyard window holding a frying pan dripping with hot grease. "There was a time if you caught a dopefiend on your fire escape, he had to *fly* to prove his innocence!" she yelled.

Dazed, she turned and saw Watt, then staggered from the window as Watt helped her to a chair. "Hello, son, it's good to see you," she said.

"I'm here, Grandma. It's okay."

"No, it's not okay, son," said Grandma. "I'm gettin' old, and they're closin' in on me. Dopefiends—whose fathers I cut new assholes—are closin' in now. But I beat em all, son—the black ones, the white ones, the red ones, even the yellow ones. I cut any color on dope new assholes and told them the same thing: A dopefiend does not deserve to live!"

"Take it easy," said Watt.

"I don't know *nothin'* I hate more than dopefiends," said Grandma. "I don't even hate white folks as much as I hate dopefiends. You know what to expect from white folks. They're sneaky, lowdown, and evil. But you never know *what* a dopefiend will do. Once I could stop 'em. But my powers are fadin' now. If I could summon up one last spell I'd make 'em show me some respect. They'd know what it meant to mess with *Madame Zeporah.*

"It's okay, Grandma."

"No, it's not okay, son. I'm scared. I've never been afraid of anything in my life. This crack is unbelievable. These new dopefiends are a different strain. I don't know what they're on. I guess it's time for me to check out.

"But I beat em all, son—the World War II dopefiends, the Korean War dopefiends, and *worst* of all—those damn Vietnam dopefiends. But this new batch might be too much for me."

"It'll be alright, Grandma," said Watt.

"No, it won't, son. Our people didn't accept this kind of stuff years ago. We had standards. If you came into the black community, you had to measure up. Now everybody's measurin' down. The girls look like whores; the boys look like clowns. And they don't believe in nothin'. And they've all forgotten about the Civil Rights Movement. It's gone. Whites don't believe in equality and blacks don't believe in democracy."

"It'll be alright," said Watt.

"No it won't," said Grandma, "not until every pipe-smokin'-needle-suckin', nose-sniffin' fool is dead, including the one on the stairs below. I'll never forgive him for the way he broke his mother's heart.

"You see, son, this world's no good," said Grandma, "and it closes in on you when you get old. Most people don't even have family to protect them anymore. I know you'll look after me, son. But thank God I don't have to stay here much longer."

"I won't let anything happen to you," said Watt.

"Don't worry about *me*," said Grandma. "Just look after your*self*. I've lived my life and there were good times with the bad. But never like this."

Taking Watt's hand, she looked up to the ceiling and let out that exasperated sound old folks sometimes make: three staccato notes going down the throat as the head turns with each note. Suddenly releasing his hand, she stood up pointing at the doorway and asking, "Do you see?"

"See what?" asked Watt.

"Do you see your mother, my baby?" asked Grandma.

"No," said Watt.

"She was standin' in the doorway smiling at us," said Grandma, "I guess she's come to escort me to the other world."

"No one is there," Grandma," said Watt.

"She was *there*, son," said Grandma. "I saw her just as clear as I see you. I saw my little girl, and she looked at you and me and smiled. She's happy, and I'm gonna be happy, too." The old lady put her arms around Watt and hugged him tightly, giving him a kiss on the cheek. Then she went into her bedroom with Happy trailing behind.

Watt wanted to say something else to her when the phone rang. He picked it up, saying, "This is Watt."

"Watt," said Sylvia, sobbing. "I love you. Do you know what that means? It means I'll do *anything* for you, *anything!* Why didn't you call me and tell me you were getting out of the hospital today? I could have met you. When I called, they said you were gone."

"I didn't feel like bothering you," said Watt.

"Watt, I'm your woman. How could it be a bother?"

"I wasn't thinking," said Watt. "I meant to call you, but I called Perry instead, and he wasn't home."

"Perry may never be home again," said Sylvia. "He's a dopefiend."

"I don't believe that," said Watt. "Look, I've got to go. I need to finish talking with Grandma. Let me call you later." He put down the phone, thinking, *No way could Perry be a dopefiend.*

Watt went to Grandma's room to talk with her, saying, "Maybe it's time for us to leave Harlem. We could get a nice place in the Bronx or Brooklyn where there aren't so many dopefiends, and you can open the windows without one flying in. We don't have to stay here any more. What do you think?" he asked stepping through the doorway.

But the old lady didn't say a word. "Grandma, can you hear me?" Then he flicked on the light. He found the old lady reclining on her bed with a beatific smile. She was dead. Happy lay across her feet, dead, too. "Grandma!" cried Watt, letting out a howl. He dropped to his knees, wracked with physical and mental pain he had never known, and cried. When he recovered, he thought for a moment of dousing the old lady with lighting fluid and giving her a Viking funeral. And if her bed had been a barge on water he might have done it. Instead, he sat by her side, holding her hand and crying.

How long he cried he did not know. Eventually, when he ran out of tears, he called the police. Both woman and dog were removed, and Watt, for the first time in his life, slept in the apartment without her.

He was aroused the next morning by a hand that had mastered the ability to knock and scratch simultaneously. Going to the door, he opened it and saw Mrs. Saunders standing beside an old man whose eyes looked as if they were in perpetual grief. "This is Mr. Needby of the Needby Funeral Home, and he'd like to speak with you, Watt, if you feel up to it." Nodding, Watt led them to the living-room.

They sat. Mr. Needby placed his hat on the table, saying, "Mrs. Saunders asked me to speak with you because she thought our funeral home could lift some of the burden from your shoulders."

"Your grandmother was the best friend I ever had," said Mrs. Saunders. "We went through a lot together over the last fifty years."

"Perhaps you've considered calling someone else," said Mr. Needby. "If you have, let me tell you what we …"

"She threw her husband into the street two weeks before I tossed mine out," said Mrs. Saunders.

"What we can do for you," said Mr. Needby, "is …"

"She taught me how to fight dopefiends," said Mrs. Saunders. "She was the *best* friend I ever had."

"And I'm sure you were the *best* friend *she* ever had," said Mr. Needby.

"Twenty years ago, she and I gave each other a list containing the names of people to contact when we died," said Mrs. Saunders. "Most of the people on both lists are dead. But, see, my name is right there on top of your grandma's list." And she held up a yellow piece of paper with Grandma's handwriting on it.

And may your name *remain* on the top of all lists for years to come," said Mr. Needby.

"I miss my friend," said Mrs. Saunders. "I'm ready to go, too."

"And our home will be happy to assist your loved ones when your time comes," said Mr. Needby, his eyes brightening up.

"What loved ones?" said Mrs. Saunders. "My son and daughter died years ago. Zeporah was the only thing that kept me going."

"Yes, and *speaking* of Madame Zeporah," said Mr. Needby, I'm sure your grandmother's last wish is that her passing—beyond the vacancy it creates in the hearts of her loved ones—will not place too great a financial burden on any survivor. Perhaps the sooner we discuss the funeral arrangements, the sooner your grandmother can truly rest in peace. It's so easy to sound mercenary at times like this."

"At least the dopefiends didn't get Zeporah," said Mrs. Saunders.

"I *hope* I don't sound mercenary," said Mr. Needby. "But we do have to recognize that financial security is a force in death as it is in life. How we reach the pearly gates is not important. Whether we can put gas in the tank to get there is of the utmost importance. I hope I don't sound mercenary."

"No, you don't sound mercenary," said Watt, thinking, *this money-hungry fool.* "Let me tell you what *I* want and *don't* want. I don't want to pay for an expensive casket, and then when I'm not around have Grandma's remains dumped into a pine box so you can sell that casket again later. And I don't want her dug up and the casket switched later. I don't want one of those Mcfunerals with the hearse driving ninety miles an hour to get to the cemetery so it can get back to the church to pick up another body. I don't want one of those two-fers either with Grandma's casket lying on top of somebody else's. And I don't want you to hit me with any inflated costs. I want an item-by-item listing of everything I pay for."

"We can meet all of your demands," said Mr. Needy. "We're not a fast funeral chain. We care about the deceased almost as much as you do. But tell me," he said, leaning forward, his eyes welling with tears, "What about *the insurance?*"

Of course, there was no insurance. There was an insurance booklet indicating Grandma once had insurance, an industrial policy sold to her many years ago by a fast-talking representative of a tiny insurance company that had grown gargantuan off the nickels, dimes, and hopes of poor black people who got swindled. But the policy was worthless, and if Grandma had seen that fast-talking representative again, from that tiny insurance company that had grown gargantuan, she would have cut him.

Wiping away tears, Mr. Needby examined the insurance booklet carefully, and then rose with dry eyes, saying, "Excuse me," and walked to the door. Before he could open it, Watt called, "I'm paying for the funeral—cash money."

Pivoting 180 degrees, as if riding a skate board, Mr. Needby glided back into the living room and placed his hat on the table exactly as he had done before. Tears welled in his eyes again.

CHAPTER 18

▼

It was a lovely funeral in a neighborhood church, preceded by a wake. Grandma's corpse, lying in her favorite black dress and gray wig on a couch of light blue velvet, looked as if it were buoyed on a cloud. She still had that beatific smile on her face, which prompted several of the old ladies to comment on how beautiful she looked, which was important.

For the old ladies equated ugliness in death with evil in life. Although most of them had come to mourn Grandma, some came to see the true picture of her soul which, they believed, death revealed. If Grandma had appeared ugly or unlike the way she looked when she was alive, the old ladies would have concluded that she had deceived them and had been an evil person. "She looks just like the Zeporah *I* know," Mrs. Dawson affirmed, and all of the old ladies agreed, nodding their heads.

After the wake, an organ prelude triggered the processional and everyone took a seat for the funeral. Watt entered with Sylvia, Mrs. Saunders, Mrs. Dawson, and the rest of the old ladies. Looking around he saw people he hadn't seen in years: a woman whom Grandma had prevented from committing suicide (and who the very next day hit the number), and a man whose marriage Grandma had saved. Other people were there too whose names he had forgotten but whose faces he remembered. He didn't see Perry, however, although Grandma regarded him as her other grandson.

The invocation and the prayer of comfort were brief and followed by a musical selection: *Take My Hand Precious Lord*. Rev. Puryear, a jack-leg preacher, stepped forward to give the eulogy. He had won fame in Harlem years earlier for his stand against crime and drugs. His eulogy, accompanied by a running commentary from the old ladies, cut right to the heart of who Grandma was. "Zeporah Foye Montgomery enjoyed serving people," he intoned, "people who were more fortunate …"

"Yes!"

"… people who were less fortunate …"

"It's true."

"… people with troubles …"

"That's right."

"… in need of love …"

"He knows."

"… support …"

"Go on, boy!"

"… and some plain old conversation with a good friend."

"You said it."

"She never tired of giving …"

"No, she didn't."

"… to the friends who loved her …"

"We all did."

"… calling her 'Zeporah,' 'Madame Zeporah,' or just plain 'Zep'…."

"That's right."

"She was always there …"

"Yes, she was."

"… Possessing something unique …"

"Yes, unique!"

"… rare qualities …"

"Very rare!"

"… qualities possessed by other great people."

"Great qualities."

"One of those qualities was compassion."

"That's right."

"Another was love."

"Good gobs of love."

"And a third was certainly strength."

"O God! Was she strong!"

"But all of these qualities came together."

"Yes, together."

".. through her belief …"

"Pure faith."

"… through her belief in God."

"Yes, Lord."

"For what else could have enabled her to withstand the pain she knew but her belief in God—coming from the West Indies as a little girl, then losing her mother and father when she was very young—not to mention a husband she threw out during the ninth month of her pregnancy.

"But Madame Zeporah overcame it all, raising her daughter and losing her, too, then turning around and raising that daughter's son."

"So true."

"No obituary can describe the complex person Madame Zeporah was. I met her when I first came to New York. She was an amazing woman, and she was always doing God's work, with powers that both baffled and amazed me."

"Amazed us, too."

"A few weeks ago she came to me distressed and told me she was disgusted with what Harlem had become. *Rev, the people don't respect each other any more,* she said. And when I asked her what we could do, she told me *We have to start all over again and work the way our parents worked to improve our community and ourselves. We have to cherish our children the way our parents cherished us and make sure they get a good education. If we do that, our kids will have some hope and be less afraid and maybe less dangerous.*"

As Rev. Puryear paused, the old ladies abandoned their commentary to fill the air with weeping.

"That's the kind of person Madame Zeporah was," said Rev. Puryear. "When you talked with her she gave you the truth—*straight from the hip*. And she possessed another rare quality I forgot to mention. She possessed honor. That's right! Honor. With all this talk about self-esteem today, a lot of people don't know what the word honor means. Madame Zeporah knew. She knew that honor isn't *self*-esteem. It's *social*-esteem, the social activation of self-esteem. If you truly have high self-esteem, you treat other people honorably. That's why there's only one Commandment that we need. And you could throw out all the others if we were true to the one that says *Do unto others as you would have them do unto you.* Madame Zeporah knew the truth and the power in that one commandment because she was a proud, bold, honorable, African American woman who could change for better the life of anyone she met. She was royalty. She was nobility. She was the best we had.

"So don't weep for Madame Zeporah. Weep for us whom she has left behind to finish her work. Weep for yourself because you miss her and will never see her likes again. And weep for the world that was not as fortunate as you to know a woman so strong, so great, and so kind.

"But rest assured. Madame Zeporah is fine. Right now, somewhere in Heaven, she's starting all over again and fixing up her house. She's standing over a kitchen sink, slicing an onion and grating some garlic. And she's thinking of *new* ways to serve the Lord."

Finishing the eulogy, Rev. Puryear descended from the pulpit and took a seat as the organist played *I Can't Give up Now*. Mr. Needby came forward, announcing, "Those who wish to bid farewell to Madame Zeporah may do so at this time."

As the organist played *In the Sweet Bye and Bye*, the mourners filed by. Watt led the way. Leaning over the casket, he wanted to kiss Grandma's corpse. Instead he touched her arm, which felt stiff, like a board. "Goodbye, Grandma," he said before taking his seat. Then the other mourners followed, each looking into Grandma's face, nodding, shaking their heads, and crying—in sync with the music—*we will meet in the sweet bye and bye*.

After the mourners paid their last respects, the casket was closed. Rev. Puryear said a brief prayer, and six pallbearers lifted Grandma's casket and carried it out with Watt and the old ladies walking behind. Then the church doors opened and sunlight flooded in.

The street, normally empty that time of the day, was filled with people—people who had come to pay their last respects to Grandma. They stood quietly as her casket was loaded into the hearse and Watt, Sylvia, and the old ladies climbed into parked limousines. They cleared a path through the street so the vehicles could move. Then they waved goodbye.

As the car engines started and the funeral procession prepared to drive off, Blip trudged up the street. Not knowing he was too late for Grandma's funeral, he went into the church and one of the female parishioners shrieked.

Then they were moving. The funeral procession traveled up Eighth Avenue in a straight line behind the hearse. They were heading for the 145th Street Bridge that led to the Bronx and Woodlawn Cemetery.

Everything seemed as if it were going to be alright until they neared 145th Street and saw what looked like thousands of dopefiends. On both sides of the street, they lined 145th Street from Eighth Avenue to the bridge. Although he didn't see any weapons, Watt wondered what this army of dopefiends would do. And for a moment he thought of his father's death in front of the Outhide Bar & Grill.

Then a few of the dopefiends raised their arms and waved, not mockingly either. Others, wearing hats, removed them, and Watt saw in their faces a sincere sadness and a respect for the foe that had fought them so bravely for many years. Watt smiled and thought of what Grandma might have said, "When you're alive it's the dopefiends, and when you're dead it's the worms. But it shouldn't be *both*."

As the procession reached the bridge, the dopefiends disbanded. With singular goal and sole purpose, they returned to the task that filled their days.

Finally, the funeral procession arrived at the cemetery. Watt and Sylvia helped the old ladies from the cars. Breathing deeply some held their hands over their hearts as they approached the gravesite. Two grave diggers, leaning on their shovels, stood by the rectangular chasm waiting to ply their trade. Mr. Needby waved his hand and they backed away. Then Mr. Needby had everyone form a circle around Grandma's grave as the gravediggers lowered her casket into the ground, and Rev. Puryear, in a brief grave-side ceremony, intoned, "Father, into your hands, we commend the soul of this great woman, Zeporah Foye Montgomery, to sup at your table and dwell with you in heaven from this day forth unto eternity. Begging your forgiveness for our sins, we do so in the name of the father, the son, and the Holy Ghost ... world without end. Amen."

When he finished, the first shovel of dirt was thrown followed by the second. Watt took out Grandma's knife, the one she coated with garlic and onions, and threw it into the grave with her, saying "Here, Grandma." At that moment, a sudden gust of wind swept through the graveyard. Mr. Needby's hat slipped from his hand and started rolling through the cemetery. One of the grave diggers dropped his shovel to chase it while the old ladies smiled, and Watt said, "You're welcome, Grandma."

CHAPTER 19

▼

"He's a dopefiend!"

"He's not a dopefiend!"

"Then why wasn't he at your grandma's funeral?"

"I don't know why—maybe he's hurt or sick or in the hospital."

"Maybe he's high somewhere."

"Wherever he is, he's still my friend, and I have to find him."

"Good luck. You know what your grandma thought of dopefiends."

"I know what she thought of Perry."

"Then why didn't he show up?"

"I don't know why. But I'm out of here."

"There you go running away again."

He left Sylvia's apartment where he had gone after Grandma's burial and the big meal at Mrs. Dawson's—all the time wondering, *where's Perry?* He had called him a dozen times before the funeral but couldn't reach him. He wondered if his old friend was hurt or dead. If he was alive, he would have been at Grandma's funeral. Everybody in Harlem had heard about it. Her obituary was in the *Amsterdam News.*

As he climbed the stairs to his apartment, he remembered he didn't have food or money. Grandma's funeral had taken all of his cash; his checking and savings accounts were empty. He needed to go back to work to make money. But first he had to find out what happened to Perry.

Approaching Blip's landing, Watt wondered if Blip was asleep and if he could creep by him. He didn't want to hear anything a stupid dopefiend had to say. But

Blip was awake. He seemed to be waiting and greeted Watt, saying, "Dat wuz da fastest funeral I never attended."

"You were late," said Watt. "That's all."

"Yeah, I been late fa everything, even my own life," said Blip. "I ain't nevah been no early bird. Thass why I ain't caught no worm. But I got a worm at least. An' I found somethin' out. Did you know Nickless rhymes wit' dickless, haha. A rapper tole me dat th'uther night an' I laughed my ass off. But now it ain't so funny—cause o' what happened to your man, Perry."

"What are you talking about?" asked Watt.

"Your man, th' *uther* king, Perry."

"What about Perry?" asked Watt.

"I thought you knew. I don't wanna lay nuthin' heavy on ya. You already carryin' a load."

"What happened to Perry?" snapped Watt.

"Ids a bitch," said Blip. "Two bitches—if you got one an' five bitches if you got none."

"What happened!" yelled Watt.

"Remember dat money Perry owed Rusty for work da Black Hole done? Well, Rusty approached Perry an' said, *Pay me the money you owe me or I'll call Mean Joe Vine.* An' Perry, he grabbed Rusty an' threw 'im against a wall. Then, he takes out a whole roll o' money an' puts it in his face, sayin', *I got ten times what I owe you right here! And I can make ten times more tonight. But even if I had more dollars than dogs made deliveries, I still wouldn't pay you.* Now he shouldn'a done dat cause Rusty knows a lot o' folks."

"Did Joe Vine get Perry?" asked Watt.

"No, somethin' worser got 'im, first," said Blip. "So, Perry went home to Rosaline. She been fuckin' on the stairs for years an' Perry, he been takin' every dime she made. Well she had enuff o' tha dicks, tha splinters, an' tha newspapers. She had so much newsprint on her ass dat somebody stopped fuckin' her last week ta read the race results.

"So she tole Perry, *I wanna quit. My ass is tired and I'm sick of the stairs.* But Perry, he don't wanna hear dat an' slaps her, sayin', *you'll work till I tell you to stop!*

I ain't no slave! say Rosaline.

You're my fuckin' slave, say Perry.

"Well, Rosaline, she ran away a couple of times. But Perry brought her back, pullin' her by the hair. Finally, he buys some handcuffs an' chains her whenever he goes out.

"Well, one night, he comes home, an' Rosaline is smilin' in her chains, lookin' all sexy, chained ta tha bed."

"Did Rosaline kill Perry?" interrupted Watt.

"No, it's worse dan dat," said Blip. "Perry, he starts ta watch a little TV. But Rosaline, lookin' sexy, an' Perry can't decide whether ta fuck her or watch the game. He decides ta get tha pussy at halftime an' goes ovah ta tha bed. He takes off all his clothes, her clothes, an' tha handcuffs, too. Then he lays her back on the bed an' slowly opens her legs.

Come to me, baby, Rosaline calls, *Get that big dick as hard as you can cause I wants you like I never wanted you before.*

"Well when she said dat, Perry's dick got harder than Chinese arithmetic, an' he leaps in tha air like he's divin' into a pool of cool water on a hot summer day. But dere ain't no water in dat pool. Dere ain't even pussy!

"Cause Rosaline decided ta fix Perry fa enslavin' her. She stretched her ass in handcuffs an' got a single edge razor blade from da drawer. Den she got some duck tape and wrapped it all around dat blade, 'xcept in da middle where da blade wuz exposed. Then she put tha blade up her cunt wit' a little grease an' jest laid dere lookin' sexy, waitin' for Perry to come home.

"Da moment Perry landed in her cunt, his dick split down da middle like a hot sausage. He howls an' tries ta pull away, but Rosaline, she wraps dose legs around him real tight an' starts grindin' fast. Perry's howlin', but Rosaline's got 'im. An' tha more he howls, da the faster she grinds, wigglin' them hips an' yellin' *Fuck me!* so loud dat folks are comin' from all around.

"When she finally let poor Perry go, he rolled off da bed, screamin'. His dick looked like it been through a paper shredder. An' Rosaline, she say, *I'm nobody's slave.* Then she gets dressed an' walks out, leavin' Perry on tha floor, howlin'. An' you know no doctor—particularly a white one—ist comin' up to Harlem to sew no nigger's dick back on. Beside, it was in so many pieces they'd have ta sweep it up an' glue da pieces back tagether first."

Even before Blip finished, Watt was doubled over, clutching his own genitals. As tears streamed down his face, he stood up and turned to go into his apartment when Blip called, "But dat ain't all."

No more, thought Watt, as Blip continued, "While Perry's on tha floor rollin' around in pain, who should walk through the door but Mean Joe Vine who say, *You can go to tha doctor fa your dick after I finish with your jaw.* Then he start beatin' Perry up. It wasn't no HARLEMASSWHIPPIN'. But it hurt. Joe Vine is about a low mafucker. He beat up a man who wuz already in terr-i-ble pain. After he finishes workin' him ober, tha ambulance comes. Jingle Bells. Jingle Bells.

"You know, boy, I ain't nevah believed in Christmas since I found out they called Santa Claus St. Nick. You know *Nick* rhymes wit' *Dick,* and *nickless* rhymes with *dickless,* and how's Nick gonna give anybody a thing if he ain't got no dick."

"Where's Perry now?" asked Watt.

"Where most dopefiends go—da streets."

"Where?" asked Watt.

"Near tha Outhide," said Blip, "'cept now they call it the Last Step."

As Blip suddenly descended into a slow nod, Watt raced down the stairs. He was running towards the Last Step with tears in his eyes. But first he decided to go to Perry's apartment off Eighth Avenue.

He raced down the street to Perry's building and up three flights of stairs. The door to Perry's apartment was open, and the place was picked clean. Somebody had taken everything. Even the lock and the faucets were gone.

Leaving the apartment, he walked along Eighth Avenue. The army of bow-legged old women was coming home, queens in domestics' bodies. Balanced by shopping bags in each hand, they trod through the tenements like camels of the ghetto.

Watt entered the Last Step Bar & Grill. A new set of Bookend Sisters had their heads down at each end of the bar. Watt slapped a lot of hands, saying, "What's happening?" Then he spotted Victor, an old friend who had gone to school with Perry and him.

Victor had graduated from Nixon High. But after losing a few jobs, he started selling reefer for a living. He didn't make a big production of it, and he didn't make a lot of money. He just did it. And if one of his friends wanted some reefer but didn't have any cash, Victor would give it to him and say "Pay me later." Somehow, Victor had figured out a way to be tough and honorable at the same time.

"What's happening, Victor?" asked Watt

"Not much, Watt.

"Seen Perry?"

"Not today. But you don't wanna see him."

"Why?"

"He's a dopefiend, and you heard what happened to him with that hoe."

"Yeah, I heard," said Watt.

"Well even before that he was acting strange. You were in the hospital when he first started messin' with scag. One day he asked me to cop for him, and I told him that's not my thing. I sell reefer. That's all. But he put the beg on me so strong I hooked him up. I told him *our friendship is over. Don't ask me for shit again.* That's the last time I saw him. But let me warn you—he's not the same."

"Thanks, man," said Watt slapping Victor's hand. "I'll catch you later."

As Watt rose from the table, a commotion broke out. Spud, the bully of his boyhood, was being bitch-slapped against the bar by a man he had once robbed. "You remember what you did to me in elementary school, mothafucker!" yelled the man. "I oughta kill ya for it!" Finishing, he threw Spud to the floor. Watt approached Spud as he struggled to his feet, asking, "Seen Perry?"

"I aint seen him," said Spud, blurry eyed and staggering. He held out a book of matches, asking, "Wanna light?"

"I don't smoke," said Watt. At that moment, someone in the back called "Light," and Spud staggered to his cigarette. Meanwhile, a couple of men were arguing over which policemen were the meanest in the world. "Chicago's Two-Gun-Pete," said a man.

"New York's King Cole Trio," said another man. Finally, a third man broke up the argument, saying "Jehoover and Towntamer."

Watt walked the streets for hours searching for Perry, going to all the places in Harlem he thought he might be. He was on the verge of giving up when he saw Perry peep out of a hallway and duck back in. Running to the building, Watt opened the door and yelled, "Perry!"

Stopping in mid-stride on the landing, Perry turned, saying, "You're the last person I wanted to see."

He was wearing army fatigues and a black knitted cap. His face was battered, and his jaw and nose were lopsided. As he turned around completely, Watt saw the junkie in his eyes.

"You come here to stare?" he asked.

"I came here to find you," said Watt.

"You want to be a tourist."

"Why do I have to be a tourist?"

"Because you are," said Perry. "You've always been a tourist. You take in pain, but you don't suffer the way the rest of us do. You always manage to shake it off and get outside of it. That's one of the things that always amazed me about you."

"I'm not outside now, man," said Watt. "I'm inside with you."

"So now you know. I'm a dopefiend," said Perry. "But for a long time you didn't know."

"I knew you were doing something," said Watt. "I just didn't think you got hooked."

"Whenever I got high, I stayed away from you and your Grandma," said Perry. "I didn't want her throwin' any lye in my face."

"So what are we going to do now, man?"

"About what?" asked Perry.

"Everything," said Watt. "You need help."

"The funny thing is I don't even want to kill Rosaline," said Perry. "Most dudes would have taken that bitch's life. But I did a lot of shit to her. I guess what goes around comes around."

"We need to go to a hospital, man."

"I been to the hospital. You know anybody who wants to hire a dickless dope-fiend who pees through a bean-shooter?" laughed Perry.

Watt didn't answer. Nor did he laugh.

"Maybe I'll become another Blip," said Perry.

"Fuck Blip!" said Watt.

"No," said Perry. "We're all Blips. I remember the tail end of the Civil Rights Movement—Malcolm, Martin. You know, man, we *believed* in something back then. Black churches were bombed, children were killed, and kids had their heads whipped to desegregate a lunch counter I wouldn't eat on today.

"We knew the difference between right and wrong back then, and we had the heart to do something about it. But we sold out for a little money and some comfort, especially those bourgeois niggers."

"I haven't seen any money or comfort," said Watt.

"No, but you're close to it," said Perry, "smackin' those millionaires with CMB. But I'm talkin' about those bourgeois mothafuckas who forgot us. They were supposed to look out for us or at least help us. But the Just-Us Express sped away when they got an opportunity, and they left us to rot after they got their money."

"What's that got to do with us *now*?" asked Watt. "You're blaming somebody else so you won't have to do what you need to do now. The Sixties are gone. We *missed* them. We've got to look after our *own* time and our *own* problems. So what are you going to do about your habit?"

Suddenly, the hallway door burst open, and two little boys skipped in. Hardly noticing Watt and Perry, they scampered up the stairs.

"Lemme take a look at my options," said Perry. "I could get into a drug program and have people treat me like a kid and tell me how fucked up I am. No thank you. Or I could go around the corner and buy some methadone—the dope man sells it, too—and get hooked on that. No thank you. Or maybe I can find God. Maybe I can put on a clean white shirt and go to church and pray. God ain't found me all these years, so how can I find him? Or maybe I can go Muslim, put on a clean white shirt and go to the mosque and pray to Allah. With all respect to my Muslim friends, Allah can't work for me. Those are my options, and I say no thank you to all of them."

"Stop it, man, you've got other options," said Watt. "They're inside of you with your will."

"Oh yeah," said Perry, with a laugh. "There's always the Church of the Warm Savior. Now they know what religion is *really* about."

"Hey man, stop bellyaching," said Watt. "You forgot. You're still a king!"

"Not any more," said Perry. "I ain't shit!"

"You're a bad motherfucker," said Watt. "You've always been a bad motherfucker. You hear me?!"

"You wanna know what I'm gonna do?" said Perry, with a lost look in his eyes. "Not a *fuckin'* thing but die—and the sooner the better."

He let go of the banister and moved to the other side of the stairs, momentarily bracing himself then sliding down the wall.

"Get up!" yelled Watt, as an apartment door opened above them and a woman hollered, "What the hell is going on down there?"

"Call for Philip Morris!" shouted Perry, imitating an old TV commercial from their childhood.

"Get outta here before I call the police," said the woman.

"The police ain't comin'," said Perry, "neither is my dick."

As the woman slammed the door, Watt grabbed Perry by his shoulders and lifted him up, saying, "It's the jungle, and you've got to keep fighting to stay alive—*with or without a dick.*"

He loosened his grip for a moment, thinking Perry would support himself, but Perry slid back down the wall the moment Watt let him go. As Watt tried to catch him, he accidentally knocked off his knitted cap. Fiery, straight red spears shot in all directions from Perry's head. A greasy red process protruded where African hair had once been.

Watt stepped back, saying, "What the fuck have you done?"

"I ain't in the old Miracles or Temptations," said Perry. "And this ain't the Sixties. But this is my protest against what these money-hungry crackers and bourgeois niggers have done." Then Perry reached up and tweezed a patch of his patent leather hair, holding it away from his head in a gesture of absolute self-hatred.

"Like it?" asked Perry.

"No. I don't like it," said Watt, trembling and putting Perry's cap back on.

"You can't help me," said Perry. I gotta help myself—when I'm ready—if I survive. But I want you to do something for me."

"Anything," said Watt.

"Stay away from me," said Perry. "You can't trust me any more—I'm *telling* you. If you take me home, the moment your back is turned I'll steal everything I can to buy some dope. I'll do anything when my jones comes down. When I'm better, I want to have our friendship to come back to. But it won't be there if I destroy it now. And I'm going to destroy it if you stay with me. So just leave. Please! Leave me right now. No hugs, no tears, just walk away—like we'll see each other tomorrow." Pausing, he looked into Watt's eyes and cried, "Please, Watt!"

"Later," said Watt, walking away.

CHAPTER 20

▼

Walking down the street, Watt fought back the tears. All he'd need was for some punk to see him crying and think he was soft. As he neared his building, he remembered he still didn't have any money. The only place he could get some was Dr. Von Geber's. So he turned around and went to the subway. But before he could descend into the ground, he saw S. Burrows running toward him with his attaché case extended like a lance. "He's still chasing you, and you're still running," said Watt.

"Of course we're running—from *him,*" said Burrows. "We've been running from him for hundreds of years. But it's *you* I want to see."

"About what?" asked Watt.

"A book you're going to write someday," said S. Burrows.

"What book? What the hell are you talking about?"

"Just remember," said Burrows, "it's got to show us in a positive light. When it comes to African Americans, a book is never Art. It's always public relations."

"What about truth?" asked Watt.

"Image is more important than truth," said Burrows.

"You bourgeois motherfuckers are really fucked up." said Watt.

"S. Burrows," called a voice from a distance. "Please stop running. I just want to talk with you."

"No!" screamed S. Burrows, taking off down the street, seemingly pulled by his attaché case.

As the man in rags with bad feet approached, Watt said, "What's happening, brother?"

"I'm still chasin' him," said Colly, "and he's still runnin'. But I'm a little thirsty now." Ceasing to run, he reached into a pocket and took out a bottle of pluck and offered Watt some. At first Watt refused the drink. Then he took the bottle and raised it to his head. As the cheap wine splashed down his throat, Watt felt his anxious body calm. He forgot about Perry. He even forgot he was drinking someone else's pluck. Finishing, he returned the bottle.

"You drank it *all!*" howled Colly.

"Thanks," said Watt.

"I know better than to offer you a drink next time."

"Thanks," repeated Watt as the cheap wine loosened the pain in his gut.

"A day worth of beggin' gone in a second," complained Colly, "thanks to *you.*"

"Here," said Watt, going into his pocket and pulling out his last five dollar bill.

Taking the bill, Colly popped it, like a shine rag, and then grinning, said, "You can drink *my* pluck anytime."

"Tell me why you're chasing him," said Watt.

"Cause he's ashamed of me," snapped Colly. "And I want to find out how he got to where he is so I can tell my kids."

"Who is he?" asked Watt.

"That's S. Hartford Burrows, of the exclusive Burrows family of Washington, D.C. They were free two-hundred years ago when the rest of us were slaves. Some of them, the ones in Virginia, even *owned* slaves. Ain't dat some shit, black people ownin' black people?"

"Yeah, but that was part of the man's strategy to pit us against each other."

"Well it worked," said Colly. "It's *still* workin'."

"What do you want from him?" asked Watt.

"I hate him, but I want my kids to be just like him," said Colly, "so I need him to tell me how to do it. But he thinks he's better than me. He don't know the only thing that makes him better is his family's luck. They were house niggers and got treated better than us field niggers. I want him to understand that he's still BLACK, and whatever he does, the white folks still call him nigger behind his back. So I gotta follow him wherever he goes. We're bound together by the color of our skin. And he ain't no better than me."

"Hold on, man," said Watt. "No one is better than anyone. But you need to stop worrying about *him* and get *yourself* together."

"I'm losin' him! I gotta go!" shouted Colly. Handing Watt the empty bottle, he took off after Burrows.

Going down into the subway, Watt caught the "AA" train up to 125th Street, then went up the stairs and crossed over to the downtown side to catch the express train that would take him to 59th Street.

The train, crowded already, pulled into the station twenty minutes late with passengers' faces smashed against the doors. Watt boarded the train, pushing his way in enough so the doors could close. When they finally did, the train started moving, and scenes of darkness followed scenes of light as the train passed through stations along the tunnel.

Mysteriously, the train halted between 72nd Street and 59th Street. Lights dimmed as deodorants failed, and funk thickened like a plot. "I'm sick of it!" someone yelled. "You stink!"

"If you don't like the way I smell, buddy, get the hell away from me."

"I would if I could, but I can't move!"

"You Americans with your hang-ups about cleanliness are the *filthiest*-minded people in the world!" snapped a woman with a British accent.

"You stink, too, limey bitch!" someone said.

"Doesn't a person have a right to stink?" someone innocently asked, and passengers answered in unison, "No!"

Holding his nose, Watt waited for the train to start again. It eventually pulled into 59th Street with people gasping for fresh air. A husky conductor, supporting a frail-looking man all wrapped in bandages, pushed his way to the train doors before they opened, saying, "Let Spiritus Mundi off first—this way, Mr. Mundi."

Using his key, Watt entered Dr. Otto Von Geber's brownstone. He met Erika Von Geber coming down the stairs. A smile came over her face when she saw Watt. Her arms opened wide and she embraced Watt tightly. He held her cautiously, but when she rubbed her belly against his groin and grabbed his butt, he gently pushed her back, asking, "Where is everyone?"

"Otto is conducting a group session upstairs," she said, flashing both tongue and eyes. "But you don't have to go in right away, do you? Come with me while they work."

"No, thank you," said Watt. "I'm going upstairs." As he left her and went up the stairs, thinking, *all these years I didn't know she was a freak*, something told him to look back. He turned and saw Erika staring at him with a look of utter contempt on her face.

Before going into the den, he stopped at a hallway closet to get his white jacket, the one with Watt written over the pocket, but it was gone. As he slowly entered the upstairs den, the clock hissed and the parrot cried "Ordnung!"

"Ah, Watt," said Dr. Von Geber, looking up, "it's good to see you. Come in."

They were all there—Ainsley Bridges, Lena Messa, Pearl Fryman, Willard Camalian, and a few new millionaires—seated around Dr. Von Geber who sat in his temperature-controlled chair. Their eyes were riveted on a large television. Some important global event was unfolding, and they stopped their group session to watch.

"What's going on?" asked Watt.

Bill Tetley reporting from the New York Stock Exchange, said a preppy-looking reporter, *where millionaire Wally Raunch, suffering from some inexplicable mental disease, is holding all members of the New York Stock Exchange hostage.*

Mr. Raunch, who is wearing a hunting vest that he claims contains twenty pounds of the explosive C-4 is threatening to blow up the New York Stock Exchange and send the global economy into a tailspin if brokers do not agree to purchase his corporation's stock and boost its value.

As you probably know, Mr. Rauch is the heir to the Catchall fortune and the President and CEO of Raunch International. For the last few years, he has exhibited what some have described as bizarre behavior. Several of his Associates have said that Mr. Raunch is suffering from a disease called CMB, which is unfamiliar to members of the medical community to whom we've talked. We do not know what those initials stand for. Nor do we know if Mr. Raunch has been receiving treatment for the disease.

Police have Mr. Rauch surrounded and are trying to negotiate with him. As the negotiations proceed, all of the brokers of the Exchange have been on their feet since the Exchange closed officially this afternoon. Mr. Rauch has demanded that they remain on the floor of the Exchange. And if just one broker leaves, he has threatened to pull the ripcord attached to his vest and blow the entire Exchange, in his own words, to Kingdom Come.

Understandably, all of brokers are exhausted. Many have been forced to deposit their bodily wastes in trading pits or on the floor of the Exchange. Frankly, the place stinks. One Exchange official said it smells worse than the elephants at the circus. We will update you momentarily if there are any further developments.

"I urged him to get treatment for his CMB," said Pearl Fryman, sobbing. "But he wouldn't listen."

"Raunch was always cheap," said Ainsley Bridges, "penny wise and pound foolish."

"Let's see if it's on any of the other channels," said Willard Camalian. And sure enough, every television channel from networks to cable was focused on Wally Raunch at the New York Stock Exchange.

"He said he didn't need Dr. Von Geber's help," said Pearl Fryman, adding, "Do you see what can happen when a disease is left untreated?"

"I swear I will never stop getting treated," said Lena Messa, "until I'm cured."

Her words prompted a smile from Dr. Von Geber. Then everyone's head turned back to the television.

This is Bill Tetley again with the latest update on the hostage situation at the New York Stock Exchange. After receiving calls from corporate heads the world over, police are considering an attempt to apprehend Mr. Raunch. Teams of extra brokers are being flown in from all over the world to replace any killed today. And a makeshift stock exchange is being assembled in Madison Square Garden, where Mr. Raunch held a party some months ago. Although the situation is grim, and we are all concerned about the brokers being held hostage, the New York Stock Exchange must resume operation. Experts believe it can commence operation day after tomorrow.

Isn't that some shit, thought Watt.

"Brokers are always replaceable," said Ainsley Bridges, during a momentary silence. "However, we can never let them know that."

Bill Tetley here, as you can see, police are closing in on Mr. Rauch right now. We're going to turn up the microphone so you can hear what they're saying.

"Come on buddy, give us a break. We all have families and kids. We're not millionaires. We're working folks. What's wrong with you? You've got everything."

"I told you not to fuck with me, didn't I? I told you what would happen if you did, didn't I! Well now you're going to get it, you, poor, hapless motherfucker!"

As policeman lunged forward, Wally Rauch yelled, "Top of the world, Ma!" and pulled his ripcord. Screaming, brokers dived into their excrement-laden trading pits and covered their heads. But, the bomb that should have blown the roof off the stock exchange didn't explode. The police grabbed Wally Raunch, slapped him a couple of times, and removed the potentially explosive vest. As they led him away, he screamed, "It was American made! We don't manufacture shit in this country right any more!"

Bill Tetley reporting—police officers have just captured billionaire Wally Rauch. We thought he was a millionaire, but analysts pointed out that he has billions.

"Turn the television off, Stetson," ordered Ainsley Bridges. "Call my broker and tell him I want to buy fifty-thousand shares of Raunch International immediately. They should be a bargain now."

"I'm going to do the same thing," said several other millionaires.

"Let's conclude the discussion," said Dr. Von Geber. "I think we've all heard and seen enough this evening. Besides, I have something to discuss with Watt."

"Yes, I'm ready to return to work," said Watt.

"But Dr. Von Geber, asked Willard Camalian, "what about God?"

"God is dice," said Dr. Von Geber. "The idea that dice are thrown creates him. The idea that dice throw themselves destroys him. And the idea that dice are not thrown at all destroys us."

"What about religion?" asked Pearl Fryman.

"Religion is an effort to find certainty in dice," said Dr. Von Geber. "It's a comfort for people coming together to blend their genes. I think we can adjourn now."

"But what are perceptual speeds?" asked Ainsley Bridges.

Now they're going to have a literary discussion, thought Watt. Nothing bored him more than listening to them bullshit about writers, living or dead. *What purpose do writers serve? They can't feed you or give you money. Besides, nobody reads any more.*

"If you could travel in Einstein's tram," said Dr. Von Geber, "gradually increasing its speed until you reached the speed of light, you would see all the schools of painting pass by—Naturalism, Realism, Impressionism, Surrealism, and many more. Straight lines would slope as you moved forward.

"The perceptual speed, then, is the internal aesthetic speed at which the artist sees the world and renders it in his work of art. And if he or she is successful, the work of art comes to life in the mind of the observer, whose internal speed and perception of the world have been changed by the work of art.

"Heisenberg made it clear in his theory of quantum mechanics. When the internal aesthetic speed of the observer is moving faster than the work of art, you have Naturalism. When the internal aesthetic speed of the observer and the work of art are moving at the *same* speed, you have realism. And when the internal aesthetic speed of work of art is moving faster than that of the observer, you have all the other artistic movements. That is all for now," said Dr. Von Geber.

"What about the parodies?" asked Lena.

"Very well," said Dr. Von Geber with a bored expression on his face. "Who will go first?"

For a moment, the millionaires looked like school children with homework. Each shuffled papers rushing to go first.

Quickly rising, Bridges said, "I know the imposition of pencil on poem, the sad inquisition of cleansing lead."

Crap! Thought Watt.

"You left out Thomas' *death's feather*," said Pearl Fryman.

Then Willard Camalian mentioned some writer named Faulkner and affected a Southern accent with his spiel. "Like others who shared his lot, he lived in fantasy passed and barely remembered, of land and mansions and black hands picking cotton, wanting to go back and do that which he could not do because he had not been born when it needed to be done—not knowing it didn't matter because going back or forward is no different than standing still, as old Zeno the philosopher knew, which is why he had to break away from the past and concentrate on the present by doing what he had to do now before it was too late."

He must have been drunk when he wrote that, thought Watt, patiently listening while the others took their turns.

Finally, Lena Messa moved to the window to caress an artificial plant, saying, "I'm a plant and you're a plant, except that I walk. I'm a plant and you're a plant, except that I talk. I'll do my best to speak for you."

When she finished, there was a silence. Each millionaire bowed his or her head as if God had spoken. Then they applauded, chanting *Dickerson* as Lena popped an Alka Selzer into her mouth.

Watt had enough. He was ready to go back to work and slap these millionaires.

Suddenly, Ainsley Bridges fell to the ground in front of the fireplace and began writhing and kicking his legs. Hearing his master's voice cry out, Stetson raced back into the room, crying, "It's that Indian again! He's eating Mr. Bridges from the inside!"

As Bridges rolled and twisted on the floor, choking, Watt and everyone else in the room could hardly believe their eyes. A tooth popped out of Ainsley Bridges' mouth and red fingers appeared, followed by a red hand, which grabbed and twisted Bridges' lips. As Bridges gagged even louder, and the hand continued periscoping up and down, Pearl Fryman shrieked and fell backwards on the floor.

At that moment, Stetson struck the hand with a giant spoon, prompting the hand to wag a finger and make a "naughty, naughty" sign. But Stetson continued rapping the red knuckles until the hand recoiled downward, seeking sanctuary in Ainsley Bridges' guts.

"What's going on?!" asked Watt. Then he remembered Bridges and Laughing Gravy in the park. *He ate the Indian*, thought Watt as Stetson worked to revive Bridges. *But now it's time for me to go to work and make some money.* He pointed to Lena Messa, who ignored him. Sucking her teeth, she turned her head away. As the other millionaires watched with disgust on their faces, Watt approached Lena, saying, "Let's go upstairs. I haven't heard you make Tarzan-talk in bed for a long time."

"*Excuse* me?!" said Lena. "What are you talking about?"

"Let's go upstairs and get in bed," said Watt.

"*Excuse* me," Lena repeated. "You mean you want to *sleep* with *me*?"

"I just want to do my job," said Watt.

"Well do your job with someone else," said Lena harshly. "I don't *sleep* with the help, especially *Negroes*."

"You don't sleep with *Negroes!*" cried Watt. No one had ever called him a Negro before. That was a term from the past. Before the Black Nationalist Movement, before the Civil Rights Movement, Before *Brown v. the Board of Education,* there were Negroes. But no one had ever called him one before. For him, it was worse than being called a nigger, and he wanted to bitch-slap her for it. And what did she mean *she didn't sleep with Negroes.* Watt had been screwing her for the last three years. It was part of her therapy.

"Watt," called Dr. Von Geber from the other side of the den. "Let me speak with you a moment if you please." As Watt approached, Dr. Otto Von Geber rose from his recliner and met him in the center of the room. "That is one of the things I wanted to discuss with you. She doesn't remember anything you did with her. Those nights of therapeutic lovemaking never happened. She doesn't even know your name. So don't remind her. And Watt, due to new treatment she received while you were away, she now hates black people and is an avowed racist."

"How could that happen?" asked Watt.

"Things like that happen all the time," said Dr. Von Geber. "There is something else I want to talk with you about. Many changes were made while you were in the hospital. In addition to CMB, we have begun to treat a new and more deadly disease, CBB, Chronic Billionaire Burnout. You saw the danger this new strain poses in Wally Raunch, who will go down in history as the first billionaire terrorist. Consequently, our therapeutic methods and procedures have changed. Slap therapy does not work anymore. We've begun a more radical treatment, and we do not need your services anymore. I will give you a check to cover today, as well as severance pay and a bonus. I wish I could do more. But, as I've heard you say, *those are the breaks.*"

"But doc—" muttered Watt.

"You had your Devil's Interval, and you let it pass, content to continue working in our treatment center because it was easy. You should have thought of your future. That was your responsibility. But you will not have any trouble finding work. You have the schadenfreunde, the love of malice, and that will take you a long way. Although your intelligence is amazing, you must learn to focus your hate."

As Dr. Von Geber continued talking, Watt looked at the millionaires. Sadistic joy beamed on every face. Without his job, he no longer had power over them.

Maybe he never did. Perhaps he was just a tool they used for their amusement. But he had always thought of himself, naively, as Dr. Von Geber's right-hand man. Now that power and position were gone. He was unemployed and just another Harlem statistic.

Grandma had warned him, "Do what you gotta do fast, son," she said, "cause the Devil's Interval is gettin' shorter and shorter." But although Watt had taken her seriously, he never thought working at Dr. Von Geber's treatment center was *his* Devil's Interval or that his job would ever come to an end. If he had known that, he would have finished high school, gone to college, and got a professional degree.

But he didn't prepare. Now no one would ever know of the great work he did: how the New York Stock Exchange had rallied from a drop of 501 points because he took a few millionaires into a restroom and slapped them until they became confident and successful. Nor would anyone ever know, or admit, that they became wealthy because of what a black man had done. Nameless, he would disappear like other Black men of earlier generations who contributed to the health and wealth of the nation and received no recognition, not even a footnote. He tried to ponder what he would do to make a living in the future, but he couldn't think clearly. "But, doc," he said.

"I'm sorry, Watt," said Dr. Von Geber. "But our institute is developing new techniques and treatments, and you no longer fit into our plans."

At that moment, the door to the den opened, and Lena cried, "Howe!" with the excitement of a young girl on a merry-go-round.

A big, bearded, mean-looking white man stood in the doorway. Wearing overalls, with bare feet, he stood approximately six-feet-six inches and looked to be in his thirties. A country boy, he seemed to be a product of a different kind of poverty from a different kind of place—maybe Appalachia or the backwoods of Mississippi. Hard living was etched in his face. In a different sort of a way, he had suffered like Watt.

For a moment, Watt thought of giving everybody the "Fuck you all!" litany. But like America's first answer to Sputnik, his litany disintegrated before leaving the ground. Besides, he needed Dr. Von Geber's check to pay his bills this month.

As Howe entered the room, scowling at Watt and receiving cheers and adulation from the burnt-out millionaires, Watt noticed that all eyes were glued to his whip, which he wore on a ring attached to his pants.

"Howe replaced you while you were in the hospital," said Dr. Von Geber, "and we are very happy with his work."

"But doc …," said Watt, as a commotion broke out. Several of the millionaires were restraining Howe, saying, "He's going. He's going. He can't take your job."

"You probably feel as if affirmative action has come to an end," said Dr. Von Geber. "Perhaps it has. But you have to shake off your ghetto mentality of hopelessness and make your Devil's Interval again. I have faith in you and believe you will prevail. I am grateful for the years you contributed to the development of our treatment center. You must go now. I have things to do. Erika has your check and will see you on the way out." He pointed to the door, and then turned to speak with a couple of the billionaires who were restraining Howe.

As Doctor Von Geber walked away, Watt looked up at the clock to note the time. He wanted to be able to say in years to come that on this night in 1984, at approximately 9:00 p.m., I lost the best job I ever had. But the clock, which had hissed when he entered, was now mysteriously broken. He heard no bird's "Ordnung!" or farewell from anyone..

When he reached the bottom of the stairs, Erika was waiting with an envelope for him. "First, give me the key," she said.

CHAPTER 21

▼

Riding a crowded train uptown, Watt thought of what he could do to make a living. He was a high school dropout without any skills except slap therapy. Although he needed money, there were things he refused to do. He wouldn't pull a clothing rack through Manhattan's garment center, and he wouldn't flip burgers in a fast food restaurant, and he wouldn't deal drugs. *Grandma could never forgive that,* he thought. He realized the old lady still exercised power over him. Perhaps he was a clock she had wound and left running.

I wouldn't be in this predicament if I had thought ahead during those years I was making money slapping millionaires. I will never live solely in the present again. The millionaires had used him to wake them up because, as Grandma once said, "White folks will pay you to wake them up, even when they'd prefer you let them sleep. It's got something to do with the Puritan ethic, son, and a guilt complex I don't fully understand."

As the express train made the haul from 59th Street to 125th Street, and the lights blinked on and off, a man stood behind Watt and said, "You started all this! You're responsible! You did it with your damn *slave* labor"

"You talking to *me?*" asked Watt.

"Yes, I'm talking to *you!*" said the man, his blue eyes blazing. "You did it! You helped them speed things up with your damn slave labor. And now that we're all crazy, now that nobody believes in a thing, you have the nerve to hate whitey and talk about your rights!

"Well I'm *sick* and *tired* of you thinking you're better than everyone else! I'm *sick* and *tired* of affirmative action and racial preferences! I'm *sick* and *tired* of you thinking *I'm* supposed to sit in the back of the bus! We're not going to stand for it anymore. We, the *white* people on this train, are going to *change* things! And the first thing we're going to do is outlaw blues! We're going to put people in jail for playing the blues. Then we're going to fire each and every one of you from your jobs. We're going to turn the clock back to the Nineteenth Century and put every one of you in your place. That's what we're going to do—we, the people, we, the *white* people on this train!"

Now Watt *knew* he was crazy. Practically all the people on the train were Black or Latino, and the train was heading straight for Harlem. "Listen, man, leave me alone!" said Watt. "You're crazy, and I don't want to fuck you up!" Meanwhile, passengers began to chant, "Kick his ass."

"But he's crazy," said Watt.

"That don't matter, son" said an old woman whose voice reminded him of Grandma's. "He's crazy, but he's *responsible.*"

"How does it feel to be surrounded by white people that hate you," the madman continued, "and let you know it every day? Martin Luther King had a dream, but we're going to give you a nightmare—again."

Knowing he was crazy, Watt wanted to let it go. But the maniac persisted. When he said, "Well I have a dream, too … and your mother's in it," that was all Watt could take. A left hook behind the maniac's right earlobe knocked him colder than an arctic night as passengers cheered.

When the train pulled into 125th Street, the maniac staggered to his feet and got off. He stumbled across the platform and boarded another train, heading farther into Harlem, and began his racist spiel again. Shaking his head, Watt caught the downtown local one stop to 116th Street and walked to his home, thinking, *what will I do?*

Blip was asleep, so Watt climbed over him and went into his apartment. He continued asking himself, *What will I do?* Then he became distracted by O Harold's woman's voice echoing through the yard. "More! O Harold, more!" she howled. O Harold was working overtime, giving her everything he had, but still she cried, "More! O Harold, more!" But then O Harold cut loose with a cry that was more gutbucket than blues, "Goddammitt, bitch! I ain't got no more!"

A few nights later, Watt was still asking himself *what will I do?* when someone knocked on his door at 2:30 a.m.

"Yeah, who's there?" he asked.

"Marshall Express," said a voice. "I have a special delivery for Mr. Watt."

"At 2:30 in the morning!"

"We deliver 24 hours-a-day, anyplace, anywhere, under any conditions. And I wish you'd take this package so I can get the hell out of here."

"Leave it at the door," said Watt.

"No, sir, we can't do that. You have to sign for it."

"Who's it from?" asked Watt, thinking *it might be a trick.*

"Sir Ainsley Bridges, President and CEO of the Saxon-American Corporation," the voice answered, and Watt slowly unbolted the door. Two white men dressed in black, SWAT team regalia, carrying automatic weapons and wearing bulletproof vests, stood outside his door holding an envelope with his name on it.

"Just sign right here," said one of the men. As Watt signed the receipt, one of the men gave him the letter and rapidly spieled, "Thank you for using the Marshall Express. Please call on us if you have any special delivery needs. Good night." Then they turned, doing SWAT team maneuvers, guns ready to fire, and went down the stairs. Meanwhile, Watt went back into his apartment and read the letter.

> Dear Watt:
>
> Your being fired the other day was inevitable. As you saw, I did everything I could to prevent it. But you must understand. We've been rehearsing getting rid of you for such a long time. I guess at the heart of things is the fact we've never liked you. But at a certain point in history we needed you to do certain jobs.
>
> Although that point has passed, your welfare remains my concern. It would be such a waste for someone with your immense talent not to be able to put it to use.
>
> Permit me to make a suggestion. Why don't you work for me as a personal consultant? After all, the Saxon-American Corporation owes you a lot. Through one or two meetings each week, I'm sure we can develop a mutually beneficial relationship.
>
> Why don't we start this morning—a few hours from now? Meet me at the usual place in the park at 4:00 a.m. so we can make plans and discuss developing our mutually beneficial relationship. I'll be waiting. Don't be late.
>
> Your friend,
> Sir Ainsley Bridges

At least he could make some money now, and this time he would prepare. He'd stash some kiss-my-ass money in the bank so he wouldn't find himself broke when it was over.

He looked at the clock. It was 3:00 a.m. now. He had an hour to go before he met Bridges in the park. He would approach it differently this time. He'd slap Bridges harder than usual to compensate for Howe's whip. He'd also enter the park differently. Usually, he entered from the bottom and worked his way up. This time he'd start from the top and work his way down.

Leaving his apartment, he stepped over Blip going down the stairs. Then he walked up to 123rd Street, the northern boundary of the park. Circling around to Morningside Heights, he walked down to 116th Street and stood before a statue perched above the park. "Carl Schurz, a Defender of Liberty and a Friend of Human Rights," read the inscription. But the statue had its back turned on Harlem.

He climbed over the fence, which the New York City Parks Department locked at sundown, and landed gingerly on the park stairs. The screams and even Harlem seemed different from above. The last lights from bars were flickering out. Mad poets were burning verses in the dark.

> *Father, you heard the irony in stone,*
> *A bird under glass*
> *With thoughts of the sky, not the ceiling,*
> *And the smell of laughs that didn't understand*
> *The cry in the rain*
> *When the pain did not suffice*
> *And Words came to peck the mind*

As he descended, he saw a blonde-haired woman in a leopard coat staggering up the stairs. On the stairs below, he saw the shadow of a shivering Stetson, his white raincoat blowing in the wind. Seeing Watt, Stetson asked with a look of astonishment, "What are you doing coming *this* way? You've never come *this* way before. We always expect you to come from below."

"I thought I'd do something different," said Watt.

"Well you shouldn't have done it!" snapped Stetson. "But never mind that now. It's 4:00 a.m., and Sir Ainsley is waiting. He wants you to improvise tonight. Forget all the old scripts. Say *anything* you want. Pay no attention to what he says. Then end the session with a slap. I'll be waiting here with your check."

"No problem," said Watt. Descending, he found Bridges slouched on the stairs, wearing a green bowler hat, with a look of loss embroidered on his face. "You finally made it on time," he said. "And you came *down* instead of *up*."

"Slight change of direction," snapped Watt.

"You see yourself differently now," said Bridges. "Do you remember when Jazz and Bojangles were all you had. You were humble then—very frightened, too. But time, the omnivore, has changed you."

Playing along with the game, Watt said, "We always had much more than that. But what I remember most from the past is what your people did to mine."

"We were just exacting revenge," said Bridges.

"For what?" asked Watt.

"For what you did to us when you chased *us* out of Africa. Europe was cold. We wouldn't have gone there if you had shared. You didn't, however, and we migrated and became white. You see, we were the oppressed people."

"Bullshit," said Watt.

"And it's an unforgiving world," said Bridges. "We haven't forgiven you, and you haven't forgiven us. So where do we go from here?"

"No where," said Watt, "as long as you continue to freak out when Polly doesn't want a cracker but a nigger with a stiff dick."

"You see, Watt, that's your problem," said Bridges. "You see everything in terms of sex when there's so much more to life besides sex. Money is so much more satisfying than sex."

"And that's all you think about," said Watt.

"Yes, I admit it. Money enslaved me when I was a boy, and I've used it to enslave everyone I could. I didn't have what you had."

"What's that?" asked Watt.

"Freedom," said Ainsley Bridges.

"*You* have the nerve to talk to *me* about freedom," said Watt, laughing. "You want *my* pity—*you*, a billionaire who's been free all his life!"

"I don't want pity," said Bridges, "but I think I deserve a little sympathy. I've always understood what freedom is—and is not. You thought it meant being able to do *anything* if you had money or credentials. You didn't know that freemen, even rich freemen, are chained differently. The only freedom we have is deciding on what to do to those who are more chained than we are."

"That's more freedom than I've ever known."

"Perhaps, but I became imprisoned also by an equation," said Bridges. "One and one makes two dollars."

"So now *I'm* supposed to feel sorry for *you*," said Watt.

"Don't feel sorry for *me*," said Bridges. "But have some compassion for a fellow human being. After all, I had CMB, and now I have CBB."

Watt was ready to slap him now. "Where's your hand sandwich?" he asked.

"I don't want to eat myself anymore," said Bridges. "Something is eating *me*."

"You shouldn't have fucked over that Indian," said Watt. "That's why you're sick."

"Yes, the Indian!" cried Bridges with a mad glow in his eyes. He sprang from the stairs and put both hands around Watt's throat and started choking him. His strength seemed to double as Watt struggled to break free. "You know about the Indian!" cried Bridges as Watt raised his hand to slap him. But before he could land a slap, the billionaire muttered, "One and one makes—" Releasing Watt, he fell back and slumped on the stairs. He began gasping, and with a final gasp, he said, "two dollars!" Then he became silent and didn't move.

"Alright," said Watt, rubbing his own throat and breathing deeply. "I didn't know you were that strong." But Bridges neither answered nor stirred. Assuming the billionaire was playing possum, Watt said, "Where's my bowler hat?" Then Watt shook him, saying, "Get up! Come on." But the billionaire remained still. Standing over him, Watt thought, *He can't be dead! We were just playing a game, acting out a fantasy based on black-white bullshit. He can't be dead!*

"Oh Lord!" someone cried, and Watt looked around to see who it was. Then he realized it was his own voice he had heard.

As he stood frozen in the dark, Stetson came running down the stairs, his white raincoat blowing in the wind. He looked at Bridges and shook him several times; he took his pulse and placed his ear against the billionaire's chest. He even slapped Bridges once himself. When Bridges didn't respond, Stetson looked at Watt with terror in his eyes. Then he turned and ran back up the stairs, screaming, "They've killed Sir Ainsley Bridges! They've killed Sir Ainsley Bridges!"

CHAPTER 22

▼

Watt ran down the stairs under a chewed moon's rays. He could still hear Stetson screaming, "They've killed Sir Ainsley Bridges!" Then he heard a loud Indian whoop followed by sirens above the park.

As he exited the park, a mugger tried to grab him. But Watt threw him aside, saying, "I don't have time to be mugged!" Minutes later, he was at his building, hurdling Blip who called, "Whas happenin', my man?"

Watt ran into his apartment, grabbed a few things, and came out. As he went down the stairs, Blip asked, "Whatcha do? *Kill* someone?"

"I can't talk now," said Watt.

"Yeah, you killed someone," said Blip. "But slow down. Be cool. It's done, an' bein' scared will just get you caught. I killed a mothafucka once. So I knows what I'm talkin' about when I tells you if you slows down, tha police will run right *by* you. They ain't tha smartest mafucks in the world. All they got is a trick—an' tha trick is usually your friend."

"You don't understand," said Watt.

"I know about killin'," said Blip. "You ain't in no real trouble. A lot of people kill people today. Now your man, Perry, *he's* in trouble. He gotta mafucker busted last night who was supposed to be his friend. But you know how it is. You can't trust no dopefiend, even if he is supposed to be your friend. Ax Victor Vernon if you don't believe me. He's rottin' in jail cause of what Perry done. When Jehoover an' Towntamer drove up an' grabbed Perry, sayin', '*Give us somebody, dopefiend, or we're going to take you!*' Perry gave 'em Victor Vernon.

"He didn't do dat at first. At first, he said, *Fuck you!* Normally Jehoover and Towntamer would have shot him dead. But dat day they let him slide, maybe because of what Rosaline did. So Towntamer, he just gave him a hard slap. Tha instant Towntamer's hand landed on Perry's face, the words *Victor Vernon!* leaped out. He tole them everything: lies, truth, fantasy! Whuteber dey wanted ta hear.

"He even tole 'em Victor sells reefer, but dey weren't interested in dat. *Just the hard stuff, dopefiend*, say Jehoover. So Perry tole 'em more lies an' dat Victor sold crack.

"Well, an hour later dey drove up an' busted Victor an' didn't gibb him no slack. Dey planted some dope on him and tole him, *We got some help from your boy, Perry*. So Victor's mad an' hot an' Perry might as well be dead cause when Victor Vernon gets out of jail, he's gonna fill his ass wit' lead."

"But back to you now. Lemme tell ya, boy, only once in a lifetime you come this way. Thass why you gotto relax. You didn't kill the pope but some street nigger that nobody will miss, right?"

"No, Blip," said Watt. "I killed a white dude."

"Well dat's kinda bad, but it ain't *dat* bad," said Blip. "Theys wheelin' an' dealin' out dere jus' like us. Some of them are eben *worse* than us. They aint gonna hunt you down for killin' no white trash."

"But he was a *rich* white dude!"

"How rich?" asked Blip.

"A billionaire," said Watt

"A *billionaire!*" cried Blip.

"Yeah," said Watt.

"Boy, who'd you kill, *GOD?*"

"Ainsley Bridges," said Watt.

"*Ainsley Bridges!*" snapped Blip, "*Sir* Ainsley Bridges of The Saxon-American Corporation?"

"Yeah," said Watt.

"Boy, you better run your ass off!" cried Blip. "An' don't stop till you get to Mars!"

Turning, Watt vaulted down the stairs and raced out of the building. He ran around a corner and stopped to look back. He saw a police car pull up to his building and Jehoover and Towntamer get out. Guns drawn, they went into his building. Moments later he heard shots. Then he started running, and as he ran he thought, *they killed Blip because of me.*

Sirens blared behind him in the wake of the rising sun. A plane flew overhead, and he wished he were on it. But then he began to choke and realized it was the Pollution Plane flying overhead.

He knew he couldn't get justice if Jehoover and Towntamer caught him. He thought of going to Chicago and maybe taking Perry along. But first he had to find Perry. So he went into the building where he last left him and went up to the roof and came down again. But Perry was nowhere to be found. He couldn't risk looking for him in the street. The police would get him for sure. So he huddled in the building all day and waited.

Only a few people came into the building. Later, a police car stopped across the street. Watt ran up to the roof, crossed over several buildings to the other side of the block. Then he entered another building and started down the stairs.

In between landings, he saw a body slowly bobbing up and down—a dope-fiend high to the max. "Perry!" said Watt. "Perry!" he repeated. And a sluggish "Yeahhhh" was the response.

"I've been looking for you," said Watt. "We've got to get out of here, man. I killed Ainsley Bridges. I didn't really do it, but everybody *thinks* I did. The police are after me—the same way Victor Vernon is after *you*."

"Yeahhhh."

"Hey, man! Get yourself together! People out there want us dead!"

"Yeahhhh."

"Wake up, nigger! Understand? They *hate* us and want to *kill* us!"

"Yeahhhhh."

"You motherfucker! Why'd you have to go and do this to yourself? Don't you know life is hard enough *without heroin!* I ought to beat the shit out of you for being so stupid!"

"Yeahhh."

Then it hit Watt. *This isn't Perry. This is somebody I don't know.*

"Well I'm leaving now," said Watt. "And I can't take you with me like this. You'll get us *both* killed. If you want to shoot dope, you've got to make it for yourself. I just want you to know I love you. I wouldn't have made it this far if it weren't for *you*. I hope you hear me, man. I love you, brother. Goodbye."

"Yeahhh."

Watt didn't know if his words had penetrated the shroud of dope cloaking Perry's soul. He hoped that somewhere Perry heard him and would remember. He turned and waved good-bye to his best friend and went up the stairs. Perry looked like a pillar of black salt about to dissolve.

Tears clotted Watt's eyes as he sat on the roof of another building until the sky evicted the sun. Then he ventured into the street to go to Sylvia's house, cutting across 115th Street, near Wadleigh Jr. High.

Suddenly, prowl cars appeared everywhere. Dozens of policemen wearing riot gear surrounded him. He slowly raised his hands. But the police ran by him and surrounded a nearby building as Watt relaxed. *Maybe Blip was right. If you slow down, they run by you.* Almost casually, he joined a crowd that had formed behind a police barricade.

Meanwhile, a police car decorated with gold braided paint drove up, and a police captain with more medals than Methuselah got out. Taking a bullhorn from one of his officers, he raised it and called. "Come out. We've got you surrounded."

Turning to an old woman standing next to him, Watt asked, "Who's in there, Public Enemy Number One?"

"A great man," the old woman responded, with tears in her eyes.

"Who?" asked Watt.

"That's not important," she said.

"What's a great man doing hiding in a basement?" asked Watt.

"A great man was born in a manger," responded the old woman, and Watt nodded his head.

Then the great man's voice cried from the basement, "I'm coming out! Don't shoot!"

As weapons clicked all over the block, a tall, thin, bald old man in a union army Civil War tunic kicked away some basement boards and climbed the stairs with his hands above his head. Handcuffs greeted him. A cheer went up from the crowd when they saw him. "I beat them for 50 years!" he said. "I lived in that basement *rent free* and never spent a dime for electricity."

As the crowd applauded, Watt asked, "Who is he?"

"You need to read some Black History," was the response.

"Okay, I need to read some Black History," said Watt. "But who *is* he?"

"If you don't know who *he* is, boy," said the old woman, "Then you don't know who *you* are. It's that simple."

Watt started to ask someone else, but one of the policemen began staring at him intensely. When Watt slowed his inner rhythms and relaxed, the policeman turned to look at someone else.

As they put the old man into a police van, a white man in a business suit and a hardhat appeared. The police captain shook his hand, saying, "We finally got him," to which the man in the business suit replied, "Yes, but he burned a lot of free electricity before you did."

CHAPTER 23

▼

Before reaching Sylvia's apartment, Watt saw a copy of the *Barely News* on the ground. The headlines leapt at him: *Lipsky Sentenced to Die.... Dow-Jones Drops 512 Points in Wake of Billionaire's Murder....* Another headline read: *President Announces National Dragnet for Watt, $500,000 Reward Offered.* And yet another front page article asked the question: *Who's Responsible for Watt?* And he saw a picture of himself with a caption that read: *Is This the Technological Caveman?* One of the articles attributed Watt's *evil nature* to his social background. *My social background or your social sin,* he thought. Then he realized he was taking what other people said about him too seriously. It was all bullshit to sell newspapers and ads. *I probably generated millions of dollars of news today. All people still know is what they read in the newspapers.* Mysteriously, he felt a surge of power. He was infamous. But in a world without honor, fame and infamy have the same mother. Then he turned to the financial page. In one international story, he read the lamentations of people who blamed him for their lots.

After putting down the newspaper he realized the police were probably waiting for him at Sylvia's. He couldn't go there. Her phone was probably tapped. But he had to speak with her so he called.

"Hello," she said softly.

"Don't mention my name," said Watt.

"I was hoping you'd call."

"Do you know what I did?"

"I know what they *said* you did."

"I need to see you."

"And I need to see *you.* I'm hurting inside."

"The baby?" he asked.

"No, something else, something I can't talk about on the phone."

"Do you remember where we used to take long walks and hear great concerts on summer nights?"

"Yes."

"Meet me there in an hour, and bring some money."

"Alright, baby," she said.

Hanging up the phone, he started walking, heading for Grant's Tomb on Riverside Drive, the alleged official resting place of the eighteenth president of the United States. But the tomb served another purpose. Years ago, when abortions were illegal, frightened young men used to troop their pregnant girlfriends up to the top of the tomb and push them down the stairs. *Roe v. Wade* ended that practice. Now jazz concerts are held at the tomb during the summer. People sit on the stairs and listen to the best jazz musicians in the world.

As Watt neared Grant's Tomb, he saw a cab pull up and Sylvia get out. Her eyes were swollen, and her face was puffy. She looked as if she hadn't slept in days.

"Watt," she said, putting her arms around him and her face in a position that compelled him to kiss her.

"It's good to see you," he said, giving her an obligatory kiss.

"What are you going to do?" she asked.

"Get out of here, maybe go to Chicago," he said.

"Watt, you may have to leave the country," she said.

"Maybe," he said.

"Take me with you," she said.

"I can't," he said. "I don't know where I'm going."

"That doesn't matter," she said. "I'll go *anywhere* with you."

"Do you have the money I asked you to bring?"

"Yes," she said, giving him an envelope. At that moment a police siren blared, and Watt grabbed Sylvia by the hand and they fled into Riverside Park.

"You didn't answer me," she said when they stopped running.

"What was I *supposed* to say?"

"That you *need* me and *want* me to go with you," she said.

"But I can't," he said.

"You don't believe I love you. You don't even know what *I've* done … for you."

"Love has nothing to do with it," he said. "It's survival."

"It's always survival with you," she said. "When are you going to stop surviving and start living?"

"Someday," he said.

"*Someday* may never come," she said, "and in the meantime you still don't believe I love you."

"I don't know what love is," he said.

"That's a cop-out," she said. "You know what love is. Love is what your mother didn't give you. Love is what Ullysa took from you. Love is what you don't believe *any* woman can give you. Love is what I try to give you every day. If you know what any of those things mean, then you know what love is."

"Maybe I can't understand."

"Maybe you can't," she said. "You can turn your back on me, Watt. But someday you'll look back and know you missed the greatest love of your life." Her words broke off and drifted like music into the air. She started crying, "O God! O God! Forgive me for being such a fool!" Then a flood of tears gushed from her eyes, and Watt wanted to hold his nose. The smell of her tears made him sick. "I believed that if I was patient and waited for you," she cried, "eventually you would come to me and love me."

"I care about you," he said, thinking, *maybe this will shut her up.*

"You *care* about me!" she exclaimed. "You don't care about anybody or anything, except *yourself.* You've never given anything to anyone. All you've done is *take!* All your life you've been a taker! You didn't care about anybody, except Perry and your grandmother. Well they're *both* gone now. But I'm still here … for you."

"Like I said, I'm going to miss you."

"So this is goodbye!" she cried. "Then why don't you say goodbye to me at the top of the stairs."

"Why?" he asked.

"Because I want to see the view from the top," she said. "I've been on the bottom so long."

"It's nothing but the highway and New Jersey," he said.

"But it's safer up there," she said. "The police won't spot you."

Together, they climbed the monument's stairs, up to the pillared entrance that resembled a pagan temple from where they could see the lights across the river glimmer in the Garden State. Looking south, they could see lower Manhattan, filled with its hopes and dreams. The bonfires of dead illusions lent a peculiar hue to the Apple's sky.

When they had reached the top, Sylvia turned to him and said, "You have no idea what I've done for you."

What is she talking about now? he thought.

"You don't have to have the baby," he said. "You're only in the fourth month. It's not too late to get an abortion."

"Get an abortion!" she cried. "That's all you know!"

"What's wrong with that?" he asked.

"It's a life, Watt—a baby!"

"There you go with that Catholic school stuff again."

Looking out into the darkness, Sylvia said, "Forgive me, Father, for I have sinned." Then she turned to Watt, saying, "I want you to do something for me. I want you to push me down the stairs."

"Get out of here!" he said.

"Just do it," she said.

"Why would you ask me to do something like that?" he asked.

"I want you to do it because I can't kill our baby, but you can, and because I've been stupid and don't want to carry your baby anymore. He might turn out to be as stupid as *me*—or as mean as *you*. I can't get an abortion. It's against my faith. But if you push me down the stairs and I lose the baby, perhaps God will forgive me for what I've done."

"Let's go," he said.

"No," she said. "Push me down the stairs. It's what you want!—no baby, no responsibility, no commitment. You can have it all, just *push me down the stairs!*"

"Why don't you shut up!" he said. "I didn't call you to hear this!"

"Just push me down the stairs," she continued, "and presto!—no baby. You're free."

"I don't want to hear that shit," said Watt.

"Well I want you to hear it," said Sylvia. "I want you to punish me for being such a fool! Then I want you to walk the hell out of my life!"

"Are you crazy?" he asked.

"No, I'm sane for the first time since I met you," she said. "All this time, I thought you loved me, but I was just a piece of ass to you. You used me the way those white women used *you*—I know all about it, *Mr. Black Stud.*

"You don't know anything," he said angrily.

"You blood-sucker!" she cried.

"I'm tired of you!" he said. "You're nothing but a ring-around-my-collar!—you and those smelly tears!"

"Tears from my eyes may be turds to you!" she cried. "But it's all I have!"

"Then you've got nothing!" he yelled.

"I did it for *you!*" she cried, "for *you*, bastard!"

"I'm tired of you nagging me about that leech in your belly," he snapped. "Every bitch that has a baby thinks she's doing some high-wire pussy act. As far as I'm concerned, you and that motherfucker can get the fuck out of my life!"

Screaming, Sylvia sprung on him, scratching his neck with her finger nails and reaching for his eyes. For a moment his dick got hard and he wanted to fuck her on the tomb. But then he felt the pain from one of her nails, and pushed her away.

She screamed and flew backwards for a moment, like a diver doing a back flip from a board. Then she started descending. Her pocketbook flew into the air as she hit the first row of stairs, jewelry jingling, and then the second and the third, her momentum propelling her forward. She hit two more rows of stairs with her body revolving. Finally, she hit bottom and lay at the base of the tomb.

"Don't move! Don't move!" cried Watt, running down the stairs. I'll call an ambulance. You're hurt!"

"More than you know," whispered Sylvia as blood ran from her nose and the abrasions that covered her skin. "O God! God forgive me!" she moaned.

"For what?" asked Watt, with tears in his eyes. "You've been wonderful. I've been the fool. No woman has ever loved me the way you have. I'm sorry, but I couldn't handle it."

"I don't love you anymore," said Sylvia.

"Well I love you, baby," said Watt.

"It's too late," said Sylvia. "I just want to die!"

"Why?" he asked.

"I want to die," she cried, "for loving you and for killing BJ9!"

"For what?" howled Watt.

"For killing BJ9!" she repeated. "Now do one decent thing in your life and leave me the fuck alone, you dirty, lowlife motherfucker! I'll make you leave." She let out a shriek and cried, "Killer Watt is here!" Watt saw the shadows of people approaching the tomb and stood up as a woman holding a German shepherd on a leash asked, "What's going on over there?"

"She fell down the stairs," said Watt.

"Fell down the stairs!" exclaimed the woman with the dog.

"Hey, mister,"said a man in the shadows. "You don't have to do that any more. Abortions are legal."

"I didn't push her," said Watt.

"Yes, you did," said the man.

As the crowd grew and came closer, the woman with the dog suddenly yelled, "It's *him!* It's Killer Watt! Call the police! Call the FBI! Call out the army!"

Watt turned and started walking. Then he broke into a trot. He heard the dog barking, which made him accelerate. Now he was running, running as fast as he could. As he took the hill at 116th Street and Riverside Drive, pumping his legs, he heard sirens, sirens, sirens.

CHAPTER   24

▼

Passing through Columbia University, he approached Morningside Park. Police cars were stationed around its circumference, and spotlights illuminated the dark. Throngs of people were on lines, carrying flowers, as if marching to a martyr's shrine. Some were weeping; others twisted in agony on the ground. Looking at them, Watt thought, *this isn't Morningside Park anymore. It's the shrine of St. Bridges of the Sandwiched Hand.*

It was 10:00 p.m. when Watt crept into his building, hearing, "More, O Willie! More!" echo through the yard. He wanted to talk with Blip. But the dope-fiend was no where to be found. His bottle tops were smashed. Dry blood was splattered on the wall on which Blip usually leaned. Then Watt looked up at his apartment. Moving shadows broke the light beams that shot from beneath the door. *The police are waiting for me.*

Quietly, he went down the stairs. As a December wind blew into his face, he rounded a corner thinking *who can I turn to?* Then one person came to mind, someone he had known since the fourth grade, someone who was always good for a laugh, someone he had abused, but needed now. He decided to go to Loray's.

He reached Loray's apartment building on Lenox Avenue, and went up one flight of stairs. He stopped in front of Loray's door, thinking, *if he helps me, fine; if he doesn't, fuck him!* Then he laughed, thinking, *that's exactly what Loray would want.*

As he raised his hand to knock, he noticed the door was slightly ajar. He opened it cautiously. It was quiet and dark inside. As he entered, the light from the hallway illuminated the scene. Two sets of men's clothing were strewned across the floor in parallel trails leading to the bedroom. *Loray and his boyfriend couldn't wait to jump onto each other's back. Judging from the quiet, they have finished fucking and are probably asleep.* Watt wanted to wake Loray and get some money without disturbing the other man. So he carefully shut the front door and crept further into the dark apartment.

In the darkness, he could see two bulges in the bed, but he didn't know which belonged to Loray and which to the other man. So he gambled, thinking, *I'll go right.* Groping along the side of the bed. His hand reached out and found the night table, but it also found something else. A cold piece of metal lay next to the lamp, and beside it were two others. Three guns lay on the night table. He picked up one. A big gun, it felt like a .357 magnum. He took the other two guns, a .45 and a .38, and put them into his waistband. Then he leaned over the bed and whispered, "Wake up, Loray."

A fist shot up from the sheets and struck him. Stumbling back, Watt hit the wall, hearing the hand scrambling across the night table in the dark.

"What's wrong, baby," asked Loray, "you havin' another one of those Al Capone flashbacks?"

"Someone's in here!" said the other man, "and he's got my guns!"

"You sure you left your guns where you *think* you left them?" asked Loray.

"They were right here on the night table," said the other man.

"Then there *is* someone in here with us," said Loray. "Whoever you are, I don't do trains. Ain't nobody pullin' no train on me."

"It's not a train!" said the other voice. It's *a man!*"

"Well, what do you think a train is?" asked Loray.

"And he's got my guns!"

"Well what do you want from *me?*" asked Loray. "I can't take them away from him!"

"Both of you faggots shut up," said Watt, "before I shoot you in the ass."

"My, oh my, the Devil has a way of keepin' in style," said Loray. "Hello, Dreamweaver, you picked an inopportune time to come and visit me."

"WHO IS IT?" asked the other man.

"Public Enemy Number One," said Loray.

"KILLER WATT!" cried the other man.

As sheets rustled, Watt found the wall light switch and flicked it on. His mouth opened wide, and he almost dropped the gun. Cuddled in bed with Loray was Jehoover, the Old Testament cop.

"You sick, twisted, motherfucker!" said Watt.

"Who you callin' *twisted?*" snapped Loray.

"Not *you*. You're normal," said Watt. "You're what you see and what you say you are. But that fat, white, ugly, bulldog-looking motherfucker lying next to you, he's twisted!"

"Hold on!" cried Jehoover. "Just because I *occasionally* sleep with a man doesn't mean *I'm* a homosexual.

"Have some respect for the law," said Loray.

"All these years you've been destroying people," said Watt, "because they were gay, because they were communist, because they were black, or because you didn't *like* them."

"Wait a minute," said Jehoover.

"And all the time you were nothing but a hypocrite, liar, and closet faggot!"

"Wait a minute, Squirrel," said Jehoover. "You didn't hear me. I just like to fuck a man occasionally. But I'm not gay."

"You're a faggot!" hollered Watt. "And I don't mind that. But I ought to shoot you in the ass for being a hypocrite, too."

"Wait a minute!" cried Loray. "Before you shoot anybody, let me remind you of one thing. We go back a long way, Watt. I've always loved you and made no secret of it. Do you remember when I told you how much I loved you back in P.S. 10, and you laughed at me and showed my note to the other boys. You hurt me badly back then. But if there's one spark of decency in you, and you don't want to hurt me again, you'll do me one favor—*shoot straight!* Shoot straight, goddammit, cause I'm not going down with this fool!"

"Why don't you shut the fuck up!" said Jehoover.

"See what I mean," said Loray. "I've been with his ass for twenty years, and all he ever tells me is *shut the fuck up*. In *twenty* years, he's never acknowledged that *I'm* his true love. In twenty years, I've received no floweres for my birthday, Valentine's Day, or Christmas—twenty years of Friday nights or Saturday nights or whenever he could leave his mother and sneak over to see me, and *this* is how he treats me."

"That's enough," said Watt.

"Twenty years of buying him size 24 dresses and feelin' his killer hands take off my clothes. Twenty years, and all he can tell me is *Shut the fuck up!* Well twenty years was too much. I've wasted my youth. So let me repeat what I said, Watt, cause I'm not going down with this fool! *Shoot straight!*"

"He's not going to shoot anybody," said Jehoover, laughing. "I've been watching you, Squirrel."

"Who's Squirrel?" asked Watt.

"That's just my name for all you coons," said Jehoover.

"You piece of white shit!" growled Watt.

"Like *I* said, I've been watching you," said Jehoover. "And I'm a good judge of who can kill and who can't. I don't know about this mess with Sir Ainsley Bridges—And I don't give a damn. But I can tell you've never killed *anybody*. The fact is, Squirrel, you wouldn't be doing all this talking if you had ever killed anybody. You would have shot me by now."

"Maybe you'll be the first," said Watt.

"I don't think so," said Jehoover. "Why don't you just give me those guns?"

"Don't, Dreamweaver," said Loray. "He'll l kill us *both!*"

"Don't listen to that faggot!" said Jehoover.

"Who you callin' a faggot?!" jumped Loray.

"*You,*" said Jehoover.

"There's nothing' you've done to *me*," laughed Loray, "that I haven't done to *you.*"

"Yeah, but you *act* like a faggot," said Jehoover.

"I'm not schizophrenic!" snapped Loray.

"Like I said, Squirrel," continued Jehoover. "Give me the guns and you can walk out of here alive."

"Don't do it, honey," said Loray. "He was lyin' in bed earlier tellin' me how he gets people to surrender their guns then kills them."

"You don't know what it's like to kill someone," said Jehoover, "to squeeze the trigger and watch a human being explode, knowing *you* killed him."

"Kill the psych game," said Watt, calmly.

"And I'll tell you something else," said Jehoover. "Either it feels good or it feels bad the first time you do it."

"Like everything else," said Watt.

"And if it feels bad," said Jehoover. "It can hurt you the rest of your life. I've seen men go mad because they killed someone."

"I said shut up!" repeated Watt.

"I'm just thinking of your best interests, Squirrel."

"And I'm thinking of yours," said Watt. Walking over to the bed, he struck Jehoover upside his head with the .357 Magnum. Momentarily Jehoover became cockeyed as blood burst from his skull. He fell backwards as a huge welt rose on his head. "Shut up when I tell you shut up!" said Watt.

"Oh No!" cried Loray.

"What's wrong?" asked Watt.

"He's gettin' blood on my gold *silk sheets!*"

"Let him bleed!" said Watt. As he looked around the room, he noticed a camera case on the dresser. "What kind of camera do you have?" he asked.

"A Polaroid," said Loray.

As Watt started to pick up the camera, he noticed some photographs nearby. "What's this?" he asked, as Jehoover gradually regained consciousness.

"That's just him and me having fun and doing a few little tricks together," said Loray.

Watt looked at the pictures. What he saw was beyond pornographic. "You were really freakin' with that camera," said Watt.

"Wait just one minute, Squirrel," groaned Jehoover.

"Shut up!" said Watt.

"Leave those pictures alone!" cried Jehoover.

"Shut up," repeated Watt. "I'm taking these pictures, and if you ever fuck with me again, you'll see them in *Chronos* or the *Barely News*, you sick motherfucker. But tell me something, Loray. How the fuck can you get into bed with this piece of shit?"

"We do it every week," said Loray. "And when we finish he takes the pictures home and *claims* he destroys them."

"Well he's not taking these pictures home," said Watt.

"Those are *my* pictures!" cried Jehoover.

"Not any more," said Watt. "I hate to leave you two lovebirds. But I've got to go."

"I want those pictures," said Jehoover, climbing out of bed. "And I want my guns, too." Watt fired the gun over his head, making Jehoover cringe. "The next one will be in your fat ass," said Watt. "Loray, tie him up."

"Again!" snapped Loray. "I tied him up earlier, but just for you." Humming, Loray reached under the bed and pulled out some rope.

"Use his handcuffs, too," said Watt.

"He doesn't carry handcuffs," said Loray, "because he doesn't take prisoners. But I have some handcuffs I can use."

"You're not going to handcuff *me*," said Jehoover.

"I thought I told you to shut up," said Watt, raising the gun and making Jehoover cower.

Loray handcuffed Jehoover and tied him up while Watt supervised the tying of the knots. "No matter where you go, I'll find you," said Jehoover, "even to the ends of the earth. I'm going to find you and kill you. Do you hear? I'm going to kill you!"

"Maybe," said Watt, striking Jehoover on the head again. This time Jehoover fell off the bed and onto the floor. Watt took all of the money from Jehoover's pockets and a few dollars Loray was kind enough to give him. "Listen, man," said Watt, as he tied up Loray, "that fat piece of shit is tied good. But you can wiggle free in about an hour if you try"

"I *always* try," said Loray, smiling, "just like I *always* wait."

"Take it easy, Loray," said Watt.

"Good-bye, Dreamweaver," said Loray.

CHAPTER 25

▼

He was on his way to the subway, taking a side street to avoid the police, when he noticed a sign in front of a building: Church of the Warm Savior: Rev. Goosebite inside. But underneath some Haitian had scratched: Le Rat Mort intérieur.

Watt remembered Marv Goosebite off Central Park North. He was looking for the Church of the Warm Savior. Perry had also mentioned the Warm Savior, and Chump had told Watt to come to the Warm Savior if he wanted some fast money, and that was exactly what Watt needed now.

As he started to go into the church, he heard voices from the alley nearby. Peering around the building, he saw men loading boxes onto trucks. "You guys be c-c-c-c-careful with that," barked stuttering Chump. Watt avoided letting Chump see him, because he knew he would sell him out for the reward, and went into the church.

Although it was 1:00 a.m., the church was packed. Every pew held a parishioner. But what surprised Watt most was that people from all races and walks of life were there. Poor people and rich people knelt before the same altar, prompting Watt to wonder, *Could the Church of the Warm Savior truly be the new faith?*

Then Watt realized it was Christmas Eve. He had forgotten about Christmas. It had become just another day for him. *Perhaps that's why the Church of the Warm Savior is packed*, he thought. Marv Goosebite stood at the pulpit decked in a long white gown—before him sat a vat of liquid, behind him a crate of bread, ingredients for the Eucharist. The parishioners seemed impatient, the acolytes calm. Then Rev. Goosebite looked at the congregation with a twinkle in his eye and scratched himself once on the groin.

"Welcome, to the communion of the new human race," said Rev. Goosebite. "The journey upon which you now venture is the greatest one in life. You will not cross continents or voyage to distant shores—although you will feel as if you had. You will not take flight on a vessel called the Pequod or the Enterprise—although that should be its name. The name of your vessel is, appropriately, *you*—the individual. And for *you*, the individual, the struggle is always the same: God and the Devil tugging on each side with darkness, light, and freedom somewhere between.

"But *you*, the individual, also stand on a new threshold of Infinite possibility. And from this new threshold you will ponder vast menus of delight and, most importantly, choices. No responsibility shall be your legacy; no concern for the future will be your right.

"For some, it will be marijuana—but we don't have any here. For others, it will be crack, crank, cocaine, or heroin, which we have in abundance here. And for those who can afford it, we have special, journey-specific drugs, designed especially for *you,* the individual, who want to venture to new galaxies of the mind.

"So think about your freedom, and think about your drugs. They're all here for *you,* the individual, to choose. Just remember that it's out of doubt that conviction comes, out of struggle true victories emerge, and that the great events that have transformed the world began with *individuals,* like you, who were high—high on hopes, high on dreams, high on drugs.

"So fare forward, voyagers. You will not be the same person you were fifteen minutes ago. You will be higher. You will be freer. You will be part of the new human race."

As he finished one of the acolytes cried, "God is dope!" And the congregation of dopefiends cried in response, "Yes, God is dope!" Watt looked at them closely. They weren't just your lowlife dopefiends. Some of them, judging by their clothing and jewelry, seemed rich, sophisticated, and hip. Watt had always looked at dopefiends as freaks, not as part of a religion's design. But faith—or the space faith left when it evacuated their souls—lurked in their nodding heads as they prayed to plucked religion.

Then, from the pulpit, Rev. Goosebite nodded, and thuggish-looking acolytes positioned themselves in a triangle around the church. Waving their arms, they signaled to the dopefiends to get on line. One by one, each row was called; each dopefiend handed an acolyte something valuable—jewelry, electronics, art, or money—which other acolytes collected and carried through a side door adjacent to the alley where Chump had been loading the trucks.

From those three lines, a single one was formed that led to the altar where Rev. Goosebite stood in front of a golden barrel with his prelude to each dope-fiend's particular drug. As each dopefiend came forward and opened his mouth, Marv Goosebite reached into the barrel behind him and gave each a wafer with white powder dripping off, saying, "For the new race."

After receiving a wafer, dopefiend eyes rolled around in dopefiend heads as brains ceased to think. Some dopefiends began nodding even before they left the altar. One dopefiend, a former professional basketball player, leapt ten feet into the air as if he had swallowed a lightening bolt while another ran around the church full speed with smoke coming from the top of his head, and still others struggled to walk, taking one step forward and two to one side, then three back-wards, before falling down. And at the back of the church, the heroin addicts threw up.

It's all part of the economy, thought Watt, *the misery-money-drugs economy.* Looking on the scene, he wondered, *how did all these people get hooked?* Then he remembered what some ex-dopefiends told him.

"It's that first shot, first hit, or first toot that does it. You think you're immune and can beat it, or you want to prove that you're stronger than your friend who got hooked. But you're playing Russian roulette with your veins. And you will get hooked, and when you do, you spend every waking minute of every suffering day struggling to get dope."

The words of ex-dopefiends are written on tenement walls, but nobody reads them.

As Watt sat observing this drug Gehenna, his head began to spin. His body felt as if it were being lifted higher and higher. He wanted to sleep, but not in Hell. Then someone screamed "Devil!" and Watt wondered, which one—*racist, capitalist, Old Testament, or new? There are so many varieties of Devils today. Which Devil do you mean?*

1. Devil!: Something or someone to blame, as in The Devil made me do it. Or the Devil will be the death of me yet.

2. Devil: as in the Biblical arch fiend and purveyor of sin, such as the sin of slavery in Egypt, America, or anywhere in the world.

3. Devil: as a declaration or exclamation, as in: "The white man is the Devil!

4. Devil: as an ecclesiastical pawnbroker of fools and budget souls, as in, I sold my soul to the Devil at the crossroads.

These are all Devils, thought Watt, and there are others, too. Which Devil do you mean?

As the word *Devil* misted through the air as if sprayed from a giant atomizer, Watt's eyes drooped. His legs felt leaden. He was starving at the root.

Then someone yelled: "Is Scott illogical? Is Scott illogical?"

How do I know if Scott is logical when I don't even know Scott.

"Is Scott illogical? Is Scott illogical?" they repeated, as Watt's head continued to spin. A feeling of emptiness came over him and he stood up and got on line. "Refill," a voice said, "refill." He didn't want to become a dopefiend, but there he was on line. Soon he would be at the altar. Marv Goosebite would wed him to a drug. Then he would be not only a fugitive, but a dopefiend as well. At that moment, he thought about his mother, flat-veined and reeling in her punched hide. He imagined her carrying him through the tenements like some chicken in a basket and sobbing. Then he heard Grandma say, "If you hang out with dope-fiends, you *become* a dopefiend. So get out of there, son!"

With leaden feet, he got off line and staggered to the door. A thuggish-looking acolyte asked, "Whatchoo got? Where's your loot?"

"I have nothing," said Watt, turning his head away so as not to be recognized.

"Well you don't have a prayer," said the acolyte. "If you ain't got nothin' for the Church of the Warm Savior, we ain't got nothin' for you!" Along with another thuggish-looking acolyte, they grabbed Watt under his armpits and carried him to the door and threw him into the street. Watt didn't even feel any pain when he hit the pavement. All he felt was relief. He lay there breathing in fresh air and watching trucks roll out of the alley.

As he stood, continuing to feel relief and contemplating where to go next, several shots rang out. Bullets struck the church edifice above his head, like lightning, causing hunks of brick to explode.

Watt started running, but the bullets followed him like flies. Looking back at the gun flashes, Watt saw the shadows of Jehoover and Towntamer firing their guns while a little boy cringed behind them, pointing. Watt wondered who the child was as he continued running. He ran over to Central Park North and raced along the outer wall, thinking he had lost them. But a volley of shots told him he was wrong.

"To the ends of the earth!" he heard Jehoover yell. "I'm going to kill you!"

At that moment, Watt stopped running. He had three guns. He took out the .45 and fired, trying not to hit the kid. He needed practice though. Although his shots didn't come close, he continued firing until the .45 was empty and he threw it away. Then he leapt over the park wall and continued running.

CHAPTER 26

▼

The Pollution Plane flew above as he ran down Central Park's Heartbreak Hill. Jehoover and Towntamer were following in a car and firing at will. Watt fired back in a running gun battle that moved south through Central Park. As Watt ran, he saw people scrambling in the dark: a runner out for a jog; half-dressed couples evacuating the park; the homeless, the hapless, and the luckless, all scurrying in the dark.

Watt thought if he could make it downtown he could disappear into the crowds. But as he ran, he continued to wonder who that child could be. Then it hit him. It was Cecil. He had told Watt he was going to get it *big*. But Watt didn't realize *he* would be his ticket.

As he ran across a grassy field, he heard Jehoover's car engine roar from the road. Then he heard the door open and slam as a pair of feet stamped along the ground, following him across the grassy field. Towntamer was probably on foot, he thought, and trying to cut him off. Watt had to change direction to avoid the trap. A shot whistled by his head, and several shots came from the other direction. Watt cursed them and fired back. He fired until the .38 was empty. Then he tossed it away. He pulled out the .357 magnum and continued running and firing the gun. The recoil of the gun made his arm jump.

As he came off the grassy field to hit the road that lead to the Fifth Avenue side of the park, a voice said, "Drop the gun or I'll blow your black ass away!" Towntamer stood behind him. As Watt dropped the gun, Towntamer moved in and frisked him, saying, "I'd like nothing more than to shoot your black ass down, but Hoove said he wanted you alive." Then he called, "Hoove! We got him!"

Jehoover drove up in a black car, headlights glaring, and got out. He had a bandage wrapped around his head, and a sadistic glow was in his eyes as he approached Watt. Picking up the .357 magnum, he said, "Thanks for returning my favorite gun, Squirrel." He punctuated his words by striking Watt on the head with the pistol. Watt went down and came up bleeding as Jehoover said, "See, I didn't have to go to the ends of the earth to get you. I caught you in Central Park. Now, before I end your miserable life, tell me: Where are those pictures?"

"I don't have them," said Watt.

"You've got them!" snapped Jehoover. "You didn't have time to leave them anywhere. Did you search him?"

"No, I just frisked him," said Towntamer.

"What about my rights?" asked Watt.

"Dead men have no rights," said Jehoover as Towntamer laughed.

Then the car door on the passenger side opened, and a figure, approximately four and one-half feet tall, got out. Blinded by the headlights, Watt couldn't see him clearly at first. He expected to see Cecil, but as the figure got closer, Watt recognized him. It was Spud, the bully of his boyhood. Peering out from behind Jehoover's coattail, like a dog, Spud grinned at Watt, saying, "I told you I'd get you for what you did to me at P. S. 10. Perry and BADNIGGER are next.

"You little motherfucker!" said Watt.

"I *never* forgot what you did to me with those bats," said Spud. "Now we even. And I got $500,000 to boot."

"You better carry it in your shoe," said Watt.

"I'm gonna carry it anyway I want," said Spud.

"Shut up!" snapped Jehoover, making Spud cringe. "Go turn off the car headlights. We don't need any cameras, and we damn sure don't need any lights."

As Spud hopped over to the car, Jehoover put his gun up to Watt's head, saying, "I want those pictures now! You sure you didn't search him, Tame?"

"No, Hoove, you told me *you* wanted to search him. I just frisked him."

As Spud turned off the headlights, Watt realized he was standing under a park lamp's glow. Perhaps someone would see Jehoover kill him. Maybe, as the cliché goes, justice would prevail. But then he laughed to himself, thinking, *this is America. Justice is a joke.*

Spud returned to Jehoover's coattail, saying, "I turned the lights out like you told me to do."

Watt expected Jehoover to reach behind and pet Spud. Instead, he said, "He's a master of the obvious, isn't he, Tame," and the two Old Testament cops laughed, and Jehoover struck Watt again.

"This is personal," said Jehoover smiling. "Nobody's ever done what you did to me." Placing the gun against Watt's temple, Jehoover rifled through his pockets, saying, "Here they are." As Jehoover took the pictures from Watt's pocket, loose change flew out and landed on the grass. A few coins rolled into the dirt, and Spud dropped to all fours and crawled about retrieving them. Towntamer broke out laughing.

"I knew you didn't leave them anywhere," said Jehoover.

"What's that?" asked Towntamer.

"Never mind," said Jehoover. "Now I can take my time killing this coon."

"I'll tell you about those pictures," said Watt, looking at Towntamer. But Jehoover struck him before he could say a word. "This is *it* for you," said Jehoover, "last stop, Central Park."

"Everybody's got to die sometime," said Watt, slowly rising.

"Well your *sometime* is *now*," said Jehoover as Towntamer laughed and Spud giggled.

Suddenly, the sound of metal smashing glass was heard, and Jehoover's car's windshield exploded as the light atop the car went flying. Then all four tires collapsed.

"What's going on?" yelled Jehoover, as the car's hood sprung open.

"It's that crazy motherfucker with the broomsticks!" yelled Towntamer.

"Well shoot the cocksucker!" yelled Jehoover.

It was Ralph, mad Ralph who, like an Arthurian knight, beat the heads of cars with his metal broomstick—even police cars.

"Ralph," called Watt. "It's the Beast!"

"The Beast!" cried Ralph, from atop Jehoover's car. "I must fight the beast!"

"Shoot him!" yelled Jehoover, "before he destroys my car. First you though," he said, pointing the distracted gun back at Watt. But just as he was about to pull the trigger and Towntamer took aim to shoot Ralph, all the lights in New York City went out, and a collective yelp went through the air as someone cried, "BLACKOUT!"

"I've been waiting twenty years for this! It's CHRISTMAS!" cried a nearby voice, and in that instant, Watt dove to the side of the road as Jehoover fired his gun blindly and repeatedly in the dark.

"Hoove!" yelled Towntamer falling in one of Jehoover's blasts. "You shot me!" But Jehoover continued firing blindly, yelling, "Where are you, black mother-fucker?"

"You shot me! You shot me!" cried Spud rolling in darkness.

As Jehoover fired, screaming, "Your black ass is MINE!" Watt crawled away, dazed, thinking, *this is what I was rehearsing in the hospital.* When he got far enough away, he stood up. Bloody and staggering, he saw a car's lights stabbing through the darkness and followed. He put one foot in front of the other until he exited the park at 110th Street, back in Harlem. The traffic lights were out and cars, gridlocked in all directions, blew their horns frantically as impatient drivers tried to escape. A few pedestrians, exercising their fantasies to be traffic cops, tried to bring order but were ignored.

Watt was walking back toward his neighborhood when he saw a group of men congregating on a corner with flashlights, trying to help people. "Hey, you," one of them called, pointing a light at Watt. "What happened to *you?*"

"I don't understand," said Watt.

"What *happened* to you?"

"I don't know," said Watt.

"How'd you get so bloody?" one of the men asked.

"Police," said Watt.

"Did you hear that, Gus?" said one of the men. "It's that Rodney-King shit all over again."

"They think they can just grab one of us and beat the shit out of us any time they want. Billy, come and take a look at what they did to this brother."

"I've had enough of this, Gus!"

Watt was afraid they might recognize him. But the blood streaming down his face disguised him. *There's no better disguise than blood,* he thought.

"You said the police did this to you?" asked Gus, "Where?"

"In the park," said Watt.

"I'm sick and tired of this," said Gus. Then he told the story in a louder voice to other men nearby. "This brother was on his way to work, minding his own goddamn business, when the police grabbed him and beat the shit out of him. The only thing that stopped them from *killing* him was the Blackout."

A couple of big-butt sisters, carrying flashlights, antiseptic, and bandages came out of a nearby building. As they washed the blood off Watt, they told other people, "You should see what they did to this brother!"

"It's not as though he was a killer," said Billy, "somebody like Killer Watt. Now *there's* a motherfucker who *deserves* whatever he gets."

"Well I've had enough of this shit!" said Gus. "I think it's time we did something."

"I ain't got no job anyway!" said Billy. "So what do I have to lose?"

"Five minutes ... with guns!" said Gus, and the men dispersed as the women continued wiping the blood off Watt's face and trying to stop the bleeding.

"I've got to go!" said Watt.

"No, you stay here, mister," said one of the women.

"I ain't seen my man so fired up before," said the other woman, "since he lost his job at the plant."

"Did you see the look in Gus' eyes—the determination to do something about what happened to this brother?"

"It's the same thing that happened to his real brother."

"What happened to his brother?" asked Watt.

"The police beat him to death last year for runnin' a light. He was wrong, but you don't kill anybody for *runnin' a light!*"

"You know what this means?" asked one of the women.

"No, what?" returned the other.

"We might lose our men tonight."

The two women became silent. "I've got to go," said Watt, thinking, *I can't let these brothers get killed over me.*

"Wait!" said one of the women. "They're doing it for *you!*"

"They don't even know who *I* am," said Watt.

"Who are you?' asked one of the women, wiping his face. Then a car slowly turned the corner and its headlights momentarily shone on Watt's face, which was now clear of blood. One of the women let out a shriek and dropped the bandages while the other woman dropped the basin and cried, "It's him! It's Killer Watt!" As the two women ran, Watt stood up and walked further into darkness, hearing guns firing.

Passing a building on Lenox Avenue, he heard a voice above him ranting and saw a shadow standing on a fire escape, impotently raving in the dark.

"Jesus asked his Father to forgive you because you knew not what you did. But you never heard His Father's reply because he *never* forgave you. Your sins are *unforgivable.* You, who crucify Christ each day, behold His judgment! O Rough beast, this is your hour. *It's serpent time!*"

At 114th Street and Eighth Avenue, Watt saw a crowd of men, carrying a pawnshop's broken balls above their heads. The balls that had infected their streets and their lives were coated with tar and feathers, and the men threw them through the plate glass windows of store after store in a prelude to repeated looting.

Watt decided to avoid that crowd and walk over to Morningside Avenue. He was still groggy from Jehoover's beating and didn't believe his own eyes at first. Just outside Morningside Park, he saw several men in army fatigues pointing an anti-aircraft gun at the sky. They had two spotlights, which emitted two powerful columns of light that pierced the darkness and illuminated the night.

Watt wondered what they were trying to shoot down. Then he heard the Pollution Plane flying overhead and thought, *they've got to be kidding,* until he heard the rat-tat-tat-tat-tat of their weapon blasting at the sky. Now he could see the Pollution Plane caught in the spotlight's grip. It was trying to avoid the shells and escape Harlem. And Watt thought, *what's the use? That plane's been dropping gas on Harlem since I was a kid.*

Then Watt heard the plane's engine sputter and the men send up a cheer. A whine replaced the engine's hum as the plane plummeted and spun. In a tunnel of light, Watt saw the pilot bail out and his parachute open. He also saw the pilot get swept into a northeasterly wind that threatened to blow him further into Harlem. Watt watched the pilot pull frantically on his parachute cords, trying to go in the opposite direction. At some point he stopped pulling at the cords and started praying. Suddenly, a westerly wind gusted and blew the parachute toward Morningside Heights and safety.

To cheers and sighs, the men manning the gun watched the plane descend into Morningside Park. They braced themselves for a huge explosion. But the crop-duster plane landed haplessly in the mud with a plop and stood erect like a toy with its tail up.

CHAPTER 27

▼

"Going out tonight, handsome?"

"You don't even see my face."

"What does that matter?"

"You don't even know my name."

"I know you're good looking."

"Yeah, but I'm a woman, too, *bitch!*"

"It's Christmas—anything for money?"

Watt walked in darkness, still emerging from the delirium caused by Jehoover's pistol-whipping. He continued uptown, hearing the screams of those with nothing to gain pursued by those with nothing to lose. His feet, absent any prodding from his mind, carried him to 125th Street and Seventh Avenue.

On a dark corner, he saw a small crowd of shadows listening to Brother Kahlil. "I accuse the white man of *all* those things and more, much more!" he concluded."

Crossing Seventh Avenue, Watt saw a much larger crowd of shadows listening to another speaker. In a flashlight's glow, Watt recognized the student with all the books from the House of Styles Barber Shop and Beauty Salon. He was dressed in a white shirt, blue suit, and red tie. He spoke in a tone supported by knowledge and understanding. Concern for his people seemed to gush from his pores. "Now there's a difference between a black man and a nigger," he said. "And don't *you* ever forget it. A nigger is something a white man created!"

Cheers rose out of darkness. "Right on!" yelled an old Sixties revolutionary. But as the crowd cheered and clamored for more, a handful of black policemen appeared. Flashing a warrant for the student's arrest, they handcuffed him and took him away.

"What about *Kahlil?*" someone protested.

"You're free to listen to *him* anytime," said a policeman.

"There go the Uncle Toms," said the old revolutionary.

"They're not Uncle Toms," said a young man wearing a baseball cap backwards. "They're *Overtoms!*"

"What's an *Overtom?*" someone asked.

"Uncle Toms do what they're told. Overtoms anticipate what the white racist wants done before they're told to do it."

Meanwhile, Watt hid in a nearby doorway, hoping neither the police nor the Overtoms would see him. He knew they would catch him if he stayed in Harlem. He had to get out before power was restored. But without electricity, the trains weren't running. And if he caught a bus, someone would recognize him. There was only one solution: a gypsy cab. Unlicensed, unregulated, prepared to carry anybody (dead or alive) anywhere, gypsy cabs venture where licensed cabs fear to go. But, in a blackout, even a gypsy cab would be hard to find.

Watt finally saw a gypsy cab cruising down the street: steel-clad, with bullet-proof glass, a Plexiglas partition between the driver and passenger—definitely a gypsy cab. Other people signaled the cab, too, waving their arms and yelling, "Hey, brother!" But when the cabbie stopped and told them he wanted one hundred dollars to take them wherever they wanted to go in Manhattan, they all jumped back and cursed him. Then the cab stopped in front of Watt. Fortunately, he still had the cash he got from Sylvia and Loray, not to mention the money from Jehoover's pockets. Watt agreed to the cab driver's outrageous price. "Hold on," said the cabbie. "Before you get into *my* cab, tell me is that blood dry?"

"Yeah, it's dry," said Watt.

"It better be," said the cabbie, throwing a lever that unlocked the cab's doors. As soon as Watt got in the cab, the cabbie threw another lever that locked the doors.

"Where to?" asked the cabbie

"Sutton Place," said Watt.

"Where?" asked the cabbie, as if he was hard of hearing.

"Sutton Place," said Watt.

"What are you, a butler?" asked the cabbie.

"No, I *live* there," said Watt, angry at the cabbie's assumptions.

"Listen, man, I ain't got no time to be messin' around with you when I could be makin' some real money. Blackouts only come every ten or twenty years."

"I *live* there!" snapped Watt, taking out one hundred dollars and holding it in the air.

"Put it in the slot," said the cabbie.

Without traffic lights, a cab ride that should have taken twenty minutes took an hour. On the way downtown, Watt heard screams from several posh neighborhoods where white folks were raising hell.

Finally, they arrived at Von Geber's townhouse on Sutton Place. Scrutinizing the neighborhood, the cabbie asked, "You *really* live here?!"

"That's right," said Watt.

"If I had known that," said the cabbie, "the price would have been two-hundred dollars for *you.*"

"Open the doors and let me out of here!" snapped Watt.

"I would never have thought you were rich," said the cabbie, "not the way you were walkin' around Harlem with blood on your clothes."

"Live and learn," said Watt.

"Call me if you need me again, uh, brother," said the cabbie, handing Watt a business card. "I sure would like to talk with *you* about how you got your money. Just remember the price is two hundred dollars next time, blackout or no blackout. And I don't haul bodies or stolen goods on Sunday. But for a price, I can recommend someone."

"I'm not your brother!" said Watt, climbing from the cab and slamming the cab door. He tore up the business card, saying, "Fuck you!"

"Fuck you, too!" yelled the cabbie.

As Watt opened the door to Dr. Otto Von Geber's townhouse, using the spare key he had made and kept for emergencies, he saw the cabbie still shaking his head in disbelief before driving off. Watt entered the house, which was dark, save for a candle that glowed from one of the upstairs rooms. Quietly, Watt crept up the stairs. He was surprised when he heard the cuckoo clock in the den hiss and a new bird cry, "Ordnung!"

He knew that Erika, Fritz, and any millionaires in the house were probably asleep. Dr. Von Geber was probably in the den, talking on the phone, reading five books at once, or just sitting in his temperature-controlled recliner, thinking.

Watt didn't know what he would say to Dr. Von Geber and started to rehearse what he would tell him in his head. "I didn't kill Ainsley Bridges. Everybody thinks I did. But *you* know better. *You* know he died because he ate that Indian. I shouldn't have to go to jail or get the Big Needle for what *he* did to *him-*

self. But no one will believe me. It's too fantastic. So I need some money to get out of the country." *Yes, that's what I'll tell him.* Then he heard the crack of Howe's whip and Camalian scream in ecstasy.

Reaching the den door, Watt heard Dr. Von Geber talking. At first he thought someone was in the room with him. Then he realized Dr. Von Geber was talking to someone on the phone. "As I said to you before," said Dr. Von Geber, "all you have to do is use the right spin at the appropriate time. People are so overwhelmed with information today that they no longer can discern truth from lies. Remember, the communications revolution is also the golden age of propaganda. Keep the people saturated with information and you will keep them crippled and controlled."

Whoever Dr. Von Geber was talking with must have invoked history because Dr. Von Geber said, "What made America great was the founding fathers' ability to rationally create and dramatize public illusions and personal lies, most of which Hollywood now maintains. No, no, no. That is not necessary. Perhaps thirty years ago, we had to worry about women, minorities, and poor whites starting a revolution. We do not have to worry about them anymore. They have lost *all* initiative."

Then Von Geber laughed, as if the plight of women, minorities, and poor whites was the funniest thing he could think of. "During the Sixties," he continued, "we created programs to help some; we gave others welfare. But overall, we created dependency relationships. Now all we have to do is withdraw *all* programs, *all* assistance, and the dogs will fall flat on their faces. They had what a former assistant of mine—a detestable scumbag!—called their *Devil's Interval.* Now it's over. We do not need to worry about them anymore. We can continue to cut back all assistance. And without help, most of them will retrogress to where they were two hundred years ago.

"No. We do not need to use the police or the military to control them. We can continue to give them drugs that will make them kill each other at higher rates. And their drug-related crimes will get them imprisoned and make the middle class issue more calls for law and order, which will allow us to gain more control. Of course, we must use the fear of terrorism to the maximum. What civil liberties the fear of crime doesn't erode the fear of terrorism will.

"Bear in mind we have a society that could go on functioning economically with just a fraction of the population. We do not need slave labor the way America did in the Eighteenth and Nineteenth Centuries. Nor do we need so many workers today as we did in the first half of the Twentieth Century. Get rid of them. Labor is cheaper in foreign markets. And the Gross Domestic Product of the United States will soar. Don't worry about the poor or skilled workers who will be forced to take lower-paying jobs.

"Let me put it to you another way. If we were to put one-tenth of one percent of the population we need under a geodesic dome, and let the rest of the nation blow up, our society would function even better economically with the use of automated technology that we cannot use today because of unions and worker displacements.

"In short, we do not need *the people* any more for anything. *We* are the people. And without communism to hinder us, we can at last create the kind of state the Fuhrer envisioned. America will be the *Fourth* Reich!"

Leaning against the door jamb, Watt's heart was palpitating. He had heard more evil in a matter of minutes than he dreamed possible in a lifetime.

And I come from Harlem, he thought, *innocent, expendable, Harlem.* Now, for the first time in his life, he knew what he had to do. He would wait until Dr. Von Geber got off the phone. Then he would go into the den and kill him with his bare hands. *Dr. Otto Von Geber must die,* he thought, *so that the world can remain free.*

As he waited for Von Geber to get off the phone, a hand touched his shoulder and he spun around. "Shhhh," whispered Erika Von Geber, placing a finger over his lips. She was wearing a sexy negligee and staring deeply into Watt's eyes. "How are you? I've been *so* worried about you," she said, pouting thick lips that looked as if they had been injected with collagen, which she coated with a bright red lipstick. "Did the police hurt you? Come with me. I have something for you—your Christmas present."

"A small tight thing I hope," said Watt, thinking, *what better way to take revenge on the Devil before you kill him than by first fucking his wife.*

Taking Watt by the hand, Erika led him up the stairs and down the hallway to her bedroom. As she walked in front of him, switching her thighs, she looked back at Watt, extending her tongue and making sizzle sounds with her saliva. He never noticed it before. *She's got a big ass for a white woman.*

"What about Dr. Von Geber?" asked Watt.

"He will not come in," said Erika. "He *never* comes to my bedroom any more."

"Are you sure?" asked Watt.

"Yes, I'm sure. "But first," she said, pointing to the bathroom, "take a shower and clean the blood off."

The shower refreshed him. When he came out of the bathroom, Erika had a couple of martinis waiting. After he sipped a martini, Erika asked, "Would you like to get high?"

"On *what?*" asked Watt, and she pulled out a cigar-size reefer, the biggest he had seen in years, and said, "This will get you in the mood to fuck."

"That's okay," said Watt. "I'll pass."

Then Erika pulled out a large cookie tin filled with cocaine, saying, "I know you'll like this. It's the best."

"No thanks," said Watt, thinking, *I had no idea she was a reefer-smoking coke head.*

"What's wrong?" asked Erika.

"I don't do drugs," said Watt.

"You *don't!*" said Erika. "I thought *everybody* in Harlem did."

Watt just looked at her, thinking, *more assumptions. Let me screw her, kill her husband, and leave.*

"I guess I will have to indulge alone," said Erika. Within minutes, she smoked the reefer to a butt, snorted up half the cocaine in the cookie tin, and downed both martinis.

"What part of Mars did *you* come from?" asked Watt.

"Venus," said Erika, taking off her negligee. "Give me animal ecstasy," she said. "Fuck me like the lowest whore in creation. I'll do whatever you want." As Watt entered her, and they started to make love, Erika reached out and slapped him—hard. *What the fuck is she doing?* wondered Watt. He slapped her back hard, and watched her face turn red with excitement as she fell into a state of total exultation. Her eyes rolled back into her head, revealing the whites only, and she started screwing like a nymph on death row. In the throes of passion, she moaned, "What are you doing in that black body?"

"Suffering," he said, as she drove her nails into his back, and he screamed.

As he fought to hold back orgasm, they twisted and turned in every position for what seemed hours. Then it was time. Together, they approached the precipice where body-madness overwhelms mind-saneness, and couples dangle on a cliff before letting go. Simultaneously, they came together, screaming and falling further than that archangel fell. Gasping for air, they eventually caught their breaths.

As Watt lay there, he heard the crack of Howe's whip again and Camalian scream in ecstasy.

"I'll be right back," said Erika, getting up and putting on a robe.

"Where are you going?" asked Watt.

"Don't worry, I'll be right back," she whispered.

While she was out of the room, Watt leaned up in bed, wondering if the door would suddenly burst open and Dr. Von Geber and the police would rush in. Feeling vulnerable, he thought of several movie scenes in which men were killed in bed after screwing.

Erika came back a few minutes later, carrying a little wooden box. "How would you like to do something *really* kinky?" she asked.

"I need a little rest first," said Watt. "That marathon session wore me out."

"This will be different," said Erika. "It's kinky."

"I'm not into the kinky stuff," said Watt.

"I think you would like this," said Erika, opening the box. Peering into it, Watt saw an insect, a *live* insect, crawling around the sides of the box, trying to find the exit.

"What the fuck is that?" he asked, closing the box.

"Something to make us feel good together," said Erika.

"How?" he asked.

"I'm going to put it in my vagina," said Erika, "then you're going to fuck me, and it's going to play music on both our organs and drive us crazy."

"What!" snapped Watt.

"Think of it," said Erika, "a man and a woman, the highest forms of life, making love with an insect, the lowest form of life."

"Not *me!*" said Watt. "I've heard of some freaky shit before—people whipping and peeing on each other—but this is the *freakiest* shit I've ever heard. No, baby, I don't go that way."

"I didn't think someone from Harlem was afraid to do *anything* kinky," she said.

"It ain't about *fear*," said Watt. "It's about *normalcy!*"

"But I thought...."

"You thought *wrong*," said Watt.

"You are so conservative," said Erika.

"I guess so," said Watt.

"Then let's do it the old-fashioned way," said Erika.

"I'm a little tired," said Watt.

"That doesn't matter," she said. Dropping to her knees, she gave him a blow job that would have revived King Tut. Then they started fucking again.

After the moans, groans, and orgasms, Watt didn't plan to fall asleep. He had planned to remain awake and take care of Dr. Von Geber. But what man can remain awake after a couple of powerful orgasms with a woman who qualifies as a super freak? He awoke later that morning, perspiring under an electric blanket that made him feel too warm. He felt as if he were back in the hospital again, attached to life-support equipment. He even imagined he heard faint blips moving across dark screens.

Then he looked at Erika. She was wide-awake, lying on her side and staring at him from the other end of the bed. She had placed her body as far away from his as she could. "Good morning," she said with a forced smile. "Merry Christmas!"

"Don't you feel it?" he asked.

"Feel what?" she responded.

"The electricity," he said.

"Oh yes, Watt, you were magnificent!"

"I don't mean *that* electricity," he said. "I mean the electricity in the bed." Climbing out of bed, he threw back the covers, hearing Erika yell, "Are you mad?!" He could feel wires in the blanket. But the electricity he had felt was coming from somewhere else. "Get out of the bed!" he ordered. Then he turned over the mattress, dumping Erika onto the floor. "I demand that you stop this at once!" she yelled, jumping up. "Let's go back to bed."

Finally, he found them, dozens of multicolored wires that ran beneath the mattress. They met in a single cable that traveled from the head of the bed along the wall. Thinking, *I should have known*, Watt followed the cable until it disappeared behind a full-length mirror on the wall across from the bed. He was still thinking, *I should have known, a*s he ran his hands all over the wall around the mirror, and Erika commanded him to "Come back to bed this minute! I want to fuck your brains out some more!"

Then he found a wall panel next to the mirror that receded to his touch.

"Did you hear me?!" yelled Erika, as a motor began to whine and the mirror slid away.

Sipping a cup of coffee, Dr. Otto Von Geber sat in a little room behind a thick Plexiglas wall. Wires, attached to his arms, legs, head, and chest, were plugged into a large electronic console.

"You lowlife, dog!" yelled Watt. Picking up a bedroom chair, he threw it at the Plexiglas shield. The chair bounced away without even scratching the Plexiglas. "You lowlife motherfucker!" repeated Watt.

"Let's not be so free with words," laughed Dr. Otto Von Geber from behind the partition. "You once told me about a saying you have in Harlem, Watt—how some husbands when told of their wives' indiscretions shrug it off by saying, *He can't wear it out*. Well, Watt, *you* can't wear it out. Erika will bathe and wash you away, we will be man and wife as always, and I will have completed a book called

The Nature of Jealousy that will shock the world. You have helped greatly with the final chapter, *Sex and the Race Card*, which details the emotions white husbands feel when they find out black men are screwing their wives. I have felt the complete range of emotions, thanks to you. Your assistance has been invaluable. Of course, you will not be paid for your services, but your contribution is appreciated."

Even as Dr. Von Geber spoke, Watt could hear the shower running in the bathroom and Erika scrubbing herself clean.

"You Nazi excrement!" yelled Watt. "I'm going to kill you!" Then Watt picked up another chair and threw it at the Plexiglas wall. Once again, the chair bounced away. Then Watt banged on the Plexiglas, repeating, "I'm going to *KILL* you!"

"I don't think so," said Dr. Von Geber, smiling. He hit a button on the console. A telephone's dial tone blared from a loud speaker, then someone picked up the phone on the other end of the line, and said, "Captain Jehoover here."

"Captain Jehoover, this is Dr. Otto Von Geber. I'm calling to tell you Watt is here!"

CHAPTER 28

▼

I should have known I couldn't outsmart Dr. Von Geber, thought Watt as he ran across 59th Street, hearing sirens and seeing rich people freeze in their tracks and cry "It's Killer Watt!" before running into high-rise buildings and seeking protection from husky doormen. Watt felt like a monster in a grade "B" horror film.

"I'm innocent!" he said to an attractive white woman coming out of an exclusive building for a morning jog. "Nobody's innocent," she quipped, and before Watt could say another word, the black doorman blew his whistle louder than a lead trumpet player during Amateur Night at the Apollo Theater.

Now Watt was on Park Avenue and running south. The sirens were getting closer, and all he could think of was, *I should have known Dr. Von Geber had it all planned. He knew I'd be back. They set me up. I was a research project for his next book, a guinea pig. I should have known.*

But before that thought could repeat itself, a hat wafted down from a building and struck him on the head—not hard enough to knock him down or stop him, just enough to make him look up as others fell. He put up his arms and covered his head as they fell by the hundreds, blotting out the sky. "It's raining bowler hats!" he cried from beneath a haberdashery heap.

Then Chubby Hands, Sir Ainsley Bridges' British solicitor, stepped from a nearby building with a cigar in his mouth. "Sir Ainsley instructed me to deliver these to you. Now that I've done my duty and carried out his last request, I hope they *burn* you for what you did, you blackguard."

He tipped his bowler hat and said something else, but Watt didn't hear him because he was up and running again. As sirens blared, Watt's legs carried him faster. He felt like a passenger in his own body, looking at buildings and people flash by.

Now he saw 42nd Street. The silhouetted pictures of copulating couples gyrating on theater marquees got bigger as he ran towards them. Then he passed Times Square and turned onto Eighth Avenue where hands dicing in doorways moved at break neck speeds.

As he ran by Rusty's Peep Show Joint, he heard a warbling voice call "Watt," and he stopped to look around. He started to run again when that voice called "Watt" again. Then he spotted him. It was Rusty, crossing Eighth Avenue, carrying some fast food in a plastic container.

"What do you want?" asked Watt, breathing deeply.

"Get inside if you want to live," said Rusty.

"Why should I trust *you?*" asked Watt.

"Cause I may be the *only* friend you have," said Rusty.

"You helped *kill* the only friend I had," said Watt.

"I understand how you feel," said Rusty. "But believe me, man, no one is *sorrier* about what happened to Perry than me. If I had known what that bitch did to him, I would have called off Mean Joe Vine. I wanted my money, but I didn't want it *that* bad."

Then Watt heard sirens coming closer, and Rusty repeated, "Get inside." But it was too late. Six police cars pulled up. As Watt ran inside, Jehoover climbed from one of the cars and fired a shot at Watt, yelling, "He's mine! He killed my partner! You guys stay out here while I get him!"

Running into darkness, Watt heard Jehoover's heavy footsteps trailing behind. Momentarily, the Black Hole flicked on the light, and in that instant, Watt saw her lying on a cot. Looking like an alien repository for fear, she was fat and unattractive. She smiled at Watt, and then flicked out the light, sending the peep show joint back into darkness.

"Squirrel," called Jehoover entering the darkness. "This is it! End of the line. I'm going to kill you! Towntamer, the only good nigger I ever knew, is dead … because of you. Now he's waiting—Do you hear?—For *you!*"

Watt didn't make a sound. He tried to remember what he had seen in the room when the lights were on, something that he could use as a weapon.

"You know something, Squirrel," said Jehoover, "when you're dead, I'm going to clear up a lot of murders by pinning them on *you.* I'm going to make you the *greatest* killer the world's ever seen.

"People will talk of Killer Watt the way they talk of John Dillinger. You'll be a legend. I guess you know what that'll make *me*—the cop who killed the legend:

Killer Watt, the most dangerous man alive. And don't worry, Squirrel, you'll have a gun. I'll plant one on you when you're dead."

As Jehoover finished talking, Watt heard the Black Hole let out a sigh. Then she punctuated her sigh with a sob. And Jehoover asked, "Is that you or that freaky bitch?"

But Watt didn't answer. He continued feeling his way in darkness, searching for something he could use to split Jehoover's head open. Aside from a cot and a few pieces of furniture, Rusty's Peep Show Joint was devoid of anything he could use.

"Squirrel, I'm getting tired," said Jehoover. "You know we white people aren't as comfortable as you niggers in the dark. So why don't you just end it now. You can't escape. Face it. I am the law, and I've passed a death sentence on you. So get your ass over here and accept your punishment.

"I tell you what, Squirrel. If you come out now I'll make it quick. And I promise you, no one will abuse your body when you're dead."

Suddenly, Watt realized Jehoover's voice was projecting away from him, not toward him, which meant somehow Watt had managed to get *behind* Jehoover. If he could stay behind him, he might be able to grab his fat ass from the rear. Removing both shoes, Watt waited for his opportunity to attack. The sound of Jehoover's voice would be his guide.

"Well, what do you say, Squirrel," called Jehoover. "Is it a deal? Don't keep me waiting all day, boy."

Now Watt sensed Jehoover was five or six feet away. If he said just a few more words, Watt would target him. "See, that's the problem with you people. You never know a good deal when you see one."

With less than two feet between them, Watt reared back to throw a punch that would kill Jehoover. "Alright, the deal's off," said Jehoover as Watt's blow landed and he tried to grab Jehoover's neck and break it. But the punch didn't land squarely and Watt missed snatching his head. Jehoover jerked away, lost his balance, and stumbled across the room, firing his gun before hitting the floor.

The shots missed Watt, who crouched on the ground, knowing he had missed his opportunity. For a moment he thought of surrender, of accepting Jehoover's bullet in the head. Then he thought, *No way! I'll fight you to the end!*

Suddenly, he heard Jehoover scream and wondered what was going on. Jehoover sounded as if he had fallen into a trap set by the Tuxedo Muggers. Then Watt thought, *it's a trap alright, for me.*

But as Jehoover's screams grew more horrific, Watt realized they were real. And beneath the screams Watt could hear a gnawing, growling sound—like a beast devouring its prey.

Finding the theater exit, Watt groped through a door toward sunlight. Momentarily, he was blinded by the light as voices said, "Move and you're dead, Killer Watt."

"I'm not moving," said Watt.

"You better not, you black son of a bitch!" said a red-faced cop holding a shot gun. Twenty policeman surrounded Watt while a crowd of spectators stood in the background, and the media had several cameras recording his capture.

"Where's Captain Jehoover?" asked a cop as they threw Watt to the ground and handcuffed him.

"If it wasn't for all these people watching, you'd be dead meat," whispered another policeman, frisking Watt. When he finished, he gave Watt a kick in the ribs as jeers and boos came from the crowd. "Hey buddy, I'll be a witness in your police brutality case," called a spectator. My name is—" But Watt could not hear his name.

"Where's Captain Jehoover?" another cop asked him. "Did you kill him, bastard?"

"I didn't do a thing to that closet fag!" said Watt, and another policeman kicked him again, drawing more boos and jeers from the crowd.

After scrambling around like sheep in the desert, a special SWAT team advanced into the theater. Watt heard their weapons firing repeatedly as Rusty cried "No! Don't shoot her!" and a wail went up through the crowd, followed by, "They've killed the Black Hole! They've killed the Black Hole!" When the SWAT team came out, the forensic team went in. One SWAT team member stood trembling in shock. Another cop, a white boy in his twenties, kicked Watt repeatedly, saying, "It's *your* fault!"

As more jeers and boos came from the crowd, Watt yelled, "Yeah! Kick my ass, whitey! You've been doing it for four-hundred years! Well I'm used to it now! I don't even feel the pain anymore! You're playing my song!"

Greeting the kicks as if they were old friends, Watt looked up and saw Rusty stagger from the theatre. Letting out a squall, Rusty collapsed on the pavement. Beating the cold concrete with his bare hands, he cried, "Oh God! It's Christmas, and I've lost everything!"

CHAPTER 29

▼

Although Watt felt sorry for the Black Hole, whom newspapers described as the brutal accomplice of the greatest mass murderer in history, he didn't feel sorry for Rusty and found himself thinking, *So what! Eventually, everybody loses everything. All you can do is try to win while you lose. We're all going to die.*

Death now came to Watt as a process that would lead him down a corridor and strap him to a stretcher for the Big Needle. Some people called it justice because it involved the law and was done by a book, but what book, whose law and, for that matter, whose justice? Millions of men and women languish in prisons—the victims of fate, politics, their own corrupt personalities and, yes, injustice. No one knows who owns this circus we call the legal system anymore.

The authorities took Watt to an interrogation room and rattled off new charges and details about crimes he was *supposed* to have committed. It was Jehoover's script without Jehoover. One hundred murders were laid at his feet. Quickly, conservative politicians used Watt as an example of liberal policies run amuck. The crime victims and the accusers had one thing in common, however. They were all white. Of course, the Overtoms were there, too. They're always there, shaking their heads as if they're ashamed and asking any white person who would listen, "Why did he have to be black?" That was their way of saying, "We're not all like that, particularly me. I'm different."

But white people kill each other all the time, and when they go off, they really go off. Look at all the mass murderers in U.S. History. Few were black. And let's not forget about the white people who kill their own children even, and then say some strange and mysterious black man did it, which brings to mind that painful and satirical joke a black newspaper columnist once made: Any white person who wants to commit a murder, the columnist said, can dial 1-800-BLAME-A-NIG-GER, and a black man will be furnished and framed (false witnesses sold separately).

Now Watt had been framed, and he was going to be executed for crimes he did not commit. He needed a team of super lawyers to beat the raps and avoid the Big Needle. "Where's my lawyer?" he asked a guard standing in front of his cell. "Call Johnny," he implored, until one of the black guards, an Overtom to be sure, said, "Ain't you heard? Johnny's dead! No super trial for you, just the Big Needle. Besides, a lawyer for you would just be a waste of taxpayers' money. Everybody knows you're guilty."

"Give me a lawyer!" snapped Watt. "It's my right!"

He finally got his lawyer. Without looking at his face, he could tell he was a prim and proper attaché-carrying-African-American man who was probably born in Washington, D.C. (the capital for Uncle Toms and Overtoms), and who, under different circumstances, Watt would have dismissed as a typical uptight, bourgeois Negro for whom he had no use. But when he looked at his face, he recognized him immediately. So when he said, "My name is S. Hamilton Burrows, and I've been appointed to represent you as counsel in court," the words weren't necessary.

"How's it going, Burrows?" asked Watt. "It's nice to see you again, especially when you're not running from—what's his name—oh yeah, Colly."

"Have we met before?" asked Burrows.

"You damn right we met before," jumped Watt. "We've met all over Harlem. We even talked."

"I don't know what you're talking about," said Burrows.

"I first saw you on the staircase," said Watt. "Rosaline was pulling a train on the *Times*."

"Who?" asked Burrows.

"Rosaline," said Watt. "We met twice again when Colly, was chasing you through Harlem."

"Who?" asked Burrows.

"You sound like a stuttering owl!" snapped Watt. "Colly, that's who. Yeah, we met before!"

Burrows glanced over his shoulder at the guard outside the cell as if he were going to call him and say "Get me out of here!" But instead he maintained his cool and calmly said, "You've got the wrong guy. I think you've confused me with my twin brother, S. Hartford Burrows. He's always hanging around strange places. He gets his kicks that way, watching. Our family has tried to help him and get him to stop before it's too late, but we haven't been successful."

"Let me see your brief case," demanded Watt. S. Hamilton Burrows held out his brief case, and Watt saw immediately that it wasn't the motor-powered attaché case he had seen before. Saying, "Okay," Watt sat back down as Burrows continued, "All I know about you is what I got from your file. Since it's clear you can't afford counsel, the court has appointed me to represent you and give you the best legal defense possible. But let me repeat, *we've never met before*, and I don't know any of those people you just mentioned."

"Sorry. My mistake," said Watt, thinking, *if that's the game he wants to play, I'll play along. He's middle-class and probably hates me. He's probably ashamed of me, too. Maybe the crackers have sent him to help fry me. I'll play along for now with the game.*

Then S. Hamilton Burrows laid out a plan for Watt's defense.

"But I'm not crazy," said Watt. "I'm innocent! I told you! Bridges ate Laughing Gravy who tore him up from inside and eventually climbed out through his guts and …"

"Do you expect me to tell a jury that and claim you're sane?" asked Burrows. "That might be proof that you're *insane*. Please don't insult my intelligence or the intelligence of a jury with a story like that. Do you expect people to believe that the Chairman of the Board of the Saxon American Corporation was a *cannibal?*"

"But he was!" snapped Watt. "I used to stop him from eating *himself!*"

"Forget Laughing Gravy—and forget the cannibal stuff," said Burrows in exasperation. "We're going with the insanity defense."

"But I'm not crazy!" repeated Watt.

"You're either *crazy* or you're *dead*," said Burrows. "And we're *not* going to put you on the witness stand."

"Why not?" jumped Watt. "I've got shit to say!"

"And the prosecutor, James Dumson, III, has a lot to say, too. He'll kill you in the cross-examination. Your chances are better if we keep you *off* the stand. Besides, you're . ."

"I'm not crazy!" said Watt.

After weeks of preparation, including jury selection, the trial, initially hailed as the new trial of the century by newspapers and media outlets, got downgraded to "just a trial" because Burrows found evidence that Watt could not have committed ninety-nine of the one-hundred murders with which they charged him. They didn't charge him with Jehoover's death either. The Black Hole accidentally ate the Old Testament cop, a coroner's inquest ruled. The single crime, with which

Watt was charged, however, was the murder of Ainsley Bridges, the founder, Chairman of the Board, and CEO of the Saxon-American Corporation.

Now the policemen guarding Watt looked at him from new heights of rage, as if he had cheated the system. Disappointed media stars got reassigned. A second wave of lesser reporters took over press coverage. Watt's headlines shrank. *The Greatest Mass Murderer in History* headline, which appeared on page one in *THE BARELY NEWS*, got downgraded to *Poor Black Man Kills Rich White Man Who Helped Him* on page eight.

On the day before the trial, Burrows brought Watt a suit, saying, "The jury will identify with you if you *look* middle-class."

"Why should I have to *look* middle-class to get justice?" asked Watt.

"I agree," said Burrows, "but that's the way things are." He also warned Watt not to stare or scowl at any jurors, but not to avoid looking them in their eyes. "Act as if you *believe* you're innocent," cautioned Burrows. "But occasionally stare into space so they think you *might* be a little crazy, too. Oh! And don't forget to smile occasionally. I'll signal you with a tap on the desk when it's time to smile." As Burrows said the word smile, Watt thought, *yes, the smile is the main ingredient in the Great American Cook Book of Uncle Tom Recipes—Polly want a smile!*

On the day of the trial, Watt was led into the Manhattan Criminal Court building in shackles and held in a chamber outside the courtroom. At a signal from the bailiff, a Marshall removed the shackles and led Watt into the courtroom to jeers and boos from onlookers.

Burrows greeted him, shaking his hand and saying, "Let's win this." As Watt sat down, he looked around the courtroom and saw some people he knew: Mrs. Dawson and Mrs. Saunders were there, and Sylvia was there, too. Her face was still badly marked by the fall, and her arm was in a cast. She was clearly pregnant now. Her stomach, which contained his baby, jutted out through her clothes. She had refused to testify for either the defense or the prosecution, which wanted her to tell the court how Watt had thrown her down the stairs at Grant's Tomb to abort their baby. Instead, she just sat there looking sad, rubbing her stomach or turning sideways from the occasional baby kick in the womb. *That baby's kicking her ass from the inside already,* thought Watt.

Then Watt looked at the jury, thinking, *an integrated lynch mob, a mixed bag of men and women from different ethnic groups, ready to show how impartial they are by killing me.* One of the jurors, a strong-looking black woman, scowled at Watt and seemed as if she wanted to spring from the jury box and tear him to pieces.

The reporter from *Chronos* and his photographer were there with other media vultures. In the front row of the visitors section sat twenty cookie-cut white men with their arms folded. Each wore a red tie and a dark blue suit with a white carnation in the lapel, and each scowled at Watt with hate in his eyes. *What are these guys, an ivy league street gang?* wondered Watt.

"The Board of Directors for the Saxon-American Corporation," said Burrows.

"They don't scare me," said Watt, smiling.

But when the clerk made everyone rise for the entrance of the judge, saying, "The Honorable Willard B. Camalian presiding," Watt's cool demeanor caught fire. "How the fuck did *he* become a judge?!" yelled Watt.

"Calm down!" said Burrows, grabbing Watt by the wrist.

"But I used to slap that motherfucker!" cried Watt.

"Calm down. Don't overdo it!" said Burrows.

"That's the fastest outburst I've ever witnessed in one of my courtrooms," said Judge Willard Camalian, taking his seat. "The defendant is to be commended for setting a new record," Judge Camalian added, as two husky bailiffs rushed to Watt's side. "But he is warned about any further such behavior. If there is another similar display of emotion, I will have the defendant removed from the courtroom and he will watch all proceedings on a television monitor. I hope I've made myself clear."

"Yes, Your Honor," said Burrows.

"The jury will disregard all words uttered by the defendant during his emotional outburst," added Judge Camalian. "Let's proceed." He nodded his head, and the board members of the Saxon-American Corporation nodded back.

Both sides made opening statements about why they were there, what they intended to prove, and how *their* proof would convince the jury of Watt's guilt or innocence. Through it all, Sylvia continued to cry, prompting a man seated beside her to ask, "Lady, where'd you get so many tears?"

Then the prosecution and defense got down to petty squabbling, the he-said-she-said variety that infects the American judicial system. The prosecution went first.

"Your honor, I'd like to call Mr. Louis Kleindeck to the stand. After they swore Kleindeck in, the prosecutor asked, "Mr. Kleindeck, were you the defendant's principal at Nixon High School?"

"Yes, I was."

"is there anything you remember about the defendant when he was a student at your sschool?"

"Objection, your honor," said Burrows. "The prosecution is asking for speculation on the part of a witness whose testimony is not germane to the case."

"Objection sustained," said Judge Camalian.

"What do you remember about the defendant's behavior when he was a student at Nixon High?"

"In the twenty-five years I've been the principal at Nixon High, we've only had one serious disturbance—a riot—in which several teachers and students were injured. And Watt caused it."

"How did he cause it, Mr. Kleindeck?"

"By standing in front of my school with a bullhorn and espousing communist philosophy," said Kleindeck, sending a stir through the courtroom.

"I knew that bastard was a communist!" cried one of the Saxon-American Corporation board members.

"Order in the court!" said Judge Camalian as Dumson continued.

"In your recollections of the defendant would you describe him as mentally ill?"

"Objection!" called Burrows. "Witness is being asked to give a professional opinion on the defendant's mental health, for which he is neither competent nor qualified to do."

"Sustained," said Judge Camalian.

"How would you describe the defendant's moral character?" asked Dumson.

"Objection!" called Burrows. "The witness is being asked to make a judgment on the moral character of the defendant, something for which no one is qualified to do. Furthermore, the witness has been out of touch with the defendant since the defendant was a boy and can in no way testify on the defendant's character as an adult."

"Sustained," said Judge Camalian, adding, "The jury is instructed to disregard the prosecution's entire line of questioning with this witness and everything the witness has said in response."

"That will be all," said Dumson with frustration.

"Just a minute," said Burrows, rising for cross-examination. "During the years when the defendant was a student at your school, did you ever call him a *nigger?*"

"Never!" snapped Kleindeck. "I supported the Civil Rights Movement."

"Well suppose a couple of young black boys had disrespected you and treated you as if you were anything but the principal of Nixon High, do you think you could call them *nigger* under *those* conditions?"

"I would never do such a thing," said Kleindeck.

"Objection!" called Dumson. "Counsel is trying to make the witness speculate on behavior he has already said he neither committed nor condoned."

"Withdrawn," said Burrows. "Did you have any kind of confrontation with Perry Lamprey and the defendant?"

"No, never," said Kleindeck.

"Did you ever raise a golf club over your head and threaten to kill the two boys?" asked Burrows.

"That never happened," said Kleindeck, "and if anybody says it did they're lying. I respect my students, and I encourage them to speak out. I would never raise a golf club and threaten to strike one of them."

"Objection!" called Dumson. "Counsel is pursuing a line of questioning that is completely irrelevant to the case at hand."

"Thank you. That will be all," said Burrows.

As Kleindeck left the stand, his face turned as red as it did the day Watt and Perry were in his office. He looked at Watt and cried, "I *knew* you would end up here! I told you weren't going anywhere!"

"That will be all, Mr. Kleindeck," said Judge Camalian as Sylvia let out a cry.

CHAPTER 30

▼

The next day Lena Messa took the witness stand. Describing Watt as the janitor at the Von Geber Treatment Center, she said the word all black men dread coming from the mouth of a white woman: *rape!*

"Will you please repeat what he did to you?" asked Dumson.

"He raped me," said Lena, with the froth from an Alka Seltzer drooling from her mouth.

"Oh No!" cried Sylvia.

"On how many occasions?" asked Dumson.

"Dozens, I think," she said, "maybe hundreds. It's so painful. I don't want to think about it. I was there to get help, but instead I got raped."

"I understand," said Dumson.

"We ought to get a New York rope!" cried one of the Saxon American Board Members with a Texas accent. As Camalian banged his gavel for order, Watt jumped up. "Do you motherfuckers *always* have to lie before you kill? You make up lies about a person or a country to justify killing them because you need that feeling of being right when you do evil. It's that Puritan ethic bullshit and pure hypocrisy! And it makes me sick!"

"That's enough!" shouted Judge Camalian, banging his gavel as the two bruiser bailiffs forced Watt back into his seat. "I've warned the defendant about such outbursts. The jury is instructed to ignore everything the defendant said."

Then Burrows crossed examined her. "Ms. Messa, You said the defendant raped you dozens, maybe hundreds, of times. Wasn't *one* time enough for you to report him to the police?"

"Objection!" called Dumson.

"Let me withdraw that," said Burrows. "Ms. Messa, you're the head of a corporation. You're educated. You're rich and you're powerful. Why didn't you report the defendant to the police immediately after the *first* rape?"

"I was scared," said Lena Messa.

"Did you report it to the head of the treatment center, Dr. Otto Von Geber?"

"No."

"Can you please tell the court why you didn't?"

"I was scared."

"Well, did you tell anybody about your experiences with the defendant?"

"No."

"Why not?" asked Burrows.

"Watt used to carry a big knife," she said, "with KILL written on the handle."

"Did he ever threaten you with this knife you say he carried?"

"No."

"About how long did these rapes go on?" asked Burrows.

"For five years," said Lena Messa, "depending on when I was being treated."

"And you expect the jury to believe that the defendant went on raping you for five years, and you never mentioned it to a soul?"

"Negroes have always frightened me."

"I'm an African-American man, Ms. Messa. Do *I* frighten you?"

"No, you're different. I just remembered. I did tell one person about the rapes." said Lena Messa.

"Who?" asked Burrows.

"My friend, Sir Ainsley Bridges," said Lena.

"It's unfortunate that we can't confirm that allegation," said Burrows. "That will be all, Ms. Messa."

The next witness surprised Watt. How someone so lowdown could show his face in public, let alone in a courtroom, was a feat that boggled Watt's mind.

"Mr. Kahlil," said Dumson.

"Brother Kahlil will be alright with me."

"Mr. Kahlil, what is your title?"

"I am Chairman and Supreme Commander of the United Separatist Party."

"Would you describe the United Separatist party as a civil rights organization, Mr. Kahlil?"

"I would not," said Kahlil. "Civil rights organizations want to integrate the races. We want to keep them apart." Before Dumson could proceed to the next question, a racist round of applause swept through the courtroom. Kahlil was even more popular with the whites seated in the courtroom than he was with the blacks.

"Was the defendant ever a member of the United Separatist Party?"

"Yes, he was," said Kahlil. "But I had to expel him."

"Exactly why did you expel the defendant from your organization?" asked Dumson.

"I expelled him when I discovered he was undermining my organization by sleeping with several white women." As that strong-looking black woman in the jury started breathing dragon fire, another Saxon-American Corporation board member leaped to his feet and cried, "Black bastard!"

"You have to try to understand the confusion that some of our brothers experience," said Kahlil. "It's the fault of the integration-mad Negro. The word *integrate* means to make whole by bringing parts together."

"Objection!" called Burrows.

"The word *integer* means a whole number, as opposed to a fraction. A hole, usually empty, is a chasm."

"Objection!" called Burrows.

"Some of our brothers confuse *whole* with *hole* and end up doing a whole number on the white woman and their people."

"Objection!" called Burrows as the courtroom stirred with both confusion and laughter. "The witness is perpetuating false definitions that distort the English Language and promote irrational fallacies that are obviously beyond his control and the understanding of the jury."

"Objection sustained!" ruled Judge Camalian.

"In your dealings with the defendant, Mr. Kahlil, when he was a member of *your* United Separatist Party, did you ever observe any behavior on his part that seemed strange or unusual under the circumstances?"

"He was violent," said Kahlil.

"Can you be a little more specific, Mr. Kahlil?" asked Dumson, with a twinkle in his eyes.

"Not really," said Kahlil. "I don't want to make any mistakes. You guys might lock me up for perjury."

"I can assure you that won't happen," said Dumson. "Thank you."

"Mr. Kahlil," asked Burrows rising from his chair. "Isn't it true that you're on the payroll of the New York City Police Department?"

"Who told you that?!" jumped Kahlil.

"Is it true, Mr. Kahlil?" pounded Burrows.

"No it's not true!" retorted Kahlil.

"I have here several papers," said Burrows, including copies of your income tax returns for the last fifteen years to prove otherwise."

"Oh, *those* papers," said Kahlil. "I totally forgot about that."

"Let me repeat the question," said Burrows. "Isn't it true that you're on the payroll of the New York City Police Department?"

"I'm paid for the community work I do," said Kahlil.

"Exactly what community work is that, Mr. Kahlil?"

"I provide leadership, COMMUNITY LEADERSHIP."

"Leadership," said Burrows with a mocking tone. "And does that leadership include monthly reports on audiotape of things that are transpiring in Harlem?"

"Who told you that?" asked Kahlil, rising up from the witness stand.

"Objection!" called Dumson. "Counsel is browbeating the witness over matters that are not pertinent to this case."

"To the contrary, Your Honor," said Burrows. "I'm trying to establish that the witness has a vested interest with the New York City Police Department, which requires him to give testimony that is unfavorable to my client."

"Overruled, I'll allow this line of questioning," said Judge Camalian.

"Isn't it also true that you were on the city payroll at the time of the incident in front of Nixon High?"

Kahlil sat silent for a moment. Every ear in the court strained to hear his response. Kahlil looked over to the Saxon Anglo American Corporation board members. A couple of them had their heads in their hands. "And you call yourself a brother!" snapped Kahlil.

"I'm not *your* brother, Mr. Kahlil," shot Burrows. "And apparently, you're nobody's brother *either*, except in your rhetoric. The court is waiting for an answer, Mr. Kahlil."

Then, in a voice barely audible, Kahlil said, "Yes."

"We can't hear you. Yes, to what, Mr. Kahlil?" asked Burrows. "Let me repeat the question. Isn't it also true that you are on the payroll of New York City at this very minute, and you *were* on the payroll of the New York City Police Department fifteen years ago at the time of the riot in front of Nixon High School?"

"Yes," said Kahlil, dropping his head, as gasps reverberated through the courtroom.

"Sellout!" yelled a young black man from the rear of the courtroom.

"That will be all," said Burrows.

As Kahlil stumbled from the stand, Watt wanted to yell, "You Afro-centric Overtom! How many other brothers did you sell down the drain?" But he kept quiet and listened as the bailiff called Mr. Stetson B. Stetson."

"Mr. Stetson," said Dumson, "you were an employee of Sir Ainsley Bridges?"

"Yes," said Stetson.

"For how long?" asked Dumson.

"For thirty years," said Stetson.

"And you were with Sir Ainsley Bridges the night he was murdered. Is that correct?"

"Yes," said Stetson. "I drove Sir Ainsley to Morningside Park to meet Watt."

"What happened after that, Mr. Stetson?"

"Sir Ainsley and I entered the park from Morningside Heights and came down the stairs. I used my special key to open the gate. It was dark. We waited for Watt, who was a few minutes late. When he finally came, he and Sir Ainsley left me and went down the stairs to talk. I could see their shadows in the darkness. But I couldn't hear what they were saying. They talked for ten minutes. Then I saw them struggling. I saw Watt hit Sir Ainsley, and I heard Sir Ainsley scream."

"What did he scream?" asked Dumson.

"Two dollars," said Stetson.

"What were those last words again?" asked Dumson.

"Two dollars," repeated Stetson.

"Is that all?" asked Dumson.

"Yes," said Stetson.

"What happened next?"

"I raced to Sir Ainsley," said Stetson. "He was lying motionless on the stairs. I took his pulse and listened for a heartbeat, but he was dead."

"Where was the defendant at this time?"

"Standing a few feet away," said Stetson. "I think he was laughing."

"The sadistic son of a bitch!" someone muttered.

"What did you do next?"

"I ran up the stairs to Morningside Heights and called the police."

"Do you have any doubt as to whether or not the defendant killed Sir Ainsley Bridges?"

"None whatsoever," said Stetson.

"Thank you," said Dumson.

"Mr. Stetson," asked Burrows, rising and approaching the witness stand. "You say you were in the employ of Sir Ainsley Bridges for thirty years. Is that correct?'

"Yes," said Stetson.

"During that time, did Sir Ainsley meet other people—or the defendant—in Morningside Park?"

"Sometimes," said Stetson.

"Did Sir Ainsley ever meet the defendant in Morningside Park late at night?"

"Yes," said Stetson.

"Did he ever meet him in the early morning hours?"

"Yes," said Stetson.

"Did Ainsley Bridges ever tell you *why* he met Watt in Harlem and in Morningside Park so late at night?"

"No," said Stetson.

"Who initiated those meetings, Ainsley Bridges or my client?"

"Sir Ainsley did," said Stetson.

"And what was the purpose of those meetings?" asked Burrows.

"Sir Ainsley used to meet Watt to give him help and moral support," said Stetson.

"Was any of that support financial?" asked Burrows.

"Yes," said Stetson.

"Couldn't Sir Ainsley have given that support at some other time of the day and at some other place, besides Morningside Park?" asked Burrows.

"I suppose so," said Stetson.

"Objection!" called Dumson. "Counsel is asking the witness, a mere hireling, to speculate on the intentions and motives of Sir Ainsley Bridges."

"Your Honor, Morningside Park is considered to be a very dangerous place by members of the police department who will gladly testify to that fact. If Sir Ainsley Bridges either regularly or even occasionally chose to meet my client inside this dangerous park, as opposed to a restaurant downtown, I'd like to know the reason."

"Overruled," said Judge Camalian.

"Did Ainsley Bridges ever tell you what drew him to Morningside Park or why he liked to meet my client there?" asked Burrows.

"Sir Ainsley told me that Morningside Park excited him," said Stetson. "It took him back to the Id. It made him feel more alive."

"Would you repeat that please, Mr. Stetson."

"Sir Ainsley said Morningside Park excited him. He said it was the closest thing to Hell, and it stirred something in his blood."

"Thank you, Mr. Stetson," said Burrows. "That will be all."

As Stetson left the witness stand, all twenty board members of the Saxon-American Corporation scowled at him. "I had to tell the truth!" pleaded Stetson. "I was under oath. Don't turn me out! I have grandchildren to support!"

As he broke down and cried, leaving the courtroom, Judge Camalian called for a recess.

Following the recess, the bailiff called, "Dr. Otto Von Geber." And both doors to the courtroom swung open as if the president or a king were entering.

Watt had always known that people applauded evil, especially when they mistook it for good. But he had never seen people applaud evil so passionately as when Dr. Otto Von Geber walked down the courtroom aisle and received a round of applause. Everyone in the courtroom stood, even Judge Camalian. Members of the Saxon-American Corporation extended their hands to shake Dr. Von Geber's. But the international therapist and genius ignored them as he walked to the witness stand and sat in the chair which, through posture and bearing, he converted into a throne.

"The court knows what a busy man you are," said Judge Camalian. "We appreciate your taking the time to come here."

"I echo Judge Camalian's respect and appreciation," said Dumson.

"Thank you," said Dr. Von Geber, nodding his head.

"Dr. Von Geber, you employed the defendant, didn't you?" asked Dumson

"Yes," said Dr. Von Geber.

"For how long?" asked Dumson.

"About fifteen years."

"Exactly how did you meet the defendant and what did the defendant do in your treatment center?"

"I met Oscar Watt fifteen years ago," said Dr. Von Geber. "He was a poor, uneducated young man from Harlem. He needed a break in life, so I hired him to work in my treatment facility, *cleaning* things up."

"In your professional opinion, Dr. Von Geber, is the defendant certifiably insane?"

"Positively not," said Dr. Von Geber. "Watt is as sane as you or I, with *two* exceptions: One, he suffers from delusions of grandeur that most of us would find amusing. He is poor. Yet he looks at the world with the indifference of a king. And, two, he is also slightly paranoid and schizophrenic. But most people who live in New York are that way."

Sylvia's sobs became louder when Dr. Von Geber used the terms *paranoid* and *schizophrenic* to describe Watt.

"Is there anything else you'd like to add?"

"Only that in evaluating Watt's sanity," said Dr. Von Geber, "we must be careful not to make the mistake that people in the legal profession invariably make when dealing with issues that involve psychiatry."

"What mistake is that, doctor?"

"They substitute good reasons for real ones—in cases of guilt or innocence—or they try to find reasons when none exists. Sometimes, the reason why someone does something is unknown to them and of absolutely no concern to the law. Rationalizations can be created for any event or action on the part of human beings or nations. That is why the only thing that matters is guilt or innocence as determined by actions.

"Watt being slightly paranoid or schizophrenic—in a city where most people suffer from those conditions—means nothing. Whether he committed the crime or not is what you have to prove. *Why* is not important."

"Thank you, Dr. Von Geber. That will be all," said Dumson."

As a welter of applause swept through the courtroom, Watt stood up and yelled, "You people think he's a great man! But Dr. Otto Von Geber is the Devil! And he's a Nazi, too!" As the bruiser bailiffs made Watt sit, and spectators booed, Burrows rose and said, "No questions, Your honor."

"Thank you, Dr. Von Geber," said Judge Camalian, nodding his head. As the applause for Dr. Von Geber increased, Dumson and his team were all smiles. Dr. Von Geber rose and left the stand, like a triumphant hero. Some of the Saxon-American Corporation board members extended their hands to shake; others tried to give him their cards. But Dr. Von Geber ignored them and exited the courtroom. After he left, Judge Camalian declared a recess until the next day.

CHAPTER 31

▼

The next day it was the defense's turn. The "D" Show began. Burrows mounted Watt's defense the way he told him he would. He made the pitch that Watt was crazy and brought in a bunch of expert witnesses to support the claim. But all were careful not to contradict anything Dr. Otto Von Geber had said as they gave their analyses on the detriments to the individual of growing up in multi-generational poverty, sub-standard housing, inferior education, and epidemic violence. But instead of handkerchiefs and tears, dry eyes and scowls filled a compassionless courtroom.

"I could give a damn about somebody poor," said one of the Saxon-American Corporation board members.

Then the old ladies came on. "I don't care what you say he did or where you say he did it. I know he's innocent," said Mrs. Saunders.

"Zeporah Foye Montgomery's grandson wouldn't hurt a soul," said Mrs. Dawson. "He might talk about doing it. He might even be capable of doing it. But he wouldn't do it, except in self-defense. And he might not do it then. Look at that HARLEMASSWHIPPIN' he took on Central Park North."

Although Sylvia had said she would not testify, when Burrows asked for her help, saying, "Watt might get the Big Needle," she agreed to appear as a witness for the defense and took the stand. Despite the bruises, everyone could see how beautiful she was.

"Thank you for agreeing to testify, Miss Donner," said Burrows. "Let me begin by asking you how long you've known the defendant."

"Five years," said Sylvia.

"During this time has he ever exhibited any behavior that would lead you to think he was mentally ill?"

"When I first met Watt," said Sylvia, "I thought he was just angry and bitter—black men have a lot to be bitter about."

"Objection!" called Dumson. "Witness is offering speculative judgments."

"Sustained," said Camalian. "The jury will ignore that last comment."

"But then I came to realize that it wasn't anger," said Sylvia. "He was stark-raving mad. Sometimes he seemed possessed and would run in his sleep. And when I asked him what was happening, he would say he was hearing wild music."

"What did you do then?" asked Burrows.

"I tried to give him more love," said Sylvia, starting to cry.

"Are you able to continue?" asked Burrows.

"Yes," said Sylvia, wiping her eyes. "I offered him everything: a family, a home, myself. But it was no use. It was then I realized he was crazy and couldn't deal with love."

"You are six months pregnant with the defendant's child, aren't you?" asked Burrows.

"Yes, I am," said Sylvia, with fresh tears swelling in her eyes.

"How did the defendant respond to your being pregnant with his child?" asked Burrows.

"He tried to force me to have an abortion," said Sylvia, dropping her head as more tears flowed. "Finally he threw me down the stairs at Grant's Tomb—to kill the baby ... maybe me."

A collective gasp went through the courtroom. Several voices called, "That dirty bastard!"

Judge Camalian banged his gavel, calling, "Order!" And for a moment, he reminded Watt of Von Geber's parrot, crying, "Ordnung!" As the courtroom quieted, Sylvia stammered, "He can't help it. He's mad."

"Thank you, Miss Donner," said Burrows.

"The state waives cross-examination," said Dumson.

As Sylvia left the stand, holding a handkerchief under her eyes, a male juror leaned over and looked at her ass and legs, then sat back and said to the juror seated beside him, "Yeah, he's *got* to be crazy as fine as *she* is!"

Then Burrows called a couple of surprise witnesses.

First, the Street Poet addressed the court. "I know nothing about Watt's involvement with any billionaire. I know nothing about him being sane or crazy. I just came here to tell you this is a very talented brother, and you should be careful not to hurt him any more." After giving testimony, the Street Poet stepped down from the witness stand, spinning an old song as he left the courtroom.

These are the rocks
that hurt since '54,
the ironies in stone

The next witness surprised Watt. "Will you please tell the court your name and occupation," said Burrows.

"My name is Loray Valdee, honey. I'm a beautician, but I'm also the queen of the Asscapades."

"The what?" inquired Burrows.

"The Asscapades," said Loray, "now appearing in an Oscar Wilde Theater near *you*."

"Well, Mr. Valdee, how long have you known the defendant?"

"Since the fourth grade," said Loray. "We were in Miss Green's class at P.S. 10."

"Have you ever seen the defendant exhibit any homicidal tendencies?"

"Not really," said Loray. "There was that big fight on 110th Street between him and BJ9. But he wasn't exhibitin' anything. Like the old lady said, it was a HARLEMASSWHIPPIN', the first one in years."

"Were there any other occasions when the defendant had the opportunity to be homicidal?" asked Burrows.

"No," said Loray, "even when he had three guns in his hands—and the opportunity to use them—he didn't."

"What three guns and opportunity are you referring to, Mr. Valdee?"

"He walked in on Jehoover and me in my apartment."

"Do you mean *Captain* Jehoover?" asked Burrows.

"Yeah, him," said Loray.

"What was your relationship with Captain Jehoover, Mr. Valdee?" asked Burrows.

"He was my man," said Loray

"Are you implying, Mr. Valdee, that Captain Jehoover was gay?"

"I'm not implying anything," said Loray. "I *said* it. He was the love of my life … and we had an understanding."

As gasps went through the courtroom, Loray asked, "What's so shockin'? He was *my* man, and I was *his* woman." said Loray, adding in whisper tones, "He got me when I was young."

"Objection!" called Dumson. "Captain Jehoover is dead and cannot defend himself again such scurrilous accusations."

"Overruled," said Camalian, smiling. "The court would like to hear more of these allegations before deciding on their merit. I would caution the witness, however, about committing perjury. Please continue."

"Let me see if I understand you correctly, Mr. Valdee. you are saying that you and Captain Jehoover had a homosexual relationship?"

"If that's what you want to call it, baby," said Loray. "Sometimes he came over just to try on a dress, but we usually had sex at least once a week."

"So you're saying," said Burrows, starting to breathe deeply, "You, a black beautician in Harlem, and Captain Jehoover, one of the most decorated policemen in the history of this city, engaged in sexual intercourse at least once a week?"

"That's right," said Loray.

"For how long have these alleged assignations been taking place?"

"ASS-SIG-WHAT?" asked Loray.

"Sexual encounters," said Burrows.

"Ten years, baby," jumped Loray.

"So, Mr. Valdee," said Burrows, "you want the court to believe that you, a black man, had a sexual liaison with Captain Jehoover, a white man."

"You *almost* have it honey," said Loray, "except for one small thing."

"And what is that, Mr. Valdee?"

"Captain Jehoover wasn't really white. Actually he was a black man who passed for white all of his life."

"Objection!" yelled Dumson, as a shockwave shot through the courtroom. "The witness is besmirching the reputation of one of the most decorated law enforcement officers in the history of the city of New York in an attempt to aid the defendant."

"Objection sustained," said Judge Camalian. "But the court would like to hear a little more. Perhaps you can tell your story from another angle without denigrating the memory of Captain Jehoover."

"I didn't think I was denigratin' anyone," said Loray. "I was just trying to tell you about the night Watt—the defendant caught Jehoover and me in bed and grabbed all three of Jehoover's guns before Jehoover woke up. He could have shot Jehoover dead if he had wanted to. But instead he pistol whipped him and left him sprawled on the bed. That's why I said he isn't a killer, and he isn't crazy."

"How do you feel about Captain Jehoover?" asked Burrows.

"I miss him every day," said Loray, "even though he treated me badly."

"Again, where did this incident occur?" asked Burrows.

"In my apartment," said Loray, "up in Harlem, O Harlem."

"Captain Jehoover was in *your* apartment, Mr. Valdee?"

"Just like you're standing here, baby," said Loray.

"Can that be verified?" asked Burrows.

"All my neighbors know about us," said Loray. "They also know what would happen to them if they said anything."

"So the defendant caught—came in upon you and Captain Jehoover while you were asleep together in bed after having sex?"

"Yes, now you got it, baby," said Loray."

"Please tell the court what happened after my client took possession of Captain Jehoover's three guns."

"Watt got his guns and pistol whipped him. Then he tied us both up and left."

"Did the defendant threaten to kill Captain Jehoover or you at any time?" asked Burrows.

"No, honey, he wasn't gonna *hurt* anybody," said Loray. "He just wanted a little money and some help, and I gave him both."

"How do you feel about the defendant, Mr. Valdee?"

"I been in love with that nig—man since the fourth grade," said Loray.

"Has that love ever been reciprocated or consummated?" asked Burrows.

"Con-sum—what?" asked Loray.

"Have you and the defendant ever had sex together?"

"No, we haven't fucked yet," said Loray.

"Objection!" said Dumson. The witness's language is as foul as his accusations."

"Objection sustained," said Judge Camalian. "The witness will refrain from using profanity or lurid descriptions of his behavior that offend the sensibilities of the court."

"Thank you, Mr. Valdee," said Burrows.

"Mr. Valdee," asked Dumson, quickly coming forward. "Are you sure you and the defendant never had a homosexual relationship?"

"We never did," said Loray, "but it wasn't for my lack of trying."

"So you and the defendant had a Platonic relationship?"

"A what?" asked Loray.

"There was a meeting of the minds with no sexual congress between you."

"I don't think Congress should ever get involved in anybody's sex life."

"No, I just meant that you and the defendant never had SEX," said Dumson.

"I know what you MEANT, baby," said Loray. "We never fucked."

"Whatever your relationship with the defendant, Mr. Valdee, isn't it true that the defendant almost took your life several months ago with a straight razor in the House of Styles Barbershop and Beauty Salon, which is located in Harlem?"

"Oh that," said Loray. "He just got mad at me."

"Why did the defendant get mad at you?" asked Dumson.

"Because I touched his little big man without askin'," said Loray.

"His what?" asked Dumson.

"His dick," said Loray, as more gasps went through the courtroom. The Saxon-American Corporation board members all looked as if they wanted to spit.

"So you *did* see the defendant's potential for committing homicide," said Dumson.

"I wouldn't say that," said Loray.

"The defendant had a straight razor at your throat, Mr. Valdee. He was a nanosecond away from cutting your throat, and you don't *think* he exhibited any homicidal tendencies."

"I do not," said Loray.

"Apparently, Mr. Valdee," said Dumson, "your notion of what constitutes a homicidal threat is far different from everybody else's. That will be all."

Although things had improved, the trial was still looking bad for Watt. He couldn't win and go free. He could lose and be declared insane, or he could lose and spend the rest of his life in prison, or he could lose and be executed. The Big Needle loomed large in his mind. All that remained between him and death were the attorneys' closing arguments, which were to be given the next day.

And things seemed even worse when Burrows told him, "The prosecution just made a big move. They're bringing in the best cut-throat prosecuting attorney in New York for the closing statement."

"Fuck him!" said Watt with a casual off-handedness.

"Not *him*," said Burrows, *"her.* I've never gone up against her before. But they tell me she's a bitch. She doesn't cut any deals or accept any plea bargains, which is going to make our insanity defense difficult to use."

"Fuck her!" was Watt's response again.

"And if you saw her, you would probably want to," said Burrows. "She's beautiful. And she's about your age. In fact, she was raised in Harlem, too. I doubt if you would know her though."

"What's her name?" asked Watt.

"Ullysa Knight," said Burrows.

"Oh shit!" said Watt. "She's going to fry me without grease!"

CHAPTER 32

▼

Watt watched Ullysa enter the courtroom the next day. Imaginary fifes, flutes, and drums played as she walked to the prosecutor's table and took her seat. She was beautiful, even in a business suit designed to keep her from looking sexy, and all eyes were transfixed by her, by the way she smiled broadly, by the elegant way she reached out to give each colleague an arms-length handshake, by the way she went into her briefcase and took out some papers, and by the way she placed those papers on the table, carefully placing them in order while her colleagues stood or sat waiting for a word from her.

A lot had happened to her since high school to make her the polished and sophisticated woman who stood in the courtroom. She had graduated from college and law school and gone on to become a successful corporate lawyer. But after her father was mugged and killed, she trashed the corporate law career to become the most formidable prosecutor in the New York City Office of the District Attorney. She was unmarried and totally devoted to her job. What she had become was far beyond Watt's station in life. She was no longer the girl he had loved in high school and who had betrayed him, but a super achieving woman whom he could neither appreciate nor converse with.

At no time did she indicate that she had ever known Watt. Only a predator-to-prey glance shot his way as she looked up momentarily from her papers to scan the courtroom. Beneath her business-like demeanor, Watt could see a hard woman had replaced the girl he once knew.

The callousness of an ex-dopefiend determined to assume the world, he thought. *Ex-dopefiend, that's what she is. She was fucked by my father. That's why she's so mean. Dope flowed in her body along with my father's sperm.* Although she probably never got high again, Watt knew the desire for dope haunted her, like an itch she could never scratch or an Eden she could never forget.

Thoughts of her as a young girl raced through his mind. Although time had moved on, the question he had asked himself as a boy fifteen years ago had grown even more with age and implication: *How could that bitch have done what she did to me?!* Fifteen years had passed, but he had never got over the pain she had caused him. Although he was a boy when she hurt him, as a man he had never been able to love or trust another woman—because of her. That's what Sylvia couldn't understand. He didn't love Sylvia because he didn't want to. He didn't love her because he *couldn't*—because all the machinery and receptors for love had been pulled from his soul, because he once loved a woman too much. Trust is more important than love in a relationship, and if you can't trust, you can't truly love. Yes, it's true. In the game of romance, women look for Mr. Right while men look for Miss Right-Now, as a popular saying goes. But what's not mentioned is that so many men get hurt and never recover. Whether it's their mothers or girlfriends, they go from woman to woman, trying to forget the pain and living in denial that they were ever hurt. That's why some men are so mean and angry and call women bitches all the time. But in the end, the stronger sex prevails. Women recover from their pain to love again while men cover it up and seldom get over their pain.

Those thoughts caused squads of emotions to bubble up in Watt's brain. Emotions that he thought he had squashed years ago resurfaced. He closed his eyes and pounded the table, trying to hear the wild music, thinking, *she's come back to me, not for love, but for absolute destruction. She's come back to me to give me the Big Needle.*

With Ullysa in the courtroom, Watt felt as if the trial had just begun, as if everyone who was guilty was now in court and everything that had come before was just a prelude to what would happen now.

Burrows tapped Watt's arm as the clerk ordered everyone to rise for that *Here comes the judge* crap, which ushered in Judge Camalian, as if a better man—pardon!—person had walked into the court. *I used to slap him after every meal and at bedtime*, too, thought Watt.

Then Ullysa approached the bench and introduced herself, nodding to judge and jury with a girl-next-door smile that made that strong-looking black woman on the jury beam with pride. *Yeah, you understand each other,* thought Watt. *You know a thousand different ways to destroy a black man.*

Smiling, Ullysa returned to her seat, conferred with an associate, then stood up to speak. "Your Honor, members of the jury, ladies and gentlemen, my name is Ullysa Knight, and I'm here to assist the prosecution and see that justice is served, not only for the defendant who deserves justice, but for the deceased who demands it. The prosecution has proven that the defendant, Oscar Watt ..."

"You know I don't like to be called that name!" yelled Watt, jumping up.

"Sit down," urged Burrows, as Judge Camalian's eyes widened and a slight smile came over his face, as if to say he had finally discovered Watt's Achilles heel. "The Defendant will sit down *now!*" ordered Judge Camalian, "or I'll hold him in contempt of court. Do you understand me, Mr. *Oscar* Watt?!"

"That the defendant, Oscar Watt," Ullysa continued, "did maliciously butcher ..."

"Objection!" called Burrows. "Counsel is using unduly prejudicial and inflammatory language. My client is not charged with *butchering* anyone."

"Although the word *butcher* doesn't bother me," said Judge Camalian, "perhaps the prosecution should be a little more temperate in the language used to describe the defendant's alleged crime."

"Excuse me, Your Honor," said Ullysa. Continuing, "... did willfully murder Sir Ainsley Bridges.

"And who was Sir Ainsley Bridges?" she continued. "Sir Ainsley Bridges was a man first of all who happened to be extremely rich. In fact, he was a billionaire, the president and CEO of one of the world's great corporations, the Saxon-American Corporation. He was successful, but he was also compassionate and caring when it came to his fellow human beings. Indeed, if we are to believe the many magazine articles written about him, clips and documentaries on his life that have appeared on television, and humanitarian awards he received during his lifetime, Sir Ainsley Bridges just might have been a saint."

"Objection, Your Honor," said Burrows. "The prosecution is using prejudicial and salutatory language to extol the virtues of the victim and thus diminish the status of the defendant."

"Objection sustained," said Judge Camalian.

"Sir Ainsley Bridges," said Ullysa, "was a very compassionate man. Indeed, if we are to believe just some of the reports, Sir Ainsley Bridges made brotherhood the centerpiece of his life. That's how he met Oscar Watt—unemployed, unskilled, uneducated, Oscar Watt, a man who doesn't even have a high school diploma."

"And you know why, bitch!" yelled Watt.

"The defendant will be quiet!" ordered Judge Camalian. "He will refrain from such outbursts, or I'll have him bound and gagged."

"But that meeting between Oscar Watt and Sir Ainsley Bridges proved to be fatal for the humanitarian billionaire. Sir Ainsley Bridges was murdered by the very man he had tried to help.

"Opposing counsel would have you believe that Oscar Watt is insane, a victim of racism and the product of the cruel and insensitive environment in which he was raised. But let me remind you that millions of other Americans—particularly African Americans—come out of similar environments every day, and the vast majority of them have not committed heinous murders. They have not perpetrated horrible crimes. They have not terrorized our community. They go to work every day and contribute to their families and the nation as a whole.

"So don't buy that hogwash about Watt's environment, and especially don't buy that bit about Oscar Watt being insane. Insanity has nothing to do with this case. This case is about the *law* and *responsibility*. It's about the burden of responsibility that all citizens—including you or me—must bear if they break the law, particularly the law prohibiting murder. So you see there are no excuses for what Oscar Watt did to Sir Ainsley Bridges. And there is no hope for our society if we allow Oscar Watt and others like him to get away with it.

"We cannot give Sir Ainsley Bridges another award for being a caring and compassionate human being, although he probably deserves one. We cannot change the cruel environment that produced Oscar Watt, although we must never stop trying to do so. All we can do is be responsible for the case before us now. All we can do is give justice where justice is due. Oscar Watt deserves it; Sir Ainsley Bridges demands it, and our society requires it. Thank you."

As she sat, a round of applause erupted in the courtroom, and the Saxon-American Corporation board members smiled and nodded their heads in approval. A crony sitting behind the new CEO wrote down Ullysa's name. That strong-looking black woman on the jury raised her head and hands as if she were in church and cried out, "Thank-you, Jesus!" Then she caught herself and sat back in her chair, folding her hands in her lap. Even Sylvia seemed inspired and fought back an urge to nod and applaud.

It's a show, thought Watt. *Justice is Amateur Night at the Apollo.*

"Your Honor, I object!" called Burrows. "I object!" Slowly, Judge Camalian banged his gavel, calling, "Order, order in the court. I would ask all observers and participants in the court to please refrain from such outbursts."

"That outburst, Your Honor," said Burrows, "are grounds for a mistrial."

"There'll be no mistrial here," said Judge Camalian. "Get on with it."

Shaking his head, S. Hamilton Burrows patted Watt's shoulder to give reassurance. He moved to the center of the courtroom, like a man who was going to say something he had said before and was pondering how he would say it differently, under different conditions, and with different stakes.

"Ladies and gentlemen of the jury, I just touched a man on the shoulder, a human being, not a butcher, as opposing counsel would have you think. I touched a human being, not a lord or a Peer of the Realm who carries the title *Sir* before his name. I touched a human being, *and* an American, who is equal in the eyes of God and the law under our system of justice to any billionaire or nobleman in the world. This American is accorded certain unalienable rights, the same rights that you or any one of your family members deserve. No rush to judgment or use of the title *Sir* on the part of the prosecution can abolish those rights.

"For the last week, you've heard evidence concerning the guilt or innocence of my client, this human being and American. Very shortly, you will go into a room to begin the task of weighing and sifting through that evidence. Your goal will be to attain justice as it is understood and practiced under our legal system.

"At the core of our legal system, I would remind you, is the belief that a man, a human being, has to be proven guilty beyond a reasonable doubt. And what does that mean? It means that under our legal system, a human being cannot be convicted because of a prosecutor's flowery rhetoric. Nor can some trick of logic, such as truth by assertion, condemn a human being under our system. A human being is convicted under our system of government if the evidence proves him to be guilty beyond the shadow of a doubt.

"Well I think it's quite clear, then, that if a human being is not proven guilty beyond a reasonable doubt, then you must find him not guilty on the basis of the evidence before you.

"Yes, I know it is an awesome responsibility that you have before you. But I know you will carry out that responsibility fairly. However, I believe that you will not be able to carry out that responsibility if you do not ask yourself a few simple questions—questions that cast several reasonable doubts. What was Ainsley Bridges doing in Morningside Park, which is reputed to be one of the most dangerous places in New York City, at four in the morning?

"Considering the reputation and violent nature of Morningside Park, how feasible could it have been for other individuals to have carried out the murder of Ainsley Bridges? What reason could my client have had for killing a man he had known and worked with for several years?

"To those practical and specific questions directly related to this case, I'd like you also to consider a few corollary ones: Does the responsibility for justice reside solely in this courtroom, or do we as a people—excuse me—a society have an obligation to create a just society by providing equal opportunity for all of our citizens?

"Do we believe that we can mete out *injustice* to a child for 18 years, and then when he comes into a courtroom as a man give him enough justice to last the rest of his life—or even take away that life?

"Finally, have we as a society become so insensitive and so barbaric that we would condemn an innocent human being to death who is clearly not in his right mind? You heard the testimony of several psychologists. My client is mentally ill because of a host of wrenching experiences inflicted upon him from the day he was conceived. Most of us as children were given food and nourishment while we were in our mothers' wombs. My client received dope from his mother's womb. Then, shortly after he was born, his mother died. And he grew up motherless and fatherless in a drug-infested community, seeing many of his friends murdered or psychologically destroyed. Of course, those experiences do not make him innocent. They could, however, make him insane, as they could drive *any* of us mad.

"But since your task is justice, and for the purposes of this trial that means guilt or innocence, ask yourself, putting the issue of insanity aside, has it been proven beyond a reasonable doubt that my client is guilty? I don't think so. I think there are too many reasonable doubts here. Witnesses for the prosecution left much to be desired. There were holes in their testimony through which you could drive a dump truck. The one thing they all seemed to agree on was that Ainsley Bridges—or Sir Ainsley Bridges was a wonderful man. And I am not here to say that he was not. But ask yourself. Have you ever heard of anyone—even a wonderful man—trying to help someone by meeting him in Morningside Park at four in the morning? Wasn't there a better time and a better place to provide assistance? Couldn't they have met during daylight hours in some place other than Morningside Park?

"Those facts lead me to say that something else was going on during those meetings between Ainsley Bridges and my client—something for which they needed the cover of darkness and a place as dangerous as Morningside Park. What that thing was I do not know. It hasn't been revealed by these proceedings. Whatever it was, it casts a large shadow over this court's proceedings and is a barrier to establishing my client's guilt beyond a reasonable doubt. Consequently, you must find the defendant, Oscar Watt, not guilty of the crime with which he is charged. Thank you."

As Burrows returned to his seat, the yawn of a Saxon-American Corporation board member was the only sound competing with his footsteps. Descending into his seat, Burrows leaned over to Watt and said. "I believe you now. You really did slap millionaires for a living."

"Would prosecution like to rebut defense council's closing argument?" asked Judge Camalian.

"No, Your Honor," said Ullysa, rising.

Then Judge Camalian instructed the jury, saying, "The jury will now adjourn and deliberate to reach a verdict."

As the jury rose to leave, a commotion broke out in the rear of the courtroom. "Don't let that savage in!" cried one of the Saxon American Corporation Board Members. Chief Laughing Gravy stood in the rear of the courtroom, holding a rifle and a shotgun with a white flag of truce attached to each.

"What do *you* want?" asked Judge Camalian.

"You know me, Camalian," said Laughing Gravy. "I come to give truth. Black man no kill Ainsley Bridges. Ainsley Bridges—like all white men—kill self … from within. You love things, not people. You let things, like clock on wall, rule you. And you create corporations to make more things. You turn people into things. You all unhappy people. Bridges unhappy man. He eat me, but the Great Spirit teach me to survive in the white man's guts. The Great Spirit help me to tear open Ainsley Bridges' stomach and come back to life. Black man innocent. That's all. I go now."

He turned and left. The moment he was out of the courtroom, Judge Camalian jumped to his feet, calling, "Marshals, police! To hell with those flags of truce! Arrest that Indian!" Then Watt heard reports of gunfire: shotgun blasts and hand gun rounds whizzing through the corridors of justice.

CHAPTER 33

▼

It was all in the *Barely News* the next day—the story of Laughing Gravy and the story of Watt: how the police shot and killed Laughing Gravy, who took three policemen with him; how Laughing Gravy had attempted to free Watt; how the mayor, the police, and particularly Judge Willard Camalian took credit for bringing New York's most dangerous fugitive to justice; how Watt and Laughing Gravy were part of a larger plot, and how millionaires all over the world could breathe a sigh of relief. The last Apache war chief was dead.

One of the stories even shed some light on Laughing Gravy's background. He was born on the San Carlos Reservation in Arizona and had been educated at some of the nation's best universities before being awarded a Rhodes Scholarship to study at Oxford. But shortly after he returned to the United States, he told a relative, "I've been a fool!" and rejected the white man's culture—even his language and clothes. He recreated himself as an Apache warrior and made Morningside Park his battlefield.

But why he tried to help Watt remained a mystery. One journalist attributed it to history, saying "Indians used to help runaway slaves, even adopt them into their tribes. A lot of African Americans have American Indian blood in them anyway. Who knows? Maybe they're related."

The newspapers also contained the jury's verdict in the case of *the People of New York v. Oscar Watt*. After ten minutes of deliberation, the jury found Watt guilty of murder in the first degree. All that remained was for him to be sentenced, which Camalian did a few days later as Sylvia sat in the courtroom and sobbed. "I sentence you to be executed by lethal injection until you're dead!" said

Camalian with a smile. "And may Lord & Taylor have Macy's—I mean may the Lord have mercy on your soul. Take the prisoner away."

"Fuck you!" yelled Watt. "I should have slapped you to death when I had the chance!"

As the marshals took Watt away, Burrows asked if he could speak with Watt for a moment. "You're not going to get the Big Needle," he assured Watt. "We have grounds for a mistrial on the basis of what happened with Laughing Gravy alone, not to mention the way Judge Camalian allowed periodic outbursts favoring the prosecution. Now tell me, Watt, before you go. Did you really slap that asshole Camalian around?"

"Yeah," said Watt, nodding.

"How did it feel?" asked Burrows.

"Good," said Watt.

"Man, I'd like to slap him, too," said Burrows. "Look. Even if we don't get a mistrial, there'll be dozens of appeals between you and the Big Needle. That should buy us ten or fifteen years. I'll be in touch."

"Later," said Watt.

They manacled Watt and led him to the van to be transported to prison. Watt was surprised to see Ullysa waiting by the van, holding her briefcase. Nodding her head slightly, she looked into his eyes with regret, and for a moment he saw the young girl he once knew. "Did you come to gloat?" he asked.

"No," she said. "I came to tell you something I've wanted to say for fifteen years. I'm sorry for what I did to you. I changed the course of your life."

Although a part of him wanted to tell her, *It's too late now,* another part of him held sway, and he said, "Thanks, Ullysa, I needed to hear that. I've waited fifteen years to hear that." As he climbed into the van, he gave her a wry smile, feeling as if an old weight had been lifted from his shoulders. Then he watched her grow smaller as the van drove away.

They took Watt to the newly named Jehoover State Penitentiary and put him on death row, a solitary section of the prison where they kill you with boredom before they kill you with the Big Needle, and the guards are careful, knowing a death row inmate has nothing to lose. In fact, an inmate might buy some extra time by killing a guard and getting a new trial.

What can you say about human nature? A *Free Watt!* movement flared up for awhile, consisting of an unemployed accountant whose wife had left him for another woman. Probably to avoid killing someone or himself, he became devoted to freeing Watt. But after a year, he got a job, met a nice lady, and decided to give the old marriage merry-go-round another ride. *The Free Watt!* movement was quickly forgotten.

After two years, the boredom was getting to Watt. He was tired of the newspapers, tired of the magazines, and tired of the dumb vanity TV shows that got dumber each season. He remained confined to his cell—a world just big enough for him to stretch, eat, and shit—for twenty-three hours each day. For one hour each day, a muscular guard named Jabbo took him out for exercise and walked him like a dog.

Watt needed something different, but he didn't know what. Then one day he was in his cell, trying to think of what he could do to pass the time, when the inmate in the next cell called, "Hey, you."

"Yeah," said Watt.

"Is your name Watt?" the voice asked.

"Yeah," Watt responded.

"Are you the one they say used to slap millionaires?"

"Yeah," said Watt.

"My name is Lipsky. Have you heard of me?"

"Yeah, I've heard of Dutch Schultz and Meyer Lansky, and Lepke, too."

"Then you know *I'm* not a punk," said Lipsky. "I don't care about *anything* or *anybody.*"

"Yeah," said Watt.

"Watt, you and I are going to die a little sooner than the rest of these assholes. In fact, the only thing between us and death is some paper with bullshit written on it."

"Yeah," said Watt.

"Don't get me wrong. I'm not being soft," said Lipsky. "But *nobody* has come to visit either of us in two years. And we know what it is to be alone."

"Yeah," said Watt.

"Well maybe we need to talk. Maybe you've got something I don't have. Maybe I've got something you don't have. Maybe it's an idea. Maybe it's a different way of looking at things. I'm not looking for a friend, but maybe we can use each other to beat back the boredom."

"Maybe," said Watt.

"Don't give me your answer now," said Lipsky. "Think about it and let me know. Let's talk later."

"Sure," said Watt. He could hear Lipsky's feet pivot on the concrete floor as he took two steps across his cell and plopped on the cot. A couple of hours later he heard him snoring.

Watt didn't give Lipsky an answer the next day because he didn't know what to say. But he thought about it. *The most powerful gangster in the world wants to talk with me. If we were outside, I might be impressed. But he's going to die just like me. We're going to get the Big Needle. So why should I talk with him? What's in it for me?* But then he thought, *Maybe I can learn something. Maybe talking will do me good. Maybe Lipsky's good for a laugh. It won't hurt to talk with him. We've got something in common. We're both going to die before these other assholes.*

The next day Watt called, "Lipsky, you in there?"

"Where'd you think I'd be, at the race track?"

"What do you want to talk about?" asked Watt.

"Suppose *I* don't want to talk with *you* now, grubba yung," said Lipsky. "You took long enough to decide."

"I couldn't get it together that fast," said Watt. "But I'd like to talk."

"Let me think about it now," said Lipsky. "I don't like anybody fucking with me—and you fucked with me."

The next day, Lipsky called over to him, "Okay. Let's talk." During their conversation, which was probably being taped, Watt asked, "Why do you want to talk with *me*?"

"Because your cell is close to mine," said Lipsky. "You're no *grubba yung*. You may be the only one around here with half a brain besides me. Most people are afraid to think too much because thinking makes them feel alone. If you came from Harlem and used to slap millionaires, you know what it is to be alone. So you're probably not afraid to think. The only question is whether you know *how* to think. I pay a professor type on the outside to send me books. I'll ask Jabbo to bring some over to you. You do like books, don't you?"

"Yeah," answered Watt, remembering all of the books Dr. Von Geber had given him to read. And that's how it began. The Jewish mobster and the black billionaire-killer formed a death row book club and discussed great books with a voraciousness seldom seen in institutions of higher learning. Their bodies remained in prison, but their minds traveled all over the world. Together, they journeyed through corridors of knowledge and aisles of dreams—free men enjoying the fruits of free men.

Although Lipsky was a killer, he knew his stuff when it came to Literature. "What do you think of Faulkner?" asked Watt.

"Time and hypnotism," said Lipsky. "Look at the way he changes tense within a sentence, and shifts you back and forth in time—pure hypnotism. By the way, you were right."

"About what?" asked Watt.

"*Invisible Man*," said Lipsky. "Ellison wrote one hell of a novel."

"But you were right, too."

"About what?" asked Lipsky.

"Writers are killers," said Watt. "Their books kill something in you and bring something else to life."

"Whatever they kill," said Lipsky, "they permanently change."

Watt and Lipsky even read detective novels.

"Who did it?" asked Watt.

"The over-phonemed, under-morphemed, West Indian butler did it," quipped Lipsky.

"What about redemption?" asked Watt.

"Redemption in *who*," asked Lipsky. "Dostoyevsky?"

"In life, man," said Watt.

"Redemption or damnation," said Lipsky, "is in our DNA, no where else."

Four years passed with the two men sharing books and becoming great friends. Their friendship was no longer predicated on the fact that they were both condemned to death but on the truth that they loved the same woman—language—and wished they had come to her sooner, before fate led them to the Big Needle.

Unfortunately, time, paper, and words ran out for Lipsky. His last appeal was denied and his execution date was set. "I'm sorry," said Jabbo, the guard, standing outside Lipsky's cell.

"When?" asked Lipsky.

"Next week," said Jabbo.

That week Watt and Lipsky tried to read all the books they could. Each man sat in his cell turning the pages of the same five books, trying to finish them before Death intervened.

They came for Lipsky early on a Monday morning. He walked by Watt's cell manacled. Accompanied by Jabbo, a rabbi, and three guards, Lipsky stopped in front of Watt's cell to say, "Take care of yourself and keep turning those pages."

"As long as I can," said Watt.

"I sent my professor type a chunk of money and told him to keep sending you books," said Lipsky.

"Thanks," said Watt.

"Fight for every second of life," said Lipsky. "Take risks as long as you're alive. And remember, what does it matter if you should lose your soul or not when your only duty is to lose it intelligently."

"I won't forget you, brother," said Watt, turning his head away with with tears swelling in his eyes.

"I'll see you in Hell, brother."

"I'll be there," said Watt, still keeping his eyes averted.

"I'll miss *all* of this," said Lipsky, "including *you*. But let's not get soft. Some of the guards would love to see me break down."

"Not me," said Jabbo.

"I could use a little relaxation," said Lipsky. "Let's go, Jabbo. The Devil is waiting."

As the procession moved down the cell block, Watt thought, *You Jew, you Jew, I loved you like a brother.*

CHAPTER 34

▼

After Lipsky's death, Watt read even more. Never mind that he was innocent and had spent seven years on death row; never mind that his trial was rigged by a millionaire judge he used to slap for breakfast and a prosecutor who slept with his father and snorted cocaine (but who had apologized for her betrayal of him as they were taking him to death row), and never mind that in his case justice was not simply blind but also cripple and crazy.

So why should justice come to him now? The only thing that mattered was paper, paper in the form of writs that kept the state from killing him, which had nothing to do with justice and everything to do with procedures that threw bubble gum between the wheels of justice. Those appeals bought him more time to live and read. And after reading so many writers he contemplated doing something he had never done before: write.

He never thought he would write when he started devouring books. But Lipsky used to tell him he was a writer. "Readers ingest books; writers digest them. You are one constipated asshole. So write! Since feelings are nothing but bio-chemistry, why not make metaphors?"

But Watt never thought that *he* would make metaphors or that portions of the books he had read would permutate themselves and push out of his mind in images and aphorisms—No! afroisms!—that shocked him and made him laugh.

Reading affected him, but writing changed him. The sheer act of organizing and externalizing his thoughts with words on paper changed him the way the first green plants changed Earth, giving him oxygen and resuscitating the humanity he had repressed for so long. *I have walked in a haze of hostility all of my life and I have hurt people, trivialized their emotions, and ignored them. No one have I hurt more than Sylvia, whose only sin was that she loved me. But I could not deal with her love because I could not deal with my own. And I may have missed the greatest love of my life.* He recalled the many ways he had been so cruel to her, and each incident—from the fiasco at Dreamland to the fall at Grant's Tomb—came back to sting him through something he did not know he had: a conscience.

He realized that fear had made him treat her that way—the fear of living coupled with the fear of loving and being responsible for raising a child. Their boy or girl would be seven now, growing up and walking the same hostile streets he did … without a father. *What kind of life can my child have growing up without me?* he asked. *The same kind of life that I had,* he answered. And for a moment—perhaps for the first in his life—he felt a gnawing sadness and guilt simultaneously. A solitary tear fell from one of his eyes and splattered on the concrete floor of his cell. That's why I didn't want to have any kids. *I didn't want to deal with the pain of my child being destroyed.*

Then it happened, like madness. The penitent in the penitentiary created his own imaginary world in which Sylvia, his child, and he found happiness together. These feelings for family and children slowly came out in every essay he wrote and poem he composed.

"Nothing is more worthwhile than having a family," he wrote, "harnessing genes, transporting souls, helping a human being to become independent. That is reincarnation; that is divinity. The greatest sin in life isn't killing someone. It's neglecting your own child and creating a cycle of neglect that can affect all of your descendants in perpetuity. For all of the sins those children and their children commit as adults can be traced to your first sin of neglect."

Is it true or am I deceiving myself? Am I using thoughts of Sylvia and my child to get me through this lonely period before the Big Needle? If I were out and with my child and her, would I love them, as I say I would, or would I take them for granted and abuse them? Would that other Watt come back?

Although Watt had written to Sylvia many times, begging for her forgiveness and imploring her to tell him the name of their child, she never answered any of his letters. But the letters didn't come back, which meant she got them. Thoughts of Sylvia and his child constantly swam through his head. Somewhere in the world they were struggling to survive, without him.

Then one day he got a letter from Sylvia with no return address. He hoped she would say she forgave him and would give him another chance. Instead it briefly read,

You've got some nerve! You destroyed my life, and now you tell me you love me. I don't want to hear it. Please don't write me anymore. Perry died three years ago. I thought you should know.

Sylvia

The news hit him like a lightening bolt. *When did Perry die? How did he die? Did Victor or someone else kill him? Why didn't someone tell me the best friend I ever had is dead?* Then he realized, *because there is no one in my life to tell me.*

He thought of the fun Perry and he had as kids—how they read each other's thoughts and watched each other's back and how they won and lost everything together. *If you're lucky, you have one friend like Perry in your life. The rest are just acquaintances. He stuck with me even in Kleindeck's office when I first heard the wild music. And he paid for it with his life.* But the boy and the man who was his friend didn't die last week. He died the day he put a needle in his arm, a coke spoon up his nose, or a crack pipe in his mouth.

Watt continued to look at the 37-word letter. Sylvia didn't say where or how she was living, and she didn't mention their child. But spots from her tears stained the page. Watt caressed the letter and kissed the tears. Then he began crying for Perry, for Sylvia, and for himself. Later, he placed the letter on the wall over his bed and went to sleep. He awoke in the middle of the night and burst into more tears.

Another year went by with Watt on death row, writing and wondering where Sylvia and his child were. His anxieties continued to build as something new took shape in him, a novel, *Godfodder.*

You are all Godfodder. Why do you do the things you do? Why are you so destructive? Don't you know it all comes back to you, your children, and the Earth? If the world is an evil place, and there's no doubt about that, it's because you made it so, Godfodder. And if people are more of the Devil's company than God's, it's because they have chosen him, particularly those in whose hearts evil dwells disguised as good.

He finished the book a year later, at which time Burrows came to see him. "I've got good news," said Burrows, "Stetson has recanted much of his testimony. He admitted that Ainsley Bridges choked you and you struck back in self-defense."

"That's not exactly how it happened," said Watt.

Then there was a new trial, more like a hearing, with Watt being shackled and led into court again, appearing before a judge without any of the witnesses who had testified before because the new judge said Stetson was the only eye witness and the only person who would be allowed to testify, which disappointed Watt because he had hoped he would see Sylvia at the hearing.

But Stetson was there. He appeared impoverished and virtually dressed in rags. The years and the Saxon-American Corporation had not been kind to him. Dumson was also there, a little older but not a whit smarter. In attitude and action, he took Stetson's recantation personal. "Isn't true, Mr. Stetson, that you have signed a financially lucrative contract with *Chronos Magazine* for a lengthy article, supposedly written by you, giving the only eye witness account of what *really* happened to Sir Ainsley Bridges in Morningside Park?"

"Yes, sir, it's true," said Stetson. "But money has nothing to do with my coming forward now. I just want to do the right thing."

"Well why didn't you set the record straight sooner?" asked Dumson. "It's been nine years. Could it be that you were waiting for the statute of limitation to run out on the charge of perjury you could have faced if you had come forward sooner?"

"No, the statute of limitation regarding perjury has nothing to do with it," said Stetson. "I just want to do the right thing."

"Then why don't you tell them what really happened in Morningside Park," said Watt. "You won't tell them because they wouldn't believe you."

"Hold on, Watt," cautioned Burrows. "It's to your benefit that he testifies. We're trying to get you off death row."

"He doesn't give a damn about me," whispered Watt. "He just figured out a new way to get paid."

"I couldn't live with myself anymore," said Stetson, "knowing an innocent man was on death row because I didn't tell the complete truth."

"Really," said Dumson.

"Really and truly," said Stetson.

New trial: similar results. Although Burrows argued that Watt should be set free, he was found guilty of manslaughter and sentenced to twenty years in prison, with nine having been served. He would be eligible for parole in eight years.

Jabbo escorted him from death row and handed him over to another guard, saying, "Watch your back, Watt. You're in the regular prison population now. And these motherfuckers are treacherous."

"Thanks, Jabbo," said Watt.

The regular prison population lived in a world of lines. A line was painted on the floor for every place an inmate might go: a blue line led to the laundry; a green line to the kitchen; a red line to the hospital, and a brown line to the yard. And if an inmate was going to any one of those places, he had to say where he was going repeatedly and stay on the line until he got there. If his feet strayed just a foot from his line, a nightstick would crash down on his skull. One of the funniest things to see was two inmates going in opposite directions on the same line try to get around each other.

Although the guards were mean, the inmates were meaner. A thick, wool sock hung over every bed, and late at night, inmates would drench their socks with water, place them over their dicks, and masturbate. As an inmate beat his meat, the wooly hairs of the sock would spike into the wet pores of a tightly held dick, simulating the feeling of the best pussy imaginable. In fact, a few inmates even swore their socks were better than pussy. They were usually inmates who had been imprisoned a long time.

But the problem was that if an inmate had a thick, wooly sock hanging over his bed and another inmate had a worn-out, ragged sock hanging over his bed, the thick sock got the nod and was stolen sometimes. Then it became a matter of respect. The inmate whose sock was stolen had to get it back or be regarded as a chump. A lot of people got stabbed over socks; a few were even killed. Of course, some inmates didn't like socks and didn't want a woman.

As a guard led Watt down a long cellblock, inmates whistled and called, "Hey, baby, I got what you want!"

"My name is Butch—and you *mah* woman!" a voice cried. "You *mah* woman!"

"Fuck you!" snapped Watt, "I'll make you *my* woman!"

"We're gonna see what you're made of, KILLER WATT!" growled Butch, "from the *Inside!*"

"Both of youse shut up!" interrupted the guard. "We're gonna see the kind of motherfucker you are now, Killer Watt."

That night Watt listened to Butch a few cells away revving up, repeating, "He's *mah* woman."

The next day Watt got his work assignment. He followed the blue line to the laundry where he put inmate towels and uniforms into washing machines. Some of the garments were laden with blood. Weeks passed.

But between going to his work assignment and back to his cell where he could read and write, he never tried to make friends. He didn't even speak to anybody, despite the fact that a few people had addressed him, saying, "What's happening, Killer Watt?"

The world hates individuals, and prison is no different. Not hanging out with other inmates in the recreation room, not talking about sports or playing chess, and not making any friends was taken as a major snub, which left him vulnerable. It all came to a head in the laundry room one day. The guards were outside, and

Watt was finishing his job when three inmates, led by Butch, surrounded him. "What do you motherfuckers want?" asked Watt, feeling for a prison-made knife he had stashed under a folded towel.

"We want you, mothafucka!" said Butch. "You *mah* woman!"

"The only thing you're going to get here, motherfucker, is death!" said Watt, still feeling under the towels for his knife.

"You lookin' for *this?*" asked Butch, pulling out Watt's knife, a spoon he had sharpened into a shiv. "We took it. Now we're gonna take you!" The four men started circling Watt who put up his hands to fight, saying "Let's do it!"

They were just about to pounce on Watt when suddenly, a familiar voice cried, "Dreamweavers, why do you want to mess with an amateur when a professional is in the room?" It was Loray in prison denims. He spun around and dropped his pants, revealing his fat ass, which he made throb and bounce at the same time. Then he stuck out his tongue and made a *slurp* sound, saying, "Come and get it, boys."

"Oh shit!" jumped one of the inmates. "That's the fattest ass I've ever seen!"

"I ain't never seen an ass that fat either!" said another as all three of Butch's boys ran to Loray, pulling out their dicks.

"It's just you and me now, motherfucker!" said Watt, as Butch raised his arm to stab Watt. But Watt caught hand and blade in mid-flight, and the two men struggled for control. Holding back the blade with one hand, Watt punched Butch in the face repeatedly with the other. Then he kneed Butch in the groin. But Butch still wouldn't let go. He tried to head butt Watt, who counter butted him and snapped an elbow to his jaw. Butch tried to bite his ear, but Watt butted him again. As the two men tumbled into a pile of soiled laundry, Watt dug his feet into the ground and threw all of his weight upward and forward. The blade went into Butch's stomach, and Watt wrenched it from him completely and stabbed him a few more times as Butch howled, "Dirty motherfucker, you killed me!"

"Then why aren't you dead!" yelled Watt, stabbing him again. Following a final wheeze from Butch, there was silence. All Watt could hear now were the loud sounds of the washers and dryers churning and Loray keeping the other three inmates in maximum heat and oblivious to Butch's death. "Come on, Gates. Don't wear it out. Save some for us."

"I can't help it! It's so good! I'm coming!" As an inmate yelled in ecstasy, Watt jumped up and ran over to help Loray. "Get the fuck off him!" yelled Watt, brandishing the bloody shiv.

"Don't kill me!" cried an inmate, rolling off Loray.

"Just get out of here, Dreamweaver," said Loray, looking up sadly. "Let me do my work. I can handle this."

"Yeah, get out of here," said another inmate, looking over at Butch. "We ain't fucking with you no more."

"What about your boy, Butch?" asked Watt.

"Fuck him! We got the finest woman in Jehoover State Penitentiary right here."

CHAPTER 35

▼

Killing Butch taught the other inmates a lesson. Just because a man reads books doesn't mean he won't kill you. They all respected Watt, or Killer Watt, as they continued to call him. And there were no repercussions from either inmates or authorities. Nobody cared about a piece of shit like Butch.

Watt now had an old friend from the neighborhood in prison with him who shared something else. They were both set up and framed. "They never forgave me for telling the world that Jehoover was my man and black," said a sobbing Loray. "I didn't do anything. All I did was love a straight man who was really gay and a white man who was really black. To tell you the truth, Dreamweaver, he was pretty fucked up, but I loved him anyway. They took ten years to set me up. They planted a kilo of heroin in my apartment. I nearly died when the judge gave me twenty years." As Loray continued sobbing, Watt consoled his friend, saying, "You're not alone, man. A lot of dudes in prison are guilty, but some are innocent." Later that month Watt tried to get Loray to read a poem, *Paradise Lost*, saying, "John Milton talks of penal fire and adamantine chains."

"Penal fire!" jumped Loray. "He must've had the clap!"

Of course, everyone thought Watt was screwing Loray, but that wasn't the case. Watt still didn't go that way. He had everything he needed to survive: his sock, his books, and his shiv—several to tell the truth, stashed at different places around the prison. But neither Watt nor Loray tried to dispel the rumors that they were lovers, which grew after Watt punched out an inmate who had tried to rape Loray. "Only Loray has the right to decide who jumps in his asshole!" said Watt, standing over the beaten inmate. "Touch him again, and I'll kill you!"

Watt continued to write as time passed, and new headlines were reported in the *Barely News*:

MILLIONS OF AMERICANS WITHOUT HEALTHCARE

HOUSE CALLS FOR MORATORIUM ON SENATE NOSEPICKING

BLACK MAN LIGHTS HOUSE WITH OWN EXCREMENT

People laughed when Willie Jones Smith told them what his new invention could do. They said he was full of, well, excrement. But they stopped laughing yesterday when Smith displayed his new mini generator, the Excre-Power, which, when attached to a common household toilet, produces unlimited quantities of electricity and doesn't pollute the environment. According to Smith, "The food you eat can determine the power you have in your home." A spokesman for Monopolated Power and Light called the invention a health hazard, saying "We are concerned about the ...

CAMALIAN ANNOUNCES RUN FOR PRESIDENCY

Yesterday, millionaire Willard Camalian announced that he is a candidate for the office of President of the United States. "The American public could do worse," he said, "and has ..."

Watt's mouth opened involuntarily. *Whoever thought a lowdown, mediocre fool like that could run for the Presidency of the United States? What happened to standards? If Camalian can be President, then anybody can. What's the country coming to?*

He was still dumfounded by the news weeks later when he got a visit from his attorney, S. Hamilton Burrows, who looked at Watt, smiling, and said, "You know the manuscript you gave me to read. I took it to a publisher. An editor liked it and wants to publish it. What's the matter? I thought you'd be happy."

"Camalian is running for the Presidency of the United States."

"I know," said Burrows, shaking his head. "Maybe you should have slapped him harder."

"I wish I had," said Watt.

Then he realized what Burrows had said about his manuscript. For some reason, the word *write* had never connected for him with the word *publish*. They seemed light years apart. *Writing is the act of developing your craft and rehearsing for performance. Publishing is performance, opening the door for judgment of just how much more rehearsal is needed. Why should I publish? I don't need anybody to validate me and tell me I do or do not have talent. But an unread writer is like an un-tasted wine. No one knows how good the bottle is until it's opened. It's the difference between masturbation and sex. And God knows there are enough masturbators in the world, certainly in Jehoover State Penitentiary, people who feel through a sock without ever experiencing life. So why not publish? Why not let people perched on toi-*

let seats, as if they were kings or queens, read and judge your words? As a writer, you are the maker of a world. Let people dwell in it. After all, as Lipsky said, if feelings are nothing but biochemistry, why not make metaphors?

Facial muscles, which had been dormant for years, slowly twitched as a smile formed around Watt's mouth and spread across his face, making his eyes widen. He forgot about Camalian's run for the presidency and started laughing, saying, "I too am a bowelful man."

"I'm glad you're finally happy," said Burrows.

"Goddamn!" said Watt, repeatedly shaking Burrows' hand, "I'm a writer!"

"Congratulations," said Burrows, smiling.

"You know, when I first saw you ten years ago," said Watt, "I thought you were just another jive ass uncle tom, like your brother, S. Hartford Burrows. A lot of brothers make snap judgments when they see middle class black men like you. It's a mistake. You're a good brother. You've stuck by me all these years, and I've never given you a cent. I appreciate you, man."

"I know you're innocent," said Burrows. "My work's not done until you're out of here. But I've got something else to tell you, something you've got to know. Ullysa Knight was the one who got Stetson to recant his testimony. She didn't want me to tell you at the time. But now I think you should know. She thought you were innocent, too."

"I thought she *hated* me," said Watt.

"Why?" asked Burrows.

"I hated her," said Watt, "because I loved her once when we were kids."

"She told me all about it," said Burrows, "what happened with your father—and how she hurt you."

"That was a long time ago," said Watt. "When you see her tell her I said thanks."

"I guess you're wondering why I'm telling you all this," said Burrows.

"I think I know," said Watt.

"Ullysa and I have become close," said Burrows. "I love her and asked her to marry me and she accepted."

For a moment Watt was silent; then his smile broadened again. "I don't think she could have found a better man," he said, "or you a better woman. I hope the two of you will be happy and stay happy. Congratulations."

"Thanks," said Burrows, as the two men shook hands.

The publication of *Godfodder* a year later coincided with the nomination of Willard Camalian for the Presidency of the United States. It also preceded by a week the birth of William Knight-Burrows, whose picture the proud parents sent to Watt with a congratulatory card on the publication of his book. Although the picture made Watt happy for Ullysa and Burrows, it made him feel sad for himself. He thought of Sylvia and his own son or daughter and wondered where they were. How was his child, who was now approaching eleven, growing up?

Godfodder received modest critical acclaim. Although some critics said it was too violent and panned it, others called it a major work with a limited range. One critic, however, called Watt "a modern day Rabelais who had written a subtly different picaresque American novel."

A few reporters, whom Watt remembered seeing at the hospital and at his trial, came to Jehoover State Penitentiary to interview him and get some new bullshit to stir people up. They were disheveled and looked older than their years. Writing for newspapers, which is a young person's game, had taken more of a toll on them than prison had taken on Watt. They had condemned Watt as a villain and mass murderer years ago. Now they were praising him as a writer and a victim, but hinting at the same time that any of them could have written his book if they didn't have the responsibilities that accompany a demanding job and family life—and if they had been locked up in prison with plenty of time on their hands. They met with him and acted as if they had never seen him before. One reporter even tried to become his friend. "You bloodsuckers will do anything for a story," Watt told them. "But would any of you trade places with me?" he asked. "I don't think you would." He answered. Not one reporter made a comment.

Lipsky's professor type, who had continued to send books to Watt years after Lipsky's death, sent Watt a letter saying:

> My late brother, Joseph Lipsky, would be proud to know he had assisted in the development of a talented writer. Although I became the literature professor, Joe was the one in the family who read all of the great books when we were kids and pointed me in the direction of academics, rather than crime. His real name was not Lipsky. It was Lipstein. But Lipsky was his nom de crime, which he took to protect his family from enemies who might seek revenge. Let me know the titles of any books you want, and I'll ship them to you. I salute you at the dawn of a great writing career.
>
> Sincerely,
> Robert B. Lipstein

Dawn? Thought Watt, *It's more like sunset. Lipsky, wherever you are, I salute you.*

A lot of other mail came, too. But the only other correspondence that moved Watt was a note from a young girl whose meaning he did not understand at first. "I'm 14 years old," she said. "Please, Mr. Watt, keep us falling."

Eventually, the book made a little money, which New York State confiscated. But according to an article in the *Barely News*, Watt was supposed to be a millionaire. That misinformation contributed to old Rusty's family trying to sue Watt for "damages and the loss of property incurred by Watt's actions."

Watt was in his cell working on a new book based on *The Seven Deadly Fears* one day when a guard told him he had a visitor coming to his cell.

"Why can't he see me in the visitor's room?"

"Because he wants to see you in your cell!" snapped the guard. "And don't get out of line with me, motherfucker or you'll be a killer with a nightstick up your ass! He's coming right now. Get ready."

Looking down the cellblock, Watt didn't believe his eyes. To hoots and applause from inmates, and cries of "Help me! I'm innocent!" Dr. Otto Von Geber moved toward Watt's cell, leaning on a cane and walking with a twisting gait.

"Yes, I know you are *all* innocent," laughed Dr. Von Geber. He stopped at Watt's cell, which slowly opened so he could enter. Dr. Von Geber had aged considerably; the lines in his face had deepened, blazing a trail to his mouth that easily could have been mistaken for a portal to hell. Entering Watt's cell, Dr. Von Geber ran his fingers across the wall. Then he lifted the mattress and looked underneath the bed before saying, "Hello, Watt. Prison agrees with you. You have aged well."

"Yeah, it's been a long time," said Watt. "What are you doing here?"

"I have come to say good-bye to you, Watt, and give you good news. Soon you will be free."

"What are you talking about?" asked Watt.

"You *do* know that Willard Camalian has been nominated for the presidency?" asked Von Geber.

"Yeah, I know," said Watt.

"And do you know he's leading in all the voter polls?"

"Yeah, I know that, too," said Watt.

"And you do know that the election is next week?"

"So what?"

"Well, when Camalian is elected President, you and the rest of the world will be free."

"How, what's he going to do, give the world a pardon?"

"Exactly!" said Dr. Von Geber. "He is going to pardon the world by blowing it up. Once he's in office he's going to launch a pre-emptive strike against all nations with nuclear weapons and film the first and last global nuclear holocaust. The atomic mushroom will be all encompassing. Life as we know it will lose its lease. Everything will begin again."

"Are you crazy?" snapped Watt.

"I have spent most of my life fighting CMB. But I cannot control it any more. It is too wide spread. The millionaires and billionaires are everywhere, and they have gone mad! All I hear from them is *give me, buy me,* and *I want.* The sickness is beyond my ability to treat it. The departure of the human race from the Earth is the ultimate and only cure for CMB.

"But the people!" said Watt.

"Fuck them!" snapped Dr. Von Geber.

Then Watt looked deeply into Dr. Otto Von Geber's eyes and made a horrible discovery. "Dr. Von Geber, you've got CMB!"

"It was only a matter of time!" explained Dr. Von Geber. "If you hang out with crazy millionaires, you become a crazy millionaire."

"Dr. Von Geber, you need help!" implored Watt, as muscle memory returned to his hands and he prepared to slap Dr. Von Geber.

"You can slap me till doomsday," said Dr. Von Geber. "My case of CMB is far beyond your slap therapy. Camalian's election is the cure I need. It's the Fuhrer's dream of doomsday finally coming to fruition—the annihilation of all plant and animal life. I must go now, Watt, and buy a $5,000.00 bottle of champagne with which to celebrate. Congratulations on your freedom."

Dr. Von Geber turned and the cell door opened automatically. As he twisted down the corridor, with inmates calling his name as if he were God or some Rock star, Watt cried, "Somebody stop him! He's going to destroy the world! He's got CMB! He's going to destroy the world! HE'S GOT CMB!"

"Who gives a fuck!" yelled an inmate as others chimed in, "Blow it up! Blow it up!" Then they buried Watt's cries in a fugue of epithets.

The following week, Watt followed events leading up to the election closely. The fear that two maniacs might gain the power to destroy the world robbed him of sleep. Then Election Day came, and the American people proved they were not as dumb as the polls had indicated. They rejected Willard Camalian's bid for the presidency and simultaneously Dr. Otto Von Geber's dream of doomsday for the world.

CHAPTER 36

▼

Five more years passed. Then one day, Watt was trooped before a parole board hearing. Five nameless people looked into his eyes and asked him questions—inquisitors for the state and status quo. "What would you do, Mr. Watt, if you were a free man next week?"

"I'd try to find work and a place that's comfortable to live and write. Then I'd see if I could locate my child."

"Have you ever seen this child?"

"No, I don't even know if it's a boy or girl. He or she was born five months after I went to prison. I haven't heard a word about my child since then."

"Then you don't even know if the baby survived the first year after birth?"

"I have the faith of a parent. I know my child survived. If I were free, I'd find my child."

"Does that mean you'd stalk or hassle the mother and force your way back into her life?"

"That relationship ended years ago. What she's done with her life is *her* business. I just want to help my child."

"Does that mean you wouldn't want to help her, too? After all she's been raising your child alone for—how many years?"

"My child should be almost sixteen by now. I've made a little money from my book."

"Yes, we're aware you're a published author."

"My lawyer has some of the money in an escrow account."

"What about the rest of the money?"

"It goes to the state for my upkeep?"

"Does any money go to your victim's family?" Watt paused before answering. A member of the parole board leaned over and whispered something to another member. "Please forget that question, Mr. Watt. It's not applicable in this case. However, do you accept responsibility for your crime?" This was the crucial moment. If Watt said he did not kill Ainsley Bridges, the parole hearing would be over, and it would be years before he would have another. If he admitted to killing Ainsley Bridges, he would be lying, but he might make parole. "My victim, the man I killed in self-defense," he said slowly, "was a billionaire. I accept all responsibility for his death."

"Are you sorry you killed him?"

"I'm sorry he's dead, but I'm not sorry I defended myself. I just wish I had not done it so forcefully. I do not know anything I regret more than Sir Ainsley Bridges' death. When I killed him, I killed a part of myself. Ainsley Bridges was a good man who tried to help me. I will always regret the fact that I killed a great man and humanitarian."

"I thought you regretted not being with your child more than anything."

"The two things are related," said Watt. "By killing Ainsley Bridges, I removed myself from the world of my child."

"What would you do for your child if you were released from prison tomorrow?"

"I'd provide for my child in every way possible. Maybe he or she wants to go to college. I would do whatever I could to make that happen."

"You know we hear this I-want-to-help-my-child stuff all the time from inmates who come before this board. I'm not saying *you're* not sincere, but some of *them* aren't. Some of them are just using the child gimmick as a con to get out of here. They don't love their children or *anyone* for that matter. Why should we believe *you?*"

"I can't speak for anybody else, *but* me. I love my child because I've learned to love myself. I didn't realize how much I hated myself, and my father, until recently. I didn't know I craved a father's love all of my life. And when I didn't get it, I became angry and bitter. I thought Hell was some place you went for lunch where nothingness was served and nothing was real, not even the deaths of other people. I wasted a lot of years before I realized I'm not a bad person, and my life has meaning. It's worth living, and it's all I have, except for my child. I have the ability to earn an honest living and provide for my child. I just want the opportunity to do so."

"Well, Mr. Watt, if you loved your child so much, why didn't you marry the mother and make an honest woman of her? Inmates have the right of marriage.

The state would have provided you with a minister and a wedding ceremony, whatever your faith."

"I wrote hundreds of letters to the mother of my child during the first ten years I was in prison. In those letters, I asked her to marry me and to let me see my child. But she never responded. I can't blame her. I abused her when we were together."

"Did you beat her?" asked a female member of the parole board.

"Yes," said Watt. "And I'm ashamed of it. If she took me back, I would never raise a hand against her. I would treat her like a queen."

"Thank you, Mr. Watt. That will be all."

That evening Watt got the unofficial word. One of the guards nodded at him and gave him a wink, a sure sign that he was going to be paroled. The next day, Jabbo stopped by his cell and shook his hand, without saying a word. "Free at last!" thought Watt.

But before he could leave Jehoover State Penitentiary, he got some unexpected bad news. His boyhood buddy and best friend looked into his eyes and said, "Dreamweaver, I have AIDS."

What could Watt say or do? In the two weeks before he was released, he did whatever he could for Loray. Then, after sixteen years and three months in Jehoover State Penitentiary, Watt was released. As he rode an early morning bus down to New York City, where thousands of people, gay and straight, were also dying from this plague, he thought of Loray. Whatever it took, he would help Loray. He would write him, visit him, and get medicine for him to prolong his life. He would send money to make sure Loray was comfortable.

Arriving in New York, Watt called Burrows and Ullysa who invited him to dinner the next night. Then he reported to his half-way house, a run-down building in lower Manhattan where a couple of former inmates were already plotting crimes.

That night, Watt slept in a room that was less ventilated than his old prison cell, on a bed less comfortable than the one he had in prison. Thinking about his child helped him to sleep. *I'm going to find my child. I'm going to find him or her.*

The next day he reported to his parole officer, a man who shall remain nameless because he deserves to be, who looked at Watt with cold eyes and colder emotions. "You may be a published writer and have a little money, but that doesn't cut any slack with me. If you slip and fall before your parole expires, I'll slide you right back into prison faster than a chicken can lay an egg. And you can write whatever books you want in the same damn cell you left. Is that clear?"

"Yes," said Watt.

"If you didn't have a job as a writer, I'd send you to one cleaning toilets in a bus station. But I guess you won't have to do that. Tell me something. Did you write that book yourself? Who helped you?"

"No one," said Watt.

"You're lucky, Squirrel," he said, making Watt's insides jump with thoughts of Jehoover. "Just make sure you report to me every Tuesday at 10:00 a.m.," said the bureaucrat. "And if you're more than fifteen minutes late, I'll send you back to prison. Don't consort with criminals or people who could get you in trouble. Call me when you find an apartment. Give me the address before you sign any lease. If you get a phone, I want the number immediately. Let me know if you develop any kind of sexual relationship with a man or a woman. Give me their address and telephone number. If you mess with children, I'll lock you up again, and you'll never get out. And don't leave the city without my permission. Is that clear?"

"Yes," said Watt.

"Alright, get out of here. Agnes, send the next one in."

Leaving the parole office, Watt thought, *there was a time I would have kicked his fat ass on general principle. But I'm older now, and he isn't worth it.* Immediately, Watt headed for the subway, thinking of Sylvia and his child and wondering what Harlem would be like.

As he got off the subway at 116th Street and Eighth Avenue, he braced for shots and the sight of run down tenements. Instead he saw high-rise luxury condominiums, apartment buildings, and brownstones with carved wood doors. And then he was shocked even further when he saw hordes of white people coming and going. *What are they doing in Harlem?* he wondered. *Harlem doesn't look any different from downtown.* Then he realized *they live here. Harlem is their home.*

Harlem had become a fancy community with upscale stores, filled with people from other racial groups: Sikhs from India; Thais from Thailand; Africans from all over the continent, and white people from all over the world. *But where did all my brothers and sisters go, the people who made Harlem what it was?*

He walked over to Morningside Park and was shocked even further by what he saw. What had been one of the most dangerous parks in the world now looked like a paradise. With its promenades and walkways all neatly manicured, and people frolicking on the grass, Morningside Park reminded Watt of pictures of European parks that he had seen in magazines while in prison.

Entering the park he strolled down one of its walkways. His eyes, which expanded, made his feet stop moving as another shock set in. A colossal bronze statue stood in the middle of the park. Looking at its smiling face and reading the inscription, he winced.

In Memory of
Sir Ainsley Bridges
A Great Humanitarian
And a Lover of Mankind
Who Gave His Life
Helping His Fellow Man

He went to Sylvia's old building, but it was gone, replaced by a modern high rise with a doorman screening visitors. Perry's old building was gone, too, as was the House of Styles Barbershop, and practically every landmark Watt had known.

As he turned a corner, still in shock, he saw some movers unloading furniture from a truck. One of the movers was black. "Hey, brother," said Watt, approaching him. "I've been away for sixteen years. And things have changed. Where have all the black people gone?"

Eying Watt suspiciously, the mover said nothing at first. Then Watt burst out with, "Please help me. I'm trying to find my child. I've been in prison for sixteen years."

"I can tell," said the mover. "I've been there, too. Well I guess you missed the change. Harlem ain't a black community no more. They finally put The Plan into effect. You got rich and middle class people from all over the world livin' here now. Just fifteen years ago I used to visit a gal that lived on Edgecomb Avenue, around 145th Street, near Colonial Pool. She might have been payin' five-hundred dollars a month for her two bedroom apartment. They forced her out and converted her apartment into a condo. Do you know how much it costs?"

"No," said Watt.

"One million dollars!" said the mover. "Did you hear me? I said one million dollars. Black folks had to get out of Harlem. They didn't have a chance or a choice. About thirteen years ago, white folks started movin' in who wouldn't have been caught dead in Harlem a few years earlier."

"Where did all the poor black folks go?" asked Watt.

"Wherever they could afford to live," said the mover. "Some went back to the South. Others went to the South Bronx, and a few are still hangin on in buildings that haven't been converted or condemned. But most of them had to leave Harlem. And you know somethin', it's startin' to get expensive in those places they moved. It's only a matter of time. We'll all be homeless or dead. We're surplus people. A poor motherfucker can't make it no more. Pretty soon a middle-class motherfucker won't be able to make it either. It's called greed, my brother, and you're a victim if you don't have any money."

"Hey, Root, are you working or talking?" a white mover asked.

"You know damn well I'm workin'," said Root. "So don't fuck with me! I took a minute to give this man some directions. Good luck, brother. I gotta get back to work."

"Thanks," said Watt, continuing his odyssey through Harlem.

He assumed his old building would be gone, like the others. But when he turned the corner, a smile came over his face. His old building, which was sandwiched between two shiny new high rise buildings that dwarfed the five-story flat, looked like an abscessed tooth in the middle of a beautiful smile. Although battered, boarded up, and abandoned, it was still there. A sign hung on a strip of wood nailed across the entryway: *Condemned. Do Not Enter.*

Climbing over a board, Watt entered the building to see if anyone was there. He trudged up the stairs, which were still filthy, still urine splattered, still strewn with newspapers and probably somebody's flesh. People *were* still living there, and he went up a flight and knocked on a few doors. Then he went up another flight and knocked on a few more. "Yeah, who is it?" asked a voice from behind a ragged door.

"Do you know Sylvia Donner?" asked Watt.

"No Sylvia Donner lives here," said a man's stern voice.

"She didn't live here," said Watt. "She used to live nearby. Do you know where she moved?"

"You've got to be about one dumb motherfucker," said the man. "You're asking me about some bitch who never lived here but who used to live nearby? Listen, asshole, I've been in this apartment for ten years. A West Indian dude was in it before me. I don't know any Sylvia Donner. So don't ring my bell again or I'll put Junior on your ass. And everybody knows what *Junior* will do."

"Sorry," said Watt.

"You better be," said the man.

Walking away, Watt wondered, *Who or what is Junior—his son, his monster, or his executioner?* Although Watt could not answer any of those questions, he knew that whoever Junior was he would be in prison in a few years. The game is rigged that way. Between the ghetto and the prison, there are few stops.

As Watt continued up the stairs, he saw bottle tops strewn all over the landing, and their number increased as he approached the top floor. Then he saw the shadow nodding on the stairs. Coming out of a nod, an old man looked down on Watt and barked, "Whatchoo want, mafuck? Cause I got plenty o' nothin'!"

"Blip, it's me," said Watt.

"Who is *me*?" asked Blip. "Cause I don't know you!"

"It's me, Watt."

"You ain't got no kid wit' ya, do ya?"

"Who?" asked Watt.

"One of them pint-sized killers," said Blip, "thass made the whole world afraid."

"No, I'm alone," said Watt, climbing up the stairs.

"Well I'll be damned," said Blip, "if my boy ain't come back to me."

"Hold on," said Watt. "I'm not *your* boy. I'm Watt."

"Ain't dat what I said," snapped Blip. "But any way you look at it, you all *I* got cause you all *I* r'member. It seem like it wuz jus yesterday you wuz runnin' up an' down these stairs—b'fore they grabbed you at Rusty's Peep Show Joint an' put you in jail. Some people said you wuz fuckin' the Black Hole. Other folks say you wuz jus' the last customer. Which was it?"

"Neither," said Watt. "That was more than sixteen years ago. I've aged. But you still look the same. What have you been doing to look so young?"

"Same thing I been doin' fa years," said Blip, "shootin' dope. Dope preserves me. It even saved my life."

"I thought you were dead," said Watt.

"So did erriebody else," said Blip. "You r'member da night you killed dat mafuck wit' more money than God, an' tha police wuz all ober tha place. Jehoover an' Towntamer, they climbed tha stairs lookin' for you, an' when they axed me if I seen ya, I tole em NO. An' before I could change my mind an' say YES they shot me in da head."

"Then why aren't you dead?" asked Watt.

"Tha doctor said I wuz so high I didn't feel the bullet. I didn't even go inta shock. I wuz so relaxed when dey took da bullet out they didn't gibb me anes—anes—"

"Anesthesia," said Watt.

"Yeah, dat," said Blip. "An' I didn't feel a thing. I guess I tapped inta my reserve supply. Dey took tha bullet out an' I left tha hospital wit' nuthing but a slight headache. DOPE SAVED ME!"

"I'm glad you're alive," said Watt. "I need your help."

"I knew you'd be comin' out," said Blip. "But I thought dat it would be in ten years—But hold your whores and horses! Did ya break out or did dey set ya free?"

"I got paroled," said Watt.

"Where you stayin'?" asked Blip.

"Downtown," said Watt.

"Thass good," said Blip. "Da neighborhood ain't as nice as it used to be, an' I can't extend my accommodations, ha-ha. You didn't tink I could say dat, did ya?"

"I'm looking for Sylvia," said Watt. "You remember Sylvia. She had my baby after I went to prison."

"I tried ta forget dat wild mafuck wuz yours," said Blip. "After you went ta prison, she had your baby alright an' went back to work tha next day. But dat little mafuck wuz so wild, she couldn't even control him in tha crib. He poked three baby-sitters in da eye wit' his pacifier an' slapped anybody who tried to pick him up. As soon as he could walk, he got into trouble. As soon as he could talk, he started lyin', an' as soon as he could run, he started stealin'. Eventually, he broke his mama's heart. She died about two years ago."

"Sylvia is dead!" cried Watt.

"Yeah," said Blip. "Dey say somethin' exploded in her head. I don't know wha happened, but she gone. An' she wuz probably glad to go. Cause dat little mafuck didn't gibb her no peace. He did whateber he wanted to do wheneber he wanted ta do it."

"Where's my son?" asked Watt.

"You do better to forget him an' go back downtown," said Blip. "He might be on death row by now. All dese kids wit'out fathers are killin' each other an' doin' crimes. Tha only way to stop em is to lock em up, an' dat makes em eben meaner."

"My son's in jail?" asked Watt.

"In jail or dead," said Blip. "He wuz a mean mafuck, an' I ain't seen 'im lately. So he's at one of them two places. An' you know somethin'. He wuz jus' like your pa, 'cept he wuz like dat from da start."

"That's my son you're talking about," said Watt. "I've got to find him."

"Forget about dat kid," said Blip. "He ain't worth two seconds of an insect's life."

"That's my son!" said Watt. "I've got to find him."

"If you find him," said Blip, "he'll probably be wit' another kid named Junior. He's jus' as mean as your son. Neither of them are shit."

"Maybe not," said Watt, "maybe not. But that's my son, and he's all I've got. I've got to find my son and save him." Then Watt ran back down the stairs with the old dopefiend yelling, "Come back, you fool!"

CHAPTER 37

▼

Watt knocked on the door he had knocked on before and the same man answered with an even sterner voice, saying, "I thought I told you to stay away from my door."

"My name is Watt, and my son is with *your* Junior."

"So *you're* the monster's father!"

"I just got out of prison, and I'm trying to find my boy. Can you help me?"

"No, I can't help you," said the man. "In fact I'm mad at you for making that evil motherfucker!"

"I'm sorry for whatever he's done," said Watt. "Can you tell me where I can find him?"

"No, I can't," said the man, with a note of diminished anger. "I haven't seen Junior in months and, frankly, I don't want to see him. The last time I saw him he pistol-whipped me—me his own father!"

"You know my boy?" asked Watt.

"Yeah, I know him. He's the one responsible for Junior being the way *he* is."

"Do you know where I can find him?" asked Watt.

"In the streets," said the man. "That's where these kids live now. They get everything they need in the streets—money, cars, women. If you see Junior, don't tell him you talked to me. I got another son left, and I'm trying to raise him right."

"Thanks," said Watt.

"Good luck," said the man.

Watt left the building and walked around every block in Harlem below 125th Street, from Morningside Avenue to Madison Avenue, looking for his son.

Finally, he reached 125th Street where he hoped he would run into someone he knew who would tell him where he could find his son. But the 125th Street he saw was unlike the one he had left.

All of the stores he remembered were gone, replaced by more fashionable, downtown, upscale stores. Even the street vendors were gone. Through all the change, one thing remained: the Apollo Theatre (O bright Apollo!). But whereas tickets for the great shows he had caught at the Apollo as a kid only cost $10.00 each, tickets for shows at the Apollo now ran as high as $150 per ticket. *Who can afford that?* he thought.

Apparently, black people had lost Harlem the same way they had lost everything else: by not working together in large numbers and organizing to improve Harlem and make it the greatest community of black people in the world (which it was once), thus ensuring a bold, promising future for their children and generations of black kids to come. Now that dream had passed.

Reaching Seventh Avenue, which was now called Adam Clayton Powell Boulevard, Watt heard a familiar voice. Standing on the corner, elevated on a cheap ladder, the student from the House of Styles Barbershop stood surrounded by a small crowd of mostly white people. But he wasn't speaking to them. He was addressing the five or six black folks who were faintly listening. Older, slightly gray, and less energetic, he spoke with the same determination he had when Watt first met him in the barbershop years ago. "Yes, we've entered a new century!" he cried. "And yes, it's a New World! But the old problem of racism is riding along with us." Turning around, Watt continued walking across 125th Street, hoping to see another familiar face. But he saw no one he knew, and the Harlem he remembered was gone.

Crossing Eighth Avenue, now called Frederick Douglass Boulevard, Watt saw the hulking figure of a black man in a ragged trench coat moving quickly in the block ahead. People jumped to the side and watched him as he passed. With his head thrown back and mouth contorted, he shook a clenched fist at the sky, seemingly cursing life itself. While in his other hand, he carried an empty duffel bag, which he swung back and forth, shooing people from his path. Watt recognized him and cried out, "BADNIGGER!"

But before Watt could reach him, BADNIGGER stomped into an exclusive gourmet supermarket and grabbed a handful of meats, potatoes, and vegetables and shoved them into his duffel bag with contempt as customers and store workers stood by and watched.

As Watt stood outside of the supermarket, he heard a man standing nearby say, "He does this every week."

"Why don't they lock him up?" asked a woman.

"He's crazy. Everybody's afraid of him, including the police," said the man.

With a crowd still watching, BADNIGGER left the supermarket, pushing a guard out of the way and dragging two others down the street before discarding them like tissue paper. Watt followed him, yelling, "BADNIGGER! It's me!" But his old friend either ignored him or never heard him because he didn't turn around.

As BADNIGGER came out of a liquor store, having grabbed several bottles of the most expensive cognac, the liquor store owner's German shepherd bounded over the counter and out of the store after him. As the growling animal leapt for his throat, BADNIGGER turned and threw a powerful hook that caught the dog in mid-air, rendering it senseless. The dog hit the concrete and lay there unconscious.

Meanwhile, BADNIGGER's eyes met Watt's, and he seemed to recognize him. Pausing, he shot a half-smile. But then his eyes moved away, and his body language seemed to say "Forget it." Shaking his head, he took several long strides away from his old friend. Then, turning a corner, he disappeared.

Watt wanted to follow him, but didn't. His boyhood friend had changed. He was now bad in the original sense of the word, and Watt had to avoid him because he could be sent back to prison if the police caught them together. Then he would never find his son who, according to Blip, had become even worse than BADNIGGER.

Watt continued searching, asking anyone who would listen if they knew where his son might be. Someone told him about a gang of Harlem kids who had relocated to the Bronx to make more money. They were in an area people called Kid Land. So Watt caught a train to the South Bronx and descended from an elevated platform, hearing loud rap music and seeing kids for miles.

Some kids, wearing expensive sneakers and jackets, carried boom boxes blaring *gangsta rap* lyrics, revolts against the soul. Others drove by in expensive limousines chauffeured by adults. And still others carried cases filled with dope, which they opened periodically to do business in the street. The same impetus that drove colonial crackers to enslave and sell blacks in America now drove these children to sell dope to other kids.

As Watt walked around the block, the cadence of rap music was interrupted by the staccato of bullets. Watt ducked into a doorway and crouched. Children, who seemed to be between the ages of twelve and sixteen, were firing guns at each other in what seemed to be a turf war. In colorful outfits and expensive sneakers, they looked like minstrels with guns.

One of the kids, no more than twelve years old, wielded a pistol that looked as big as he was, and every time he fired the gun, the weapon's recoil knocked him to the ground. But he quickly jumped up and fired it again. As testimony to his accuracy with the fire arm, a child lay dead on the pavement.

What the hell is going on here? Watt thought, seeing adults crouching, cringing, and cowering in doorways. *They're just kids. Take those guns away from them.* After the gun battle passed, some rap music started blaring again.

> *When you kill him,*
> *Kill him dead,*
> *Kill him dead*
> *Kill him dead*

As the song played, Watt watched terrified adults come out of doorways and hustle home.

Watt walked all through the South Bronx, asking kids, "Do you know Junior? My son is with him. If you help me, there's fifty dollars in it for you."

"Fifty dollars ain't shit," said one of the kids he stopped. "I can make fifty dollars in fifty seconds and not have to mess with *those* guys."

"Alright, a hundred dollars," said Watt.

"Old man, you better find a kid you can afford—maybe one who wants to commit suicide."

Finally, Watt found that kid. "Just tell me where Junior is," Watt pleaded.

"If it's Junior from Harlem you want," said the kid, taking the one-hundred dollars, try Fox Street. But don't tell him *I* told you," he added, pointing Watt in the direction of Fox Street.

It was dark when Watt reached Fox Street. He remembered he was supposed to be at Burrow's and Ullysa's home for dinner. But he couldn't stop looking for his son. He was determined to find him. He would call Burrows and Ullysa later and get a rain check for dinner. Maybe he would be able to bring his son and introduce him to them. Perhaps Burrows and Ullysa could be a positive influence on his boy.

Walking along Fox Street, he saw a group of teenage boys huddled together like a wolf pack. They weren't like the other groups of kids he had seen. There was something different and more deliberate about them. In a peculiar way, they reminded Watt of the leopard, lion, and wolf, and some of the other sinister characters he had seen around his father's table when he was a boy. But these were children.

They spotted Watt before he spotted them. They seemed to be watching him from the corners of their eyes and waiting for him to make a move. As if of one mind, they simultaneously drifted apart as he approached. Then they encircled him without making a sound.

The smallest of the group of boys strode up to him. Just a few inches over five-feet tall, he had a swagger and a bearing that reminded Watt of some of the toughest inmates he had known in prison. Ancient eyes glared at Watt from a youthful skull as he said, "My name is Junior, and I heard you were lookin' for me. Gimme your gun."

"I don't have a gun," said Watt. "I was looking for my...."

"Gimme your gun!" repeated Junior more forcefully.

"I don't *have* a gun," said Watt. "I'm looking for...."

"Your money *and* your gun!" interrupted Junior, his mouth contorting and his eyes turning icy cold.

"Listen, you little punk!" snapped Watt. And at that moment, he felt a small hand cover his mouth as a sharp piece of metal cut around his throat. He fell to the ground as knife and hand released him, and he lay there gasping for air.

"See, Junior, I didn't waste a bullet on this old motherfucker! Bullets cost money, but a knife is cheap!"

"Watt, you sure are a bad motherfucker," said Junior. "You'll kill *anybody!*—even a cop."

"Fuck a cop!" said his son.

Lying on the ground, Watt looked up at his boy. He saw part of Sylvia's face and part of his own etched in his son's, with the stone jowls of his father protruding. He wanted to tell him, "I'm *your* father! You're my boy! I love you!" But his throat was cut and he couldn't make a sound. All he could do was try to keep in the air that was leaking from his body.

"I betcha he's got some ducats," said Junior.

"Somebody, get his wallet, badge, and gun," said his son. "See how much money he's got in his pockets."

"I'll get it. I'll get it," said a little boy. Then, standing over Watt, he said, "This old motherfucker's still alive, Watt."

"Why don't you finish him off," said Junior, "and put the old motherfucker out of his misery."

"You know that ain't *no* problem for me."

"You sure are a bad motherfucker, Watt," said Junior.

Then his son spat on him, mounted him, and stuck the knife in his stomach. Watt cried as he felt the knife turning in his guts. He looked into his son's eyes and forgave him and hoped that some day he would be able to forgive himself. *No redemption, just damnation. They made me, and I made you—a monster.*

As the little boys congratulated his son, yelling "Watt!" as if he had hit a home run in a Little League baseball game, Watt closed his eyes. Seconds later he was dead. He died hearing his own name.

THE END